JUMPING FREE

JAY ANN FOLEY

This is a work of fiction. Names, characters, businesses, places, events and incidents are either the products of the author's imagination or used in a fictitious manner. Any resemblance to actual persons, living or dead, or actual events is purely coincidental.

ISBN 978-1-7392403-2-5 (paperback)
ISBN 978-1-7392403-3-2 (ebook)

Cover illustrated and designed by Catherine Clarke Design

For Auntie Jean … fond memories

1

The phone began to vibrate, the mobile bouncing energetically within the constraints of its deckchair-style holder, interrupting Amelia's doodling on a yellow Post-it note. She knew she should be typing up the notes from the editorial team meeting earlier that morning; instead, she was engrossed in drawing a delightful scene, so busy adding birds soaring through the sky above some trees, she almost didn't glance up. *It's bound to be one of those nuisance calls*, she thought. Skimming the screen out the corner of her eye, she dropped her rollerball pen in surprise and scooped up the phone, smearing wet ink in her haste. Rushing to the stationery cupboard, the best spot to take personal calls during work time, she swiped the green icon, anxious not to lose the caller to voicemail.

'Hello.' Amelia spoke quietly, discretely nudging the door closed with the toe of her stiletto as her manager passed by on their way to the kitchen. She left the light in the windowless cupboard switched off, as if somehow that would help conceal the sound of her voice.

'Amelia ... am I speaking to Amelia Hodge?' The call quality was poor, but the voice was strong.

'Yes. Hello, is that Jilly? This is Amelia.' Having not heard from her aunt in years, Amelia's first thought was the call must be a misdialled number.

'Amelia. Thank goodness. What an awful day I'm having here.' Despite sounding frazzled, her aunt's voice, honed from years spent bawling at novice riders to sit up and keep their heels down, was as loud as she remembered.

'I … well, I'm sorry to hear that.' Amelia said no more, confused how a bad day at her aunt's riding stables in the Scottish Highlands could be related to her day, hundreds of miles south in the London offices of *Your Home, Your Castle* magazine.

Fortunately, Jilly began to elaborate. 'Would you believe one of my chaps went rogue this morning. Pirate —'

'Pirates?' interrupted Amelia, shocked. 'What, were you at the beach?'

'No, no, not pirates … Pirate.' Jilly spoke in a tone usually reserved for those who tried to get on a horse from the wrong side. 'Pirate the pony only went and chucked his rider off at Loch Still. Next thing, the rascal's shot off towards the castle ruins, jumped the fence and disappeared. I went in after him and fell through the rotted floorboards. Now I've two busted ankles and Pirate's only scratched his bottom. Rotten luck for me, if you'll pardon the pun.'

'Gosh, I'm so sorry to hear that,' Amelia whispered, as the cupboard door was opened by a colleague seeking staples. She threw them a packet, then quickly shut the door again. 'But, um, what can I do? Did you want me to tell mum?'

'Well, eventually you could let my sister know, not that she'll hotfoot it back from sunny Spain. No, Amelia, what I really need is some help here. Angus is still around but, you know, he'll never get on top of it all, especially the paperwork. Now, this is a big ask, and I know it's a big ask, but I can't leave Angus in charge, we're only a small team, even more so since I lost my Stan —'

Sensing a long story coming and aware she'd already been away from her desk some time, Amelia interrupted. 'Aunt Jilly, you know, I'd love to be of assistance, I really would, but I don't know anyone in the horsey world. I haven't ridden for years and I doubt most of my work colleagues can ride a bike. I'm sorry.'

'Oh, I don't need anyone else, I need you and your common sense. Could you take one of those smatical things and come up here to steady the ship for a few months? Please.'

'Um, are you referring to a sabbatical?'

'Yes, that's the one. I couldn't remember what it's called. My memory's been rather sketchy since the accident. They tell me it's the shock.' Jilly paused for a deep breath. 'I'll pay you so please don't worry about money. Plus, the cottage is vacant so there's no stress about finding somewhere to stay.'

'But why can't you still do the paperwork?' Amelia felt confused by her aunt's unexpected request. 'Couldn't you take the opportunity to sit in the office while the others do the hard work for a change?'

'Because Donna's here to collect me. I'm going to stay with her. I can't manage anything for myself and she can't stay here more than a few days because of the kids.'

'Right. I see.' At the mention of Jilly's only child, Amelia began to understand, for Donna lived in the Orkney Islands, a flight or ferry ride from the Scottish mainland. Amelia pictured her cousin the last time she had seen her, a freckle faced, fair skinned, strawberry blonde aged twelve. The reality that Donna now had children of her own that age was a jolt.

'It's impossible for me to run the books remotely. I need someone at Lochside and who else can you turn to in times of trouble if not family?'

'I get it now.' Despite the desperation in her aunt's voice, Amelia's inclination was to turn her down. Jilly's establishment, Lochside, was in the middle of nowhere, which meant the adjacent cottage was also in the middle of nowhere. Although nearing thirty, Amelia had begun to tire of city life she didn't feel ready for the total opposite, even temporarily.

'I'm really up to my chin in the muck heap without my Stan,' muttered Jilly. 'I was hoping you could come to my rescue.'

Guilt flooded through Amelia. She hadn't attended her uncle's funeral three years ago because she'd been loved up in the early stages of a new relationship with Ryan. Sadly, it turned out Ryan had simultaneously been in the early stages of a relationship with Polly and that had been the one which endured.

'I'll see what I can do,' she offered. 'I'll have a chat with Human Resources today but I can't make any promises.'

'Righto. Hopefully they'll be good sports about it. Anything you can manage, anything at all, would be gratefully received.'

Ending the call, Amelia stared at the narrow strips of daylight around the door, which hadn't fitted properly since the Editor slammed it in a huff after she ran out of red pens. She felt certain Human Resources would say no to extended time off. *Your Home, Your Castle* was a busy luxury lifestyle magazine published monthly. They wouldn't be able to afford to let her go at such short notice and she'd used up her annual leave allowance for the year. Still, she would enquire if it were possible. Then she'd be able to tell her aunt she'd tried with a clear conscience.

Back at her desk, Amelia began typing up the meeting notes but found she couldn't concentrate. She needed a confirmed answer, the sooner the better, to give Jilly time to find someone else. Walking through the open plan editorial floor, past colleagues sitting at desks surrounded by piles of magazines, bins, rucksacks and discarded trainers, Amelia waved to Judith. The Picture Editor was watering some shrivelled-up plants drooping out of pots on a windowsill beneath a lopsided slatted blind. As Amelia reached the door to the stairwell, Judith called out to her, 'If you're popping to the shops, can you get me a can of Tango?'

'Sorry, Judith, I'm not going that way.' Amelia pulled open the heavy door, then stepped through to the landing.

Her heels caught in the plush red carpet as she climbed the stairs to the Executive suites on the second floor. She rarely came up here, there was no need, for although the staff in these offices seldom visited downstairs, they messaged regularly. Closed light wooden doors and framed pictures of flowers lined the walls of the corridor. No dust swirled in the shafts of light filtering through the skylights. Amelia caught the scent of a bunch of lilies, artfully arranged in an enormous china vase. She sneezed as she knocked on the door furthest along the corridor, then waited for the call to enter the office of Human Resources.

Twenty minutes later, a bemused Amelia softly closed the door to Manju Lawson's office behind her feeling in a state of shock that the Head of the department had agreed so easily to a sabbatical of two months. She walked back down the corridor in a trance, almost knocking the lilies off their perch. She had been so certain of a refusal she hadn't even entertained the possibility of actually having to go to Scotland, never mind as soon as next week. Although she often huddled in the office kitchen moaning with colleagues about the monotony of working life, now the opportunity for change had presented itself, Amelia felt surprisingly reluctant. The reality of leaving the familiar for the unknown was scary. *No turning back now though*, she thought as she descended the stairs. She'd better return to the stationery cupboard and call her aunt. She knew Jilly would be delighted but Amelia feared she'd made a mistake not refusing her request straightaway.

On Friday morning, delayed trains to Wimbledon meant Amelia reached the *Your Home, Your Castle* offices later than planned. Torrential rain fell from darkened March skies as she dashed towards the red brick building located off the High Street. Gusts of wind turned her umbrella inside out and airborne litter tangled around her booted ankles. Pushing through the door to reception, blinded by the hair stuck to her soaked face, she skidded on the wet floor tiles, narrowly missing colliding with a decorative yucca plant. Leaning left to avoid the plant's mean looking spikes, she bashed her thigh on the corner of a table covered with the latest editions of the magazine. Rubbing her leg through her mac with one hand, she pulled her security pass from her handbag and swiped it against the sensor, noting how much longer her hair had been when she'd joined the magazine five years ago. Then Amelia had been a fresh faced twenty-five year old with thick blonde hair, clear blue eyes and an optimistic smile. Now the hair was shoulder length, the eyes were tired and the delight at securing a new job had faded within weeks of realising it comprised the same old, same old.

The day dragged by until late afternoon when, eager to begin their weekends, Amelia's colleagues bid her farewell. She thanked them distractedly as she struggled through typing up the meeting notes she still hadn't finalised. Finishing the last sentence, she glanced up to find the office deserted, her desk lights the only ones still on. Used to a background of noise and bustle, Amelia saved the document hurriedly, keen to get going. The notes weren't great but they would have to do. She heard the outer office door click open and a shadowy figure approached.

As Manju stepped into the light, Amelia noticed her dark hair was springing out of its side plait and her pink suit was crumpled. 'Hey, I guessed you'd still be here finishing up. Just wanted to wish you good luck and a speedy recovery for your poor aunt.'

'Thanks … I suppose.'

Manju smiled. 'You know, sometimes it's good to take an opportunity when it comes along. I've always felt you have so much more potential than you realise, Amelia. You've stayed in this role, never put yourself forward for promotions. Stephanie's always felt you're not stretching yourself enough and, let's face it, the Editor can never be wrong, can she?'

'I don't think it's fair for Stephanie to criticise me like that. We don't all want to be top dog.' Amelia was surprised how defensive she sounded.

'And we don't all have to be,' agreed Manju. 'But I'm sure this break will do you good. Give you a chance to take on some responsibility and come back having gained confidence. I probably shouldn't say this but there's more to working here than just photos of wallpaper and curtains, you know. Here, these are for you.' She handed over a large box of chocolates decorated with a purple ribbon.

'Thanks.' Amelia took the chocolates, torn between being touched at the gesture and annoyed by Manju's words. 'I feel I've worked hard but if that's not enough …'

'You misunderstand me. You're a valued member of staff and we look forward to having you back. Perhaps then we can look at opportunities to expand your role.'

'I guess.' Tired and distracted by all the things she still needed to do at home, Amelia sighed. 'I've got a lot on right now, so can't really think about it at the moment.'

'Of course. It's not the time for a chat, I understand. Take care.'

As Manju walked away, Amelia shut down the laptop and

cleared the desk in preparation for the temporary secretary who would be covering her role. Shoving her unwashed mug in her bag, she tucked the chair underneath her unusually tidy desk and switched off the remaining lights, plunging the area into semi-darkness. Only the emergency lighting was left casting shadows over vacant workstations. On her way out she almost tripped over a heater which had been left sticking out from someone's desk. Downstairs the security guard returned her goodbye, then locked the door behind her.

Walking towards Wimbledon Station through streets filled with people seeking a night's entertainment in the bars and restaurants, Amelia wished she could stop off and enjoy a cool glass of wine. This time though, she had a different destination. She was off, off to the past but also the future. It would be good to have a break from magazine life and perhaps, on her return, she'd show her colleagues she could shine as well as any of them.

Back at home in her ground floor flat in Putney, Amelia tried to chivvy herself to do the packing and clearing up she'd put off until the last minute. Eager for some space of their own, a friend of a friend had offered to flat-sit, promising not to hold any wild parties. More importantly they'd also agreed to take care of her fluffy tortoiseshell cat, Chewie, who was currently sitting staring out the glass patio doors at the rain bouncing off the paving slabs in the tiny courtyard back garden.

'Wanna go out?' she called over. Chewie's tail flickered but he didn't look at her. 'You know it's not my fault the weather still thinks it's winter.'

Chewie continued to ignore her, so Amelia rose from the sofa and headed to the kitchen. It was late by the time she'd finished unloading the dishwasher and, after checking the front and patio doors were locked, she went into the bedroom, eager for sleep. As she pulled the last few clothes from the wardrobe, her gaze fell on a plastic crate crammed to the brim with photo albums. It was tucked away, having been left there years ago when her parents had downsized their possessions to move to Spain. She threw some jumpers on top of the already crammed suitcase on the floor, then slid the crate towards her and, unclipping the handles, removed the lid. A slightly fusty smell wafted out. Amelia lifted out the top album and opened it, flipping through page after page of plastic sleeves filled with family memories. Here was one of her at Lochside when she was aged about eight sitting astride a liver chestnut pony, Jilly standing beside her dressed in a tweed jacket and fawn jodhpurs. She studied her aunt's brown eyes and ruddy cheeked face beneath a bob of thick brown hair, her sturdiness similar to the Highland ponies she loved so much. Amelia wondered how different she would look now, over twenty years later. The pony had been her favourite at the time but she couldn't remember his name. When had they stopped going on holiday to Scotland every year and why? Amelia guessed she must have been a teenager when their holiday destinations changed to hot and sunny places abroad.

A soft purring in Amelia's ear brought her back to the present. Chewie perched on the suitcase, kneading the clothes with his front paws, the expression on his face suggesting displeasure at the appearance of the case, which usually led to the disappearance of Amelia.

'I'm sorry.' Amelia stroked Chewie's head gently. 'I'd love to take you with me but I'm worried you'll wander off and I'll never find you.'

She kept quiet about the dog Jilly had referred to in their subsequent conversations, a Basset Hound who couldn't go to Orkney because one of Donna's kids was allergic to animal hair. She had resisted asking her aunt why one of the other staff couldn't take the dog instead of her. Reclining back against the bed, the album flopped open in her lap on a page with a photo of a herd of ponies grazing in a field, surrounded by hills and forest. As a supermarket delivery van pulled up out front, a car horn sounded nearby and a motorbike roared past, Lochside's remote Highland setting felt more six million miles away than six hundred.

2

Early the next morning, while shadows still lingered beneath the streetlights of Putney and the rumble of traffic indicated the commuter chaos had begun, Amelia crammed the last of her possessions into the boot and back seat of her blue Mini. A fox skulking by the communal bins stopped to stare at the flashing indicators as Amelia pressed the key fob to lock the car again. She headed briefly back inside to secure the front door key in the safe she'd had fitted so it could be collected by her flat-sitter later. Blowing a kiss through the letterbox to the still sleeping Chewie, Amelia felt guilty sneaking off. She reassured herself with the thought that her cat would be well looked after in her absence.

As she fastened her seatbelt and switched on the headlights, illuminating the cracked paving of the parking area which still hadn't been repaired despite the landlord's promises, she felt a fizzing in her stomach. It wasn't excitement but neither was it nerves, more a mixture of the joy of freedom and the burden of expectation. What if she couldn't do what Jilly needed her to do? She hadn't ridden in years, her once perfect knowledge of the points of the horse had drained away to be replaced with work trivia she didn't remotely care about. Glancing up, Amelia saw her upstairs neighbour peering out a window. Plastering on a smile, Amelia gave her a wave, then turned up the radio and set off on the long journey north.

It was many hours later when Amelia indicated left at an arrow-shaped, faded sign warning her the road to Lochside Equestrian Centre was private and she should drive carefully. As she flicked on the main beam, getting her first glimpse of the lane she'd last travelled up over a decade ago, she grinned. There hadn't been another car on the road since Inverness; she really was in the back of beyond. The tyres bounced in deep potholes littering the unmade surface and she slowed down, trying to avoid the worst craters as the suspension groaned. For a quarter of a mile the Mini swayed like a boat, churning Amelia's stomach while low hanging branches dangling from the dense trees either side scraped across the roof with a shriek.

At the end of the narrow lane, the headlights shone upon a pair of towering iron gates. Securely closed, they blocked the way. In the darkness beyond, Amelia could visualise the horses tucked in for the night. She parked alongside a small white cottage and was struck by the feeling of remoteness, no doubt intensified by the late hour. She had never been here before without her family and the stables open and buzzing with activity. This time it was late at night, the staff were gone for the day, her aunt was in Orkney and fond memories couldn't chase away the air of isolation.

Climbing stiffly out of the Mini, grateful to stretch after hours spent behind the wheel, Amelia accidentally put her right foot straight into an ankle-deep puddle, concealed by a thin sheet of ice beneath a pile of leaves which had not been swept up. She shuddered at the chill in the air, shaking her leg to dislodge the water from the hem of her jeans. Trying to ignore her soaked trainer and sock and fighting a feeling of dismay, Amelia hopped over to the gates, triggering a security light which bathed the surroundings in a bright white glow. The intricate swirls of wrought iron felt cool against her cheeks as she pressed her face against them, peering through. She could see nothing beyond the circumference of light which fell only around the entrance, leaving what was beyond unlit and hidden. The noise of her approach and the sudden appearance of the light had disturbed the horses. She heard a whicker, followed by a bang which sounded like a hoof striking wood.

'Go back to sleep,' she called out.

The light flicked off within seconds of Amelia walking away. She pulled her mobile from her pocket intending to switch on the torch when the lantern fixed to the cottage's storm porch lit up as she activated its sensor. She knew the key was hidden beneath a boot remover by the front door. Lifting the implement, made from horseshoes and covered in dried mud, Amelia found a key stuck underneath with Sellotape. The lock was tricky to turn and the wooden frame of the door was swollen. Wiggling the key, she gave the door a shove. The lock released suddenly and she fell through the doorway to be greeted by a woofing sound as a tan and white Basset Hound bounded over on stubby legs, almost tripping over his long ears.

'Hello there.' Amelia crouched down to stroke the dog. 'You must be Gallus.'

Rising to turn on the lights, Amelia gazed around the living room. The ceiling was low, some of the beams only inches above her head despite her diminutive height. As so often with memories, everything seemed smaller than she recalled. The space was cramped with a sagging sofa, circular coffee table, television and a tartan basket containing a selection of chewed dog toys.

Undoing her jacket buttons, she moved through to the kitchen, decorated as an old-fashioned farmhouse complete with the welcome warmth of an Aga. Through an arch she entered the dining room, squeezing by the table and four chairs squashed inside, then within a few strides she had circled back to the living room. Settled in his basket, Gallus yawned, unperturbed by the flickering lights. Amelia hoped the power wasn't about to cut out as she took in the paintings of traditional countryside scenes lining the walls, the faded depictions of life in years gone by just visible behind dusty frames. Gallus barked, drawing Amelia's attention to a wood burning stove.

'I'm with you there,' she grinned, opening the door to light the logs already stacked inside.

Gradually the room lost its chill as the flames took hold. She found a scrawled note pinned to the working surface by a tin of soup.

The soup's for you. Gallus has been fed and walked (you'll find out he doesn't like too much exercise). His grub is in the cupboard by the back door. Zoey

While the soup heated in the microwave, Amelia carried her bags and boxes in from the car. Finally settled, she curled up on the sofa beneath a faux fur throw and drank the soup from a large mug. She closed her eyes, relieved she had made it. When she found herself falling asleep while holding the scalding soup, she decided it was time for bed.

Every stair creaked as Amelia wound her way upwards. She held the wooden handrail carefully, unbalanced by the weight of the suitcase in her free hand. The tiny landing was still overlooked by Uncle Stan's watercolour of a majestic stag, its head raised mid-bellow. Amelia entered the rear bedroom which she knew overlooked the stables and the hills beyond. Dumping her suitcase beneath a window smeared with condensation, she pulled the edges of the beige curtains together, pausing when a distant yellow glow caught her eye. It appeared to be bobbing steadily as though held by hand, out near to the Bothy at the far edge of Lochside's boundary, beyond where the fenced-in fields gave way to the wildness of the Highlands. Amelia watched, fascinated for a few seconds before the light suddenly vanished, as though extinguished.

'Could be a will-o'-the-wisp,' she told Gallus, who had followed her and was now lying on the bed. 'Although I'm not sure I believe in them.'

Gallus barked in response as though ghostly lights trying to lure you off the path to your doom were of no interest to him.

Amelia closed the curtains and flopped back on the bed. She was exhausted, her eyes dry from hours spent concentrating on the road. If there were any nocturnal troublemakers out and about they would need to find someone else to lead astray. She was going to sleep.

Keen to create a good impression, Amelia had intended to rise early and be in the stables to greet her new colleagues when they arrived. A bunch of keys on a hook in the kitchen were labelled for the gate and outbuildings and she'd planned to open up, put the kettle on and get underway with any paperwork. However, she forgot to set the alarm and Gallus proved a useless alternative. They were both fast asleep when woken late in the morning by the sound of numerous hooves and voices passing the cottage on their way up the lane.

She was scraping the last mouthful of porridge from a bowl when the front door began to tremble beneath incessant knocking, as though one of the horses was trying to break it down with their hind legs. Gallus trotted to the door, Amelia following. As she turned the key, she could see through the pane of frosted glass that the visitor was human not equine. She opened the door.

'Hi, can I —'

She got no further for the man on the doorstep began to speak. 'Hello, Jilly's niece. I need you.'

He gave a friendly wave of greeting. Amelia took in his shoulder length brown hair, amber eyes, worried expression and Thin Lizzy t-shirt beneath an unzipped waterproof jacket. He looked out of place, as though he'd fit in better as part of a Celtic Rock Band than a rural riding stables.

'Sorry? I'm Amelia, by the way.'

'And I'm Mac … McAteer. Hurry up, please.'

'Hurry up what?' She made a grab for Gallus but missed as he scooted between the man's jean-clad legs and loped towards the stables. 'I'd better get the dog.'

'Don't worry about him, he'll soon be asleep in the tack room. I need your help. Zoey was meant to take the kiddies ride to Loch Still, but she's gone the wrong way and now we've ten ponies lost in the forest.'

'What?' Amelia tried to keep up with Mac's words, rapidly spoken in his broad Scottish accent.

'Jilly usually takes the Saturday morning ride so it's Zoey's first time and she insisted she'd be OK. Vowed she knew the way. To be fair, she's not worked here long and it's not all signposted like it is in Glasgow …'

'OK, er, just let me get my coat and I'll be right with you.'

'Great.' Mac turned to leave, then swung back around, adding, 'Angus is getting Spirit tacked up for you.'

In her rush to pull on wellies and layers of clothes against the cold, Amelia missed what Mac had said before he dashed away.

Arriving at the stable yard a few minutes later, Amelia found it exactly as it had always been. Twenty-five brick stables scattered in a higgledy-piggledy fashion around a muddy lawn covered in hoofprints, in the centre of which stood Angus. Hands on hips, tufts of grey hair poking out from beneath a tweed flat cap, he nodded at Amelia. As she got closer, she saw he barely looked any different from when she'd last seen him.

'Amelia,' he beamed. 'Get on over here for a proper hello.'

He swept her into a hug, all bristly cheek stubble with a waft of pipe tobacco. It was patient Angus who had taught Amelia about horses all those years ago, spending time with her when Jilly and Stan were too busy running the business. Through his example, he demonstrated that horses were living, breathing creatures who deserved respect and tender handling. Tumbles from the saddle were soothed, quickly followed by encouragement to get back on and try again. Now he was looking at her bright red, glittery wellington boots, purchased for a music festival in a year when it had rained non-stop, with disapproval.

'Get yourself properly kitted up.' Angus pointed to the tack room. 'You'll find plenty of spare hats and boots in there.'

A dusty sign swayed lopsidedly from a nail on the tack room door, which stood propped open by a bucket filled with yellow sponges. Amelia stepped inside a room with cobwebs in every corner and a spider dangling from the bare light bulb. The tang of saddle soap filled the air, tins of hoof oil lined the floor, brushes propped inside them. Gallus was snoozing on a pile of numnahs beneath the double rows of pegs lining the walls, each labelled for the saddle and bridle of a particular pony. Many of them were currently empty.

Tracing her fingers along the rack of riding hats, caressing the assorted styles and sizes, Amelia took in the traditional black velvet hats sitting alongside the jockey's skull caps with their brightly coloured silks and woolly bobbles. There were even hats decorated with silver and pink crystals. Underneath the rack were rows of jodhpur boots, lined up according to foot size. She marvelled at how much choice there was.

Back outside and feeling more the part with her feet now encased in jodhpur boots, she fastened the chinstrap of the hat she had chosen. Angus was holding the reins of a grey Arabian mare whose tail was up almost over her hindquarters as she danced on hoof-tips beside him. Mac was already astride a handsome chestnut Irish Draught, impatiently checking the smart watch on his wrist.

'Pop up on the mounting block,' instructed Angus, pointing to the set of three wooden steps on the lawn.

'I'm not riding her,' Amelia protested. 'I need something steady, like a cob.'

'No time … there's no time,' huffed Angus, 'all the others are out in the fields. It'll take too long to get them ready.'

'But I haven't ridden for years.' Amelia felt rising panic. She knew Arabians were one of the most highly strung horse breeds, with impressive endurance and a skittish temperament. Why they would have one at Lochside was beyond her comprehension. It was akin to a driving school teaching pupils in a Lamborghini.

'Zoey's just text to say she hasn't found any of the kids yet,' Mac called over, waggling the phone in his hand. 'We need to go now.'

'There'll be another accident if you put me on her,' Amelia threatened, as she climbed the steps while Angus lined the Arabian alongside.

'Nonsense. Spirit's your aunt's favourite and Mac will look after you.' Angus tried to reassure her. 'Besides it'll all come back to you, like riding a bike.'

'Yeah, but Spirit's a motorbike not a bicycle,' muttered

Amelia, as she lowered herself gently into the saddle and adjusted the length of the stirrups.

Spirit danced sideways, tail high, ears up, eyes wide in her pretty dished face. Feeling like she was on the starting grid of a Formula 1 race with the engine revving beneath her, Amelia gulped as Angus let go of the reins. Spirit shot out the stable yard, startling Mac's mount. Amelia only just managed to suppress a yelp of fear.

Mac caught up with her. 'Are you OK?' he asked, grinning.

'I think so. She's beautiful.' Amelia stroked the silky coat of her mount's neck. The mare's trot felt like floating as she arched her neck, eyes roving from one side of the lane to the other, checking whether anything scary was hiding in the trees.

'Yeah, she's Jilly's beloved. To be honest, we all thought it would be Spirit who'd eventually put your aunt in hospital. She ended up being beaten to it by that rotten floorboard, but I guess that's what happens when you ignore the warning signs to keep out of the ruin.'

'Poor Jilly and naughty Pirate causing all this trouble.' Amelia relaxed her hands a little as Spirit blew out a loud breath and settled into a walk.

'See you've got it sussed already. Your aunt told us you were a professional.'

'Hardly. I think Jilly has exaggerated my abilities. So, what brought you to Lochside?'

'Me, ah, well, I'm on the run.'

'On the …' Alarmed, Amelia tailed off, mind racing. Surely Jilly checked the staff out before taking them on. 'I assume you're kidding?'

'Yeah, on the run from mundane office jobs where you spend all day working to make someone else rich. At least here we're all poor.'

Amelia snorted, causing Spirit to leap in the air. 'Yeah, I hear you.'

'Surely you City workers are well paid?' teased Mac. 'Seriously though, Lochside gives me an income and leaves me time to spare for the band.'

'You're in a band?'

'Yeah, I'm the lead singer in Chequered Pipes. We're a Celtic rock band.'

'That's amazing. I thought you looked like you ought to be in a band but didn't want to judge you on your appearance.'

'You know, so far, you're turning out to be the total opposite to your aunt. She's always on at me about the band. You know, "stop wasting your time", "no one could stand listening to that racket for long", that kind of thing. She's cool though. I think she loves it really.' Mac laughed. 'We're taking a left here.'

They turned off the lane onto an overgrown track and followed a trail which had been flattened through the hock high grass. The sky was streaked with thick banks of cloud but the rain held off, though the wind was cold. Amelia pulled her scarf up higher around her chin. Mac led the way at a fast trot. Spirit was keen but agreed to remain behind. Shortly, they reached a point where the surface turned to peat and the track wove into the trees. Occasionally Amelia could hear a female voice shouting shrilly in the distance.

As they moved deeper into the woods the trees became dense and the voice got closer. At the point where the track rounded a sharp bend, then doubled-back on itself, they found a group of children on ponies clustered together.

'All right, Zoey?' Mac asked.

A girl with a slight frame and a black plait swinging down her back, her green eyes rimmed with liner, answered from her perch on a dun cob. 'Just about. I'm missing two. One went that way and the other that way.' She dropped the reins and held both arms out at shoulder height, pointing forefingers with blue painted nails in opposite directions.

'OK. Amelia, you take the left, I'll go right. We'll find them.'

Before Amelia could respond the faint sound of a child's high-pitched scream filled the air.

3

They all froze except Spirit who was disturbed by the tense atmosphere and spun on her hocks, ears back. Fearful the mare was about to take off, Amelia shortened the reins.

'Zoey, take your gang safely back to Lochside. Amelia, get going,' snapped Mac, before whirling the chestnut around and cantering away.

Zoey glared at Amelia, clearly expecting her to jump into action.

'I … er. Oh, what the hell.' Amelia touched the mare's sides with her heels and suddenly she was galloping along the track, branches whipping by her face.

'Sit back, heels down,' she chanted out loud, trying to reassure herself she wasn't going to fall off.

Spirit was quick. She flew along the track effortlessly until they reached a point where it forked. To the left it carried on through the woods, whereas an offshoot led to a narrow gap in the trees. Slowing Spirit to a walk, Amelia steered her through the gap, on the other side of which she could see green swathes of fields. Ducking under a couple of particularly low branches, they emerged on open land. Pausing, Amelia glanced around, restraining a skittish Spirit, who at the sight of so much space was cantering on the spot, snorting.

'Whoa, steady now.'

Running widthways across the field some distance away was a low stone wall with a small dot on top which appeared to be waving its arms above its head. Spirit tossed her head in excitement.

'Walk on slowly.' Amelia did her best impersonation of Jilly, but the mare ignored her, taking off from a standing start. Her hooves barely touched the long grass as she skimmed the surface of the ground.

Spirit's mane blew back into Amelia's face as she sat tight, shifting forwards and lifting up slightly out of the saddle so her weight was over the mare's withers.

'Calm down,' she pleaded, her breath stolen away by the wind the moment the words left her lips.

They covered the distance from the trees to the wall in what felt like seconds. Amelia pulled back gently on the reins and to her surprise the mare responded. She'd expected to be jumping the three-foot-high solid stone obstacle, instead Spirit halted in front of a young boy, who was sitting on the wall clutching a riding hat in his lap.

'Are you OK?' Amelia asked him with concern.

'Whisky jumped the wall and I fell off.'

'Are you hurt?'

'No, but I was scared. I screamed.'

'There's nothing wrong with being scared,' Amelia said reassuringly. 'We're all frightened sometimes, especially if you ride ponies. I was scared just then when Spirit took off galloping across the field.'

'Were you really?'

'Oh yes, I wasn't sure I'd be able to stop her. It could've taken a long time before she ran out of petrol.'

'Horses don't run on petrol,' the boy chuckled, then his

face turned serious. 'But you didn't scream, even though you were scared. I did.'

Amelia dismounted. 'Don't worry. The main thing is you're not hurt. Let's go and get Whisky. I spotted a gate a bit further down. Hopefully, we can get through there and catch him.'

With Amelia leading Spirit, they walked alongside the wall until they reached a wooden gate. It was unlocked. Amelia undid the latch and they passed through to where a chestnut pony she assumed was Whisky was gorging on clumps of grass. Amelia helped the boy lift the greedy pony's head, then cupped her hands together to form a foothold for him to get back onboard. He appeared none the worse for his tumble. As he took hold of the reins, he pointed over Amelia's head in the direction of the woods and said, 'Someone's coming.'

Amelia turned to see Mac trotting the chestnut across the field, leading a little girl astride a strawberry roan pony. The pony's short legs were pumping to keep up with the bigger horse. She waved to get his attention, then unclipped a coiled lead rope from a ring on the front of Spirit's saddle and secured it to Whisky's bridle.

'Are you guys OK?' Mac shouted, stopping in the gateway.

'Yep, we're all fine.' Amelia moved alongside Spirit, preparing to mount.

'Phew. That's a relief and everyone accounted for.'

As Amelia placed her foot in the stirrup, Whisky suddenly shot backwards pulling her over. She hit the ground with a thump, still clutching Spirit's reins and the lead rope.

'Amelia, are you injured?' Mac was peering down at her when she opened her eyes.

'I don't think so. A bit winded.' Lying on the grass and feeling no desire to move, Amelia closed her eyes again and stayed put.

'Are you going to get up?' Mac asked her.

'Nope. I'll just stay here, I think, unless you're offering a helping hand.'

'You don't strike me as the type who needs that. In fact, you remind me of a song I wrote about a damsel in distress who wasn't really in distress at all. It's called —'

'Urgh, you're not going to sing, are you?' The boy interrupted, sounding horrified.

'No, you'll be glad to hear I'm not. Please can you get up now, Amelia. We need to get off Douglas land pronto.'

'Douglas land?' Amelia asked, rising to her feet so Mac could give her a leg up back onto Spirit.

'Yeah, Jilly's neigh —' Mac got no further for an angry shout stopped him mid-sentence.

'Oi, you there. Are you aware you're trespassing on private land?'

Amelia turned her head in the direction of the voice. A man was striding towards them with a golden retriever loping at his Wellington-booted heels. In his hand he held a wooden crook walking stick. He wore lemon corduroy trousers, a green tweed jacket and a furious expression on a pale face with bright blue eyes. His blonde hair was covered with a flat cap.

'Hello, Hugh,' greeted Mac in a bored tone. 'Awfully sorry. We're having a few issues this morning.'

'I'll thank you to have your issues on Jilly's land and not mine.'

Annoyed at the man's demeanour, Amelia sprung to Mac's defence. 'We've had some problems today. My aunt usually takes this ride but she's unwell, I'm afraid. She had an accident. I can assure you it won't happen again.'

'Your aunt?' the man repeated as though it were a question.

'Yes, I'm Jilly's niece. Amelia … hi.' Amelia gave a tiny wave.

The man glared at her. 'Well, Amelia hi, just to make you

aware, your aunt's land ends at this wall. That side is yours and this side is mine.' To emphasise his words, he indicated each side of the wall using the walking stick.

Rather taken aback at his rudeness, Amelia steered Spirit towards the gate, towing Whisky behind, with Mac and the little girl following. Mac slammed the gate shut by giving it a good shove with his foot.

'We shan't bother you again,' Amelia called over her shoulder as they rode away. Once they were out of earshot, heading for the path into the woods, she turned to Mac and said, 'He's a charmer.'

'You just had the pleasure of meeting the insufferable Hugh Douglas, son of the insufferable Leith Douglas. As you just discovered, their estate borders Lochside. They never stop whinging even though they've got more acres than they can keep track of.'

'Why?' Amelia slowed to let Mac's horse lead the way back onto the narrow track into the trees.

'I gathered from Angus that Stan and Leith had a big falling out years ago. I don't know what it was about but, if you ask me, they're the type of people who are never satisfied. Their other neighbours, the Fergusons, find the same as us. We try to avoid them as much as possible. Hey up, mind your heads on this low branch.'

They rode the rest of the way back in silence, the only sound the squish of the horses' hooves on the damp ground and the odd snort from Mac's chestnut, who Amelia discovered was called Hebrides.

Back at Lochside, the rest of the group had already departed. Zoey was waiting for them, leaning against the left-hand stone gate pillar decorated with a horse's head minus an ear. She was tapping a biro against a black clipboard. 'If anyone fell off they need to fill in a form before they leave,' she announced.

'I did,' the boy on Whisky piped up.

Zoey walked over and took the lead rope from Amelia. 'I'll take it from here.'

Wearily, Amelia dismounted and led Spirit into her stable. For a first day, actually only a first morning, it had been a disaster. She'd overslept, been woken by a colleague she'd never met before, the ride had been chaos, a customer had fallen off and she'd inadvertently trespassed on the private property of Jilly's grouchy neighbour.

'Way to go, eh?' she asked the mare, who was eating hay and ignored her.

When she returned Spirit's saddle and bridle to the tack room, she found Angus there studying his unlit pipe.

'Jilly won't let me light it in the stables,' he said mournfully. 'Too much combustible material around.'

'I think it's sensible to keep it that way,' Amelia responded sharply, images of Lochside going up in smoke playing in her mind. Having to tell Jilly she'd destroyed her lifelong business on day one was a horror beyond imagination. She slid Spirit's saddle back on its rack, then asked Angus, 'What time's the next ride booked in for?'

'That's it for the day actually.'

'Really? Aren't weekends the busiest time for customers?'

'It's quiet today.' Angus began shuffling towards the door.

'OK. Perhaps once we've settled down it would be a good opportunity to catch up so I can get an idea of how things work here. What do you say? Shall we all meet in the office in an hour?'

At the lack of a response, Amelia looked around to find Angus was gone.

The office was a small room next door to the tack room. The desk, located under a large window overlooking the stable yard, was bare apart from a red pen pot filled with biros. The delicious smell of brewing coffee wafted from a cafetiere on a table surrounded by an assortment of chairs. The leather swivel chair by the desk was occupied by Gallus who was eyeing up a plate of wonky jam tarts also on the table. Angus caught Amelia looking at the pastries.

'Made them myself,' he informed her proudly, 'in honour of your arrival.'

'Which explains the uneven blobs of jam and misshapen pastry cases,' said Zoey, reaching for a strawberry one and taking a bite. 'Delicious though.'

Chasing Gallus off the chair, Amelia sat down. The hound slunk over to flop under Mac's chair instead. With his droopy eyes and characteristically sad looking face, she immediately felt guilty. She'd need to be on her guard or the dog would take charge in no time. It was clear he already had the others under his spell. She could see Mac surreptitiously feeding him dog treats from a packet in his pocket. Amelia cleared her throat. 'Sorry about earlier. It was a long drive and I forgot to set the alarm. Mac and I have had a chat and got to know each other a bit and obviously Angus and I go way back. Zoey, as you've no doubt gathered by now, I'm Amelia. Mac tells me you're quite new here?'

'Yeah.' Zoey shrugged. 'On a gap year from Glasgow Uni. Would've gone travelling around the world but apparently you need money for that, so …'

Unsure whether Zoey was being serious or sarcastic, Amelia hesitated. She was saved by Mac, who now had Gallus sitting on his lap. 'Chequered Pipes are playing at the Hiker's Hope tonight if you need cheering up, Zoey.'

'Not everyone wants their hearing ruined by "Bagpipes and Monsters" played at full volume, you know,' Zoey snapped.

'I'm lost,' interrupted Amelia. 'What's "Bagpipes and Monsters"?'

'Our most popular song,' Mac explained with pride. 'Had a few downloads so far.'

'Whoopee.' Zoey began to clap.

Worried she was about to witness an argument, Amelia raised her voice. 'Back to business, please. Where are the future bookings listed? We need to plan working rotas and things.'

'It's all sorted, don't fret,' Angus informed her, plonking a blue hardback A4 page-a-day diary on the desk, which creaked beneath the book's weight.

'And where's the electronic booking system?' asked Amelia, looking down at the unopened diary before her.

'Eh?' Angus appeared confused.

Amelia turned to him. 'Don't you have it all on a spreadsheet? Excel?'

'Excel,' Angus repeated. 'Oh, I know that. It's in London. My Deirdre went to a show there once.'

'No, I don't mean the arena. I mean a booking log on a spreadsheet on a computer, emails, that kind of thing.' Amelia flipped open the diary. The pages were filled with her aunt's scrawly handwriting. 'I'm reluctant to ask whether Lochside's on social media.'

'Don't,' warned Mac, lowering his hands, palms down, gesturing to Amelia to drop it.

'Aye, what would you need that for? You can see the ponies when you get here,' said Angus, with a smile.

Amelia flipped through the pages of the diary going forwards. 'But there aren't many bookings. What's going on? Where are they all? Are they listed somewhere else? Are there two diaries?'

'Jam tart?' offered Angus, picking up the plate and pushing it under Amelia's nose while avoiding her eyes.

Less than an hour later, fuelled by two jam tarts and a strong coffee, Amelia walked along the grassy avenue, around an abandoned chicken coop, up to the fields out the back. The hardy ponies lived out all year. Only the more delicate breeds were brought in overnight, to avoid the worst of the Scottish weather.

Amelia folded her arms and rested them on the top bar of a post and rail fence. There seemed to be a vast number of grazing shapes in the fields who all needed looking after. What had she done? Her aunt hadn't mentioned how slow business was and they may well have lost a few more customers after the morning's fiasco. The catch up with the team hadn't gone well. Amelia sensed they were being evasive about something. Perhaps they resented her taking over as temporary boss, or possibly they were being protective of Jilly. Either way, without their support, how was she going to run Lochside? The ponies were unruly, Mac was a dreamer, Zoey would prefer to be travelling the world and Angus was lost without Jilly. At least the cushions in a *Your Home, Your Castle* photo shoot could be rearranged. Amelia doubted this lot could be. What a mess.

The sound of panting rose from around her ankles. She looked down at Gallus, who gazed up at her with his wistful eyes.

'I fear I've been stitched up,' she told him.

The hound barked gleefully, squashing under the bottom rail. Curved tail wagging, he lumbered off across the field, nose down, following a scent. With a sigh, Amelia dropped her chin on her arms. She could just leave. Drive back to London overnight and never answer Jilly's calls again. No doubt Manju would secretly consider her a quitter if she turned up back at work so soon, but that wouldn't bother Amelia. She'd been quitting difficult situations for years. Why break the habit now? As footsteps approached from behind, she ignored them.

'Not going to do a midnight flit on us are you?' Mac asked, leaning his shoulders against the fence, hands in his pockets.

'I'd be lying if I said I'm not sorely tempted,' Amelia replied honestly.

'Listen, me and the others agreed not to tell you this but I like you and I feel it's only fair that you know the whole picture. Then you can make your decision and I hope you stay. I know Jilly does too, but you've a job to return to if you want. Angus and Zoey, they're hard work, good sorts but …'

'I get it,' stated Amelia, watching Gallus frolicking amongst the ponies, who ignored him.

'About a year ago, a new riding stables opened nearby, on the outskirts of Beauly. I'm sure you remember that town, it's about ten miles away. To begin with Jilly wasn't that bothered about Three Stones Barn, as it's called. She insists we've got some of the best scenery in the country right on the doorstep and they can't beat that. They, however, have indoor and outdoor schools and provide lessons which we don't.' Mac paused.

'I'm with you so far,' prompted Amelia.

'Unfortunately for us, the kids want to learn to jump and do dressage. Pretend they're at the Olympics. We can't compete with that; we don't have the facilities. Gradually we've seen the loss of our customers and recently even our weekend helper, Tamsin. She used to clean tack and do other odd jobs in return for a ride. It was good having her around the place because most of the kids come at weekends and they all got along. Then one day, Tamsin didn't turn up. We were worried, then Zoey found out she'd gone to Three Stones Barn too.'

'So, what's my aunt done in an attempt to resolve this?'

'Nothing. Jilly has no desire to try and raise Lochside's profile. I wish I could tell you different, but I can't. She doesn't want to face up to it and neither does Angus. My guess is eventually they'll be forced to. Running this place can't be cheap and with fewer customers …'

'Thanks, Mac, I appreciate you telling me how it is here.'

'Think it over and give me a call if you want to chat anytime. You can find my number on the emergency contacts list Jilly keeps in the desk drawer with the keys.'

They walked back to the stable yard together. Angus and Zoey had left for the day. Apart from a cooing pigeon and Hebrides kicking his stable door, quiet had descended on Lochside.

'I've got to be on my way, get ready for tonight's session,' said Mac, taking a motorbike helmet down from a shelf in the tack room.

'Mustn't keep the band's fans waiting,' teased Amelia, as they crossed the yard.

'Try fan – singular!'

Amelia locked the gate behind them. 'I don't believe that. There must be at least two.'

Gallus looked as though he was considering peeing on the motorbike's front wheel but thought better of it.

'Jilly and her animals.' Mac shook his head as he threw his right leg over the bike seat. 'If you could liven this place up, it would do it the world of good.'

Amelia stood watching the rear lights of the motorbike winding around the craters in the lane, until they disappeared. She wondered whether it would do her the world of good to stay or if she should hotfoot it back to London. *To quit or not to quit*, she thought as she took the cottage key out of her pocket. There was no one except her to answer that question.

4

Once the work was done and Zoey had successfully managed the one ride they had booked in the next day, Amelia locked up the stable yard and cottage. She needed to take a trip to Beauly to stock up on supplies.

Driving along narrow lanes hemmed in by a mixture of stone walls and steep woodland banks, Amelia never needing to use a passing space for there was no one around. Wildflowers were beginning to bloom, providing patches of bright colour amongst all the green. She couldn't help comparing the beauty of the surroundings to her usual dreary train commute with a view of mostly of graffiti and litter. Once she reached the main road, she continued driving along the banks of the River Beauly.

Entering the suburbs of the town, Amelia concentrated on following the blue signs indicating where the car parks were located until her attention was caught by a large white billboard decorated in bright green writing above a stencil drawing of a prancing horse. She slowed down for a better look and read: 'Three Stones Barn. Riding school and livery yard. All ages and levels of experience welcome'. Large gates preceded an immaculate gravel driveway which wound between white railed fences to a distant cluster of buildings. Amelia eased her foot off the accelerator and hesitated, tempted to turn left and check out the competition Mac had told her about. Her fingers hovered over the indicator when the driver in the car behind honked his horn with impatience. She sped up and drove on by the gates.

Fully stocked up on everything she needed, by the time Amelia returned to Lochside it was dark. Having unloaded the car, she retrieved a powerful flashlight from the cupboard in the cottage kitchen then, collecting the keys, went over to the stable yard. All was quiet until she switched on the lights. Heads appeared over stable doors as she did the rounds, checking rugs hadn't come askew and water buckets didn't need topping up. She walked out to the fields, where the ponies were dozing under the moonlight. Satisfied all was well, she returned to the cottage. Exhausted from still adjusting to the physical demands of looking after Lochside, she was soon asleep, Gallus sprawled over the end of the bed keeping her feet warm.

As the page on the Thelwell calendar stuck to the wall in the office flipped over to April, the first week went by. A few customers came each day. Although Amelia had set up a new booking spreadsheet on her laptop, she hardly needed to use it. The office phone rang so infrequently when it did the shrill sound of the bell echoing across the stable yard made them all jump and Gallus howl. Amelia spent a lot of time thinking about marketing but with no budget it was tough to come up with much, if anything, to raise Lochside's profile. She felt the only thing missing was tumbleweed blowing across the lawn, as she kept visualising the smart entrance to Three Stones Barn and comparing it to the pothole-strewn lane to Lochside.

. . .

Amelia woke early on Saturday morning. A family of four were booked in for a birthday treat and she was determined to create a good impression. Tack had been polished, ponies scrubbed clean of the mud that seemed to get everywhere, the stable yard swept and the edges of the lawn tidied up with a trimmer by a complaining Zoey. Torn between leaping enthusiastically out of bed and snuggling against the last remnants of comfort from the lukewarm hot water bottle, the sound of Gallus barking from downstairs forced her into action. The hound was hungry and not keen to wait much longer for food. Pushing her left leg out from under the duvet, Amelia felt with her toes for the sheepskin of her boot slippers. Goosebumps raced up her shins. Feet suitably protected, she braved getting up, wrapping herself in a fluffy dressing gown.

'Today's the day,' she told Gallus, standing in the kitchen watching him lick his breakfast bowl clean as though he'd never been fed before. 'We've got to win regular business like this local family.'

Once the food was gone, Gallus moved to the back door, indicating he needed to go outside. Amelia struggled with the latch, then pushed the door. The hinges were stiff and it took two attempts to open it. Gallus scampered into an overgrown mess of a back garden, while Amelia, standing on a threadbare doormat, gazed around the space enclosed by a wall buried beneath greenery. Daylight was just peeking through the clouds. A pair of faded gnomes held out wonky fishing rods over a circular pond thick with algae. She stepped onto a path of broken paving stones, leading to an ornate bench which, like the gnomes, had seen better days. Hopping from stone to stone to avoid getting her slippers wet on the damp grass, she lowered herself onto the bench, feeling cold wrought iron through her dressing gown. Now rising, the sun's rays shot through a multitude of spider's webs strung between the spirals of the arms and across the back of the bench. Taking a deep breath of the clean, cool air, Amelia looked up at the squat solid stone of the cottage, originally a home for free tenants who worked the land. When Stan and Jilly had lived there in the early days, before deciding they needed a dividing line between work and personal life, her uncle had told her it was a former owner who added the stables later. She looked down at the mobile phone in her hand, tempted to message Jilly and tell her she'd decided to return to London. Gallus disappeared indoors. The time on the phone's screen reminded Amelia she needed to follow him and get to work. Hungry ponies were relying on her and so was her aunt. She would stay. It was only for two months, surely even she could muddle through such a short time.

Getting ready quickly, Amelia opened the front door while fastening her wax jacket against a dry, cool day with a tinge of mist hovering inches above the lawn. Gallus dashed outside, barking continuously. Assuming he'd seen a fox, Amelia ignored him as she struggled to lock the front door. Turning around, she saw a young girl peeking through the bars of the closed gates.

'Excuse me, can I help you?' she called over.

The girl's head shot in Amelia's direction, her red hair flying back to reveal a freckled face. She looked about twelve years old and was dressed for riding in a cagoule, jodhpurs and boots, with a black velvet hat tucked under her arm.

Worried she may have frightened the girl, Amelia approached her. 'I'm Amelia. Jilly's my aunt. She recently had an accident so I'm helping here for a few months while she gets better.'

The girl appeared reassured. 'Where's Angus?'

'He should be here soon. You're awfully early. Today's ride isn't until ten o'clock.'

The girl rolled her eyes. 'I'm not booked on a ride.'

'OK. Well, we're not fully booked so I am sure we can sort something out for you.' Confused, Amelia unlocked the gates.

'I don't —' The girl's words were cut off by the sound of an engine as Mac's motorbike drew up, pulling to a stop next to Amelia's Mini.

Angus followed close behind, pedalling an ancient bicycle with a basket attached to its handlebars. Spotting the girl, he cried out, 'Tamsin!'

Amelia paused, gate in hand. 'You're Tamsin? Mac mentioned you before. He said you used to help out at weekends.'

'Yes.' Tamsin crossed her arms and bristled. 'That's what I've been trying to tell you if you'd only listen.'

'You're back,' cheered Angus, lifting a Tupperware container bulging with oat slices out of the bicycle's basket, 'just in time for my homemade flapjack.'

Amelia was beginning to suspect it was Angus's wife Deirdre who was providing the treats but didn't feel this was the moment to tease him about it. They gathered in the office. Amelia filled the kettle while Mac placed tea bags in five mugs. He gave Amelia a smile and she grinned back, raising her eyebrows.

'I thought going to Three Stones Barn would be fun. Jilly always let me have fun. She said I could gallop Peewee and once I jumped some logs in the woods on Jellybean.' Tamsin's green eyes brightened at the memories. 'It wasn't though. It was boring. No one even spoke to me much.'

'Oh dear. How awful,' soothed Angus.

'I want to come back. All I do at Three Stones Barn is sweep and muck out and now they don't even give me a free ride in return. They said I'd have to start paying but I could still help out for the experience. Please let me come back … please.'

'That's not very fair of them. You're more than welcome back. In fact, we'd be delighted to have you again,' said Angus, not bothering to check with Amelia.

'Really?' Tamsin's broad smile revealed braces on her teeth. 'I thought you might be annoyed with me.'

'Of course not. Why would we be? We've all tried things and changed our minds. Come on, help me with the feeding.' Angus turned to leave but Mac stopped him.

'Can Tamsin get us in?' he asked.

'In where?' Angus exchanged a confused look with Tamsin.

'To Three Stones Barn, to check it out. We've heard it's the bee's knees but none of us have seen it. All our intel's come from Zoey's friend who knows someone who rode there once.'

'You can't go snooping around. It's sneaky.' Angus looked to Amelia for support.

'Actually, Mac, that's not a bad idea. I was tempted to do that myself when I drove past the other day. It's not sneaky, Angus, it's research.'

'Yeah. Do you believe they wouldn't do the same if we were taking their customers away?' argued Mac.

They all stood looking at each other for a few minutes.

'I think I can get you in,' offered Tamsin timidly. 'My friend Mona's still a helper there. I'll message her and get her to show you around.'

'Fab.' Mac gave a double thumbs up and winked at Amelia, as Angus and Tamsin went outside.

'You might be able to steal Three Stones Barn's ideas but you can't steal their money or their customers,' Zoey pointed out, having arrived mid-conversation.

Lost in thought, Amelia picked up a grooming kit, then paused in the doorway. 'True, Zoey, but if you've got a better plan for how to improve our bookings then I'd love to hear it.'

. . .

Monday was the quietest day so far with only a regular called Peg booked in. Zoey took her out for a wander round the woods on Pippin, a sensible black cob with feathery fetlocks and a fondness for food.

Angus found Amelia and Mac in the feed store carrying between them an enormous bag of apples Peg had brought in especially for Pippin.

'Who knew fruit could be this heavy,' Mac complained, teeth gritted.

'It's not, unless you've been given enough to feed all the horses in Scotland,' replied Amelia, dumping the bag in the corner then dusting off her hands.

'I've a job for you two,' Angus announced, 'and it's come directly from Jilly.'

'If it involves carrying anything then my answer's no. I'm done weightlifting for the day,' stated Mac, sitting down on an unopened sack of pony nuts.

'It doesn't actually. Jilly's fretting about that fence up beyond the Bothy —'

'But it was only repaired last month,' snapped Mac incredulously. 'I'll eat these nuts if it's broken already.'

'I know but she's worried if it's broken again the ponies might end up on Douglas land and we'll have Leith complaining. She wants you to go and check on it.' Angus pointed at them with his pipe.

'But the ponies aren't anywhere near there and I can't imagine they'd go that far voluntarily even if they did escape. They're lazy,' Mac argued, keen to stay put.

'I'll go and get it done before the rain comes,' offered Amelia. 'I don't mind. You'll just need to tell me exactly whereabouts I'm checking.'

'Now you're making me look bad,' said Mac.

'I'll take Snowdrop. He's not been out yet.' Amelia glanced at Mac.

'Oh, all right.' He relented. 'This bag of nuts is bloody uncomfortable to sit on anyway.'

With her horse tacked up and ready to go, Amelia settled on the striking grey Snowdrop, while Mac took Hebrides. The horses strode out keenly along the grassy avenue between the fields, calling out greetings to the grazing ponies, some of whom raised their heads to reply. Mac opened a narrow gate and they rode out into the wilderness. As the horses picked their way through the dense undergrowth, Amelia looked around at the expanse of unkempt land, amazed it all belonged to Lochside. What wasn't used for the stables had been left to its own devices and she'd forgotten how much land Jilly actually owned.

They crossed a narrow stream, the sound of the water gushing beneath a natural stone bridge making Snowdrop shy, but he followed when Hebrides took the lead. They cantered upward until they were approaching the Bothy, which was tucked on a hillside near the boundary of Lochside.

Recalling what she'd seen from the bedroom window, Amelia said, 'I'm sure I saw a light up here on the night I arrived.'

'Really? It sounds unlikely,' Mac replied, steering around a thicket of thistles. 'There's no electricity or water except the well. They're just basic shelters and this one's way off the beaten track.'

'But it could have been a traveller looking to stay. That's what a Bothy is for, isn't it?'

'Yeah, it is, but this Bothy's locked and out of use.'

'Locked? I thought they were always left open for emergency shelter.'

'It used to be but when they came up here to repair the fence, they found the door had decayed and a stag had got in and was trapped. It was uninjured fortunately but distressed, having likely been there a few days. Jilly made the decision to replace the door and lock it. As she said, if you're looking for shelter around here, you'll head for the lights of the stable yard and cottage. Between you and me, I think her decision was partly financial too. There isn't much spare money to maintain the Bothy to a standard where it can be used safely … here we are.'

Now that Amelia was looking at the Bothy she felt a little foolish for mentioning the light. It was just a basic stone building with, off to one side, the well Mac had mentioned.

'Guess it was a will-o'-the-wisp,' she whispered to herself.

Mac heard her, for he turned with a grin. 'Up here they're known as the Spunkie. Still, whatever you call them, I'd advise steering clear.'

Amelia laughed and patted Snowdrop as they walked around the front of the Bothy. Though she tried, she could see nothing inside through the tiny window near to the door. At the side there was a chimney and a larger window set higher up. Mac led the way a little further until they reached a fence, all of which looked ancient apart from a section patched up with new wood.

'Nothing wrong with it,' stated Mac, sounding annoyed. 'Wasting our time because Jilly's got nothing to do except sit in Orkney and worry. Let's go back the exciting way.'

He cantered off, leaving Amelia and Snowdrop behind just at the forecast rain arrived. Big drops splodged on Amelia's thighs, seeping into the fabric of her jodhpurs. Ahead the light brown rump of Hebrides was zigzagging erratically along the path. Ears pricked, Snowdrop tried to catch up. Soon the Bothy was behind them, as they wove in and out of trees, then back into the open. Surrounded by hills, it felt surreal to Amelia, as though she were riding in a painting. The last place she had ridden many years ago was Hyde Park. Distracted by the memory she was taken unaware when suddenly confronted by a huge hedge blocking the path. Hebrides had jumped it effortlessly, Mac's whoop carrying back on the wind. Beneath her, Amelia felt Snowdrop change legs and gather himself ready to launch. Fear shot through every nerve of her body, an instinctive feeling that she could not follow. A feeling of déjà vu swept over her, certain she'd been here before and fallen. She remembered pain, not only physical but a loss of confidence. It all came back to her in a rush. She had loved jumping, had wanted to prove herself yet she'd tried to do too much, too soon. After a bad fall she hadn't wanted to ride anymore and the next year her parents had booked a holiday in Spain. The regular visits to Lochside ceased. She hauled on the reins, stopping Snowdrop so abruptly the horse had to turn sideways to avoid crashing into the hedge. He lowered his head with a snort as Amelia collapsed on his neck.

Hebrides soared back over, landing beside them. 'What happened? Lost your landing gear?' Mac asked cheerfully. Amelia burst into tears. 'Oh, no. What's wrong?'

Mac listened as Amelia gabbled out what she could remember of the accident she'd only recalled when being faced with the same jump triggered her memory.

'Wow. I'm sorry to hear about that. Let's get you back,' said Mac, leaning over to take hold of Snowdrop's rein. 'We can bypass the hedge. What you need is a cup of tea and one of Angus's flapjacks. That'll stop you crying. Your teeth will be glued together. Take it from one who knows.'

Amelia tested a grin, it felt OK. 'I'd can't believe I'd forgotten I was terrified of jumping.'

'Well, to be fair, I can't see there's much call for leaping obstacles in London and we often bury our fears. It's makes it easier to deal with them, doesn't it?'

'Thanks for being understanding.' Amelia wiped her eyes,

feeling embarrassed at what to Mac probably seemed an extreme overreaction to a simple jump.

'You know, the other night Chequered Pipes played at this big wedding and I forgot the lyrics to "Island Hopping Hero". I had to hum along to cover it up. Digger on the drums thought it was hilarious. What I'm saying is, sometimes you can fudge it, but a whacking great hedge in your way, well, that's a different matter.'

'I'm an adult now though. I should be braver than this.'

'You will be.'

They got back to the stables without further incident and once Snowdrop and Hebrides were dried off and enjoying their hay, Angus suggested Amelia, Mac and Zoey pack up for the day.

'I'll finish up here,' he offered. 'You have an early night for a change. Make the most of it being quieter.'

Amelia followed Mac to the cottage. Before getting on his motorbike, he turned to her. 'I didn't mean to frighten you. I thought going that way would be fun.'

'You should have been more careful, Mac,' said Zoey, 'you know that route is for experienced riders only.'

'It wasn't Mac's fault,' Amelia defended him. 'He wasn't to know I don't like jumping. All I want now is a soak in the bath and to forget about it.'

'And remember my offer to call me anytime. I'm not just interested in the fun stuff, you know.' Mac reached out and squeezed Amelia's hand gently.

Amelia tilted her head, the cogs in her brain whirring. She'd heard the word fun used first by Tamsin, now Mac. What was it trying to tell her?

5

The next morning, Amelia sat at the dining room table bashing the top of a hard-boiled egg with a teaspoon.

'Yummy,' she said to Gallus, who was loitering under the table. 'This reminds me of … wait a minute … that's it.'

She snatched up the egg and, with the hound close behind her, dashed over to the office where Angus, Mac and Zoey were sitting drinking coffee and eating croissants. The trio looked up as she burst in, waving the egg and yelling, 'This is it. I've got the answer to Lochside's future.'

'An egg?' sneered Zoey.

'And a half-eaten one at that,' Mac pointed out, getting to his feet and stretching. 'Is this a flash of inspiration like Newton with his apple?'

'Yes, sort of. Let me explain.'

Mac sat back down. 'OK. I'm all ears.'

'We're losing customers to Three Stones Barn, right? Well, we need to win them back using fun. I say let's hold a proper gymkhana with all the traditional games. You know, like the egg and spoon race, the flag race. We can order rosettes and invite everyone, all the local kids, whoever wants to come along, whether they're riders or not. It will be free too, no entry fee. What do you think?'

A long pause followed. Gallus yawned and rolled on his back.

'The concept sounds good. I fail to see how it's going to help the business if it's all free though,' said Angus.

'We make it fun. That's what Tamsin said she missed about Lochside and that's what you said about jumping that hedge, Mac. A reminder riding isn't only about going perfectly around the school leading with the correct leg. Good experiences lead to return visits.'

'So, you're suggesting we use the gymkhana to give new customers a taste of what Lochside has to offer and tempt back the ones we've lost?' Zoey tilted her head, thinking it through. 'Can't see much wrong with it.'

'Exactly.' Amelia began to pace the room in circles. 'We need to encourage customers through the gates. This is the best and, to be honest, cheapest way of doing that.'

'Stan and Jilly always said they set up Lochside to fulfil their goal of making riding available to anyone who wanted to try it,' added Angus. 'I'm sure Jilly will approve.'

'I'll call her later and run it by her.' Amelia was bubbling with excitement. 'I can ask Tamsin to draw up some posters and perhaps get her friends involved. The more the merrier. We'll need to spread the word if it's to take place a couple of weeks from now.'

'I think there could still be some bits and pieces stashed in the corner of the barn that haven't been used for years. They might be no good by now.' Angus picked up the diary and flicked through the pages, seeking a suitable weekend date. 'We haven't held a gymkhana since before Stan died.'

'I'll go and check them out,' said Amelia.

'I'll join you,' offered Mac.

They walked around to the barn which was used for the

storage of everything from wheelbarrows and spare bits of tack to anything else that needed putting somewhere.

'Good grief,' sighed Mac, gazing around at the dusty heaps of clobber. 'Most of this looks only good for chucking out. Do you reckon Stan and Jilly ever threw anything away?'

'Who cares? Look.' Amelia pointed to the corner where a pile of colourful poles, wings for jumps and other gymkhana paraphernalia were stacked. 'We're halfway there. They just need a freshen up.'

'I love an optimist, Amelia, but that lot doesn't just need a freshen up. It needs a facelift.'

'Then it'll get one. I'm sure Tamsin and her friends will be happy to help us out.'

'I wanted to ask you actually ...' Mac started, then paused, his expression awkward. 'I feel bad about what happened yesterday. Chequered Pipes are playing at a fundraising dinner at Stirling Castle on Saturday night and I've got a spare ticket. Would you like to come? I'm hoping the offer of dinner, a few drinks and a boogie will make it up to you.'

'I'd love to come.' Amelia didn't even need to think about it. She was finding the evenings lonely and missing her friends despite telling herself it was only for a couple of months. A night out sounded most welcome.

'Fab. We're trying out a new song so you can be our mystery shopper and let us know how it goes down. Hopefully a storm. Also, we thought you should take Cisco out this morning to get your confidence back. Angus is tacking him up for you now.'

Once back in the yard, Amelia found that Angus did indeed have the dun cob ready for her.

'You remember the way to Loch Still,' he said, holding the gelding while Amelia mounted from the steps.

'Yep. I'm sure I can find my way there and back.'

'Take it gently, although this fella will look after you.' Angus gave Cisco's sturdy neck a pat.

Riding Cisco was like sitting in a favourite chair. He plodded along, taking no notice of a squirrel scampering up a tree nor the rattling chains of a tractor as it chugged by when they reached the end of the lane. Once it had passed, Amelia trotted Cisco until they reached the entrance to a bridlepath which wove its way uphill. At a point where the path forked, Amelia steered Cisco to the right and as they neared Loch Still, she felt excited. The scenic route out to the loch and the ruins of the castle had always been her favourite and she was eager to see them again. Cisco discreetly snatched at the tall stems sticking out the hedgerow, chomping on them as he walked. The track ended at open land which rose in the distance to the imposing ruin of the castle opposite the pebbled shore of the banks of Loch Still.

Cisco pricked up his ears and, taking Amelia by surprise, broke into a fast canter. Instinctively she grabbed at the reins then told herself to relax. As the ruin got closer, Amelia looked up, trying to imagine what it must have felt like all those years ago during battle with horses charging and riders poised to attack. *At least I'm not galloping into a hail of arrows from the parapet*, she thought. At the incline, Cisco slowed to a walk. Amelia let out the reins and the cob lowered his head, breath blowing from his flared nostrils.

'Overexerted yourself, young man.' Amelia straightened his unruly mane.

Once up close to the ruins, Amelia found them more sprawling than she remembered. The roof was long gone but the walls remained intact although some were broken. Her eye caught a flash of colour among the stonework. It looked like a streak of gold as it moved away at their approach.

'Is anyone there?' Amelia called, urging Cisco up the bank, leaning slightly forward until they reached the fraying twisted rope strung level with Cisco's chest. It looped all around the ruin, interspersed with regular signs warning any prospective explorer to keep out for the area was dangerous. Taking in the crumbling walls, Amelia couldn't disagree.

Cisco gave a shrill neigh, as though calling out.

'Hello?' Amelia's shout disturbed a flock of pigeons. They departed in a flap of wings and disgruntled coos. She slid gently from the saddle. Cisco lowered his head to graze. As she bent low and scooted under the rope, Amelia could hear her aunt's voice in her head, scolding her, reminding her that one accident was enough. Jilly would understand though, for Amelia was certain she had seen a horse, that the gold belonged to the coat of a palomino.

Carefully she walked under one of the archways, the stone wound with ivy, the damp ground beneath her boots clear of any hoofprints. Wind whistled around her, swirling a low mist, like dancing ghosts. Amelia paused, turning in a circle, her eyes taking in the hidden crevices, shivering at the sense of occupation by unseen watchers. It was no surprise the locals called this place the Castle of the Shadows, that there were numerous stories of fleeting shapes seen from the corner of the eye. The place had a reputation, she knew there were those who wouldn't fish at the loch alone late in the day. As a child, Amelia had listened agog to all the stories, believing the place to be haunted. To her adult self it felt nothing more than a desolate ruin with a typical eerie air. She reached the far side, where the ground fell steeply to woodland. She could see no sign of a horse. She must have been mistaken. On her return she skirted a place where the wooden floor was broken, likely the scene of Jilly's accident. She decided not to mention this to anyone. The wildness of the Highlands was clearly stirring her imagination.

Reunited with Cisco they strode back along the shore, the water whipped up by a strengthening wind. Ripples flitted across the usually motionless surface of the water after which the loch was named. Leaves fluttered on the path ahead and spun around Cisco's hooves. The path gradually descended and the rolling grasslands returned. Eventually they rejoined the road and returned to Lochside at a brisk trot.

That evening, after a bubble bath, Amelia poured herself a glass of wine and, while a pizza cooked in the Aga, curled up on the sofa, Gallus beside her, and called her aunt. Jilly answered immediately. They had a long chat, towards the end of which Amelia raised the idea of holding a gymkhana.

'I don't see it can do any harm,' agreed Jilly. 'If you want to give it a try, feel free to go ahead. There might be some old equipment in the barn. It's worth having a look.'

'Yes, we've found it although it needs a good tidy up before we can use any of it.'

Jilly abruptly changed the subject. 'Amelia, I need to ask you another favour. I know I can't keep doing that but it's important. Can you visit me?'

'What … in Orkney?'

'No … in Las Vegas. Of course I mean in Orkney. Where else would I be?'

'What about leaving Lochside?'

'Oh, they can manage without you for a day or two. Angus tells me there aren't many bookings coming up and we've already discussed the best date for you to be away. I'd like Mac to come too. He has awful taste in music but he's quite sensible. You can fly direct from Inverness. I'll get Donna to book a couple of hotel rooms because you'll need to stay overnight. I can't expect you to do it in a day.'

'OK.' Amelia was taken aback. 'For any particular reason? Do we need to bring anything?'

'No, no need. I'm feeling very remote from everything and

I've never been a fan of phones. In person suits me better. Listen, I'm sorry I didn't forewarn you about the bookings drying up. One lives in hope, you know, and I'm sure it's a temporary glitch. You crack on with your gymkhana plans. If nothing else comes of it, the ponies will love it. It'll give them something to do besides stuffing their faces and costing me money.'

After the phone call ended, Amelia sat staring at the television, her excitement levels raised not by the exciting car chase Tom Cruise was currently involved in, but by the go ahead for the gymkhana. Whenever she'd raised suggestions for future editions of *Your Home, Your Castle*, they had never been taken up. She had always felt the underlying message was that a secretary couldn't be creative. Perhaps in reality she simply needed the opportunity to be allowed to stretch herself. Manju had made it sound as though it was Amelia's reticence that stopped her moving forwards, but she couldn't without opportunity. Sipping her wine, she decided she was going to make the most of this one.

As Amelia approached the office the next morning, she could hear the murmur of conversation. Angus, Mac and Zoey ceased talking when she stepped into the room.

'Good news,' she greeted them cheerfully. 'Jilly said yes to the gymkhana. I'll go ahead and ask Tamsin if she wants to draw posters and perhaps see if her friends are willing to get involved.'

'Well done,' said Angus, with a distinct lack of enthusiasm.

'Cheers. Who's for coffee?' Switching on the kettle, Amelia began scooping grounds into the cafetiere.

No one answered. There were none of the usual treats laid out on plates either. The atmosphere seemed tense.

'Jilly told me you and Mac are going to Orkney,' said

Angus. 'What do you think she wants to discuss that can't be done over the phone?'

'I don't know. It sounds like she's bored and wants visitors,' replied Amelia, looking around at their glum faces. 'I'm sure it's nothing. She sounded fine to me. Fed up with the forced rest but nothing serious.'

'Aye, she would be. She's always been a doer,' said Angus.

'I hope nothing's wrong with her health and she's recovering OK,' said Zoey.

Perhaps she was being oversensitive, but Amelia picked up an undertone that Zoey hoped Jilly's return wasn't going to be delayed.

'Excuse me.' A voice from outside the door drew their attention. 'I wondered whether I might speak privately with Amelia.' Hugh Douglas was in the doorway, dressed in a smart blue suit, the ends of the trousers tucked into green wellies. A bemused look passed between the team.

Concealing her surprise, Amelia walked over. 'Absolutely.'

As they strolled towards the fields and to break the awkward silence, Amelia spoke first. 'Have we accidentally been trespassing again? I wasn't aware of any incidents —'

'Oh, no. Forgive me.' Hugh's voice was precise, the softness of his accent was soothing. 'I was frightfully rude when we met before. You see, my family are protective of our land. We have to be. What with trespassers, wild campers, fly-tippers and even raves can happen if you don't keep your wits about you.'

'That sounds challenging.'

They stopped at the fields filled with ponies in muddy rugs gobbling grass as though they were starving. Amelia cringed. Hugh's place was sure to be spotless. No doubt he would judge them and find them inferior.

'It is and I'm sure you'll have similar experiences. I remember one night in the Hiker's Hope with Stan, rest his soul, telling me about the tourists who book in for rides. He said they'd try to convince you they were James Bond's stunt double when in reality they'd never ridden before. Get them out in the open for a gallop and they soon discover riding isn't just sitting on a horse. Carnage sometimes, apparently. Stan used to laugh about it but I know it used to worry him.'

'I haven't come across any of that yet but thanks for the warning. It strikes me it's better to be safe and tell the truth about your abilities than exaggerate.'

'Those who don't understand the countryside never will and now the tourist season is underway it's best to be on your guard.'

'I will be.' Amelia was puzzled about the purpose of Hugh's visit. If he wasn't complaining then what did he want? Surely not to give her advice on tourists. 'Was there a particular reason for you dropping by?'

'Yes, there is. I'd like to invite you to our Garden Party. We hold one every late May Bank Holiday Monday at Keilburn. If you've been here before I'm sure you know of our estate. The parties are an informal opportunity to get together. I'm hoping you'll accept and we can use it to start again on a more neighbourly footing.'

'I'd really like that.' Amelia accepted graciously. Perhaps she could help heal the animosity that had previously existed between them. She grinned at the thought of Jilly returning to find all her problems solved.

'Well, that's most excellent. I'll look forward to seeing you there. Do bring a guest if you want to.' Hugh took Amelia's hand and smiled. *He's quite nice when he isn't angry*, she thought. 'Until then.' He kissed her hand lightly and walked away.

Mac was lurking nearby. As Hugh drew level with him, they exchanged a brief nod but no words. Mac jogged over to Amelia.

'All right?' he asked. 'What did he want?'

'Yes, all good. He simply came to extend an olive branch of neighbourly friendship.' Amelia laughed at Mac's scowl. 'I've had two invitations now. My social life is on the up.'

'Bet he wants something in return.'

'I think he just wants to be friends.' Amelia shrugged. 'Better than being enemies.'

6

The benefit of having Tamsin back was proved again on Saturday. With Mac off for the weekend and Amelia due to leave at lunchtime for the long drive to Stirling, Angus and Zoey had a lot to do. Zoey had agreed to stay overnight in the cottage and keep Gallus company because pets were not permitted in her rented flat.

'Perhaps she's warming to me,' Amelia joked, as she and Angus carried the gymkhana equipment out of the barn for an eager Tamsin to begin cleaning. She had been thrilled when she heard about the gymkhana and had begun designing posters and inviting her friends.

'Maybe,' sniggered Angus. 'More likely, she knows she's only got to put up with you until Jilly returns.'

With a jolt Amelia realised Angus was right. Soon it would be May, at the end of which she would be on her way back south. With so much to do she knew the month would race by. Despite her original reticence to come to Lochside, she knew she would be sad to leave.

'Check out my posters,' called Tamsin, waving a cluster of

brightly coloured papers in Amelia's face. 'I'm going to start putting them up this afternoon.'

Amelia admired the funny drawings of cartoon ponies and riders taking part in the proposed activities. 'Well done. These are great.'

She had considered posting about the gymkhana on her personal Instagram page but as all her followers were either family or friends, they didn't live near enough to attend. Instead, she had tracked down a local community page on Facebook and posted a basic advert using a photo she'd taken of Spirit looking pretty. To her dismay, it appeared amateurish compared to the professionally produced advert for Three Stones Barn. Still, it was the best she could do and was better than nothing.

Tamsin paused jigging on the spot long enough to check a message which tinkled its arrival on her phone.

'It's my friend, Mona,' she declared. 'You can go to Three Stones Barn on Monday if you want. She's helping out because it's a Bank Holiday and they'll be extra busy.'

'I bet they will … with our customers,' muttered Amelia.

In truth, she had forgotten about Mac's request to Tamsin to arrange a visit. With little time left to plan, they would have to bluff their way through it.

Tamsin was typing a reply to Mona, her fingers flying over the screen. 'She says get there at eleven o'clock and she'll meet you outside the main entrance.'

The accommodation Amelia had booked in Stirling was right next door to a large cemetery and as close as she could get to the castle itself. Her first glimpse of the most strategically important castle in Scotland's history, even more so than the one in Edinburgh according to Angus, was as she drove up a steep road where the tarmac turned to cobbles. The buildings in the older part of the city turned to stone and walls dominated the roadside. It felt like travelling back in time. Pulling up in one of the parking spaces outside the hotel, she got out the car and half expected a knight in full armour to trot by on his horse, lance in hand. Instead, she saw only a few cars exiting from the castle grounds a short way further up the hill, atop an imposing crag. Before checking in to the hotel, Amelia crossed the road to admire the view which looked out towards the National Wallace Monument rising above the trees.

When Amelia descended from her bedroom on the second floor to pause in front of the full-length mirror in reception, she was looking forward to the night ahead. To her relief, the strapless electric blue chiffon dress and high heeled silver sandals looked good considering the outfit had been pulled together rather last minute. With her hair styled in a chignon using diamante clips, she was pleased with the overall result.

Deciding to walk the short distance from the hotel to the castle entrance she arrived in front of a statue of Robert the Bruce, who was watching over the glamourous guests dressed in outfits which glittered beneath flaming torches. The scent of smoke mingled with many perfumes and aftershaves. Amelia was rifling through her silver clutch bag for the ticket Mac had given her when she heard someone calling her name and spotted him leaning against the entrance arch, waving her over.

'Hey, look at you all shimmery,' he said.

'Never has anyone felt as inappropriately dressed entering a castle as I do right now,' she told him, gesturing at the fabric floating delicately around her knees and the silver satin wrap covering her arms. 'I feel I ought to be in battledress with an army behind me.'

'Well, Boudicca, in my opinion you could stop an army dressed like that. You look beautiful.'

'You look pretty good yourself,' said Amelia, taking in Mac's outfit of a white t-shirt, black leather trousers and a jacket.

He spun around slowly like a model, a grin on his face. 'Why, thank you. This is the Chequered Pipes uniform. By the way, you're in for a treat tonight. Got a storming set list raring to go. So, I'll have to leave you for now. Don't forget to give me a wave.'

With Mac's familiar presence gone, Amelia felt exposed. She didn't know anyone and there seemed to be a lot of people. She joined the crowd making their way to the Great Hall. All of them seemed to be part of a group or a couple except her. Stopping outside to take in the unusual yellow limewash walls of the building which stood out amongst the traditional grey stone of the rest of the castle, Amelia took a deep breath. As the last of the evening light was fading behind the hills, she walked inside, clutching her invitation, to be greeted by a butler in full tartan regalia.

'Good evening,' he said, offering Amelia a flute of chilled champagne from a silver tray.

As condensation from the glass soaked into Amelia's fingers, she gazed around in awe. The Great Hall was dazzling in the soft golden glow of the uplighters, above which the wooden ceiling reminded her of the skeleton of an ancient warship. Circular tables had been arranged across the floor and laid with deep red tablecloths, candelabras and centrepieces of cascading flowers.

'Wow,' she said aloud.

'Glorious setting, as usual,' agreed a lady dressed in lilac, her grey hair swept into a bun. 'We come every year. How about you?'

'Er, this is my first visit. My friend's in the band.'

'How exciting. Checkered Nights, isn't it? I recall they

played last year. I do tend to remember. This is one of my favourite events of the year and it's all for a good cause.'

'I saw on the invite it's to raise money for a cancer charity.' Having been relieved to have someone to talk to, Amelia now felt unsure what to say. She sipped champagne and tried to shuffle away.

'Well, you know,' the lady said conspiratorially, pulling her back and to one side so the incoming guests could pass, 'take my advice and make sure you join in the auction. There are always fabulous prizes to bid for. Last year we won an all-inclusive trip to Mustique. It was fabulous from what I can remember but I drank that much rum it's rather hazy.'

'I'm not sure any of them will be within my price range,' said Amelia honestly.

'Oh dear. Perhaps you could bid for one of the lesser prizes. Goodness, there's Ffion. Do excuse me, I only get to catch up with her once a year.' Abruptly the lady appeared to lose interest in their conversation and disappeared.

Alone again, Amelia looked around at the gentlemen in kilts and the ladies in their finest evening wear and diamonds, as they gossiped amongst themselves. She wished Mac could have stayed longer, she never felt uncomfortable in his presence. Although she knew he wasn't far away getting ready backstage with Digger and the others, she would have preferred him to be with her.

As the guests were called to take their seats for dinner, Amelia checked the seating plan. The tables were named after Scottish Lochs and she had been allocated a seat on Lomond. The table seated eight although was set for seven. She greeted her fellow diners, who included the lady in the lilac dress she'd met earlier, while trying to conceal her dismay that they were all couples. A slender blonde lady, whose low-cut pink sequinned gown caught both the light of the candles and the eye of the man beside her, placed a hand decorated with long pink nails and a gold ring encrusted with diamonds on her companion's biceps to whisper in his ear. He glanced at a large platinum Rolex on his wrist with raised eyebrows.

Polite conversation took place as bread rolls were served and wine poured by the waiting staff. Amelia laid a red napkin over her lap and tapped her foot beneath the table, trying to remain engaged with those around her. For some reason her mind kept wandering off to thoughts of Mac. She really liked the aftershave he'd been wearing tonight and those leather trousers, which she'd never particularly been a fan of before, had looked perfect on him. If he took that jacket off, she would bet his muscular arms would suit that white t-shirt.

'What brings you here?'

Feeling herself blush, Amelia jolted back to the present. 'Excuse me?'

'I asked what brings you here?' the lady in the pink dress repeated her question.

'She's with the band, Portia,' declared the lady in lilac.

'Really?' Portia seemed surprised.

'Yes,' Amelia confirmed rather smugly. 'I'm here with Mac, the lead singer, actually.'

'Doesn't he work at that funny little riding stables?' Portia asked.

'If you mean Lochside then yes, that's my aunt's business.'

'Well … well … small world. My father owns Keilburn.'

'You must be Hugh's sister then?'

'For my sins.' Portia sighed. 'I've not come across you before though.'

'I live in London. I'm up here helping out while my aunt recovers from an accident.'

'Oh, yes, we heard about the unfortunate incident at the castle ruins although daddy says she won't be able to sue because the warning signs are quite clear —'

'I'm sure my aunt is not the type to sue,' snapped Amelia. 'She was rescuing one of her ponies when it happened.'

'Of course, I wasn't suggesting she needs the money —'

'Oh, goody. Heads up. The auction's about to start,' the lady in lilac bellowed across the table, cutting the conversation off.

While the auction took place, the dessert bowls were cleared away by the waiting staff, who then served coffee and mints. Amelia watched her fellow diners waving their gold numbered paddles in the air with abandon, making sure to keep her hands tucked under her thighs, keen not to accidentally put in a successful bid for a yacht when she could barely afford a lifejacket.

Finally, the auction was over, the lights lowered, a spotlight flashed on the stage and Mac stepped into its circle to a loud cheer. 'Is everybody ready to get this party going?' he yelled, hands poised over a low-slung guitar.

To a resounding 'yes', Mac strummed the first chords of what he announced was 'Freedom in the Hills' as multi-coloured disco lights flashed over the dance floor.

'Let's go,' encouraged the lady in lilac, gesturing at Amelia to follow. 'Now we get to strut our stuff.'

Amelia downed the last of her wine before making her way to the dance floor. Feeling conspicuous, she swayed self-consciously to begin with but every time she glanced up Mac's eyes were on her. His gaze followed only her as if she was alone, dancing just for him. After the hurt of Ryan's rejection had left her feeling unwanted, Mac's attention made her feel special again. Her confidence soared and she let herself go, lost in the music, arms pumping, feet moving in time to the beat. It was freedom. Freedom from caring what others thought. She wanted to dance so she was dancing.

'Yeah,' she roared, as she became absorbed in the joy of the music, swept along with a crowd up for having a good time. All around her people bounced on the balls of their feet, arms raised, singing along to the chorus of 'Bagpipes and Monsters.'

By the time Chequered Pipes left the stage, Amelia was exhausted and happy. She hadn't enjoyed herself as much for ages and felt sad as the evening came to an end and the revellers began to disperse. High heeled shoes were removed to avoid having to negotiate ancient cobbles while tipsy. One particularly merry guest who decided to walk backwards smacked straight into a wall, crumpling to the ground, unharmed.

'Who put that there,' he complained, rubbing his shoulder.

'Don't worry, mate,' his friend responded, helping him up. 'This castle's only been here for hundreds of years. It was inevitable you'd be taken unawares.'

Amelia was buzzing too much to return straight to the hotel. She knew she should because it was late and the staff would want to lock up but she really didn't want to go. Instead, she walked a short distance away over the lawns to the Grand Battery, then stood, tilting her head back, admiring the stars, marvelling at how majestic the sky was.

'I've been looking for you.' Mac's voice grew louder as he approached. 'Did you have a good time?'

'I really did. Thanks for inviting me.'

'You're welcome. It was nice to see you enjoying yourself. I was watching you the whole time … couldn't take my eyes off you, if I'm honest.'

'You looked … amazing on that stage.' Amelia cringed at herself. Of all the romantic possibilities that was all she could manage. Mac was bound to leave now. Except he didn't.

'I'd really like to kiss you,' he blurted.

'I would really like that too.'

Their lips touched briefly, then with more passion. The

heat from Mac's body seeped through the material of Amelia's dress as he encircled her waist with his arms. She laid her head against his chest.

'I'd say let's dance but heels and cobbles …' Mac grinned, then frowned at the sound of a vehicle's horn tooting loud and long. 'Ah, that's Digger signalling the van's loaded up and ready to go.'

'You have to leave?' Amelia didn't want such a brilliant night to end.

'Where are you staying?' Mac asked, as a staff member marched towards them while signalling they needed to head for the exit.

'A hotel just down the hill. I can walk. It's not far.'

'I could —' Mac swore and threw his hands up in frustration as Digger pressed the horn for longer this time.

'Don't worry, I can walk,' Amelia repeated.

Mac took her hand. 'No, not alone you can't. I'll walk back with you and perhaps we can, you know, talk.'

In the car park Amelia recognised Digger waiting beside a large white van, running his hands through his red hair. 'Mate, we have to go,' he shouted over as soon as he spotted them.

Mac hesitated. 'I'm going to walk Amelia to her hotel.'

'We can drop her off on the way. My sister's waiting to put us up for the night and she's got work tomorrow so we need to go. It's not fair otherwise.' Digger opened the passenger door and gestured to Mac to jump in. Then he turned to Amelia. 'Sorry, forgot my manners. I'm Digger. Nice to meet you. If you hop in the back, we'll give you a lift.'

Sensing there was tension and not wanting to be the cause of friction in the band, Amelia whispered to Mac, 'It's fine. I can't believe I'm turning down the chance to be a rock chick but there'll be another time.'

For a few seconds they held each other's gaze, their eyes

saying all the things this wasn't the time or place for them to express.

'OK,' Mac relented.

While he clambered into the passenger seat, Amelia found herself sandwiched in the back between Ross, the guitar player, and a drum kit for the brief drive to the hotel.

Once in her hotel room, Amelia collapsed on the bed, her feet relieved to be released from the heels they weren't used to. She wiggled her toes and gazed at the ceiling fan whizzing round above her head. It was probably for the best anyway. She didn't need the complications and distractions of a long-distance relationship. They rarely worked out. You needed someone nearby. You couldn't go out for meals or to the cinema or just laze around on a Sunday afternoon with someone in Scotland if you were in London.

As she curled up alone in the king size bed, gazing at a goodnight text message from Mac, Amelia couldn't stop herself feeling that she had turned down a night of what she felt sure would have been fantastic sex for the wrong reasons.

Having worked for weeks without a break, it was strange to have Sunday off. Given the gift of time, Amelia did some sightseeing and stopped for lunch at a café. Yet all the while she felt unsettled and a few times found herself glancing down at her feet expecting to see Gallus there. She sent numerous messages to Zoey checking that all was well. Eventually she received one back written in capital letters telling her to enjoy her day off and stop bothering them. She also heard from Mac, his light-hearted messages relaying progress on the journey back in the van. They both skirted around any mention of feelings or future dates. He also sent a few of the photos he'd taken from the stage. Amelia looked at herself dancing in the crowd and smiled. She certainly appeared to be having more fun than Portia, who was scowling on the edge of the dancefloor watching the man with the Rolex twirling with another girl.

Early afternoon she set off on the drive back to Lochside. With music playing on the Mini's stereo, the sun lighting the way and a bag of snacks on the passenger seat, she felt she was heading home. Lochside had given her a sense of freedom. No one was regularly checking up on what she was doing, interrupting her or expecting her to work late for nothing in return. Although the ponies brought responsibility, she had got into a routine and was enjoying it. Then there was the bonus of having met Mac and the possibilities he represented. Although aware the business was Jilly's, she allowed herself to consider the possibility she could stay, even though it was unlikely Jilly could afford to take on additional staff. She could take the opportunity to ask her aunt about it when they met in Orkney.

As she pulled into a layby for a short break, Amelia's phone pinged. Although tempted to ignore it, she opened the message and skimmed it with a sinking feeling.

Hello Amelia. Looking forward to your imminent return to the office. On your first day back, please come straight to see me for a catch up. Thanks. Manju

Without replying, she threw the phone on the passenger seat and opened a bag of sweets. Seeing the words had been an unwelcome reminder that Amelia had a life to return to and it was expecting her back soon.

7

Gallus was pleased to see Amelia back. He bounded up to her, long ears flapping, then shot straight between her legs out through the cottage door. Amelia lost sight of him in the dark but could hear him snuffling about. Knowing he wouldn't go far, she left him to it and went upstairs. As she placed her overnight bag on the bed to unpack a sudden flash of light outside caught her eye, drawing her to the window. She looked out, expecting to see lightning in the distance but when the light appeared again it was zigzagging across the land towards the Bothy. She took out her phone, pushed the window open and, leaning out, took a couple of photos. The results were an expanse of black nothingness except for a tiny, blurred spot, which Mac would probably argue was an insect, attracted by the bedroom light. She tried again but was too far away. Only a professional zoom lens would have a chance of getting a clear shot.

'All right, Spunkie, I'm coming after you,' she said, pulling the window shut to a creak of protest from the rusty hinges.

Striding across the lawn with Gallus beside her, Amelia jangled the keys and unlocked the gates. She didn't turn on any of the yard lights, instead carrying on through to the fields following only the beam of a torch. It helped her avoid tripping on the uneven ground but she was still a little freaked out by the time she reached the gate. What had seemed a good idea in the safety of the cottage felt very different now she was outside. Gallus flopped down on his belly and closed his eyes, making it clear he'd had enough exercise and was going no further.

'Oh, fine, be a lightweight then. I'll go on my own.' The sound of her voice startled Amelia. A startled shrew scurried across the torch beam. Gallus woofed at it and was answered by a lengthy neigh from nearby.

Now she was at ground level, Amelia could no longer see the light. She slipped through the gate and took a few steps forward consumed by the feeling of being watched. It was probably Gallus who she could hear breathing. Seconds later a shrill noise pierced the air, causing her right hand to vibrate. Shrieking, she ducked down to hide, then burst out laughing when she realised it was her phone ringing. She was creating so much drama she had frightened herself. The screen showed the caller was Mac. She answered but it was difficult to make out much of what he was saying. The call was crackly and kept breaking up. When she told him where she was, Mac's shouted words came through loud and clear despite the poor signal.

'Turn around now and go back to the cottage,' he yelled.

'What the hell were you doing last night?' Mac demanded, arms folded.

Amelia sat at the desk feeling chastised and disappointed. This wasn't the conversation she had planned for Monday morning. She wanted to tell Mac how much she had enjoyed the fundraising evening and perhaps suggest they go out again. Not a date, necessarily, but they clearly enjoyed each other's company so why not? Instead of which she was faced with a furious Mac, while Angus and Zoey appeared confused, until he filled them in on the previous night's events.

'Do you have any idea how dangerous what you did is?' Mac was yelling again. 'You could have been hurt and who would have found you?'

'I had my phone,' Amelia protested. She knew it was a feeble defence but it was all she had.

'The signal's not good once you get that far away from the buildings,' Angus chipped in. 'Mac's right, you were foolish. Still no harm done.'

'Fortunately,' muttered Mac.

'Indeed, imagine if the ghost of Gordon the Glorious had found you,' joked Angus, attempting to lighten the mood.

'Gordon the what? Ghost of who?' asked Zoey, sensing Amelia would appreciate a change of subject.

'Gordon the Glorious. He's a famous warrior whose clan lived on these lands. He won many battles,' explained Angus, 'but eventually he was driven over the border to England by his rivals, supposedly leaving buried treasures behind. We've never discovered anything though.'

'Probably because you've never gone looking,' sniggered Zoey, through a mouth filled with doughnut.

'Stan did once go through a phase of metal detecting but he found nowt.' Angus shrugged. 'I kept telling him you'd need some idea of where to start looking. No doubt someone down the pub told him a tale and he fell for it.'

'It'll be the usual local legend nonsense made up for the tourists.' Zoey wiped jam from her chin. 'There are no ghosts, there is no treasure —'

'And you've no imagination,' interrupted Angus.

Amelia stood up. 'Let's move on, shall we? I'm fine. I've taken onboard the criticism. Meanwhile we have a gymkhana to plan and Mac and I are due at Three Stones Barn later today to meet Mona. Let's not waste time arguing about Gordon and whether he had any treasure or not. I can't be worrying about that when I've got jumps to paint.'

Leaving the office for the refuge of the barn, Amelia sighed. The team's bickering had upset her and cast a shadow over what had been a lovely weekend. Picking up a paintbrush, she began retouching the red paint on a striped pole. Tamsin had been working hard and what had been a heap of redundant equipment was looking good. Calls had also begun trickling through as the posters were spotted locally. As planned, it was starting to come together. Amelia had high hopes the gymkhana was going to prove beneficial to Lochside's future.

Mac strode in. Saying nothing, he picked up a paintbrush and began redoing the white stripes, starting at the other end of the pole Amelia was already working on.

'I'm sorry.' He said it so softly Amelia only just heard him. 'You're an adult, Amelia, you can do what you want. It's not my business to tell you what to do but it is dangerous to wander off alone. Even in daylight it's easy to lose your way. You need the proper gear if you're going off the beaten track.'

'I wasn't off the beaten track. It was the way we went the other day.' Amelia was still feeling touchy about it.

'Yeah, I know, but once you go through the gate at the end of the fields it's uncharted territory and you've only been that way once in daylight. Just be careful, that's all. My mates and I got lost on a school trip once. It was funny until it wasn't. Volunteers had to come out and rescue us. We were kids, we didn't know any better …'

'You're saying I'm old enough to have known better.' Amelia put the brush down with force.

'No … I'm …' Mac stopped painting to lean over and kiss Amelia on the lips. 'I'm saying I want to take you out, preferably without Digger interrupting, and I can't do that if you're missing.'

'Well, in that case I'll behave.' Amelia resumed painting with a smile.

'Hmm … I don't know about that.' Mac flicked paint at the pole. 'Depends on the circumstances.'

Shortly before Amelia and Mac were due to leave, Fergus decided to play hard to catch. The minutes ticked by as they chased the prancing liver chestnut Highland pony around the field, getting to within inches of his silver tail before he squealed and galloped away again. Amelia began to doubt they'd make it to Three Stones Barn at all. In the end, Mac managed to pounce and get a headcollar on Fergus to bring him in.

It was a rush to get to Three Stones Barn in time, as Amelia wrenched the Mini's steering wheel to the left, almost doing a wheelie on the immaculately gravelled drive. Mac clung to the seat in alarm.

'It's only just eleven o'clock now,' he told her. 'Calm down.'

'I hate being late,' she hissed, pressing the accelerator. The driveway between the white post and rail fenced paddocks seemed never ending.

'Looks more like a rich person's ranch than a riding stables,' Mac observed, wincing as Amelia crunched the gears. The wheels spun throwing up a shower of stones.

'Either way, I don't fancy repainting those fences,' Amelia retorted, breathing heavily. 'Who chooses white around horses anyway?'

'I'm going to guess those with enough money to pay someone else to do all the work.'

'Damn right.' Amelia pulled into a space in a surprisingly

empty car park. 'I didn't expect there to be much room. I thought it would be packed on a Bank Holiday.'

'Maybe it's all a clever marketing ploy and they're not really as popular as they make out.' Mac pointed through the windscreen to a young girl standing by the entrance. Dressed in fawn jodhpurs, a green sweatshirt and chewing the hair of one of her long brunette bunches, she appeared to be waiting. 'I reckon that's Mona.'

'Let's make sure before we introduce ourselves to a random child.'

Mac opened his door and jumped out, giving the girl a hearty wave. 'Hello there.'

'Are you Melia and Zac?' she asked, once they reached her.

'Are you Mona?' questioned Mac.

Amelia cut in and introduced herself.

'Tamsin said you can get us in. We wanted to look around,' explained Mac.

Mona checked over her shoulder then leaned in towards them. 'I can, but you have to pretend.'

Mac leaned even closer, cupping a hand to the side of his mouth before replying. 'OK. We can do that.'

'You need to pretend you're the parents of one of my friends who wants to come here.' Mona's eyes darted sideways checking they weren't overheard. 'I told them you wanted to see the place before you book anything.'

'OK.' Amelia nodded. 'As Mac says, we can manage that.'

'Stop looking guilty,' hissed Mac.

'I'm not,' protested Mona.

'I meant Amelia.'

'I do not look guilty,' snapped Amelia. 'Though I do feel like I've stumbled onto the set of a low budget spy movie.'

Neither of her companions heard her for they were already strolling under a white wooden archway topped by a large clock decorated with a blue face and gold Roman numerals.

'Is Tamsin OK?' Mona asked Amelia. 'She felt mean leaving Lochside but she wanted to do other things. Then she was desperate to get away. She didn't really like it here.'

'She's settled in and is very excited about the gymkhana. She's ever so helpful. I don't think I could manage without her, there's so much to do,' Amelia reassured Mona.

'She told me she was really scared to ask to come back.'

'Well, if it makes you feel any better, the way I see it is you must do what's right for you at the time. Sometimes that means you make a decision and then you change your mind, like Tamsin did. She'll always be welcome at Lochside.'

'She keeps saying I should go too.'

'Maybe you could come along to the gymkhana, try us out, see what you think. It's free.'

They had now stepped into an American-style barn with ponies stabled down each side in bright airy loose boxes. The top half of each partition consisted of a metal grill, allowing the ponies to see each other. As they walked down the aisle, heads appeared from the occupied boxes. An appaloosa whinnied to get their attention.

'This is Sparkles,' Mona said proudly. 'My favourite.'

The pony snorted and shook his head. Amelia peered over the door. Sparkles was an attractive pony. His white coat was spattered with dark spots and his kindly eyes watched her as she reached out to stroke his neck.

'I can see why you like him,' said Mac, gazing around, 'and this barn's posh, isn't it? Handy when it's chucking it down. No getting soaked between stables.'

Amelia could see his point. There were storage rooms located in the barn so no need to venture outside if you didn't have to. She tried not to feel jealous as they carried on moving towards a huge pair of doors at the opposite end to where they'd entered. Mona slid one door open. It moved smoothly on its runner. Outside there were paddocks and barns. Three riders were trotting their ponies in single file around a track in an outdoor school, observed by an instructor standing in the centre.

'This way,' said Mona, leading Amelia and Mac towards a large hanger. They entered via a door signposted as the viewing gallery.

Inside the air was chilly and dusty with an aroma that reminded Amelia of a workshop, the mingled smells of leather and oil. They sat at the front of a tiered seating area on uncomfortably small plastic seats which folded down, overlooking an oval shaped, sandy surfaced ring. Mirrors were set on the walls at regular intervals, interspersed with the square letter markerboards used in dressage.

'This is the first time they've used the new indoor school,' whispered Mona reverently.

'I feel honoured to be a witness to the occasion,' said Mac, holding his hands together and bowing his head.

'It's very smart,' said Amelia, discretely nudging Mac to behave.

They watched a pink-cheeked girl desperately trying to encourage a skewbald Shetland over a row of trotting poles. Despite numerous attempts, her reluctant mount kept ducking out at the last second. Eventually he stuck his head between his forelegs, bucked four times in succession and unseated the girl. She landed on the first pole with a thud and could only sit and watch as he cantered off with a triumphant expression which suggested if she was so keen to go over the poles, she should do so herself. Mona sniggered, covering her mouth with a hand to try and disguise the sound, which echoed in the cavernous space. Unharmed but cross, the girl joined the instructor in trying to catch the pony, who kept skipping away, reins flapping.

'Marble is really naughty,' whispered Mona.

'Shetlands usually are,' said Amelia, as they stood to leave. 'By the time they catch him the lesson will be over. It's a good ploy to get out of doing any work.'

They took a different route back towards the car park, walking down a path running alongside a lawn set with wooden benches and a waterfall artistically arranged in the style of a cairn.

'I always find waterfalls soothing and rather hypnotic, don't you?' she asked Mac.

'Nope.' He shook his head vigorously. 'Just makes me want the bathroom.'

'Oh, the toilets are over there,' said Mona helpfully, pointing to a building on their right.

Looking in that direction, Amelia saw a man dressed in jeans, a blue shirt and black brogues exiting a door. He strode briskly towards them, his demeanour suggesting he wasn't best pleased to find them wandering about unsupervised.

'Do you need any assistance?' he asked in an American accent.

'Ah, good morning,' Mac stepped up to him. 'We're thinking of bringing our daughter here and Mona very kindly offered to give us a tour. We are most impressed, er …'

'Jake.' They shook hands. 'Well, that's good of Mona, however we do prefer an adult member of the team deal with prospective customers.'

'I did tell Charlotte,' Mona protested.

'I'm afraid my daughter did not inform me. She can be forgetful. Thank you, Mona, you can go now. I'll take it from here.' Jake gestured to Mac and Amelia to follow him into the building. 'Why don't you come into the office. Apologies, I don't know your names.'

'Mr Pipe,' said Mac, taking Amelia's hand.

'Thanks for the tour, Mona,' Amelia called over her

shoulder, giving a smile she hoped would reassure the girl not to worry.

The office looked new. The relaxing sound of Pan Pipes played over a speaker fixed high in the corner of the ceiling. Plush suede armchairs were set in a circle and a few beanbags had been scattered stylishly beneath the windows. An expensive coffee machine sat on a sideboard, beside china cups and saucers and individual packets of biscuits piled in a wicker basket.

'Complimentary tea or coffee?' asked Jake.

'No, thanks. We can't stop long,' said Amelia, glancing at her watch. 'Actually, we really don't have any time to spare at all.'

'Oh, darling. Are you saying we can't stay?' Mac frowned, feigning disappointment.

'I'm afraid not. We've got lunch with the … er … Campbells.'

'So we have.' Mac shrugged. 'You know, I'd quite forgotten that. We've had an excellent look around with Mona and it was good to meet you, Jake. We'll be in touch.'

'Here.' Jake thrust a glossy brochure into Mac's hand. 'Do take this. It lists our prices for the various activities we offer.'

Once back at the car, they burst into laughter.

'For a second there, I thought I was going to have to make up an entire imaginary family,' gasped Mac.

'Did you now, Mr Pipe.' Amelia's reply just made them laugh even harder.

As she drove away, Amelia concluded that Three Stones Barn had the air of a show home rather than a riding stables. It was spotless, regimented and there didn't appear to be a single strand of straw out of place. It had everything, yet Amelia felt it was lacking something.

In the passenger seat, Mac rested his head back and closed

his eyes. Amelia turned up the volume on the radio, then immediately turned it back down.

'You know, Mac, being around horses should be fun. It always was for me as a child, at least until the accident.'

'Go on.' Reluctantly Mac opened his eyes.

'I mean, learning to ride properly is important, of course, but those ponies going round and round in that outdoor school looked bored.'

'So did their riders.'

'Maybe we're on to something with our gymkhana. Perhaps we can tempt them back with the promise of fun, as well as learning.'

'All I know for sure is if anyone can pull it off, you can.'

Mac's welcome words of praise really touched Amelia. She realised it had been a long time since anyone had said anything positive about her work.

8

Dawn was breaking as Amelia drove the Mini to the airport. Mac had wanted to travel to Inverness on the motorbike, until Amelia pointed out she couldn't ride pillion carrying two overnight bags. The roads were deserted, apart from a crow picking at a carcass and the occasional startled rabbit disappearing into the hedgerow. Now it was May the weather was bright and occasionally warm and soon the notorious midges would make their unwelcome appearance.

'I wonder what Jilly wants that she couldn't tell us over the phone,' Mac speculated.

'My guess is nothing much. She's bored and wants to see us because she's missing Lochside.' Amelia indicated and turned into the entrance to the airport car park.

'Though I can't figure out why she wants me to visit and not Angus,' said Mac. 'I know Lochside's not hierarchical but surely Angus should be going, not me.'

'Angus has never been on a plane and won't go on one. He'd have to get the ferry and he considers that going abroad. Zoey told me she found out when they chatted about her dream to see the world. Angus said Aberdeen was about his limit for travel and he couldn't understand why she wanted to visit hot and sweaty places, as he put it.'

Later, as she took her seat by the window of a propeller plane that felt tiny to Amelia, having only flown on larger planes before, she glanced over at Mac for reassurance. He was fastening his seatbelt with a smile on his face.

'It's very small,' she mouthed across to him, as the plane began its taxi to the runway.

'Are you nervous?' he asked.

Looking out the window, Amelia realised she wasn't. The flight to Orkney should take forty-five minutes. She'd sat in traffic jams and on delayed trains for longer than that. When compared to the relentless grind of city commuting, today's journey was an adventure.

'Not at all.' She smiled and resumed looking out the window as the propellers picked up speed.

As the plane descended for its landing at the airport of Kirkwall, located on the largest of the archipelago of islands known as the Mainland, Amelia gazed below and got a first glimpse of the ragged coastline. However, the first thing to hit her as she descended the few steps from the plane was the wind. With his hair blowing magnificently around his face, his leather jacket billowing stylishly and clutching the bouquet of flowers they'd brought for Jilly, Mac looked as though he could be participating in a photo shoot for *Your Home, Your Castle*. Whereas Amelia suspected her appearance resembled someone who'd had a fight in a wind tunnel and lost.

It was a short taxi ride along a road surrounded by fields to the housing estate where Donna and her family lived. Mac rang the bell of a detached house built in the same modern style as those around it. Minutes ticked by before the door was opened by Jilly, who was balancing on crutches.

Having not seen her aunt for years, Amelia recognised the Jilly of her memories in the older and frailer version stood before her. The boisterousness and stocky frame had softened; the brown hair had turned grey.

'Come in, don't stand on ceremony. You're not getting a twenty-one-gun salute, you know.'

As they followed Jilly into a living room decorated with photos of Donna's children, Amelia smiled, pleased her aunt's bossiness remained, her deep, gravelly voice as strong as ever. Jilly slumped in an armchair, lifting her legs up onto a pouffe. She indicated a bone china tea set of delicate flowery cups, saucers and a teapot. The contents of a packet of digestive biscuits had been fanned out on a matching plate.

'Donna got it ready before she left for work. She's good to me. I know it can't be easy having me moping around the place alongside bringing up two kids on your own. I'll have tea, strong, two sugars, please.'

Amelia got to work making their drinks while Mac attacked the biscuits and filled Jilly in on their flight and all the Lochside news.

'Got it all under control then, Amelia? I knew I could rely on you. We might not be a glamorous family but we're reliable, loyal and practical. All attributes no one values yet everyone wants.' Jilly sounded satisfied and rather proud. 'I was chatting to your mum last night. She said they'd visit me soon. I appreciate it's not an easy journey from Spain.'

'I'm sure they'd love to see you and will as soon as they can,' Amelia assured her.

'Indeed.' Jilly took a gulp of tea. 'How's that dreadful band of yours doing, Mac?'

'Rocking on. Yet to hit the big time but the good news is "Bagpipes and Monsters" is doing OK on the streaming apps.'

Jilly guffawed and spurted tea simultaneously. 'In my day you bought a record from the shop for about ten pence. All this streaming stuff. I don't get it. Still good luck to you. I like a person with some oomph.'

Amelia glanced through to the conservatory where spots of rain were now hitting the sloping roof with a regular splat. Jilly noticed her looking and nodded.

'It's good you're staying. The weather's closing in, as predicted. Sometimes the wind shakes the house so violently it almost takes the roof off and flights get cancelled. Donna's booked you two rooms in the Inn just up the road.'

Mac sat back, sinking into the beige cushions of the sofa until his legs were higher than the rest of him. He looked comical. Amelia stifled a laugh. No one spoke. A lengthy silence followed while Amelia listened to the ticking of the ornate clock on the mantlepiece. She fidgeted in the armchair, moving a cushion that was digging into her lower back. Surely they hadn't come all this way just for Jilly to tell them about Orkney's weather; she could have done that when she returned to Lochside and saved them the journey.

'The worst thing is not being with my troops every day for the first time in decades,' sighed Jilly.

'If it's any consolation they are well.' Amelia thought she was being helpful. Judging by the expression on her aunt's face she'd failed. To try and cheer her up she added, 'I rode Spirit.'

'Oh, I do adore the way she floats. It's in the breeding of course, so as not to sink into the sand in the desert although Lochside's mostly mud. It's a bit of an irrelevant skill really but I always wanted an Arabian and Stan would never let me have one. He worried they're too temperamental. He'd be glad I treated myself in the end.'

'When are you coming back?' asked Mac. 'Still on schedule?'

'At the end of this month, all being well. I need to tell you something though and don't get cross —'

'Uh oh. Whenever that phrase is used it means what

you're about to hear is going to turn you apoplectic.' Mac grimaced at Amelia, who shrugged in return.

'Now, don't be so dramatic,' tutted Jilly, 'but I do need to tell you that, after a lot of soul searching and sleepless nights since my accident, I'm considering selling Lochside.'

'What?' Amelia and Mac yelped simultaneously.

'You can't do that.' Amelia was aghast. 'It's your life's work and Uncle Stan's too.'

'Has Donna put you up to this?' Mac demanded.

'No, she hasn't.' Jilly's expression gave nothing away. 'She's concerned about my welfare, of course, but she would never interfere and tell me what to do. It's all my own decision to make. We're clear on that.'

'I can't imagine anyone telling you what to do,' said Amelia, 'and I can't imagine you'd take much notice if they did.'

'I've always been determined but now look at me.' Jilly indicated her legs. 'I'm no use to anyone. I'm in such a muddle. Then out of the blue I get a phone call offering me a sum of money for Lochside that I wouldn't normally have a chance of getting my hands on unless I won the Lottery.'

'You only feel like that because you're still recovering. Once your legs are better, you'll be fine,' Amelia reassured her aunt. 'As for this mysterious offer, you'd have to sell your ponies ... your beloved troops. You can't do that. You won't, I know you won't.'

'I don't know, Amelia. It feels like there's so much against me,' sighed Jilly. 'I feel battered and bruised from all directions.'

'You are battered and bruised but you'll heal,' insisted Amelia.

'Have you asked yourself why someone would all of a sudden offer you what you're insinuating is a large sum of money for Lochside?' asked Mac.

'No, the truth is it didn't occur to me. There are lots of wealthy people who want to buy remote places to renovate, who are keen to move out of the cities, that kind of thing. Can't say I blame them. I didn't think it was my business to question them about their motives.'

'Do you know who the offer is from? Did they tell you?' Mac wasn't prepared to let it go.

'It's a confidential offer. I'm not at liberty to say any more than I already have. Look, I'm just giving it some thought. I have too much time sitting around and it's not helpful. The truth is, I've got to stop pretending. The business has been failing for years and costs are rising. I could take the money and downsize. Keep some of the ponies and start again but at my age it's too much effort and where would I go? I'd need somewhere brand new so I could move straight in with no maintenance and that would be expensive. Nothing comes cheap these days.'

'I don't understand why you're talking like this. This isn't the infallible aunt I remember,' cried Amelia.

'I'm not infallible. Perhaps that's what this accident has taught me most. Life is a winding road and none of us can be sure what's coming around the next bend. We can only do our best.'

'Then give me time to do my best. The gymkhana's going to change everything. We ought to give it a chance. I know Angus told you that Tamsin returned and her friends are helping us. Once they realise how much fun they're having, we'll win them all back.'

'I agree with Amelia,' said Mac. 'Now come on, Jilly, cheer up and tell me where I can find us more biscuits.'

They chatted for a bit longer telling Jilly about their visit to Three Stones Barn, but the conversation never really recovered from the bombshell she had dropped. When Jilly started to look tired, Amelia took that as her cue to suggest to Mac it was time to go and check in to their accommodation.

'Donna asked me to pass on her apologies for not being able to meet up while you're here. She's so busy with the kids' after-school activities. Leisure time is a real luxury for her. She also thought it best I don't overdo it and says I mustn't do too much, which is ironic considering, since the accident, I've never done less in my life.'

Once they'd said their goodbyes, Amelia and Mac ventured out into the rain carrying their bags.

Sitting at a table in the restaurant at the Inn that evening, candlelight giving the nook a cosy feel while wind and rain smashed against the window beside them, Amelia tried to shrug off feelings of anger. She'd taken a sabbatical, left her cat and friends behind at short notice to help her aunt's business and now Jilly was considering quitting. She felt growing fury that Jilly might have purposefully wasted her time, that she had never intended to stick it out at Lochside.

'You're brooding,' observed Mac. 'I can tell.'

'Maybe.' Amelia sipped her gin and tonic.

'You're thinking Jilly's used you to tide her over.'

'Well, what do you make of it?' Amelia demanded. 'Can an accident change someone this much?'

'There's no way she'll sell Lochside,' Mac replied with confidence. 'She's in a rut, cooped up inside all day when she's used to being outdoors. It's affected her mental state. Plus, she's sulking because Lochside hasn't fallen apart without her.'

'I have to say I prefer your theory to mine.' Amelia grinned. 'It makes no sense. Jilly's never been motivated by money.'

'But I assume she's never been offered a significant sum of it before?'

'Not that I'm aware of.'

'Who knows how we'd react if we were in her situation. I can see the attraction. She's clearly stressed and it would solve many of her problems.'

'Weird that this offer has come now, when she's vulnerable and confused.'

'Yeah but that's coincidence, I'm sure.'

They paused while two bowls of steaming pasta were placed on the mats before them by the waiter.

'Why don't you stay?' Mac asked casually, winding spaghetti around his fork.

'What do you mean? I've got no option but to stay. Our flight isn't until tomorrow morning and judging by this weather no one will be flying out tonight.'

'No. I meant properly stay. Quit your job and come to Lochside permanently. We need you to turn this around and I can't help but feel if you were that happy in London you'd never have agreed to come.'

'I can't do that.' Amelia shook her head fiercely. 'Can't give up a secure job. You heard Jilly. What if she sells? I'll have nothing.'

Mac reached across the table and took Amelia's hand, interlacing their fingers. 'You'd have me and if it all goes wrong we'll take Chequered Pipes on the road. The band and I have talked about doing it before, you know, a promotional tour. You could be that rock chick roadie after all. How's that for an offer?'

Amelia turned her head to look out the window but the single pane was misted up. She couldn't see through. Her mind felt as fogged up as the glass, beyond was the unseen and unknown. Much as she longed to answer Mac with enthusiastic agreement, she knew life was difficult. Throwing caution aside for an unsecure future squashed in a van with the band, travelling with little income, would eventually lead to arguments and discontent.

'I'll give it some thought,' was all she said.

Mac didn't have to tell her this was not what he wanted to hear, his downcast face said it all. After an ice-cream dessert which they ate in silence, Amelia followed him out the restaurant. The receptionist bid them goodnight as they crossed the hallway.

'Yeah, it could have been,' Mac grumbled, as he climbed the stairs.

Pausing on the landing, they faced the doors of their respective rooms. As she stood staring at the shrivelled leaves of a spider plant in a large pot on a table beside her door, Amelia felt compelled to say something to ease the tension. 'Well —'

'Amelia, I —' Mac interrupted.

'Stop talking,' said Amelia, launching herself into his arms. They tumbled into her room, kissing passionately as they landed in a heap on the floor, Mac's foot knocking the plant off its table in his haste.

Turns out I was right, Amelia thought later, *the sex was fantastic.*

Back at Lochside the next day they found everything the same, although Amelia couldn't help feeling guilty that she knew Jilly was considering selling when the others didn't. She guessed Zoey wouldn't be too upset. With university to return to, for her Lochside was only a temporary job. Angus, on the other hand, would be devastated. She watched him painting the plank of a show jump designed to resemble a brick wall. He was humming while he worked, enjoying being involved. She couldn't tell him their efforts might be for nothing. They had invested a lot in the gymkhana. Jilly wasn't there and didn't understand how hard the team were working to ensure it was a success.

'What do we do?' she asked Mac, when they were alone in the barn filling a wheelbarrow with hay. 'We can't tell Angus and Zoey. It's Jilly's responsibility to do that.'

'Carry on as usual. We caught Jilly on a bad day, that's all.' He placed a final slab of hay on top of the teetering pile. 'You're all set.'

Recent rain had turned the ground soft and numerous hooves had churned the entrance to the field into a muddy mess, especially the spots where the ponies usually gathered. The herd had huddled together at the far fence with their hindquarters facing the drizzle blowing on the wind. Battling through the gate and steering around the deepest mud, Amelia called them over. A few heads turned in her direction, ears back, expressions unamused. If food didn't motivate them, she'd need to come up with a more imaginative way to chivvy them up. The wheelbarrow's tyres squelched across the sodden grass as she steered it over to the hay feeder and began stuffing armfuls inside, trying not to let too much get blown away.

'Over here, you lot. It's too expensive to waste. Grab it while you can,' she shouted.

Expecting at least greedy Pirate to approach, she glanced around, then started upright. The herd had moved yet not towards the food. They were now pressed up against the fence, all looking in the same direction with pricked ears.

'Over here,' Amelia called out again, waving a fistful of hay, which provoked no response from the mesmerised ponies. 'Give me strength.'

Keen to return to the shelter of the office and a cup of tea, Amelia turned to leave, pushing the now empty wheelbarrow. The ponies were behaving weirdly. She knew they were used to the sights of the Highlands. She couldn't figure out why they were acting hypnotised. It couldn't be a deer; they saw them all the time. Leaving the wheelbarrow behind, she approached the ponies, who ignored her.

'What are you looking at?' she asked, following their gaze to a place on the hill where, glowing golden like a flower blooming between the greens and browns, a palomino horse was staring back at them. Despite the distance, Amelia could tell it was expensive and well-bred and should not be roaming Lochside's land. Wiping moisture from her eyelashes, she looked again and the horse was still there. Her first thought was it must have escaped from somewhere. Her second thought was she had better get a headcollar, catch it and bring it inside for safekeeping.

Back in the tack room, Mac was playing with Gallus, Angus was dozing and Zoey was cleaning a bridle.

Watching Amelia collect a headcollar from the peg, Mac asked, 'What's that for?'

'There's a loose horse up on the hill by the geldings' field. It's not one of ours. I've never seen it before. It's a palomino.'

'Really?' Mac looked surprised. 'Are you sure?'

'Yes. I don't know where it's from.'

'I thought they only had Clydesdales at Keilburn so I don't think it can be from there,' said Angus, who'd woken up and was listening.

'I'm going to go and bring it in. We can't leave it out there alone.'

'If it's from Keilburn, they'd never do the same for us,' Zoey pointed out.

'Well, we're better than that.' Amelia headed for the door. 'We care.'

'I'll give you a hand,' said Mac, pulling on a wax jacket and zipping it up. 'It could be a two-person job if it doesn't want to be caught.'

Amelia held the door open and they stepped outside.

Sheets of rain blew in their faces as they hurried over to where the ponies were still gathered at the far fence, watching the stranger.

'There.' Amelia glanced at Mac to check he was looking in the right direction. 'See.'

'Where?'

Amelia tutted. 'There. Out with no rug on in this weather. It's irresponsible of whoever owns it.'

'But there's nothing there,' said Mac, shrugging. 'Unless you're going to catch an invisible horse and pretend it's yours like my sister did once. We all had to play along and call it Teddy. She kept it going for weeks'

'Oh for …' Amelia turned around, furious, to find the ponies were now all at the hay feeder and the palomino was gone. 'We should search for it, at least nearby.'

'I don't think that's necessary. Perhaps you were mistaken.'

'But it was right there, bright gold, you couldn't miss it.'

'Yeah, I believe you saw something but the light up here can be quite deceptive. You saw lights up at the Bothy that time so you know it can play tricks on you.'

'It's not clever enough to form the shape of a horse though.' Amelia pushed away piebald Chess who had wandered over hoping to supplement the hay with some polo mints. 'It wasn't only me. The ponies saw it too.'

'Sorry, Amelia. It's nice of you to care but if there was a horse it's probably on its way home now.' Mac began to walk back to the gate. 'My coffee will be getting cold.'

'Bizarre.' Amelia removed Chess's nose from her pocket and followed Mac.

9

Everything stepped up a gear in the days preceding the gymkhana, the team working with purpose. Any spare moment was spent painting, cleaning, planning or stacking equipment ready for the games to begin. Tubs filled with beanbags rested against show jumps, flags stacked up along the walls alongside piles of sacks and cones. They had set aside one of the unused fields for parking and another for the games themselves. On Thursday a delivery of portable toilets arrived and the farrier, a cheerful chap called Euan, dropped in to give the ponies a pedicure.

'We're almost ready,' said Amelia, standing in the centre of the grass, hands on hips, surveying progress. 'I mustn't forget to collect the rosettes.'

'I'll join you,' offered Mac. 'Can we stop off for a beer at the Hiker's Hope afterwards? I'm parched and knackered. You're such a tough taskmaster, you've worn me out.'

'I haven't even begun wearing you out yet.' Amelia gave Mac a cheeky wink, prompting him to chase her all the way back to the cottage.

Amelia had ordered the rosettes from a local saddlery and

riding supplies shop, along with replacements for the items chewed beyond repair by rodents.

'Tell me,' said Mac, as they pulled into the shop's parking area, 'what sort of games we will be having because I'm no expert on these things.'

'We've got the egg and spoon race, the sack race, apple bobbing and loads more.'

'OK. I've no idea what any of those involve but they sound fun. Look, there's one of our posters on their noticeboard.'

Looking at the poster which had been pinned in the centre of the noticeboard for maximum exposure, Amelia felt proud she had made this happen. Surely she deserved a visit to the room filled with riding clothes which always attracted her like a magnet.

'I could just have a quick peek at the jackets,' she suggested, edging nearer the archway which led through to rows of merchandise.

'Focus, Amelia, focus. You've already got jackets for every occasion. How many more do you need?'

'Spoilsport. I knew I should have left you behind.'

'We're here to pay for and collect our order,' Mac advised the staff member behind the counter, who produced a trolley loaded with numerous boxes from a room out the back.

Amelia and Mac managed to squash the boxes in the boot and on the back seat of the Mini. Both were overflowing by the time Mac lifted the last box.

'This one's the lightest,' he commented, raising the flap to reveal colourful rosettes. Holding a yellow one against his chest, he asked, 'What do I get if I win one of these?'

'That one means you finished third,' said Amelia, closing the boot with a firm shove.

'That's no good. Which colour's first place?'

'Hmm, now you're testing my memory.' Amelia drummed

her fingers on the car roof, scrunching up her face. 'First place is definitely red, then second place is blue, for third you get yellow and fourth is … I know … it's green.'

'OK, then I'm wearing this one because I want to be a winner.' Mac removed a red rosette from the box and fastened it to the buttons on his shirt.

'Whatever makes you happy.' Amelia opened the driver's door. 'If I were you though, I'd remove that before we get to the Hiker's Hope. You don't want people assuming you're a politician.'

Mac spent the journey to the pub desperately trying to untangle the knot in the rosette so he could take it off.

The Hiker's Hope was perched on top of a steep hill, which was not how Amelia imagined it. She was pretty sure if you were an exhausted hiker seeking hope you'd rather find a pub in a downhill direction than up. It meant the views were stunning though because the whitewashed stone-walled building was nestled in the mountains. To reach it you had to walk over a wooden humpbacked bridge, straddling a stream of crystal clear water.

Mac took Amelia's hand as they strolled across the planks which creaked beneath their feet. 'You should see the stream when it's full of the snowmelt coming down from the mountains,' he said.

Inside the pub was spacious and uncrowded. They took their drinks to a table beside a narrow-latticed window overlooking a derelict mill wheel. Amelia sipped her orange juice and watched Mac gaze with delight at his alcohol-free beer.

'Cheers,' he raised the bottle to chink it against Amelia's glass. 'Here's to a successful gymkhana on Saturday.'

'Here's hoping.' Amelia's tummy fluttered with nerves. She mostly kept it to herself but she was feeling the pressure.

As though sensing this, Mac changed the subject. 'Seen any more of those mysterious lights at night lately?'

'Nope. Been falling into bed exhausted though so for all I know the Spunkies could still be there.'

Mac laughed. 'Perhaps they're riding that palomino you saw. The blighters can't get into the Bothy anyway. The key's kept in the top drawer of the desk in the office.'

'The one with the Loch Ness keyring?' Amelia had wondered what that key was for, it was the only one she hadn't needed to use.

'Yeah. I thought —'

'Good afternoon, Amelia. Hello, Mac.' Neither of them had noticed Hugh Douglas was sitting at the table behind, until he turned around and acknowledged them. 'I am looking forward to you joining us on Monday for the Garden Party, Amelia.'

'The Garden Party. Has it come around already? Are you definitely going, Amelia?' Mac asked in a rush.

'Yes, that's my plan.'

'Oh.' Mac looked disappointed.

'You are, of course, welcome too,' Hugh said to Mac in a tone which indicated the opposite.

The other occupant of the table rose to his feet. A tall, slender man with grey hair, he did not acknowledge Amelia and Mac, instead ignoring them. He walked away with Hugh following.

Amelia gave Mac a quizzical look.

'Leith … Hugh's father,' he explained. 'Keilburn House and the estate are his until Hugh inherits them.'

'He's not very friendly.'

'No, but then neither is Jilly to him. It's the history thing. She tells him off as though he's one of the ponies.' Mac chuckled.

'No wonder they don't get on.' Amelia pictured Jilly chasing Leith away from Lochside with a lunge whip.

Mac checked the time on his phone. 'Drink up. I've got something to show you.' Once outside, he offered a hand to Amelia, saying, 'This way.'

'It's late in the day for wandering off.' Amelia took his hand.

'Don't worry we're not going far.'

They climbed up a steep narrow path at the rear of the pub. As loose stones slid out from under Amelia's trainers. Mac put an arm around her waist to steady her.

'It'll be worth it,' he promised.

Twenty minutes later they reached the crest and Mac was proved right, it had been worth it. Amelia had a bird's eye view. She felt she was soaring above the Highlands, looking out over glittering lochs, dotted with tiny islands bordered by banks dense with Scots pine trees. As they stood cuddled together, watching the twilight, Amelia sighed. 'This is a moment,' she whispered.

'I know,' agreed Mac.

On Friday morning a minibus arrived bringing eight children booked in for a holiday treat. As Amelia surveyed the reluctant expressions on a few of the faces, she wondered whether some were perhaps keener than others. Angus took charge, ushering those without hats and boots into the tack room. A girl in a smart jacket and sparkly jodhpurs leaned on the doorframe yawning and swinging an expensive helmet by its chinstrap while watching the chaos taking place to kit everyone out in the right size gear.

The team were rushing to prepare the ponies when Mac asked Amelia in a quiet voice, 'Can you go with them on Jellybean.' Checking they were out of earshot, he added,

'Zoey needs you to bring up the rear. When they booked in, Angus was told they were all experienced riders but one of them just tried to mount Chess on the wrong side so it appears that was a fib.'

'Sure. No problem.'

Amelia retrieved Jellybean's tack, propping his bridle over her shoulder and hefting his saddle down from the rack. Carrying it over the crook of her arm, she jogged to his stable door and pulled back the bolt. The strawberry roan Welsh pony was a steady mount who rarely put a hoof wrong.

'You're a good boy, aren't you,' she cooed, as she straightened his forelock over the browband.

Mac appeared in the doorway. 'I suspect you're going to have your hands full.'

'Really?' Amelia paused in buckling up the throat lash. 'On Jellybean?'

'I'm not referring to Jellybean. I mean that lot. Talk about all the gear and no idea. You'll need to be careful.'

Amelia finished tacking up then led Jellybean outside, fastening her hat as she went. The group had gathered and Angus and Mac were moving through them checking girths and adjusting stirrup lengths. As Angus tightened Pumpkin's girth the saddle slid around. The girl onboard grabbed Angus in a panic to the amusement of the other children.

Pirate's rider, the girl in the sparkly jodhpurs, was holding the reins too tightly and the pony was shaking his head in agitation. Amelia rode over to them. 'Can you let the reins out please. Pirate prefers a looser rein. He likes to think he's in charge. The trick is to make him believe he is but secretly you are.'

Scowling, the girl turned on Amelia. 'And who are you to tell me how to ride?'

'I'm not telling you how to ride. I know the ponies here

better than you and I'm giving you advice. Pirate's quirky but, once you get to know him, he's lovely.'

'I don't need advice from you. I'm experienced. My daddy has polo ponies and I ride them all the time.' Abruptly, the girl turned her face away.

Irritated, Amelia glanced over at Angus, who shook his head in dismay. With a sigh, she moved Jellybean away and looked at the other riders. It was clear they were novices. Their hands were too high, their reins too loose and their feet stuck out with heels up instead of down. Zoey caught Amelia's eye and pulled a horrified expression.

'OK, listen up.' Zoey stood up in her stirrups to get everyone's attention. 'We're going single file. Stay one behind the other and leave room between your pony and the one in front. Watch out for them stopping to eat. If they do try that, give a pull on those reins and show them who's in charge. Chess is especially greedy.' Zoey pointed to Amelia. 'Amelia, over there, will be at the back and take care of any stragglers. Without further ado … let's go.'

Herding cats would have been easier. Peewee made a dash for the hay in the barn and Mac had to bring him back, then do his best to organise some sort of line. Amelia gulped at the thought of having to survive the next hour.

Finally, when they were assembled in an almost orderly style, the ride set off out the gate just as the first drop of rain landed on Amelia's waterproofs. At first the riders chattered excitedly to each other but by the time they turned onto the bridlepath the wind had strengthened, driving the rain into their faces and they fell quiet, keeping their heads down to shield themselves. Protected from the worst of it at the rear, Amelia kept an eye on the riders she could see and soon realised that the girl in front of her was tilting precariously to one side. Whisky's saddle appeared to be slipping and a loose girth was dangerous. She could call ahead and ask for the ride to halt while she sorted it out but they were already running late. Over the noise of the howling wind, metal shoes clinking on the stony surface and the creak of tack it was unlikely Zoey would hear her. She reached for her mobile phone, zipped securely in her jacket pocket. She could call the Lochside mobile which the ride leader always carried with them. Whisky trod on a loose stone and stumbled. The girl shrieked and turned around, her face pinched and pale. She was clinging to the pommel of the saddle with both hands.

'I want to go back,' she pleaded.

'What? Are you OK?'

The girl shook her head. 'I want to get off.'

The decision was made for Amelia, she needed to deal with the situation immediately. 'You're uneven. Try pushing your weight down on your right foot so you're sitting in the centre.'

'I can't,' the girl wailed, too scared to move.

'Just lean to your right a little.'

'No. I can't.'

'I'll help you.' Amelia manoeuvred Jellybean upsides Whisky.

The ponies were pushed close together by the narrowness of the track. Whisky's ears flickered back in warning. Jellybean ignored the threat, plodding on unperturbed. Amelia's right knee was now brushing through the branches of the hedgerow, while her left rested against Whisky's stomach.

'I'm going to check your girth. If it's OK, we'll put your right stirrup down a couple of holes. I can tell that side's shorter and it's making you unbalanced.'

Leaning down over Jellybean's withers, Amelia slipped a hand between Whisky's belly and the girth, feeling the heat from his body warm her fingers. The girth wasn't loose. She would have to deal with the stirrups.

'Take your foot out for a minute.'

The girl's face was level with Amelia's, eyes wide with fear. 'I can't. I'll fall off.'

'You won't. Trust me,' Amelia reassured her. 'Whisky's only walking. You'll be fine.'

'No, I won't. I can't ride and I didn't want to come. Philly made me because she wants to show off.'

Amelia assumed Philly was the girl on Pirate. 'You'll feel much better once your stirrups are level. Give it a try and, if you're still not happy, I'll tell Zoey I'm taking you back. Once you're comfortable, you'll relax and enjoy it. By the way, what's your name? Mine's Amelia.'

'I'm Lucy.'

'OK, Lucy, slip your foot out of the stirrup iron and let your leg go loose. I'll drop your stirrup.'

Hesitatingly, Lucy raised her foot and removed it from the stirrup iron. To compensate she clung even tighter to the saddle as Amelia reached over and pulled down on the leather until the buckle was visible. Quickly she dropped it into a vacant hole two lower but as she was pulling the buckle back up, the wind suddenly changed direction. A huge gust blew up from behind lifting the horses' tails, causing Whisky to scuttle sideways and crash into Jellybean, forcing the roan into the hedge. Amelia lost her grip on the leather as branches scratched her face. Lucy yelped, startling Whisky again. He bounced forward into Pippin's hindquarters, setting off events like a chain of dominos. Pippin lashed out with a hindleg. Affronted Whisky tried to bite Pippin's backside. To escape Whisky's teeth, Pippin charged into Fergus, who bashed into Peewee, who leapt into Chess, who tried to get by Pumpkin, who blocked his path by ramming into Pirate. Squeals of fear sounded from each rider in turn.

Amelia shunted back into the saddle and steered Jellybean out of the hedgerow, at the same time stretching out to grab Whisky's bridle. Lucy was trembling and in tears.

'Hey, it's all right. No one's fallen off. Let's get this stirrup adjusted so you can put your foot back in.'

Lucy consented and Amelia had just got her settled when there was a loud crash from up ahead, followed by Zoey's voice bellowing, 'Sit back.'

A ripple passed back from rider to rider, excited and fearful.

'Pirate tried to jump the hedge!' yelled Pippin's rider.

As the hedge had to be six feet tall and Pirate was only a little over fourteen hands high, Amelia doubted it.

'Oh no. I feel sick,' whimpered Lucy.

'They're exaggerating. Don't worry, just focus on yourself.'

Zoey ordered everyone to trot on. As Whisky followed the others, Lucy moaned, flopping about like a ragdoll. With every stride Amelia cringed. She was poised to catch Lucy if required. Up ahead, Zoey was herding the riders through an open gateway in a hedge now sporting a chunk of missing foliage at the top. In a whirlwind of panic, Zoey rode Hebrides from pony to pony, trying to calm the situation. Lucy's sniffles continued as Amelia followed her into a large field overgrown with nettles and ragwort.

'Keep an eye on this lot and make sure they stay together while I sort out this mess,' Zoey muttered, nodding towards the middle of the field where Pirate was grazing, reins askew. Philly sat on the wet grass a few feet away from him. Her furious face was beetroot red. She was clutching her arm and looking with dismay at her grass-stained clothes.

'That pony is a disgrace,' sobbed Philly. 'He needs schooling. I'm not getting back on him. You have to get me another pony. I don't want that one.'

The boy on Peewee was giggling. Chess's rider had dropped the reins to cover her mouth with her hands in shock; Chess was consuming grass faster than a lawnmower. The boy on Fergus was picking his nose and the rest of the ponies were eyeing up the hedge, contemplating a feeding frenzy.

'OK, everyone, let's gather up our reins and focus, shall we?' instructed Amelia. 'We'll be on our way again soon. Just a minor hiccup. It happens when you ride horses.'

'No, it doesn't,' snapped a humiliated Philly, stamping over, 'only ones who haven't been taught properly. The lady in charge says you have to get off and give me your pony and you have that one. Let's see you ride him perfectly seeing as you know it all.'

Zoey had grabbed hold of Pirate's reins in the nick of time as he edged towards a poisonous ragwort and was leading him over. 'Hop off, Amelia, please. Philly wants to swap to Jellybean.'

Amelia dismounted, then gave Philly a leg up. The girl sniffed and brushed Amelia's hand away when she tried to assist with shortening the stirrups. 'I'm perfectly capable of doing it myself,' she snapped.

Biting back her annoyance, Amelia took Pirate's reins while the others formed a line. Having lost time, Zoey was keen to get moving again.

'Righto. Off we go. Remember keep their heads up, not too close and away we go.' She was behaving as though nothing had happened. 'Amelia will catch us up when she can. OK, ride trot on.'

The ponies followed Hebrides through the gateway. As Whisky's rump disappeared, Pirate let out a shrill neigh. Upset at being left behind, he spun round furiously.

'Hold your horses,' Amelia muttered through gritted teeth. 'I can't have stirrups as short as a jockey.'

Once back on the bridlepath, Pirate calmed down and ceased shaking his head. The wind still howled but the rain had eased to drizzle as they cantered past Loch Still and the castle ruins. Despite her efforts Amelia couldn't catch up with the ride. They had got too far ahead. She hoped Zoey was managing on her own and they would all get back unscathed.

As she trotted back along the lane to Lochside, the sounds of children could be heard coming from the yard. Once through the gates Amelia was greeted by a mixture of grumpy and happy faces. She wondered whether the hard to please Philly had been content with Jellybean or, much like Goldilocks, tried every pony until she found one that lived up to her expectations.

'Do come along to our gymkhana tomorrow if you're in the area,' Amelia called out, as the group retreated to the minibus. Zoey held out some leaflets. Only one of the children took one.

'I'm going to warn all my friends not to come here,' Philly said loudly. 'This place is awful.'

'What a nightmare,' Amelia groaned, collapsing on the ground beside the equally exhausted Pirate, as she watched the minibus depart with relief.

'Don't worry,' said Angus. 'There'll be plenty of unspoilt kids who'll still come.'

'Plus, on the bright side, that's this week's bad day out the way. Which means by the law of averages tomorrow will be brilliant,' added Mac, just as another heavy downpour began.

10

Amelia couldn't be sure whether it was the gutter outside the bedroom window overflowing from a sudden deluge of rain or the boom of thunder directly over the cottage that woke her up. She glanced sleepily at the clock on the bedside table. Six o'clock in the morning on gymkhana day and, from the sound of the water drumming on the roof, the Highland weather was not in the mood for being kind. A peek between the gap in the curtains revealed a grey sky, sheeting rain and the rapid appearance of enormous puddles.

'It'll brighten up, won't it?' she asked Gallus, who merely raised his eyes and yawned in response.

Once outside, Amelia found conditions were worse than they'd looked from the window. She dashed across to the gates, struggling to unlock them with everything so slippery, then splashed over to seek shelter in the office. She was standing, the hem of her coat dripping on the floor, when Angus arrived, closely followed by Zoey.

'Perfect day for it,' commented Zoey sarcastically.

'It'll blow over. I feel it in my bones,' said Angus.

'By ten o'clock?' Amelia asked hopefully.

'Trust me, Angus's bones aren't that accurate,' said Zoey, 'and this weather looks set in for the day.'

Feeling gloomy, Amelia switched on her laptop and opened the spreadsheet on which she had prepared the timetable for the day's activities. None of them could be moved inside, even if they had time to clear a space in the barn, which they didn't.

'Without a snazzy indoor school like the one at Three Stones Barn we're going to struggle,' she sighed.

'This is Scotland. The sun will be out in a minute,' Angus reassured her.

Zoey made a scoffing noise, receiving a glare from Angus. She tried to turn it into a cough just as Mac burst in, saying, 'Sorry I'm late. Cows on the road.'

'That'll be the inspiration for the next song title, will it?' teased Zoey. 'You know "Don't blame it on me, blame it on the cows". That kind of thing.'

'Ha, ha.' Mac threw his motorbike helmet on a pile of rugs. 'With talent like that you can understand why we've never invited you to join the band. Well, that and I overheard you singing in the barn the other day. It was enough to scare away the ghost of Gordon the Glorious, that's all I'm saying.'

'I think that's saying more than enough,' snapped Angus, 'and I'm sure Zoey doesn't want to be in your band anyway.'

'Too right.' Zoey nodded vigorously.

Amelia dropped into the swivel chair, massaging her eyes in frustration. 'What do we do? Press ahead regardless?'

Mac puffed loudly. 'I'd arranged for the band to turn up and provide some entertainment as a surprise. I'm sorry, Amelia, but I've just cancelled them. We can't play in this; it'd damage the equipment. The rain's coming in sideways so we'd have to be indoors and there's nowhere suitable.'

'I'd spoken to Euan and he offered to do a live farrier

demo but here's a text from him saying he can't make it now.' Zoey held up her phone with the screen facing outwards.

'And I'd ordered a crate of cupcakes decorated with iced ponies. The bakery rang to say the delivery driver's stuck on a flooded road and unlikely to get here in time,' added Angus apologetically.

Despite the negative news, Amelia was touched the team had gone to so much effort to try and add their own ideas to the day.

The sound of hooves clopping in the yard drew them all outside. Tamsin and her friends were each leading a bedraggled, dejected looking pony into an empty stable. Amelia walked over to the stable Tamsin had just disappeared into with Peewee.

'Hi,' she greeted the girl, whose face was hidden inside an enormous faux fur lined hood. 'Do you think we can spruce them up in time?'

'They're soaked,' Tamsin stated in a voice which suggested Amelia was being stupid. 'We can't plait manes and tails in this state and the mud won't brush off their legs when it's wet.'

Amelia knew Tamsin was correct. Peewee's mane and tail were running with dirty water. Her brain raced, trying to come up with a positive slant but she couldn't find one.

'No one's going to come out in this.' Tamsin voiced Amelia's fears.

Amelia was spared replying for her phone pinged with a message from Jilly. She read it hurriedly.

Weather awful here. Hope you've got the sunshine. x

She felt like crying. By ten o'clock not a single participant had turned up and the office phone hadn't rung with any enquiries whether the gymkhana was going ahead. Mac braved the swirling craters of the lane, leaping over the widest torrents of water, to check whether anyone was on their way and unsure where the parking was. He returned to the office and declared the road was devoid of vehicles.

'Although it might be brightening up a bit,' he added, trying to finish on a high.

'Yeah, in Florida,' said Zoey, 'not here.'

Sticking her head out the door, Amelia looked to the sky. She knew Mac was trying to be positive but with no wind to blow them away the stationary clouds hung low over the hills. The rain wasn't going anywhere anytime soon and Mac knew it. She couldn't hear any cars approaching, even in the distance. She fastened her wax jacket and went outside, walking around to the fields, head down, rain battering her hood. Amelia stared miserably at the equipment they had carefully set up the night before. The handmade cardboard signs giving directions to the car park and toilets had turned soggy, rendering the words unreadable. Everything looked uninviting in the cold and wet. The waterlogged grass would soon churn to mud under the weight of numerous hooves, feet and tyres. The heavier cars would probably get bogged down and stuck and they had no tractor to tow them free. Mac arrived panting at her side.

'Thought I'd find you here. You know, it's still a fabulous idea. It's just today's not the day for it.'

'I really wanted it to work.' Amelia kicked the ground. 'To see customers having fun, the ponies enjoying themselves, everyone energised, instead of this.' She gestured at the sodden field. Apart from a solo pheasant dashing for the shelter of the trees, nothing stirred.

'It'll happen,' Mac reassured her. 'I know you're disappointed but when the time is right, we'll give it another try. In the meantime, I'm going inside to get a drink. I suppose it's too early for a beer?'

'Have whatever you want.'

'Coming?' Mac held out a hand.

'No. I'll stay a moment. Please tell the others the gymkhana's cancelled. I don't suppose anyone'll call to check anyway.'

'Sure.' Mac walked away.

The pheasant had deserted her too. Amelia stood alone, soaked and sad. Soon how to attract customers on a shoestring budget would not be her problem, for by the time the team tried again, if they even considered it worth trying again, she would be gone.

Back at the yard a van had arrived and a crate of cupcakes was being unloaded from its rear doors by a driver whose expression suggested his day was going as well as hers.

'Give them to Tamsin and her friends as a thank you,' Amelia instructed Angus. 'They deserve a treat for giving up their time for nothing. I'll pay you for them.'

The worst of the downpour had eased by the afternoon. Angus, Mac and Zoey began packing away the gymkhana equipment. While they were carrying poles, show jump wings and cones back to the barn, Amelia bypassed them and kept going. She sensed Mac move to follow her and heard Zoey stop him, saying, 'Leave her be. She needs some time alone.'

Zoey is right, thought Amelia, as she slipped through the gate. A persistent drizzle was falling and damp ferns brushed against her legs, smearing her waterproof trousers. She carried on, fingers brushing the key in her pocket. She felt the urge to just keep walking until she'd gone far enough she no longer knew where she was. She was lost anyway. Who even was she? Amelia the secretary from *Your Home, Your Castle*; Jilly's niece who came to save the day but didn't; Mac's sort of girlfriend, who was leaving soon so how could there be a future? It was all so confusing. She slipped the key into the hole in the Bothy door. It clicked open easily. She stepped inside onto a dusty floor covered in hoof prints resembling inverted hearts left by the trapped stag. The soles of Amelia's wet wellies obliterated them.

The air was still inside the Bothy, a feeling that somehow Amelia was disturbing something invisible, a sense she ought to have asked for permission before crossing the threshold. It was sparsely furnished with two ancient wooden chairs angled either side of a stone fireplace and a wooden table.

One of the chairs wobbled beneath Amelia's weight as she sat down. She knew she should be helping clear up instead of hiding but hadn't wanted her overwhelming sense of disappointment to infect the others. Aside from the sound of blackbirds squabbling in the bushes outside, she sat undisturbed. It felt good to stop, if a little strange in a world of constant action. Stretching both legs out before her, she remembered she'd meant to try yoga. Perhaps on her return to London she would take it up. One of the lessons from being at Lochside was the realisation she needed a more active lifestyle when she returned. She closed her eyes, then opened them seconds later when the sound of scrabbling paws made her jump as Gallus loped into the Bothy.

'What are you doing here?' she asked him, stroking his head. 'Surely you didn't walk all that way.'

'He didn't. I carried him most of it.' To Amelia's surprise, Zoey appeared in the doorway. 'He's heavy. When I put him down he refused to move so I had to pick him up again.'

Amelia watched as Zoey took the other seat, crossing her legs and unfastening her red waterproof jacket. She gazed around. 'I've never been in here before. Not much to it.'

'No,' agreed Amelia, 'but my understanding is they're for shelter not comfort.'

'Good job. It's hardly holiday chalet material.' Zoey

jiggled her foot, tickling Gallus's tail as he sniffed around the fireplace. 'I know you think I don't like you —'

'I …' Taken aback at Zoey's bluntness, Amelia chose her next words carefully. 'It's OK if you don't. I can see how Jilly asking me to step in instead of one of you must have rankled. It's like someone new being promoted unfairly over others.'

Zoey waved a hand dismissively. 'I'm not bothered about that and I don't imagine the others are either. Mac's main focus is the band and Angus will always choose the path of least resistance.'

'I hope you're right. I never wanted to cause any bad feeling by coming here.' Amelia shuffled as Gallus flopped between her feet, his tail pounding against her shins.

'This was always temporary for me. Once my travel plans fell through, I couldn't get work in Glasgow and my parents got fed up with me doing nothing. Jilly's an old friend of theirs so they called in a favour and here I am.'

'I see. Um, Zoey, is there something you want to tell me?'

'Yeah. I wanted to say that I think your idea for the gymkhana was good. We've been defeated by the weather today but we won't give up. We will try again.'

'Thanks. I'm glad to hear it.' Amelia smiled ruefully. 'Next time it'll have to be without me though. There's no time to fit it in before I leave.'

'That's a shame. I reckon on a sunny day it'll work. I'll push Jilly to give it another go. Here …' Zoey pulled a squashed chocolate cupcake decorated with an icing pony's head out her pocket and handed it to Amelia. Gallus watched it pass over his head with beady eyes. 'Stay in here as long as you need to. We've got the clearing up under control. Come on, Gallus.'

By the time Zoey reached the door, Gallus was at her heels, although he kept glancing back to check whether the cupcake was up for grabs.

'Zoey. Thanks,' Amelia called after her.

It was as if a cloud of gloom had descended on Lochside the next morning. No one felt like chatting, instead they worked in silence. To allow the ponies a rest after what was supposed to have been a busy day no customers had been booked in. As Amelia swept the yard, hindered by Gallus chasing wisps of straw, the sun broke through the clouds.

'Of course the sun's out today,' grumbled Zoey.

'My back's aching. How about a break?' suggested Angus, propping his pitchfork against the wall and stretching. 'Tea break,' he bellowed.

They gathered in the office. Amelia noticed Angus kept glancing at the clock on the wall. The third time he missed his mug of tea with the biscuit he was meant to be dunking, she asked, 'Everything all right, Angus?'

'Actually, we're expecting a new arrival,' he replied. 'Jilly told me last night. A Shetland pony belonging to a friend of hers who's unfortunately having to move away and can't keep him anymore.'

Amelia and Mac exchanged a bemused glance. After their conversation with Jilly in Orkney they had not expected the herd to expand. Amelia would have been less surprised to hear one of the ponies was leaving than a new one arriving. They could not pass any comment for Angus and Zoey still knew nothing of the offer to buy Lochside.

'When's this pony arriving? We haven't got anything prepared,' Amelia asked.

Angus consulted the clock again, which despite the dust and cobwebs was still readable. 'Within the hour.'

Sure enough, less than an hour later a loud clanking sounded from the lane. Everyone stopped what they were doing to rush out and greet a van towing a stained horse trailer, the top half of which was painted green, the bottom a faded grey, as though the person decorating it had run out of paint or time or both. The trailer swung precariously, its wheels almost leaving the ground, license plate swaying from its single fastening, as the van backfired, cracking like a firework. The sound of hooves kicking stable doors echoed around the yard. Angus and Zoey dashed off to calm things down, muttering about injuries.

'Quite the entrance,' said Mac.

'Yep. A fanfare would have been less attention-seeking,' agreed Amelia.

They greeted the driver, who was out of the cab and now banging on the side of the trailer with a clenched fist.

'Everything OK?' Amelia asked, perturbed by his behaviour.

'This one is nothing but trouble. Took some persuading to get him in and then he wouldn't stop kicking. Thought he was going to break my trailer. Get the ramp down and get him out of my hair.'

Amelia moved over beside Mac and together they undid the locks and lowered the ramp, behind which the face of a black Shetland pony was looking at them. He had somehow managed to get loose and turn around. He hurled himself down the ramp. Mac lunged for the frayed lead rein, which appeared to have been chewed through. He missed as the pony sidestepped off the side of the ramp and dived headlong into the verge of wildflowers. Mac swore as he was knocked to the ground.

Amelia moved fast to grab the pony's headcollar. She pulled on the rein to try and lift his head. Though tiny, he was stocky and black except for a star between eyes which twinkled as he raised his head and slobbered green slime all over Amelia's arm.

The driver slammed the ramp shut and jumped in the cab without saying goodbye.

Mac picked himself up and brushed down his jeans. 'He can't wait to get away from this feisty chap, can he? Frightened we're going to send him back, do you think? What's he called then?'

As she led him into the yard, Amelia read the nameplate on the headcollar. 'Brutus.'

'Brutal, more like.' Mac rubbed his hip. 'Could have broken a bone falling like that.'

Amelia led Brutus around to the field. He pulled ahead, neighing shrilly at the geldings, who looked up from grazing. A few moved to the fence for a better look.

'I'll just pause here for a bit and let them get used to him,' Amelia said, loosening the lead rein.

Brutus lowered his head and began eating the grass, ignoring Pirate who was trotting up and down on the other side of the fence, snorting. Amelia ran her fingers through Brutus's dense mane, pulling gently at the knots.

'He's generally in good condition. Needs a good groom but …'

'What I don't get is why Jilly's taken him in,' said Mac. 'One minute she's talking about selling Lochside and the next she's expanding. I don't think she knows what she wants. It's not a good situation for all of us.'

'She's always been a sucker for an animal in need,' explained Amelia. 'It used to get on Uncle Stan's nerves how she could never refuse any animal seeking a home. That's how they ended up with twenty chickens years ago. Eventually Stan gave them away to a local farmer.'

'I'd like to have met Stan. He sounds a character.' Mac climbed on the top rail of the fence, then swung a leg over, dropping into the field the other side. Making soothing sounds, he reached for Pirate who ceased pacing. 'I'll stay this side while you put the new chap next door.'

Tugging Brutus's head up, Amelia took him into the small field adjoining the geldings' home where he would spend a few days until the vet could check him over. Once he'd received the all clear, he would join the others. Slipping the head collar off, Amelia moved away. Brutus dropped down for a vigorous roll before getting back up on his little legs. Filled with curiosity, Pirate and Chess came over to the dividing fence but there was no animosity. The ponies eyed each other for a few minutes and then returned to grazing.

'Seems to have gone OK,' said Mac, meeting Amelia by the gate. 'I hope the little one doesn't try and get out.'

Observing the Shetland's relaxed attitude, Amelia didn't think he'd be any trouble and told Mac so.

'Although we should probably check the fencing in that field soon,' suggested Mac. 'According to Angus it's not been used for years so I doubt it's been done for a long time.'

'Add it to the list.' Amelia grinned, nudging Mac with her shoulder. 'It'll keep you busy until I'm gone.'

'You carry on like this and you'll turn into a bossy and demanding person like your aunt.'

Laughing, Amelia gave Mac a playful shove. 'There's worse people I can try and emulate.'

'That's true.'

11

As the days passed the weather remained changeable but the sun returned for the Bank Holiday Monday at the end of May. Gallus bathed in the rays beaming through the bedroom window, stretched out on Amelia's duvet while she raided her wardrobe, flipping through the limited clothes she'd brought, searching for an outfit suitable for a Garden Party. Everything was either too formal or too casual. With time ticking on, she eventually settled on a blue summer dress decorated with white flowers and paired it with white canvas pumps. Deciding it would have to do, she chased Gallus outside and locked the cottage door.

Mac was waiting in the office, dressed in a blue polo shirt and smart black jeans, watching Angus turn the pages of the diary, searching for the one he needed. Once at the correct date, he began scribbling hurriedly while frowning with concentration as he allocated names to ponies according to the size of the rider.

'Don't you two feel bad about leaving me alone to deal with everything on the busiest day we've had for months,' he grumbled.

'Wait … what am I then? Scotch mist?' protested Zoey.

'We don't have to go if you'd prefer we stay here and work,' offered Amelia, feeling guilty.

'Absolutely not,' Angus insisted. 'Off you go. I forgot I've got Scotch mist to help me.'

Amelia had vague memories of being driven up the road which ran alongside the Keilburn estate boundary. She recalled a stone wall reinforced with dense hedges which ran for miles and a majestic entrance arch, topped with a statue of a stag thirty feet up in the air. It had seemed grand and glamourous, especially when compared with the street of semi-detached houses where she'd lived as a child. She'd longed to explore the grounds beyond the wall, imaging castles and stables filled with beautiful white ponies.

'I'm excited to finally get the chance to see what Keilburn's like,' she told Mac, who was giving directions because he insisted the sat nav would send them the wrong way.

'I bet it's not as impressive as my neighbourly relations skills. You're about to witness them and they are legendary.'

'I'll reserve judgement until I've seen them in action.'

They were still some distance from the main entrance when they joined the end of a queue of stationary cars.

'It's seems very popular. I think we're a way off the entrance yet.' Amelia tapped the steering wheel impatiently.

'Perhaps they're holding a car boot sale as well as a Garden Party,' joked Mac, as the traffic crawled forwards.

'From the brief look I got of him, Leith Douglas didn't strike me as someone who would be a fan of car boot sales.'

Amelia lowered the window and watched the cars wind their way beneath the arch, before pausing for a man in a yellow high-vis jacket to speak to the driver. Each time something passed between them, then the car drove on into the estate. It seemed to be taking forever to get there. Amelia's

Mini was hemmed in by cars. From further back came the sound of a car horn.

'Are we really this bothered about neighbourly relations?' asked Amelia, turning to Mac, 'or shall we leave?'

'I thought you were desperate to nose around. Have patience. We're moving.' Mac nodded at the large gap which had opened up in front of the Mini.

Another staff member had arrived and now the queue was moving faster as two cars could gain access at once. They reached the arch and Amelia drove through.

'Good morning. Welcome to Keilburn.' The man in the high-vis jacket grinned and handed Amelia a parking ticket. 'Please display this on your dashboard. The car park is straight ahead. Do enjoy your visit.'

'Thank you.' Amelia pressed the accelerator and followed the line of vehicles all heading for the car park, which had been set up in a field. She found a space in a row of expensive looking cars.

'Wow. A Ferrari. Dreamy,' gushed Mac, gazing with admiration at the silver sports car next to him as he exited the passenger door. Amelia patted the bonnet of her muddy Mini.

'I saw that,' grinned Mac, 'and before your car gets jealous, I'm not saying I want one …'

'Good, Mr McAteer, because you can't afford one.' They held hands and joined the stream of people, some carrying picnic hampers, all moving towards a small wooden hut. Most had dressed for the occasion in smart country clothes. Amelia tidied her hair and brushed off her dress.

'You look fine,' Mac reassured her.

'Welcome.' The staff member in the hut, a lady wearing a grey fleece with Keilburn House printed in yellow lettering on the front, greeted them. She passed two tickets through the hatch. 'Don't forget to collect your Pimm's on the way in. Would you like to buy a raffle ticket? Only a pound each and all the money raised is going to the local Animal Sanctuary.'

'Go on then,' said Mac, pulling out his wallet. 'We'll have a strip of five as it's for a good cause. Can you put them down in the name of Amelia Hodge at Lochside Riding Stables.' Taking the tickets, he handed them to Amelia.

'You're from Lochside? Oh, my daughter used to ride there until she moved over to Three Stones Barn …' Realising what she'd said, the lady blushed and tailed off. Changing tone, she added, 'Do enjoy your visit to the marvellous Keilburn House and Gardens.' They left her tucking the money in a cash tin and writing the details in the raffle ticket book.

'Awkward,' said Mac, taking a glass of Pimm's from a tray on a table outside the hut.

The path widened out to a manicured lawn on which a marquee had been erected. A Barbershop Quartet wearing kilts were playing 'All You Need Is Love' while a handful of visitors, who'd obviously indulged in more than one Pimm's already, danced in front of them. Groups of people had gathered for drinks and canapes and were seated at the tables and chairs laid out around the marquee's entrance. Nearby a pair of bay heavy horses, with white blazes on their faces and white feathered socks on their legs, stood patiently between the shafts of a smart carriage.

'Aren't those Clydesdales?' asked Amelia. Mac confirmed they were. 'Aren't they quite rare?'

'Sadly, yes,' Mac replied. 'There are efforts to preserve the breed. I admit it's one of Leith's positive contributions to society. Don't ask me to name any of his others because I'll struggle.'

Laughing, Amelia turned her gaze to Keilburn House. Built in Georgian style from an unusual light-coloured stone with a pretty pink hue, its large rectangular windows looked out over the lawn on which she stood, then rolled away to a loch and pastures of Highland cattle. The rest of the surroundings were woodland.

'Let's go in,' suggested Mac, gesturing to the double entrance doors.

They passed between stone pillars into an oval shaped hallway. Noting the marble floor, Amelia glanced at Mac's muddy boots, then at a nearby staff member, who was pretending not to notice.

'The mud's dry,' she whispered, as they walked by.

Each room was richly decorated in reds and greens with oil paintings on the walls and high ceilings adorned with delicate cherubs' heads in the coving. Everything was polished and glittering, from the ornate chandeliers to the cutlery.

'I believe I could feel quite at home here,' joked Mac.

'Yeah. Chequered Pipes could hold concerts in the grounds and no one would complain about the noise,' Amelia played along.

There were staff members positioned in each location, ostensibly to provide historical facts but probably also to prevent pilfering of trinkets. They listened as one explained the origins of a painting to an enthralled group of visitors.

'Fantastic and can you stay here?' asked a lady with an American accent.

'No, you can't, I'm afraid. It's a family home but I do believe that Portia, that's the current owner's daughter, is considering opening up the barn conversion for parties.'

The group gasped with enthusiasm. Amelia and Mac continued.

'How odd it must be to have strangers browsing through your home commenting on everything from your choice of furniture to your family portraits.' Amelia turned to Mac to see if he agreed but he wasn't there. She found him in the music room gazing at a grand piano.

'I mean ... just look at it. It's a beauty,' he said.

The staff member standing nearby overheard him. 'It's a Steinway. Do you play?'

'A little. The guitar's more my thing but I can knock out a tune.' Mac's response held no hint of boasting, he was simply stating a fact. Amelia could sense he was itching to get his fingers on the pristine keys.

'I'll need to check first but maybe ...' The staff member indicated their radio, then moved away to speak privately.

Mac hopped on the spot until, minutes later, he received a thumbs up. A section of the blue rope barrier was unfastened to allow him access, then he sat on the piano's stool and began to play. Visitors passing through paused to listen. Amelia didn't recognise the music Mac was playing but she was mesmerised by the soaring notes of the beautiful tune, which ended to a round of applause. Mac stood and gave a slightly embarrassed bow.

'You were amazing. You never said you could play like that. What music were you playing?' asked Amelia. 'Was it Handel? It was gorgeous.'

'Er, no.' Mac tried to conceal his amusement and failed. 'It's called "Ay Up It's Burns Night" and I wrote it myself for Chequered Pipes.'

Ameila wasn't sure whether he was teasing her, as they linked arms and carried on towards a small door tucked away in a corner of the music room. Unlike the other doors, this one wasn't propped open. Mac gently pushed it and they found themselves in a dimly lit library with windows set high up. Shelves of books lined every wall, one large leather tome sat on a circular table, piles of books were heaped on the floor and on the seat of a leather armchair. Dusty surfaces and the general untidiness compared to the rooms they had previously seen gave Amelia the feeling they shouldn't be there. She was curious about the book which had been left out on the table and decided to have a peek. It looked very old and bore the title *Myths and Legends of the Lost Treasures of Clan Wars*. She opened the brown leather cover and flicked through the pages, stopping at one bookmarked by the top corner of the page being folded down. The swirly writing was so elaborate as to be barely readable. She studied the colourful red and gold illustrations.

'Hey, Mac, this looks like it's about Gordon the Glorious.'

'Really?' Mac was across the room in two strides. 'Oh, yeah. I think Zoey's right, it's a load of nonsense. See, it says when he fled the battle he left behind a dagger covered in priceless jewels. As if you'd leave something like that behind.'

'You can read this?'

'Parts of it. It's folklore, that's —'

'Ouch.' The door handle bashed into Amelia's elbow as it swung open with some force.

'This room is not part of the tour. Oh … it's you two.' Hugh Douglas frowned at them. 'The library is off limits. I need to ask you to leave this private area.'

'Sorry about that. We didn't realise,' Amelia apologised, watching as Hugh swept the book off the table in a manner which suggested he didn't want them to see it.

Tucking the book under his arm, he moved to the door and held it open. 'After you.'

As they walked out ahead of him, Mac asked, 'What's that book you've got there then, Hugh?'

'Nothing of any relevance. The tour continues back the way you came. Thank you for coming. Goodbye.'

Watching Hugh stride away, Mac muttered, 'He didn't want us loitering in that library, did he?'

'It doesn't matter. Let's see if we can get on a carriage ride and make the most of the sunshine.' Amelia tugged Mac's arm, leading him outside.

They waited their turn in the queue and then took their

seats, Amelia leaning back as the Clydesdales stepped forward and the open-topped carriage began to move. She found it relaxing listening to the clop of hooves while watching the grounds of Keilburn go by at a sedate pace. They went through the woods following a track. The driver pointed out a derelict cottage, explaining it would once have been home to a crofter working the land.

'That's similar to our Bothy,' said Amelia, 'except it's not an empty shell like that one is.'

As they broke from the trees into open land, Mac suggested she look up. A buzzard soared over them and she also spotted a hare, racing away with an impressive burst of speed. Against the backdrop of the mountains everything was so photogenic it felt almost surreal. On their return they ate delicious salmon sandwiches sitting at a table and chairs overlooking the loch. Amelia was finishing her last mouthful when Hugh walked by with the book from the library tucked under his arm. He didn't take the path to the car park, instead heading in the opposite direction.

'He's still got that book with him. I wonder why,' she said.

Gazing at the darkening sky, Mac shrugged. 'It's clouding over. If you're ready I think it's time to go.'

By the time they reached the car it had started to rain. Amelia switched on the wipers, stopping at the car park entrance while a Range Rover swept by. She spotted Hugh at the wheel.

Mac checked the time on the dashboard clock. 'Let's follow him. See where he's taking that book.'

'We can't do that,' protested Amelia. 'It's nothing to do with us.'

'Yeah, I know but we're not due back at Lochside for hours and if we go back early we'll end up mucking out. I've got a day off from all that.'

'It's still a no from me.'

Ahead of them the Range Rover swept under the arch, stopped to check for oncoming traffic, then indicated left and pulled away.

'OK, fair enough. If you turn left, there's a nice pub a few miles on. We can drop in there or would you rather feed the ponies in the rain?' teased Mac.

Giving in, Amelia turned the Mini onto the road, keeping a discrete distance from the Range Rover. She had to admit she was feeling curious about Hugh and the mysterious book he was carrying around and she did want a break from feeding the ponies in the rain. She drove for miles but there was no sign of the pub Mac had mentioned. She was about to ask him how much further it was, when the Range Rover indicated left again.

'Left here,' instructed Mac.

Without thinking Amelia followed, turning the Mini into a lane so narrow the wing mirrors were brushing the undergrowth. 'What if something comes the other way? It'll never get by. There's no room.'

'There are passing places. Don't worry though, nothing's likely to come along here. It only leads to a church.'

'What about this pub? Are you saying it's in a church?'

'Nah.' Mac laughed. 'I made it up to get you to follow Hugh.'

Slamming on the brakes, Amelia turned on him in a fury. 'That's not funny and now we're stuck. I can't turn around here.'

'Calm down. You can whizz the car around in the church car park. I'm sure St Beathan won't object.'

'I might drop you off and leave you there. You can ask this St Beathan for forgiveness for being cheeky.'

'Well, technically, I can't since St Beathan has been dead for centuries according to that sign I read back where we turned off.'

'This is ridiculous.' Amelia drove on, the tense silence between them broken by the squeak of the wipers and the sound of the tyres splashing through the water running in grooves down the sides of the lane. The parking area was next to a tiny church set within an overgrown graveyard with mist drifting between the headstones. The Range Rover had been parked skewwhiff as though Hugh had jumped out in a hurry. Carefully avoiding the ancient stone wall, Amelia turned the Mini and drove back out to the lane.

'Turn in here,' suggested Mac.

Amelia pulled the Mini's bonnet up to a rusty gate which had collapsed and was missing a few rails. A bedraggled crow perched on the top bar watching them with shrewd eyes before spreading its wings and flying away.

'This place is giving me the creeps,' she said, shutting off the engine.

'Let's go around the back and see what he's up to.'

'Do you really think we should? It's kind of invasive. He might be visiting the grave of a relative.'

'What … and gifting them a book to read? Besides this place is too low brow for Hugh's clan. Let's go on an adventure.'

'I don't need an adventure. I need a cup of tea and a relax. I'm not Sherlock —'

The passenger door slammed shut and Amelia watched Mac crossing the field towards the graveyard's rear wall. Hoping she wouldn't return to find the Mini had been towed away by an angry farmer, she followed, picking her way through thistles, over rough land which had been left to its own devices for years. The smell of damp soil wafted up and she looked down in dismay at the mud seeping through her canvas shoes.

'My shoes are ruined,' she hissed at Mac, who was crouched behind the crumbling rear wall.

'I'll buy you another pair. Best not lean on the wall. It doesn't look very safe.'

'I don't intend to.'

Together they peered through a gap and observed Hugh walking between the headstones. He stopped at one surrounded by overgrown grass. Crouching down, he opened the book, glancing from page to stone, then back again. Pulling a pen from his back pocket, he flattened a patch of grass at the base of the stone with his hand then leant closer until his nose was mere inches from it. Then he sat back and scribbled briefly in the book.

'He's defacing that old book,' reported Mac.

'Yes, I can see that.' Amelia's legs were beginning to ache. She shifted to get a better position, accidentally dislodging a rotten section of mortar. A stone fell to the ground, followed by an avalanche of grit.

They ducked before Hugh, attracted by the noise, turned his head in their direction. When they dared look again, Hugh had moved away from the headstone and was striding back towards the car park, head bowed against the rain.

Mac stood and made a move to clamber over the wall.

Amelia stopped him. 'No way. We're going. This is not our business.'

'What if he's planning a spot of grave robbing?'

'Of course he's not and we shouldn't be here.'

'It's a public place.' Mac jumped over the wall and jogged over to the headstone.

Cursing, Amelia followed, careful not to tear her dress, the damp grass soaking her bare legs. They squatted side by side in front of the stone which was spattered with lichen, the lettering faded.

'Gordon McTavish.' Mac spun towards Amelia. 'Good grief. I didn't know Gordon the Glorious was buried here. I thought he fled Scotland forever and died in some foreign land.'

Amelia rose, wincing as her knees cracked. 'Well, there you are then. Now you know.'

'But what's Hugh's interest in it?'

'I don't know and I don't care. Perhaps he's doing a spot of genealogy and believes they're related. I'm leaving. You can either come with me or ask Hugh for a lift if he's still here.'

Mac followed Amelia back across the field, swearing the entire way.

12

For the rest of the week, Amelia was distracted by a nagging feeling she'd forgotten something. She remembered what it was in the early hours of Thursday morning: they still hadn't checked the fencing in Brutus's field. The Shetland was proving to be quite a character. It had taken three of them to catch him, he'd almost succeeded in biting the vet and then he'd kicked poor Jellybean, who was only trying to be friendly. After that, the decision had been taken to leave Brutus in his own field for the time being. At mid-morning break, Amelia said she would check on the fencing.

'Aye, that ought to be done. Keep him in where he can't cause any trouble,' agreed Angus. 'He chucked his feed bowl at me yesterday, nearly knocked me out, and the other day I caught him trying to sink his teeth into Whisky through the fence.'

'Jilly sure knows how to pick them,' agreed Mac, who'd nicknamed the pony Brutus the Brutal. 'She picks them, then we have to deal with them while she stuffs herself with biscuits in Orkney.'

'The vet said we'll have to get his teeth rasped soon. I'm booking that day off as holiday,' said Angus.

'Or Jilly can deal with it. It'll be a nice welcome back present for her,' suggested Mac.

'I think you're all being mean,' tutted Zoey. 'He's obviously come from a place where he was lonely and has forgotten how to share. He needs to learn to be part of a herd again.'

'You deal with him then,' snapped Angus. 'I could have been injured when he threw that bowl at my head. Good job I used to play cricket and have good reflexes. I felt the rush of air as it whizzed over my scalp.'

Amelia left them to it. Plugging in ear pods, she walked around to the fields expecting to find Brutus up near the gate. She couldn't see him but the field sloped gently down so he was probably grazing in the dip. She began walking around checking the fencing while humming along to the radio. Looking down from the brow of the slope, she still couldn't see the pony. The field appeared to be empty. Confused, she scanned around and spotted a break in the rails where the wood was splintered. Sliding down in a hurry, she tripped, almost losing her footing and slammed heavily into the rail. Peering down to the stream below, she caught sight of the Shetland, who had taken a tumble and was now wedged between broken branches. His rear hooves were dangling over the stream, the ground around his forelegs churned from his efforts to free himself.

'Hold on, buddy.' Amelia removed her ear pods. Shoving them in a pocket, she climbed the fence. As she jumped, she dropped low, steadying herself from toppling down the steep bank.

Her approach galvanised Brutus. He wriggled desperately, attempting to free himself enough to reach her. Stretching out her hand until her fingers brushed his hairy ear, Amelia tried to help him. She slipped, falling heavily against the branch, causing it to snap in half with a loud crack. There was nothing she could do except watch in horror as Brutus whooshed away as though on a slide and, seconds later, splashed into the water. He was instantly carried away.

Squealing, Amelia ran to the edge of the stream, almost falling in herself as she spun at the water's edge, the tips of her wellies submerged, her arms windmilling to retain her balance. She could see Brutus in the distance trying to roll over so he could swim. She raced after him, tripping on tree roots, wrenching her wellies from the treacly mud. Grabbing her phone as she ran, she unlocked the screen and called the office number. After what seemed ages, Mac answered.

'Help me! Brutus is in the stream,' she yelled.

'What?'

'Brutus broke out of the field. He's fallen in the stream.'

Mac swiftly caught on to what was happening. 'Don't lose sight of him. There's a bridge where it's shallower. I'll try and get ahead. With luck, I can catch him there.'

'Please, please hurry.'

'I will.' Mac ended the call.

Amelia ducked under branches, her panic such she hardly noticed the scratches on her face, yanking her hair free when it snagged, clinging to tree trunks to stop herself falling down the slippery bank. She fought through the dense undergrowth, thorns clinging to her jodhpurs like miniscule hands. Keeping Brutus in sight, she pushed on. Further on she lost him as he rounded a bend. When she got there, she saw a man standing knee deep in the bubbling stream beneath a stone arched bridge, his arms around Brutus. It wasn't Mac. It was Hugh Douglas.

'I've got him,' shouted Hugh, spotting Amelia.

Driven by relief, Amelia clawed her way through a dense

thicket to join Hugh and together they hauled the heavy pony over to the bank.

'Here, catch this.' Mac had arrived on the bridge. He threw a headcollar down to Amelia, who dived, grabbing it with both hands.

She secured it to the pony before leading him up the slope to the bridge, where Mac put a rug on the Shetland, saying, 'We'd better get him back and check him over.'

Now she'd stopped, Amelia realised she was soaked in sweat, mud and water. She was also bleeding from numerous surface cuts. She turned to thank Hugh, but he had already left. As they limped back to the stable yard, Amelia realised she hadn't asked what he'd been doing there. She realised it didn't matter.

After dinner that evening, Amelia was looking forward to a bath and an early night so was disappointed to hear a knock on the cottage door. Unusually Gallus growled; she couldn't recall him ever having done so before. As she collected the front door key, she noticed the Loch Ness keyring beside it. Thinking she really must return it to the office drawer the next day, the knocking began again, this time twice in rapid succession. By now, Gallus was at the door, barking. Gently, Amelia moved him aside, calling out, 'Who is it?'

'It's Hugh … Douglas.'

'Hold on a sec.' She opened the door to find Hugh standing under the storm porch, dressed in a blue shirt and cream chinos, holding a bottle of Dom Pérignon Vintage Champagne. 'To what do I owe the honour of your company twice in one day?'

'Gosh, yes, and I do hope I'm not intruding …' Hugh grinned, waggling the bottle, 'only I wanted to deliver your prize personally rather than have one of the staff drop it off.'

'My prize?' Amelia bent down to restrain Gallus who was trying to sneak out unnoticed between the two pairs of legs.

'Yes. I'm pleased to inform you that one of your raffle tickets was a winner and your prize is a bottle of champagne. Here it is.' Grinning, he presented the bottle to Amelia. 'Makes it worth the effort of coming along to the Garden Party, I'd imagine.'

Not wanting to appear impolite Amelia took the bottle, the glass cold between her fingers. 'Oh, it wasn't an effort. We enjoyed ourselves.'

'I'm pleased to hear it. Actually, there is another reason for my dropping by. Could we share the bubbly and have a chat? It's fresh out the fridge so should still be nicely chilled.'

'Perhaps just a quick drink then.' Amelia moved aside. 'I'm pretty tired.'

'Cool.' Hugh strode confidently into the cottage. 'Kitchen through here? I'll get the glasses. You take it easy.'

Amelia sank back into the cushions of the sofa, chastising her weakness at not declining Hugh's offer. She didn't feel like socialising. She should have politely asked him to come back another time and was wondering whether it was too late to back-pedal when Hugh reappeared with two champagne flutes filled to the brim.

'I found these at the back of the cupboard with the other glasses. There you go.' He handed her a glass. 'Congratulations.'

Amelia sipped her drink. The champagne was delicious and, as the bubbles popped in her mouth, it occurred to her Hugh hadn't asked to see the winning raffle ticket. She couldn't remember where it was or whether she even still had it.

'I wanted to check you were OK after your scare with the pony earlier,' explained Hugh.

'I see. Yes, thankfully we're all recovered. Angus has put a temporary repair on the fence until we can get it fixed properly. Unfortunately Brutus can't go in with the others until he learns some manners and that field hasn't been used much. You must think we're terribly careless but it was one of those things. I was literally checking the fence when it happened.'

'Not to worry. At least all's well and I was happy to help. The little chap was struggling to swim in such fast-flowing water. He must have fallen awkwardly.'

'He did. He tumbled down the bank and then with the shock of entering the cold water …'

'As I say, I'm glad I was there and able to react quickly. I don't know if you're aware but eventually that stream widens into a waterfall which, at this time of year, is in full flow. Had the little chap continued on, the consequences could have been deadly. I don't wish to frighten you, Amelia, but perhaps, in your aunt's absence, you ought to accept some assistance from those of us with local knowledge.'

'Thank you for the offer but we're coping fine.' Amelia bristled, she couldn't help it. 'It was an unfortunate accident, that's all —'

'And yet your aunt was recently involved in one of those too,' Hugh cut in.

Ignoring his comment, Amelia asked, 'Why were you at the stream earlier?'

Crossing one leg over another, Hugh rested his right ankle on his left knee. 'I wanted to let you know about the raffle prize.'

'You could have called.'

'I could, but I wanted to see you, do it in person. It's a nicer gesture than by phone.'

'You invited us to the Garden Party and that was a nice gesture. From my perspective, we're getting along fine as neighbours. You don't need to go to a lot of effort, honestly.'

'Oh, but I … well, I wanted to ask you out. You see, I like

you, Amelia, and it's been good having a person of similar age to me in the area. No offence to Zoey, of course. She's just not really the type I'm going to get on with.'

'Outspoken, you mean.' Amelia swallowed a mouthful of champagne, her mind whirling. 'I don't know what to say —'

Hugh talked over her. 'My sister spends most of her time in London working in fashion design and my younger brother, Rufus, is away abroad so it's mostly me and my parents at Keilburn. I'd love some company. To be frank, I'd like to get away but my father's less generous with me. His expectation is I'll run the estate and give up any ambitions of my own.'

At the anger in Hugh's tone, Gallus looked up from his position lying by the fire and gave another growl. Amelia didn't want to become embroiled in the Douglas family's business. 'The thing is, it's not long until my aunt returns and then I'll be going back to London.'

'That's disappointing. I guess if you're heading back to London soon it won't be possible.' Hugh gulped the last of his champagne. 'I should have asked you earlier.'

'That's always been the plan. There's also the added complication of … well —'

'Mac.' Hugh stated.

'Yes. We've grown quite close.'

'I see.' Hugh gazed at the fire for a minute, then seemed to perk up. 'Still, no need to let this delicious champagne go to waste. Here, let me top up your glass.' Reluctantly, Amelia raised the flute and Hugh filled it to the brim again. 'I'm awfully glad to hear you enjoyed the Garden Party. We often invite the locals. The problem is they love a gossip with our ground staff and we have to stop them nattering all day. Those rose bushes won't prune themselves, you know.' Hugh chuckled, slapping his thigh. 'Do drink up. You've barely touched the good stuff.'

Amelia guzzled her drink in the hope that the sooner she

finished it, the faster Hugh would leave both her and Gallus, who kept eyeing the visitor with dislike, alone.

'Our Garden Parties are hugely popular. We've been holding them for years. It costs a lot to keep Keilburn going and we're community minded. We like to do what we can. I'm investigating setting up an apprenticeship. It would provide a great opportunity for someone local who might not otherwise find work …'

Amelia felt suddenly overcome with tiredness and slightly dizzy. Hugh's words were fading in and out; she really wasn't in the mood for listening to his sales pitch about how considerate his family were. Other than Keilburn being Lochside's neighbour, their lives were never going to intertwine. They had nothing in common. She really wanted him to leave now and tried to raise herself off the sofa to suggest it was time for Hugh to go but found she didn't have the strength. Feeling sick, her eyelids refused to do as instructed. She fought to keep her eyes open while trying to stop the sofa spinning. As though from a distance, she could hear Gallus barking and Hugh's voice asking if she was all right. His concern increased as she felt herself slump sideways.

'Amelia … blimey, it must be the champagne that's affecting you.' She sensed Hugh leaning over her, his breath ruffling her hair. She couldn't raise her arms to shove him away. 'Perhaps you've overdone it. Half a bottle probably is a bit much if you're not used to it.' He grabbed a throw and tucked it around her. 'Another time, eh? Sleep well.'

He crept out the door, leaving Amelia to her slumber.

She woke hours later with a splitting headache and Gallus sprawled on her legs. She was lying on the sofa beneath the throw but could barely remember how she got there. When she raised her head a giant thumping ensued. Hugh was gone, as were the champagne flutes and the empty bottle.

Frightened, she shot upright and staggered to the door, relieved to find it locked. It appeared Hugh had secured it and then posted the key through the letterbox. Had he not done so the thought that anyone could have entered the cottage while she was asleep was disconcerting. It was light outside and nearly time to start work. Slowly, she made her way upstairs, keen to take a quick shower to shake her out of the stupor so she could face the day.

Back in the kitchen, dressed and having grabbed a slice of toast, Amelia swept up the stable yard keys but couldn't find the Loch Ness key ring. With no time to worry about it, she decided she'd search for it later. It had probably only fallen down the back of the cabinet anyway.

'You're late this morning,' observed Angus, watching Amelia struggle with the padlock on the gates.

'Yeah. I'm very tired. Hugh dropped by last night.' The lock finally clicked free and the chain slid from between the railings with a clatter, allowing Amelia to push open the gate.

'Hugh Douglas?' Mac was instantly suspicious. 'What did he want?'

'He was dropping off a bottle of champagne I won in the raffle. I'd forgotten you bought those tickets.'

'And he couldn't do that earlier in the day?' bristled Mac.

'I guess not,' snapped Amelia, her headache making her cranky and not in the mood for Mac's questions. 'We were all distracted with Brutus yesterday. Maybe he thought it best to leave it until later.'

Once Zoey joined them in the office, Angus made an announcement. 'Now Zoey's here, I can give you the good news. Jilly called me last night. She's back tomorrow.'

'Tomorrow?' echoed Amelia.

'Well, you're supposed to be leaving on Saturday,' Zoey pointed out, 'and I expect Jilly wants to do a handover before you go.'

Sinking into a chair, clutching a mug of tea, Amelia felt disconcerted. Jilly coming back signalled the end of her stint at Lochside and, although she'd always known it was coming, it had been a future occurrence. Now it would have to be dealt with, the baton would have to be handed back. Muddled thoughts of leaving Mac, Hugh's recent declaration of interest in her and her imminent return to the magazine left Amelia overwhelmed by a sensation of being lost. She didn't belong here, yet neither did she feel she belonged at *Your Home, Your Castle*.

'Amelia, are you paying attention?' Angus had assumed an authoritative tone, as though emboldened by Jilly's return.

'Huh.' Amelia looked up.

'I was saying we need to get busy. Everything must be spick and span for the return of the boss. I'll be baking a cake to welcome her home.'

'More like Deirdre will,' muttered Zoe, her mouth close to Amelia's ear so only she could hear.

By the time they'd finished work, the stables, ponies and tack looked the cleanest Amelia had ever seen them. Assisted by the lack of mud now the weather had improved, Lochside was looking good. Amelia gazed around with a sense of pride.

As they left the stable yard together, Mac put an arm around Amelia's shoulders, asking, 'How do you feel?'

'Honestly, mixed emotions. I didn't improve the bookings but on the plus side, the place is still standing, it looks good and Jilly is returning to the same number of staff and one extra pony, so not a bad job overall. I'd award myself eight out of ten.'

Mac laughed. 'No, I meant about leaving. Your imminent return to the land of crowds of non-four-legged beings.'

'It is what Jilly and I agreed at the beginning.' Amelia opened the cottage door, then flopped on the sofa with Mac on one side and Gallus on the other. Her possessions were strewn everywhere. 'I guess I'd better focus on doing some packing soon. Work's expecting me back on Monday and it's a long trip if I accidentally leave anything behind.'

Mac stood and began pacing the room. 'My offer still stands. One day we'll take Chequered Pipes on the road. You'll always be welcome to join us.'

Gallus gazed into Amelia's eyes with his mournful expression as though also trying to persuade her not to go. 'I know where you are,' was all she could say.

'Before you go how about joining me and the band at the rugby? One of Digger's mates has arranged for us to go to Murrayfield in Edinburgh. I've already checked that it's no problem for you to come too. I thought you could stop off on your way south. It would break up your journey and I'd love you to be there.'

'I'd like that,' enthused Amelia.

If nothing else, it would give them one more day together.

13

Amelia gazed around the cottage thinking how bare it would look once she had packed her remaining items. She had given the place a homely feel by putting up framed photos and candles. As she took them down it occurred to her the marks left in the dust would soon be the only evidence she had been there. She stopped briefly to eat cereal, wandering around the ground floor, bowl in hand, spooning cornflakes into her mouth. A glorious day had begun. She watched a robin hopping over the front lawn and a blackbird bathing in the ornamental stone dish she had been topping up with water. Magpies chattered in the trees, disturbed by Angus as he pedalled past the window, then reappeared moments later holding up an enormous Tupperware tub containing a whole cake.

'Jilly's favourite,' he signalled. 'Coffee and walnut.'

Amelia gave a thumbs up, then Angus went off to unlock, clearly excited at the return of his longtime boss. He was fortunate to feel that way, reflected Amelia, most people couldn't wait to see the back of theirs. She was in the kitchen when Gallus began whining non-stop. She found him standing up on his back legs, front paws scratching at the door. As soon as it was open, he shot out so fast he almost tripped on his pendulous ears, charging over to Zoey's Fiesta, where Jilly was clambering out of the passenger seat.

'Oh, my boy,' she beamed, sweeping Gallus up. 'Yes, that's right, I'm here.' Amelia had never seen the dog as animated. 'Ahoy there.' Jilly raised a hand and waved to Amelia. 'I'm so happy to be back. I can't wait to inspect the troops. I've missed them all dearly.'

True to her word, Jilly visited each stable in turn, making a particular fuss of Spirit, whose ears were back giving a warning she didn't relish the attention. Jilly was oblivious as she rubbed the mare's neck.

'They all look well, Amelia.'

'We've done our best. I'm only sorry that I couldn't bring in more customers for you.'

'We'll have another crack at the gymkhana, perhaps in August when the weather's better. Oh, it's good to be back in my own space again. Living with three others, even if they are family, gets stifling. Let's get the troops fed and then we can all catch up.'

Mac came into the barn while Amelia was absentmindedly measuring feed into buckets. 'Morning,' he greeted her cheerfully. 'We've all got to be on our best behaviour today then, eh?'

'For sure.' Amelia glanced up, pausing from scooping pony nuts into various multicoloured buckets to brush hair off her forehead.

'Hey, don't give them that much,' exclaimed Mac, peering into the buckets, 'you'll make them hyper.'

While Amelia removed some feed from the fullest buckets, Mac began loading up the wheelbarrow.

'I hope you don't feel like you've been demoted,' he said, studying Amelia's face.

As she put the scoop down, Amelia considered throwing her life in the air and giving in to the temptation to tell Mac to take Chequered Pipes on the road and she would join them. The feeling of freedom which flooded through her at the thought made it so tempting. No going back to the structure of set hours working in an office. Instead, an unknown, potentially exciting future ahead of her with Mac by her side, versus leaving tomorrow to resume her previous life. For reasons she couldn't define she simply smiled and replied, 'Of course not. Jilly was always going to return. I knew that from day one.'

Mac held the gate open while Amelia steered the heavy wheelbarrow into the geldings' field. She could feel sweat running down her neck from the effort. Dropping the wheelbarrow's handles with relief, she helped Mac unload the buckets, the pair barely able to keep up as the ponies thrust their noses eagerly into each one. Once all the ponies were eating a breakfast of their own, they turned back towards the gate.

'It seems funny now to remember when you first got here and you thought about leaving straightaway,' said Mac.

'I know.' Amelia smiled at the memory. 'I thought it was going to be a disaster.'

'I knew it was going to be OK the moment I met you.' Mac grinned. 'Jilly seems in good form.'

'She's certainly over the moon to be back. As she said, being trapped in someone else's house isn't easy.'

Mac reached out, pulling Amelia into a hug. 'You did good. Now you have to solemnly promise to keep in touch.'

'Definitely. I don't want to miss out on being the first to hear when Chequered Pipes hit the big time.'

'Which could be sooner than you think. Digger swears one of the guests at Stirling Castle was a record company executive who liked what she heard, although he did get that from a friend who buys his newspaper from a guy who knows another guy who works in the building next door … well, you get the drift. It might not be true.'

'You never know. After all, you have to start somewhere.'

While Mac went to check whether Fergus had a loose shoe, Amelia returned the wheelbarrow and empty buckets to the barn. She knew Jilly's return would change the dynamics and it became apparent how much when she entered the office to find her aunt was joking with Angus, Mac and Zoey about something from before Amelia's time. She made herself a cup of tea, trying to ignore the feeling that the band was back together and she wasn't part of that history.

'OK everyone.' Jilly looked around, her expression serious. 'Because I wouldn't want you finding out from rumours in the pub, I do have to tell you that I've been approached about selling Lochside.'

'What? Jilly, no.' Angus almost broke his empty pipe in half.

'Now, Angus, calm yourself down. I'm not selling. However, I do have to be realistic about the future. My age, my health, these challenges aren't going to get easier to deal with, only worse. One possibility I'm considering is to reduce the number of ponies by selling a few of the younger ones —'

'Jilly, you can't.' Angus's voice was trembling, tears close to the surface.

'I'm only talking through possible options at this stage.' Jilly raised a hand to count them off on her fingers. 'Number one is to sell the younger ponies. Number two is to sell off some of the land —'

'Or leave it as it is,' Angus interrupted again.

Rolling her eyes, Jilly tried to conceal her irritation. 'I only wanted everyone to be aware. It's supposed to be confidential but apparently there was talk about it at a Garden Party recently. You know how rumours fly. Anyway, let's leave it at that. Some customers have just arrived.' Jilly glanced down from looking out the window and opened the desk drawer. 'There's a key missing. Where's the Bothy key gone?'

Amelia slapped her forehead lightly with the palm of her hand. 'It's in the cottage. I keep forgetting to put it back. I'll do it before I leave.'

'No rush,' said Jilly, getting up to greet the customers who were now crowding in the doorway.

Amelia spent her last night in the cottage sharing a drink with her aunt, Mac unable to join them due to a prior commitment with the band. After a glass of wine, she noticed Jilly suppressing a yawn and suggested her aunt needed to rest. Agreeing she was feeling tired, Jilly scooped up Gallus. As Amelia waved goodbye, she realised she would miss the Basset Hound. He had been company and it wouldn't have been the same without him.

Mizzle swirled around as Amelia piled her belongings into the boot of the Mini early the next morning. Not wanting to prolong the goodbyes she was packed and ready to go by the time the team arrived.

'Look after yourself.' Jilly gave her niece a big hug. 'Thank you for everything.'

Angus gave her a peck on the cheek and she received an unexpected hug from Zoey, who said reassuringly, 'Don't worry, I'll make sure the gymkhana happens eventually.'

'See you later,' Mac whispered in Amelia's ear, giving her a farewell cuddle. Although it was his day off, the others didn't know they were meeting up in Edinburgh later and would have considered it a snub if he wasn't there. 'Let me know which room you're in.'

Amelia gave a final wave as she got into the Mini. With tears brimming, she drove slowly away, Gallus running behind. He didn't manage all the way to the road, but he stayed there until he couldn't run any further. Pulling the visor down to shield her eyes from the bright morning sun, Amelia turned the bonnet in the direction of Scotland's capital city. She was on her way.

She arrived at the hotel by lunchtime and from her spot in the car park could see the sign for Murrayfield Stadium and the top of the structure above the rooftops, it was that close. Once in her room, she unpacked a few items and shortly after heard the roar of a motorbike pulling up outside. Opening the window, she stuck her head outside and shouted to Mac, who was getting off the bike. He turned and waved, then blew her a kiss.

Later that afternoon, they joined the hordes of people walking towards the entrances of the gigantic oval-shaped stadium. Many were wearing Scotland Rugby scarves and hats decorated with a thistle, despite the mild weather.

'Looks like it's going to be a good crowd,' Amelia observed.

'Yeah. Guess so.' Mac seemed distracted as they headed towards the queue for the turnstiles, however instead of joining the end of one, he led her onto a hospitality entrance.

'I didn't realise we were in hospitality. I'm glad I made an effort now.' Amelia felt relived she had chosen a cornflower blue dress and black high heels over jeans and Converse trainers.

Mac grunted, then moved away to speak to a staff member. Moments later he steered Amelia through to a covered area beneath the stadium where crowds stood in groups, arms waving passionately as they discussed the upcoming match. Grabbing her hand, Mac wove his way through the throng. Rather than going outside to the terraces, they headed for a hospitality box.

'The guys are in here,' Mac explained as he opened a door, then stood back to let Amelia enter first.

She stepped into a room already filled with people. The band and their partners were helping themselves to vol-au-vents from a tray or food from a buffet laid out on a table set to one side. They greeted her and she was also introduced to the other guests. Feeling names and faces beginning to blur, Amelia gratefully accepted a gin and tonic, then moved over to the glass frontage to gaze down at the pitch. Each end had its white railed two post and crossbar goal in situ. Looking around, Amelia tried to imagine how it must feel to play in front of so many people. She wondered whether you became immersed in the game and forgot about the venue or whether it was always daunting to play in front of such a big crowd who were scrutinising your every move. A small stage had been set up in the centre of the pitch. There was a lot of electrical equipment, a drum kit and a microphone stand.

'Look, Mac,' she called over. 'There must be a live performance before the match.'

Mac nodded but carried on talking to Digger, whose partner Verity came over to keep Amelia company. With her smart tweed suit and bobbed brunette hair, Verity was the opposite of Digger with his tattoos, torn jeans and gaudy t-shirt. They seemed a mismatched pair.

'Today's match is only a friendly,' Verity explained, handing Amelia a glossy programme.

'Thanks.' Assuming that meant the score didn't matter as much, Amelia flipped through the pages.

They chatted amicably until the time for the game approached. People spilled outside to take their seats and the atmosphere began to build in anticipation. Amelia turned to ask Mac if he wanted to get some seats, but scanning the room, she couldn't see him. Assuming he had popped out briefly her attention was taken by a sudden peak in the noise outside. Something was going on.

'Here they are,' squeaked Verity, clapping her hands excitedly.

Following Verity's gaze, Amelia's jaw dropped. Chequered Pipes were striding across the pitch towards the stage. She watched Digger take his seat at the drums and Mac step up to the microphone with his guitar slung over his shoulder.

'What are they doing?' she yelled.

'Mac wanted it to be a surprise, so I promised not to say anything. One of Digger's mates arranged for the band to play before the game. It's fantastic exposure for them.'

Fanning herself with the programme, Amelia watched Mac in disbelief. She had never expected this as he welcomed everyone, his familiar voice echoing over the tannoy. The band began to play 'Bagpipes and Monsters' to a huge cheer. Jigging along to the beat, arm linked through Verity's, Amelia joined in, singing along. After a couple of songs, the band paused.

'This next number is new,' announced Mac. 'I wrote it for someone special to me. She's leaving tomorrow. I hope not forever. It's called "Glad It Happened" and here it is. Enjoy.'

The song was beautiful. The lyrics told the story of the joy at meeting someone you connect with and the sadness when you part. It made Amelia cry. Once Chequered Pipes had finished their final song, the stage was quickly dismantled and cleared away. By the time the match had started, Mac and the band were back in the box. Amelia quickly realised two things: she was wrong about the score not mattering and it didn't look a particularly friendly game. There was an awful lot of chasing after each other and throwing the opposite team members to the ground. The scrum looked positively terrifying and it seemed obligatory for everyone to end up covered in mud. She found herself swept along with the excitement and when the final whistle blew and Scotland had won it made everything more perfect than it already was.

Afterwards, they went out for dinner with the band to a restaurant in the city and by the time Amelia and Mac returned to the hotel it was late and they were exhausted. They made the most of their time together and before she fell asleep, Amelia whispered to Mac, 'I'm glad it happened too.'

Mac's response was a snore; he was already asleep.

Amelia woke the next morning to find Mac, fully dressed, sitting on the edge of the bed.

'I've got to get back,' he told her apologetically. 'The band are playing at the Jumping Trout tonight. It's all go at the moment.'

'It's nice to be popular,' murmured Amelia sleepily, reaching out a hand to take hold of Mac's. She didn't want to let go for when Mac walked out the door her time at Lochside really was over.

Mac suddenly leaned forward and said with urgency, 'Don't go, Amelia, find a way to stay.'

Knowing Mac felt the same made Amelia even more reluctant to return to London.

'How do I find a way though?' she asked. 'I have to live.'

Mac stood and shrugged angrily. 'There's more to life than sitting at a desk —'

'You think I don't know that.' Amelia raised her voice too. 'You're simplifying a situation which isn't simple.'

'Fuck's sake, Amelia. Why do you always have to be so … so rigid? Can't you be more spontaneous.'

'Spontaneous won't pay my rent or buy my food.' Amelia felt her reasoning was justified but it seemed to rile Mac even more.

'You know what, you're a free spirit trapped in a shell of

fear.' Mac zipped up his jacket and picked up his helmet from the chair.

'You can't judge me like that.' Amelia was furious. It was all right for Mac. He sailed through life wrapped up in Chequered Pipes, daydreaming of playing the big stadiums, never bogged down by the minutiae of life. Amelia, on the other hand, couldn't live off fresh air, much as she might want to.

Mac turned, hand resting on the door handle. 'You're right. I can't. Guess I figured I knew you better than I actually do. My mistake.' He opened the door.

From her position sitting up in the bed, Amelia could see the brown swirls on the beige carpet of the corridor. 'Mac … wait.'

He paused. 'How many years, huh, how many years will you do what you have to do, rather than what you want to do?'

'You're looking for a happy ending.'

'No, you're wrong. I'm trying to get a happy beginning with you because I feel this could be special.'

'I … but …'

'I'm sorry you don't feel strongly enough to do the same.'

'But I do.'

'Then stay. Ring up that posh magazine you work for and tell them you're not coming back.'

'Even if I did that, I'd still have to go back and work my notice period.'

'There you go again, chucking obstacles in the way.'

'They're not obstacles, Mac, they're real life. Something you don't have to worry about on the stage.'

'I don't get what you're insinuating. What … that my life is easier than yours? Is that what you're saying?'

'No. Instead of rushing off, please stay longer and we can

try to, I don't know, this isn't something that can be sorted out in a hurry.'

'I can't. The birthday party group have paid us to be there tonight and I have to be.'

'But don't you see, that's what I'm saying about my life,' insisted Amelia. 'I have to be in London tomorrow. I have commitments too.'

'You asked me to wait. Life doesn't wait. You'll find that out eventually. I hope before it's too late.' Mac stepped out into the corridor, clicking the door shut behind him.

Amelia jumped out of bed, pulling on a dressing gown, and rushed to the door. She poked her head out, frantically looking both ways but Mac was gone. By the time she wrenched the window open the motorbike engine was roaring and all she could do was watch from above as Mac steered it out of the car park and onto the road. She sank on to the edge of the bed. It was Sunday morning and she was expected to return to her desk at *Your Home, Your Castle* the next day. The option to do anything else wasn't available. Jilly's talk of downsizing had made her realise there wasn't a place for her at Lochside. She had to go home.

14

It was early evening when Amelia unlocked the door of her flat. She received an awesome greeting from Chewie who, as soon as she stepped inside, leapt into her arms, purring while rubbing his face against hers. On the living room table a crystal vase had been filled with a beautiful bunch of colourful flowers, a thank you note from her flat sitter propped against it. To her relief, both the cat and flat appeared to have been looked after, which improved Amelia's mood a little. Upset by their earlier disagreement, she'd spent the journey listening out for a message from Mac. So far there had been no word from him. Knowing he would be prepping with the band for their performance at the Jumping Trout, Amelia left it. While she waited for a pizza she'd ordered to be delivered she unpacked to the background sounds of traffic, car alarms and music from the flat above. The noises seemed amplified; she didn't recall them being so loud. Her ears would need to readjust to city life again.

With her mind fizzing from a combination of not having heard from Mac and the thought of returning to work, Amelia struggled to switch off and sleep. Shifting every few minutes, disturbing Chewie, who eventually gave up and left the bed, she snoozed the alarm twice before getting up. Out of her old routine, tired from the previous day's long drive and lacking the motivator of knowing hungry ponies were waiting, it took Amelia ages to get ready. Sluggish and disorientated, she gave Chewie his breakfast, then threw together a packed lunch. She appeared to have forgotten so much, she hoped she could still remember how to do the job.

Ten minutes later than planned, Amelia raced out the front door, crashing into the wheelie bins lined up for emptying. Regaining her balance, she walked quickly in the direction of the station, her shoes already rubbing her heels. A sudden shower spattered droplets over her head, destroying her attempts at sleek hair. Pulling up her hood, she jogged into the station building just in time to avoid a heavy downpour and joined the end of the queue at the barrier. She found her season ticket buried at the bottom of her bag.

Finally settled on the train, she gazed out the window and wondered how long it was going to take to get back into the faster pace of office life. She checked her phone for messages for the umpteenth time. There was still no word from Mac which didn't improve her rapidly plummeting mood.

Arriving at the office building, she paused. She didn't have to do this; she could just walk away. Mac had offered her that opportunity.

'Welcome back to the chaos, Amelia.' A voice from behind heralded the arrival of Judith. The Picture Editor was wearing her usual chunky silver bangles, which chimed as she pulled on the door handle. 'After you.'

Amelia followed her inside and up the stairs, noting Judith's long hair, which regularly changed colour, was currently lime green and clashed with the paisley patterned dress she wore over black biker boots.

'Good to have you back. How was the sabbatical?' Judith asked, without turning her head.

'Much needed. Actually, too short if I'm honest.'

'Yeah, these annoying job things, always getting in the way and ruining everything, eh?' Judith chuckled. 'Might even ask for a sabbatical myself, see if I can get away with it.'

Amelia thought it unlikely Stephanie, as the Editor, would be willing to lose any more staff for the foreseeable future but she kept that to herself.

The first difference Amelia came across was her old desk was missing. In the space where it used to be was an enormous pair of bushy plants spewing from elaborate ceramic pots. The furniture's outline was still imprinted in the beige carpet.

'Blimey, Amelia, where's your desk?' Declan, the Marketing Executive, had arrived. His unshaven face looked mystified beneath dark, spiky uncombed hair. His crumpled shirt suggested he too hadn't been prepared for Monday morning. 'And where's mine?'

'Nice to see you,' she faux greeted. 'I've no idea. Were they here on Friday?'

'Do you think I'd be standing here if they weren't?'

Amelia couldn't argue with that. 'Did anyone say anything about them being moved?'

'Of course not, otherwise I wouldn't have asked you where they are because I'd have already known.'

'I'm out of the loop having been away for two months.' Amelia circled on the spot, baffled.

'Yeah, I had noticed you got to skive,' Declan muttered, rubbing his cheek. He pulled a can of Coke from the carrier bag dangling from the crook of his arm. 'I'm not fully awake yet. I need sugar.' As he pulled the ring open, the drink fizzed and overflowed, dripping on the floor.

'Hello, there.' Manju was striding down the office towards them, hindered by a tight black and white pin-striped dress.

'In case you're wondering, we decided to relocate your desks late on Friday.'

'But … but.' Declan was flabbergasted. 'I've sat in the same place for years.'

'Well, Declan, you'll be delighted to learn we've moved you somewhere better. It's a quieter spot. After all, you don't want to be out here in all this noise.' Manju gestured around the currently peaceful editorial floor.

'Never been a problem before,' huffed Declan. 'Can't say I've ever noticed it was noisy.'

'It is rather unfortunate you've come straight here. I had hoped to catch up with you both and explain the new seating arrangements beforehand, as per the message I sent Amelia some time ago.' Manju gave Amelia a stern look.

'Oh.' Amelia vaguely recalled receiving a message from Manju on her way back from Stirling. 'Sorry. I read it ages ago and I forgot.'

'Can't be helped, although I was under the impression that Stephanie had already spoken to you, Declan.'

'Nope.' Declan shrugged and tossed the now empty Coke can into the nearest bin.

'Where are our desks?' asked Amelia impatiently.

Manju led them to a door Amelia had always assumed belonged to a cupboard. She exchanged a bewildered look with Declan as Manju turned the handle.

'What the …!' Declan exclaimed, as he stepped inside. 'They've got larger lockers down the gym. Surely this is a joke.'

As Amelia peered round the door frame, her heart sank. Declan was right. The cramped space contained two desks and two chairs. A teeny window above Declan's desk shed virtually no light, while Amelia's desk area was so dark she'd need a mining helmet to see anything.

'Once you've settled in, pop up and see me, Amelia. We'll

have a chat.' Manju closed the door behind her, obliterating all life from the outer office. It was like being sealed in a bunker.

'Can't see this was necessary,' grumbled Declan, as Amelia shuffled over to her chair, careful not to bang her thigh on the sharp corner of the desk, while dodging the balled-up piece of paper he bowled cricket-style towards her. She batted it away with her hand, as he sneered, 'This is all your fault.'

Glaring at the water-stained ceiling tiles, one of which was broken, offering a glimpse into the abyss beyond, Declan sighed dramatically.

'My fault?' Amelia repeated. 'How'd you come to that conclusion?'

'If you hadn't gone on sabbatical, they'd never have thought to look at everything. They're only making changes because you gave them the opportunity.'

'Everything? What changes?'

Head bent down as he furiously typed on his mobile, Declan ignored Amelia.

With a tut, she switched on her laptop. 'OK, if you're not going to tell me then I'd better go and see Manju.'

'Yeah, you do that. Tell her I want to move back outside with my mates.'

Once upstairs, Amelia knocked on Manju's door.

'Come in,' called Manju's voice chirpily.

As Amelia entered, Manju stood up from behind a desk so vast it would have taken up the entire area of her new office downstairs. Trying not to bristle at the unfairness of being moved there without any consultation, Amelia said, 'Declan mentioned there'd been some changes.'

'Come and take a seat.' Manju gestured to a pair of armchairs angled around a circular coffee table, piled with copies of *Your Home, Your Castle*. 'I wanted to chat to you before any of your colleagues, but these things happen. How's it going so far?'

'OK, I guess, although I've only been here half an hour. What's going on?'

'Ah, yes.' Manju appeared reluctant to say much. 'Well, um, Stephanie and I had a chat and decided that, on your return, you would work more on the marketing side of business, supporting Declan. He has such a heavy workload and we wanted to help him although he never complains, of course.'

'He doesn't seem very happy about the new seating arrangements to me.' Amelia's temper rose. The thought of Manju and Stephanie making decisions without discussing them with her first while Declan, who she knew did as little as possible most days, played the overworked employee, irked her. 'What about my other work? The work I was doing before the sabbatical?'

'That'll be done by another secretary.'

'But there isn't another secretary.'

'Actually, there is now. The temporary secretary is staying on and you'll move to marketing.' Manju shuffled in her seat. 'We believe it's for the best and we're very excited about the new structure.'

'I would've liked to have been consulted before all this. I also feel it would be good if Declan and I could go back to the editorial floor, where we belong. I mean, is the new seating arrangement permanent?'

'We see it as permanent, yes. Why do you ask?'

'Because we'll be isolated in there. How will we know what's going on?'

Manju giggled. 'Email, of course, and team meetings. Declan's a great communicator, he'll keep you up to speed on everything.'

Amelia frowned. Manju's version of Declan was very

different to the one she knew and had worked with. She longed to be dealing with nothing more complicated than a pony with a loose shoe instead of the complex situation she was now faced with. 'Can I not just go back to my old role and the new secretary do this job?'

Manju tutted but tried to mask it. 'The decision has been made. The tasks the role requires are the same, just in a different area. Look on the bright side, Amelia. This could be a promotion opportunity. Declan intends to share all the work with you —'

'I bet he does,' interjected Amelia.

'I appreciate you probably feel disconcerted by the sudden changes. That's why the company thought it wise that you attend a marketing course to help you adapt. You've already been booked on one and you'll find all the information you need in an email.'

'I really don't think that's necessary.'

Manju picked up a china cup from its saucer, took a sip of coffee, then said in a stern tone, 'It's a requirement, Amelia, not an option.'

Convinced the meeting had merely been a formality and that however she felt was of no consequence, Amelia rose to her feet. 'I need to get on, so if that's all …'

'Fabulous.' Manju grinned. 'Keep me updated on how you go. Declan's a fantastic colleague though, I'm sure you'll have such fun working closely with him.'

Amelia nodded and moved out to the corridor, resisting the temptation to slam the door. She returned to the office to find Declan playing with the *Game of Thrones* character figurine which guarded his desk.

'Well?' he asked as she came through the door. 'P45?'

Amelia dropped into her chair. 'Nope, but I did find out I'm your assistant now.'

Declan tossed the figurine aside, accidentally dropping it

headfirst into his mug of tea. 'I don't want one. I told them that.'

'I guess we'll both just have to make the most of it, seeing as we're stuck with each other,' Amelia said reasonably.

'Thanks to your sabbatical I'm trapped in here with you.' Declan unwrapped a Twix, shoving both sticks into his mouth at once.

'It's not exactly a dream come true for me either.' Amelia picked up her phone to check whether she had any messages; she didn't.

Declan stuck his earbuds in and tapped away on his keyboard, head moving in time to the beat of the music. Amelia felt as if the day should already have ended.

The week dragged by until finally it was Friday when Amelia had a long overdue catch up with her friend, Malandra, who arrived that evening wearing a green dress, her brunette hair in a ponytail. They chatted while consuming a takeaway and a bottle of Sauvignon Blanc Malandra had brought with her.

'Feels strange you being back after so long away,' Malandra commented, as they tucked into Chinese food, watched by Chewie. 'I almost forgot you were coming back.'

'Yeah. Sorry I wasn't in contact that much. It was a crazy busy time.' Feeling slightly chastised, Amelia defended her lack of communication.

'I was keeping an eye on your Instagram but even that didn't get updated much,' commented Malandra, a sly expression on her face. 'One might almost believe you had a distraction up there.'

'You mean besides a herd of permanently hungry ponies and a business that's not doing very well.' Amelia sipped her wine.

'Yes, I do mean besides that. A distraction that perhaps

answers to the name of Mac.' Malandra obviously wasn't going to let it go. 'Whenever I did hear from you, I couldn't help noticing Mac's name was mentioned every time.'

Amelia grinned and put a forefinger to her lips. 'That would be telling.'

'Come on then … tell.'

Amelia filled her friend in on most of what had happened during her time at Lochside. She didn't go into detail about the argument she'd had with Mac in Edinburgh, she still hadn't resolved how she felt about it herself and didn't want Malandra's analysis to confuse her further.

'Were you tempted to stay?' asked Malandra, when Amelia had finished. 'I get the impression you were. Aside from the weather, the mud and the cheeky ponies, it sounds rather idyllic in a countryfied kind of way.'

Amelia chased some rice around her plate while considering the question. 'It would have been nice to stay but Lochside's struggling. I didn't feel I could ask my aunt to take on another paid role and she doesn't need anyone extra now she's there.'

'Plus, although the theory's good it's an awfully long commute,' joked Malandra.

Amelia laughed. 'Yeah, true.'

'You know, joking aside, sometimes the path not chosen wasn't necessarily the right one anyway. I mean, tempting as it may be, what if you'd moved up there and Mac had left to do his band stuff and your aunt had sold the stables. From what you've said before it sounds like this Angus is past retirement age and Zoey will return to Uni but you, you'd have given up everything to gain nothing.'

Amelia held up her glass and studied the liquid against the soft glow of the wall light. 'You know, this stuff's amazing. It's making you very wise.' She laughed. 'Seriously though, you've always wanted to be a teacher since we were at school and you're doing the job you love so —'

'True,' interrupted Malandra, 'and sometimes I do love it but other times I don't and mostly I just grit my teeth and get on with my job like the majority of us have to.'

Amelia placed her empty plate on the table and reclined into the soft comfort of the sofa. Seizing the opportunity, Chewie jumped into her lap and curled up for a snooze, his weight pressing on Amelia's full belly. 'I can't believe I've got to work closely with Declan though,' she complained. 'I've never had much to do with him before and don't particularly want to.'

Malandra grimaced. 'I guess that's the outcome of being absent for a long time. It's given them the opportunity to shift work around, by the sound of it, in Declan's favour. He's the guy with the spiky hair I met at the Christmas do, isn't he?'

'Yes.'

'I can't say I liked him. He struck me as shifty but then he was extremely drunk.'

'He's obviously been complaining about everything and to keep him happy they've decided to dump all his work on me. He's no team player though. I doubt he'll like having to explain what he's working on to me.'

For a while they sat listening to an Ed Sheeran album playing from the iPad speakers, interspersed with Chewie's snores.

'I am a supportive friend,' Malandra said suddenly, 'but I wouldn't be a good friend if I didn't say that I feel your best option is to stick it out at the magazine. You're tough enough to stand up to Declan if he's lazy. This Lochside situation sounds dicey.'

'I know, I know.' Amelia raised her hands. 'I'll give Jilly a call over the weekend and see how it's going. They did say they'd try again with my gymkhana idea …'

'And think about sending Mac a message, yeah? One of you needs to reach out. You'll feel better for it. You don't want to feel uncomfortable if you visit Lochside again, do you?'

'I guess not although I doubt I'll be visiting any time soon.'

'True, but who knows about the future. When Zoey returns to Uni there might be an opportunity. That's if you're still interested by then.'

Lying in bed later, Amelia picked up her phone and unlocked the screen which lit up the photo of Mac on Hebrides alongside her riding Spirit which she'd set as the wallpaper. They were laughing at something and looked happy. It spurred her to open a new message, then close it after a few minutes. She couldn't find the words to write to Mac. With a deep sigh, she switched the phone off. No doubt he'd be playing with the band somewhere anyway, too busy to bother chatting with someone now part of his past. She fell asleep troubled by thoughts of regret at the path not chosen.

15

Over the next few weeks, Amelia tried to settle into a routine. While she was distracted at work, there wasn't time for her thoughts to drift to Lochside. She heard nothing from Mac and found it difficult to resist checking the posts on the band's Instagram page in the evenings. She knew they were mostly done by Digger. Other than announcements about forthcoming venues where Chequered Pipes would be playing and lots of comments about their performances, she could glean nothing more. As time went by and the weariness of work and commuting consumed her again, it seemed easier to leave it. Suggesting meeting for a drink to clear the air was impractical when you were at opposite ends of the country.

At eight o'clock on a scorching Monday morning, Amelia arrived at Waterloo station and stood waiting under the clock. She removed her sunglasses to wipe the sweat from her face and dry the plastic frames. A heatwave had rolled in and even early in the day the temperature beneath the station roof was baking. Her feet, squashed into a pair of platform sandals she hadn't worn for months, were already sore and as a pigeon waddled by it glanced at her toes. Deciding they weren't edible, it wandered on. Amelia checked the time on her phone. Fifteen minutes later she was still waiting, fuming like someone stood up on a blind date and feeling she deserved better. She'd sent a message to Declan over the weekend reminding him they were due at an exhibition yet there was no sign of him. Increasingly annoyed, Amelia paced, watching the minutes tick by, taking with them the preparation time she had planned before the exhibition opened. Declan finally turned up nearly an hour late, unkempt and with sweat patches under the armpits of his creased shirt.

'What time do you call this?' Amelia snapped. 'Please don't tell me you've been drinking all weekend.'

'What's it to you?' Declan growled. 'You're not my keeper or my boss.'

'And I'm very happy not to be. You look like you slept outdoors.' As she spoke, it occurred to Amelia that might actually be true. 'Where's your tie?'

'It's too hot for a tie and why bother? No one wears them anymore. It's all smart casual these days.'

'Well, there's no time left to buy you one seeing as we're already late. At this rate there'll be virtually no set up time left.'

'I'm not spending money on a tie. Quit fussing and panicking. Remember I've been doing these exhibitions on my own for years and I've coped fine without you.' Declan marched off to the escalator, his untucked shirt flapping behind him.

Following him onto a platform packed with people, who then crammed into a stifling tube train, Amelia clung to a handrail by the door, feeling the draught of warm fetid air blast through the carriage. Her energy levels were being sapped by the heat and the conflict. Next to her a grim-faced

Declan was obviously trying not to throw up, taking deep breaths as the train swayed around every curve in the tunnel. His head lolled and sweat rolled down his forehead and cheeks.

'Maybe you should consider cutting down on your drinking at the weekends, even if only for a month or two.' Amelia wedged herself in the corner to give Declan more space and air, although it wouldn't be fresh. 'I'm sure you'll feel better for it.'

'Maybe you should consider keeping your opinions to yourself.' Declan burped. 'Do you need that plastic bag?' He indicated the carrier bag Amelia was holding in her hand.

'Yes, it contains everything we need. Unless you fancy carrying it?' Amelia extended her arm towards him, the bag dangling from her fingers. 'You're welcome to it. It's full of leaflets and heavy. You'll have to be careful not to drop it because I don't have any replacements if the bag splits and they blow away.'

Declan shrugged. 'I didn't want a lecture. I was just checking out vomit bag options.'

'You're disgusting.'

'And you're annoying. I wish you'd stayed in Scotland. We didn't even notice you were gone. Everything was fine until you reappeared and I got shoved in a bloody cupboard. You're difficult to work with, Amelia. Everyone says so.'

'No, they don't.' Amelia instinctively jumped to defend herself. 'Stop exaggerating.'

'Yes they do, just not to your face. You've always been tricky and now you've been demoted. Serves you right.'

'I haven't been demoted and you know it. It was you bleated to Manju about your workload. If you hadn't done that, none of this would have happened.'

'What I say to HR is nothing to do with you,' sniffed Declan.

'Yeah, right.'

The train slowed, then stopped and the doors slid open. Amelia stepped onto the platform, not bothering to check whether Declan was behind her. His obnoxious hangover induced mood was rubbing off on her. He could stay on the roasting hot tube train for all she cared. In stony silence they travelled up the escalator, then walked out of the station and across the road to the venue, Declan lingering behind to annoy her. As they crossed the entrance of the huge exhibition hall, Amelia tried to get into a better frame of mind for the day.

When she reached the stand allocated to *Your Home, Your Castle*, Amelia was relieved to find it had been set up the evening before by the transport team. Disappointingly, the location was tucked away in a dimly lit corner beside the fire exit doors.

'We're unlikely to get much footfall here,' she commented, as she unpacked the leaflets, fanning them out on a table.

'Are you ever satisfied?' snapped Declan. 'You'd have more to complain about if you were by the stinky loos which is where I was last year.'

'But we're out on a limb here. You can't see us until you're practically falling over us.'

'Not my problem if the magazine's too tight to splash out for a premium stand. Can't say I care that much. What I do care about is that I'm starving. I'm going to get a bacon sarnie from the café next door.' Without asking Amelia whether she wanted anything, Declan departed, leaving her to log the company iPad on to the Wi-Fi.

Amelia sat gazing around the large airy hall. It was rammed with exhibitors preparing for the doors to open at half past nine bringing what they hoped would be a rush of potential customers.

It was half an hour before Declan returned, sporting a

ketchup splodge on his white shirt and a wide grin on his face. 'I've got a date,' he informed Amelia proudly, 'with the barista. I couldn't resist asking her. Got her number … see.' He swam his mobile backwards and forwards under Amelia's nose.

'Great. Could you focus on the work now? They're about to open the doors.'

'You're telling me to focus? I'm not taking that from someone who disappeared for months because her stupid aunt fell through some stupid floorboards while playing at a castle. You can do it all today. It's payback time.' Giving Amelia no chance to object, Declan spun around and stomped off.

Sinking down on a stool, Amelia shook her head in dismay. She should have been prepared for some of the staff to have a problem with her sabbatical. Declan seemed to have taken it particularly badly. The day dragged on with interest in their stand slow. A few potential advertisers stopped by but soon wandered off without committing to anything. None of them returned and neither did Declan. Amelia called his mobile a few times in the lunch break. He didn't answer and as she was unable to leave the stand empty, she went without lunch.

The remainder of the day passed with no further visitors. When Declan eventually reappeared, they exchanged no words for neither needed to point out the event had been a complete waste of time. Clearing up without enthusiasm, they shoved gear back into packing cases, then walked through the rapidly emptying hall, the detritus of used takeaway cups and abandoned leaflets around their feet, the smell of onions drifting over from the food concession stands.

'I'm not going back to Waterloo,' Declan informed Amelia at the station entrance. They parted ways at the ticket barrier with curt goodbyes.

. . .

The remainder of the week passed by with Declan mostly giving Amelia the silent treatment, unless conversation was unavoidable. His childish refusal to remove his earbuds or engage in chat infuriated her and by Friday morning she'd had enough. Rather than lose her temper when he ignored her yet again, Amelia picked up her mug and retreated to the kitchen. She was swirling a teabag in a mug of hot water with suppressed anger when Judith came in.

'Hi, Amelia, are you coming to my birthday drinks later?' she asked, rinsing her cup at the sink.

'Oh, I hadn't heard about them.' Amelia was surprised. News of social gatherings usually scooted round the office at a speed beaten only by someone bringing in cakes.

'I did mention it to Declan the other day. I thought he would let you know.'

'He must have forgotten.' Amelia didn't add that she suspected he'd done so on purpose.

'It's straight after work at The Happy Brewer. Do join us if you can. It would be lovely to see you there. You haven't been out with us for ages.' Judith studied Amelia's face. 'Is everything OK? You look weary.'

Much as she longed to confide in Judith, Amelia felt torn. In her experience involving other colleagues in office disputes inevitably exacerbated issues. Since she was desperate for advice she ended up spilling the saga of the day at the exhibition.

'I'm sure Declan's not upset with you really. He's not been himself since the desk moves and says he misses sitting with the rest of us. He'll come around.' Judith patted Amelia's arm reassuringly.

'I guess, but you always see the best in people and …' Amelia tailed off as other staff entered the kitchen.

'Remember it's The Happy Brewer later. It'll do you good. I understand it's hard readjusting after a long time out the office.' Judith gave her mint tea a brisk stir, squeezed the bag, threw it in the bin and vacated the kitchen in a swirl of tie-dyed skirt, leaving Amelia staring at the dripping tap. She knew glossing over difficulties the way Judith did would achieve nothing. She needed to talk to Declan. Going to the pub for a chat outside of work could be an opportunity to clear the air and put an end to the unbearable working atmosphere between them.

Although the magazine staff were the only drinkers in The Happy Brewer the celebrations were well underway. Mostly they gathered in the same groups they usually socialised with. As she entered the pub, Amelia spotted Declan. After purchasing a glass of wine, she eased her way towards the huddle he was part of but, as she approached, he thwarted her by moving away to join another group. She tried to catch his eye to indicate she wanted to talk but was waylaid by a tipsy Judith thanking her for the birthday card Amelia had rushed out to buy at lunchtime. Having managed to extract herself from Judith's flowery perfumed hug, she scanned the bar again. To her dismay, there was no sign of Declan. She spotted Andy from the Advertising department and pushed her way through the crowd to stand beside him, knowing if anyone knew where Declan was it would be his closest friend.

'Do you know where Declan is?' she shouted to be heard above the noise of the crowd and a band warming up in the corner.

'He's left, mate,' replied Andy, tipping his glass to reach the remains of his pint. 'Want another?' He gestured to Amelia's half-empty glass of wine.

'Oh, no thanks.' Amelia suddenly felt exhausted.

Seeing the band had flooded her mind with images of Chequered Pipes and especially Mac. Sadness at the lack of contact between them overwhelmed her. She wished she was brave enough to call him but felt so uncertain about how he'd react. Queasy from the yeasty smell of hops and hemmed in by colleagues braying like mules in the stuffy bar now crowded with drinkers, she surveyed her colleagues. Were they sending sly looks in her direction as their lips moved, spilling gossip gleefully as the band began to play? A girl she'd seen earlier engrossed in conversation with Declan was staring at her with open hostility. Had Declan been stirring trouble complaining about Amelia to others? She had to be sure he wasn't pitting the department against her. Finding Judith swaying to the music, Amelia gestured she was leaving.

Judith placed her mouth right beside Amelia's ear. 'My advice is ride out the storm. Don't let the likes of Declan get you down. Keep your chin up.'

'Thanks, Judith. Happy birthday.'

Once outside, Amelia caught sight of Declan further up the street, his laptop bag banging against the back of his knees as walked into the entrance to the train station. As a bus roared by and a group of revellers chanted songs on the other side of the pavement, Amelia gave up on shouting out to him. He was too far away to hear her and was disappearing inside the building as Amelia began to jog, tripping in her sandals. After a few strides she stopped running. He would be through the barrier and gone before she could catch him.

Her train home was late and then she couldn't find an empty seat. She rested against a partition, wondering how to turn things around and why it was so difficult to come up with anything better than her time at Lochside. She needed to stop feeling she was missing out on a future that was never hers and focus on her life in London.

. . .

The temperature rose each day and by the end of July the office was unbearably stuffy. Declan tried to open the window above his desk. He found it was jammed shut and his efforts were rewarded only by a shower of muck falling on his gelled hair like confetti. Amelia laughed at him as she switched on her desk fan, earning a scowl. Relations and tempers were not improved by the airless conditions and it was a relief to get out of the office for a day. As Amelia drove towards Chichester the following week she was feeling more positive. She had even considered offering Declan a lift as he didn't have a car. In the end, his sullen and uncooperative behaviour persuaded her to let him sort his own transport to the photo shoot. She was looking forward to spending the day on a luxury motor yacht which *Your Home, Your Castle* had hired. It was moored in Chichester Marina.

As she pulled into the Marina car park, Amelia wasn't surprised to spot Declan getting out of the passenger side of Judith's orange and white Volkswagen camper van. Sliding Ray Ban sunglasses up his nose with one hand, he ignored Amelia as she waved to him, instead sauntering off in the direction of the boats. She noted on this occasion he had made the effort to dress smartly in navy blue tailored shorts, a short sleeved white shirt and navy blue deck shoes. Judith hurried after him, the skirt of her long summer dress swinging around ankles encased in the ribbons of platform espadrilles, as she hoisted a straw bag onto her shoulder.

'Hi, Amelia, how was your journey?' Amelia asked herself sarcastically. 'Traffic OK? Shall we wait for you and we can walk together?'

She locked the car and followed the path Declan and Judith had taken, wondering why, if her presence was so unimportant, she was there at all. With each step dust flew up from the scorched ground as she made her way to the motor yacht. She found *Lucky Lulu* moored at the end of a pontoon. There was no sign of Declan and Judith. Assuming they were already on board, Amelia stepped onto the platform at the stern, admiring the smooth caramel wood. She looked up, then gasped. The motor yacht resembled a floating five-star hotel. Ahead of her, a glass sliding door stood open, beyond it a luxury lounge. She stepped inside, inhaling the refreshing scent of a forest after rain. No doubt it cost a fortune to make the indoors smell subtly of the outdoors without being overpowering. There was an abundance of white marble surfaces with furnishings artfully arranged to create a minimalist look. Judith was fussing around setting up the fabrics and cushions for the photo shoot. Through the huge windows Amelia admired the view of the surrounding yachts. She closed her eyes and imagined herself, cocktail in hand, gazing at a sunset in the Caribbean after a day of swimming in turquoise waters and sunbathing.

'Don't just stand there daydreaming, Amelia, get the drinks ready please,' snapped Judith, in a display of uncharacteristic bad temper. 'We're using cranberry juice instead of red wine … cutbacks.' She tutted and pummelled the cushion she was holding. 'Back in the day when Cornelius was Editor we did things properly but since Stephanie took over she wants it all done on the cheap. Budget savings, except when it comes to what she wants, of course.'

Considering it wisest to make no comment, Amelia walked over to the table where the empty wine glasses sat on a tray and lifted one of the unopened cartons of Cranberry Juice from Judith's straw bag. She could see no sign of Declan who had no doubt slunk off for a crafty cigarette. While Judith fastidiously arranged the cushions and throws on a white sofa, Amelia filled the glasses with juice. A glance at her smart watch informed her it was midday. With the sun at its peak, the temperature felt like thirty degrees and she wished they'd turn on the air conditioning.

As though reading Amelia's mind, Judith fanned herself with a piece of paper. 'I asked them to switch on the air con but because the door's open they said no,' she groaned. 'If only the breeze would pick up and cool it down in here.'

'We'll soon be finished. Then we can have a nice cool drink of one of these.' Amelia indicated the tray of brimming glasses she was holding.

'Yes, let's get on,' agreed Judith, picking up an enormous camera. 'The photographer's called in sick but I can cover it. My snaps are usually better than his anyway. As I told Stephanie the other day, they were always good enough for Cornelius. I don't think she appreciated hearing that.'

Amelia grinned, bending over to begin placing the glasses on a coffee table nestled between the two sofas. A shout, followed by the sound of running feet was all she heard before something smashed into her back. Knocked forward by the force with which she had been hit, she stumbled and fell, face first. The tray slipped from her fingers, the glasses tumbling. Amelia yelped, watching in horror as the eight glasses of ruby red Cranberry Juice splashed all over the pristine white sofas, cushions and throws like a tidal wave crashing on a beach.

'Declan!' cried Judith.

'What? Amelia backed into me,' Declan protested spitefully.

Neither of them offered to help Amelia as she lay on the floor surrounded by broken glass.

'What a mess!' Judith was shocked, the camera dangling from her hand.

'Yeah. Everything's ruined.' Declan nodded. 'You saw what happened though, right? It wasn't my fault.'

Carefully rising to a crouch while trying to avoid cutting herself on any of the sharp pieces, Amelia wiped juice from her chin, thinking this could be the moment her career reached an all-time low.

'Be careful, Declan, don't hurt yourself,' cautioned Judith, pulling him away.

'Oh, yeah, don't mind me,' muttered Amelia furiously.

'Wait until Stephanie hears about this. It'll cost a fortune to put this right. Bet she takes it out your wages, Amelia,' said Declan smugly.

16

'Oh, I've just got an email from Stephanie saying she wants to see us both urgently.' Even as she said the words to Declan, Amelia had an ominous feeling. The incident the day before had not been mentioned yet but it was nearly lunchtime and she knew what had taken place on *Lucky Lulu* couldn't go unaddressed indefinitely. She would need to stand her ground; Declan could not be trusted.

Declan, however, appeared delighted, leaping from his chair as though he'd been stung. 'Excellent. About time they apologised and moved me out of here. I'm sure this used to be the stationery cupboard. What the hell were they thinking moving me in here in the first place?'

'They clearly weren't thinking when they moved us in here.' Amelia was taken aback at her colleague's enthusiasm as she hurried to keep up with Declan, who was practically sprinting the length of the top floor to the Editor's suite, situated next to Human Resources furthest from the stairs.

Declan burst through the door surprising Wendy, Stephanie's Executive Assistant, who was typing on a laptop.

She paused, glancing up over tortoiseshell framed spectacles. Amelia's eyes met Wendy's over a spotlessly tidy desk.

'Take a seat,' instructed Wendy, raising her voice to be heard above the persistent bleeps of a pedestrian crossing drifting in through an open window from the street below. 'Stephanie won't keep you waiting long.'

'Great.' Declan grinned and stood in front of Wendy's desk trying to engage her in small talk. When she made it clear she was too busy, he gave up, dropping into the chair next to Amelia.

'Only trying to be friendly,' he huffed, tipping the chair on its back legs against the wall.

'Makes a change,' Amelia said.

Declan ignored her. She studied the wall behind Wendy's desk which was covered in framed photos. Some she recognised as covers of past editions of the magazine, others were of the senior management team dressed in tuxedos and evening gowns enjoying themselves at a variety of media award ceremonies.

'Funny how they never invite the staff who actually do the work,' grumbled Declan, who was looking at them too.

Amelia was about to comment when Wendy informed them Stephanie was ready. They entered the vast space of the Editor's office, where Stephanie sat behind a glass desk, looking at the screen of her Mac. She stopped typing and leaned forward, the leather chair creaking beneath her, placing her hands, palms down, on the desk. Amelia took in her neat nails decorated in a French manicure and, as the sleeves of her lavender silk dress retracted, the diamond studded gold watch on her left wrist. The walls were covered with similar photos to Wendy's area and two of the chairs from the six usually set around a glass meeting table had been placed in front of Stephanie's desk. They sat without needing to be asked, Declan practically levitating above his cushion.

'Thank you for coming straight up,' Stephanie began, glaring with pale eyes from beneath the fringe of an auburn bob. 'I'm sure I don't need to explain to either of you why you're here —'

'I haven't unpacked much at my new desk so I can —' Declan cut in.

'We've received a complaint from the owner of *Lucky Lulu*, Declan,' Stephanie interrupted him loudly. 'Plus a bill for the replacement of two white designer sofas, would you believe? As well as for professional cleaning of a stained wooden floor. The owner wishes to avoid claiming on their insurance as they insist *Your Home, Your Castle* should cover the costs of repairing the damage caused while you were onboard. Would either of you care to enlighten me?'

Amelia glanced over at Declan, who was now looking lost. As she launched into an explanation of the incident, Declan began talking over her. They both got progressively louder, each trying to ensure their version of events was clearly heard.

Stephanie ran out of patience after a couple of minutes and raised a hand. 'OK. Stop, please, both of you.'

'Amelia backed into me,' Declan shouted, before falling silent at Stephanie's request.

'You ran into me and you know it,' yelled Amelia. 'Just be honest, for once. You weren't even working; you'd disappeared to smoke as usual.'

'Oh, that's rich coming from the person who disappeared for two months. We're all aware what your work ethic is.' Declan looked at Stephanie, seeking approval for what he clearly thought was a clever point.

'Ask Judith. She saw everything.' Amelia glared at Stephanie, challenging her to do the right thing.

'I've already spoken to Judith. She said she can't be sure what happened because she was busy setting up the camera.'

'That's not true,' Amelia stated, 'she saw everything, I know she did.'

Declan began shouting angrily that Amelia was lying.

'Declan, please,' soothed Stephanie. 'All right. I can see I'm not going to get an honest explanation —'

'I've given you an honest explanation,' interrupted Amelia.

'And the pair of you need to cool off. This is not what the company expects in terms of staff behaviour.'

'I agree,' said Declan. 'I feel we need space if we're to continue working together and if I change desks that will help move this forward. I can move today. I'm ready.'

Amelia remained quiet, a sense of foreboding creeping over her, a feeling Declan was going to play this to his advantage, as usual. A golden carriage clock on the windowsill ticked the seconds off as Stephanie gave some thought to Declan's proposal. An ambulance rushed by outside, its siren earsplittingly loud before fading into the distance. Wendy's phone began to ring and Amelia listened to her answer it using her posh telephone voice, then inform the caller the Editor was unavailable and offer to take a message.

'All right.' Stephanie nodded as though agreeing with her own conclusions. 'For the time being, Declan, you will relocate to the main editorial floor. Amelia, you will remain where you are. I need to impress upon you both my displeasure at this. We also have a photo shoot which needs to be urgently rescheduled. Declan, I would like you to lead on that alongside Judith.'

'And what will I be doing?' asked Amelia.

'We have some, er, administrative tasks for you.' Stephanie's mobile phone buzzed on the desk. 'Your behaviour will be monitored. I would impress upon you to ensure there are no repeats of this unfortunate incident. That is all.'

Amelia was closest to the door. She rose and turned to

leave, followed by Declan. As soon as they stepped into the corridor, he turned on Amelia, his face puce, his fists raised in fury.

'This is all your fault,' he spat at her.

'Stop blaming me for everything. You're responsible for yourself and you should have been more careful. Why did you push me over anyway? What for?'

'I told you I didn't.'

They made their way back to the editorial floor. Once they were surrounded by the team Declan puffed up like an actor under the spotlight on stage. 'I'm telling you it's all your fault, Amelia.' He turned to address the other staff. 'No one had ever gone on sabbatical before Amelia. Since she returned it's been nothing but trouble.'

There were murmurs of agreement and hostile glares were sent in Amelia's direction.

'Declan, you're being unfair. This has nothing to do with me being away. Instead of skiving why don't you try working for a change? See if that turns things around for you.'

'Fuck's sake.' Declan stormed off.

Passing through the *Your Home, Your Castle* reception the next morning, Amelia called out her usual cheery greeting to the receptionist who, although seated at the desk and not wearing her headset, didn't respond. Amelia repeated herself as she continued up the stairs. She received no reply.

The editorial floor was silent, the staff working without their usual chit-chat. Declan had moved to the desk next to Andy and did not look up when Amelia passed. Even Judith seemed reluctant to engage with her, moving away when Amelia approached. She stepped into the office to find Declan's furniture had been removed. Feeling the need for sugar but keen to avoid walking through the open plan office again, she took the rear fire exit stairs. As she reached the final concrete step, voices drifted through the partially open door which led to a section of the car park reserved for smoking.

'Declan says it's all her fault and he wishes she'd stayed in Scotland. In fact, the further away from him the better. He says they'll have to drag him kicking and screaming back into that cupboard,' Andy was telling his audience with relish.

Amelia gently pushed the door open and stepped through. The group of four staff stopped talking and dropped their eyes guiltily as they resumed puffing on their cigarettes and vapes.

'You know what? I wish I'd stayed in Scotland too,' she informed Andy. As she marched away towards the shops, she realised she meant it.

Days passed and Amelia grew used to the seclusion of the office. She even began to appreciate it. The only signs Declan had once shared the space were a stained mug and the figurine from *Game of Thrones* which had been left on the floor. On principle Amelia refused to wash up the mug and put it away. She also wasn't prepared to move the figurine to Declan's new desk. If he wanted them, he knew where they were and would have to come and get them. They still hadn't exchanged a word since their argument.

Breathing a huge sigh of relief, Amelia opened the office door and walked through the editorial floor. It was almost seven o'clock in the evening and finally the end of a long and challenging day. A delivery of throws needed for a photo shoot for the next edition's front page had been delayed and Amelia had made numerous phone calls trying to track them down. Her stratospheric stress levels were due to the drama and chaos created by senior management. It hadn't been well received when Amelia pointed out they were just a few pieces of material anyone could live without and it was hardly the end of the world.

'Tough day?' the security guard asked sympathetically. 'You're the last one to leave.'

'Am I really that haggard or is my mascara smudged?' asked Amelia, grinning. 'I haven't had time to look in a mirror all day.'

'Get some rest,' the security guard advised, unlocking the door and holding it open. Amelia stepped into the bright light and heat of a summer's evening like a mole breaking the surface of a lawn.

'Thanks. I will and I'll pour myself a large glass of …' Amelia didn't finish her sentence, nor did she feel the handle of the door bashing into her back because her attention was captured by something across the road. Blinking rapidly, she slid her sunglasses on to get a clearer look without squinting. Sitting astride a motorbike was someone who looked so like Mac it could almost be him. *How funny*, she thought as she turned away, *that Mac should have a doppelganger in Wimbledon, of all places.*

'… lia … Amelia.'

A passing car with its windows down and music blaring from its speakers drowned out most of the shouted words, but it did sound rather as though someone was calling her name. Glancing over her shoulder, Amelia saw the man with the motorbike was nearer now. In fact, he appeared to be making a beeline for her. She watched as he wheeled his bike towards her and the closer he got the more he looked like Mac.

'Amelia … wait.' The voice was unmistakably Mac's but seeing him out of context in a busy London street made it difficult for Amelia to accept it was him.

He touched her arm lightly with a shy grin. 'I tracked you down. I had to look up the address on the magazine's website and then hope they only had the one office in Wimbledon.'

'How long have you been waiting for me?'

'A few hours. It doesn't matter. I would have waited as long as it took to find you.'

'Why didn't you just call me?'

'It's not easy to discuss over the phone. I need to talk to you about two things. That's why I'm here.' Mac paused, looking around at the unamused faces of the people forced to squash by them in the road. 'Listen, here's not the place. I'm obstructing the pavement with the bike. Can you spare me time now? Is there somewhere nearby we can go?'

Tilting her head to give her brain a chance to catch up with how delighted she was to see Mac again, Amelia couldn't think straight.

'There must be somewhere we can go,' pressed Mac.

'Sure. There's a pub on the Common. We can go there.'

With Mac wheeling the bike, they strolled the short distance to the Common and settled in the pub garden, selecting a picnic bench in the shade. Once Mac returned with their drinks, he removed his leather jacket and wafted the material of his blue t-shirt. 'Phew. It's much hotter down here.'

Taking in his jeans and boots Amelia sympathised. Her summer dress and sandals were more suited to the weather, yet she still felt drained by the oppressive heat. 'You need to dress for the southern summer.'

'Yeah, I misjudged it. It was chucking it down when I left. I need to tell you something,' Mac began earnestly. 'But firstly, an apology. I'm an arse, what more can I say? I expected you to give up your life and relocate hundreds of miles while I wasn't prepared to make any changes myself. I'm sorry. I figured you'd be angry with me and rightly so. I picked up my phone numerous times to contact you but I was scared I'd get a reply telling me where to go. That would have meant it was over and I didn't … I mean don't … want it to be over.'

'Mac, it's —' Amelia interjected.

'No, Amelia, if you're going to say it's all right, it isn't. I ought to have been understanding and not got frustrated with you. I was trying to juggle the job, the band, you …' Mac shrugged, his expression sad.

'I didn't like parting with an argument but competing priorities are always difficult and we didn't make each other any promises —'

'Exactly,' Mac butted in, keen to speak again. 'But I shouldn't have pressured you. The argument was down to me and I've regretted it ever since. I desperately wanted to contact you but figured you were getting on with your life and I thought I should let you do that.'

'I did the same,' admitted Amelia. 'I assumed there'd be plenty of groupies throwing themselves at the band and you wouldn't be missing me.'

'Well, obviously I've been fighting them off, but there's only one you,' joked Mac.

Amelia laughed. 'Been chasing you around Digger's drum kit, have they?'

'I wouldn't have noticed if they had.' Mac sipped his drink, then reached out and took hold of Amelia's hand. 'I mean what I say. There's only one you. I wish I'd contacted you sooner, then two things forced me into action. I'd been sulking and dithering and one morning I was out in the field when I saw that palomino you told me about, up on the hill. Only briefly, then it was gone, but it seemed like a sign … a reminder of what I had to do … find you.'

'That horse is still running loose then?'

'It appears to be. We can't both have imagined it, especially as I'd forgotten all about it until then.'

'And what was the second thing? You mentioned there were two.'

'Jilly.'

'What about Jilly?'

'She doesn't seem to be coping very well. I'm worried she might be tempted to sell up. She didn't completely dismiss the idea when we met her in Orkney, did she?'

'What?' Amelia was alarmed. 'Why? How is she not coping?'

'I don't know.' Mac shook his head. 'She's changed since the accident. She's lost confidence, become more uncertain. It's a shame to see her so indecisive when before she was so forthright.'

'But surely she won't sell. I thought she'd be back to her old self by now.'

'She's not. Sometimes she disappears and leaves us to it.' Mac picked up his glass of Coke, then put it down again. 'She was never like that before. She was always there, always available. Perhaps I'm overreacting but there was no one else I wanted to talk to about it. Zoey's not interested and I don't want to worry Angus. He's decided to deal with it by forgetting Jilly ever mentioned the possibility of selling.'

'Poor Jilly. I don't believe she wants to sell but maybe taking a step away from the business has changed her perspective. If only there was some way to help her.'

'Well, the Colonel seems to be doing his best to distract her.' Mac raised his eyebrows.

'The Colonel?'

'Angus spotted them together in the Jumping Trout one evening. He did some digging and apparently they met in the waiting room at the Fracture Clinic. I'm sure you'll have seen his house, it's the large manor on the road to Inverness. I've spotted her car parked outside a few times. His family run a distillery in Strathspey but we can't ask anything because Jilly hasn't mentioned him …'

'Perhaps she doesn't see it as anyone else's business.'

'Which is fair enough,' agreed Mac, glancing around. 'It's getting busy. I'll go order.'

While Mac went inside to the bar to order their food, Amelia fanned herself with a menu and wondered again why he had come in person. You didn't usually travel hundreds of miles on a motorbike for a chat which could have taken place over the phone or even a video call.

'They said it should be about ten minutes,' Mac informed Amelia as he retook his seat, 'which is good news because I'm starving.'

'Did you travel down today?'

'Yeah. I told Jilly I had urgent band business and needed a few days off at short notice.'

'So, I'm your urgent band business?'

'You are.'

'I fear you're going to be disappointed. I have little to no influence over Jilly's life. I wish I could help but I can't see how.'

Mac reached over and laced his fingers through Amelia's. 'To be honest it's partly a ploy to see you again. We didn't leave things in a good place. I wanted to put that right.'

'Me too.'

'Amelia, I don't know what my future looks like, I just know I really want you in it. I don't care if it means you down here and me up there. We'll make it work.' Mac paused anxiously. 'That's if you want the same?'

'I do.' Amelia smiled. 'Very much.'

'I'm glad.'

A staff member appeared carrying two pizzas and placed them on the table, smiling their acknowledgement of Amelia and Mac's thanks.

'There's plenty of time for us to figure it out. First though, we must sort out my aunt.' Amelia picked up her knife and fork. 'I only hope she hasn't already decided to give up on Lochside.'

'I sincerely hope not,' said Mac. 'We all do. He might be trying to hide his concern, but I watched Angus eat a whole Victoria Sponge yesterday. It's obvious he's uptight.'

As they ate their food, the pub garden filled with customers eager to enjoy a sunny evening. It was only when Amelia had finished her last mouthful that it occurred to her to ask Mac where he was staying. 'Surely you're not heading back tonight?'

'No definitely not. There's a limit to how many miles you can do on a motorbike in a day and still walk. I haven't booked anywhere yet. I was going to ask if you have any suggestions?'

'Yes,' Amelia replied, smiling. 'You can stay with me.'

17

Amelia was woken the next morning by the alarm blasting through the bedroom half an hour earlier than usual. Groggily she tried to recall why she'd set it for that time and why there was a lump in the bed beside her, when she could feel the familiar weight of Chewie by her feet. Then Mac raised his head from the pillow and yawned.

'How do you shut that noise up?' he asked.

Reaching out, Amelia turned off the alarm, her movement dislodging Chewie, who slunk across to settle on Mac's legs. Despite usually being picky over visitors to his territory, the cat had taken to Mac straightaway. Tempting though it was to ignore the alarm, reluctantly Amelia got out of bed, knowing if she didn't she'd fall back to sleep and be late for the marketing course she was due to attend in Central London that day.

'I have to get going,' she told Mac, 'I'm due in the city by nine o'clock. You're welcome to stay. I won't be late home and then I'll call Jilly for a chat. See if I can find out what's going on.'

'That sounds good.' Mac grinned and stretched. 'I don't

need to be back until the weekend. What's so important that you have to leave me alone all day?'

'The magazine's sending me on this marketing course even though I'm no longer working with Declan so it's a waste of time. I did point that out to Manju the other day but she insisted I go. Honestly, I think the company's too tight to throw away the fee because they can't get a refund.'

'It doesn't sound like *Your Home, Your Castle* is very considerate of its staff, Amelia.' Mac sat up. 'I don't want to start another debate about the future right this minute but if you don't want to go on this course, you shouldn't have to.'

'It's complicated and for the time being I'm just trying to keep the peace. I don't want any more trouble.'

'Your colleagues ought to give you the same courtesy in return.'

Amelia grinned and blew Mac a kiss, then headed for the bathroom.

She left Mac sitting on the bench in the courtyard eating cornflakes and watching Chewie prowl around, leaping at shadows. She walked briskly to the station humming happily despite having to spend the day on a course which was rudely encroaching on time she could have spent with Mac. The unresolved issue of their parting had been playing on her mind more than she'd admitted and, now they'd had the chance to talk it through, she felt much better.

Her good mood was waning by the time she arrived at the venue in Victoria. The train had been hot and crowded with no seats available. Now she stood in a stuffy meeting room with the other participants, gathered around the refreshments table. She made herself a mug of tea and tried to avoid eye contact with anyone until a man in his thirties, wearing a smart grey suit and a snazzy psychedelic tie, approached.

'Hi. I'm Joshua.' He extended a hand.

Forced to reciprocate or appear standoffish, Amelia shook his hand and told him her name.

'I'm looking forward to today.' Joshua grinned. 'I've got loads of ideas and I can't wait to share them.'

Amelia faked a smile while hoping Joshua and his ideas didn't end up making the day last longer than she already feared it would.

There were numerous breakout sessions for role play which Amelia couldn't avoid, although she participated only half-heartedly. Fortunately the course tutor barely noticed. The enthusiasm of the others made up for her reticence and when the clock finally reached four-thirty, she felt a surge of joy. Her fellow course members gathered on the pavement, keen to swap contact details and keep in touch to provide mutual support and encouragement. Despite Joshua's overzealous request, Amelia managed to avoid giving her number by insisting she had to run for the tube. Once there, she squeezed her way on to a platform, edging to the front. She looked at the board. The next train was due in four minutes. She checked her toes were behind the yellow safety line then glanced up at a colourful advert, stretching from floor to ceiling, curved with the tunnel. Its photographs of two countryside scenes captured her attention. One was of a couple with their arms wrapped around each other strolling through a sunny forest, the other was of a group of horse riders trekking over heather strewn moorland. Their happy faces were lit by the sun or, more likely, Photoshop. A strapline in bold lettering read: 'Book your relaxing break with us. Self-catering cottages available throughout the year. Don't delay, book right away for the holiday you've earned the right to enjoy.'

Amelia's shoulder was pressed up against a man who turned to the lady next to him and said, 'After the day I've had, I'd give anything to be there instead of here.' He nodded his head to indicate the poster Amelia was also looking at, there being no room to raise an arm in the crowd.

'Yeah,' agreed his companion. 'What a tedious meeting that was. If I could reach my phone, I'd book that place right now.'

'Even if you could they won't let you have time off at such short notice,' the man complained. 'Got to get going on all those action points from today first.'

'Except I wasn't paying attention to any of them. I was too busy trying to figure out the plot of that new Netflix show I watched last night,' admitted the lady. They both laughed ironically.

Amelia had her phone in her hand. She touched the screen and it lit up with the photo of her on Spirit and Mac on Hebrides. Her eyes took in the sunny day, their faces beaming as the horses posed, ears pricked. It brought to mind their giggles as they tried to get the perfect shot. Briefly transported from the confines of the London Underground to the broad expanse of the Highlands, Amelia closed her eyes and imagined the breeze brushing against her face; it was so realistic she could actually feel it, and it tasted of … soot. She opened eyes now watering from the draught caused by the incoming train. Her eyes flicked up again to the advert, then back down at her phone and a plan began to take shape. Propelled forward by the momentum of the rush to board as the train doors opened, she managed to grab a seat and sat so engrossed in thought she nearly missed her stop.

Her phone began to ring as soon as she was outside Putney tube station. The caller was Mac. She stopped to answer, tucking into a gap between the ticket machines to keep out the way of the rush of people eager to get home. Her feet rustled on the litter strewn floor and she raised her foot as a mouse darted out from a crumpled bag and disappeared with a crisp clamped in its mouth.

‘Hey, you on your way?’ asked Mac cheerfully. ‘I’ll get the pizza ordered if you are.’

‘Yeah, I’ve just got back to Putney. Listen, Mac,’ Amelia spoke urgently, unable to conceal her excitement, ‘I think I know what to do. I think I’ve got the answer to Lochside’s problems.’

On Saturday Amelia rode all the way to Scotland on the back of Mac’s motorbike. It was not an experience she wished to repeat and the sense of relief she felt as they wound their way up the lane to Lochside was overwhelming. She couldn’t wait to stretch her legs and give her numb backside a break. Evening was drawing in as Mac pulled the bike up alongside the cottage, the engine’s noise bringing a barking Gallus out the gates. Recognising Amelia, he wagged his tail and rubbed his face against her legs. She stroked him fondly.

‘We’re just about to close,’ a voice boomed from inside the stable yard. ‘I’m afraid there are no more rides going out today.’

Amelia and Mac looked at each other and called simultaneously, ‘Jilly, it’s us.’

As they walked side by side through the gates, Gallus trotting beside them, Jilly stopped sweeping to greet them, dropping the broom with a loud clang. Peewee jumped and Euan, who was bent over midway through fitting a new shoe to the grey pony’s off hind leg, swore.

‘Sorry,’ Amelia apologised to the farrier.

‘No bother. I’m almost done,’ Euan replied, teeth gritted with determination that Peewee was not getting his leg back until the job was finished.

‘I wasn’t expecting you back until tomorrow, Mac,’ exclaimed Jilly, ‘and, Amelia, how lovely to see you and so unexpected. Have you … have you joined the band?’

Amelia and Mac burst out laughing.

'No. I can't sing,' confessed Amelia, 'and the only musical instrument I can play is the recorder. I wouldn't want to subject anyone to that.'

'But I thought Mac went on urgent band business. I mean, if you'd told us you were dropping by for a visit ...' Clearly flustered, Jilly flapped her hands at Angus and Zoey as they arrived back from the fields carrying numerous headcollars.

'Amelia!' Zoey greeted enthusiastically. 'What are you doing here?'

'Goodness,' said Angus. 'Such an unexpected pleasure. I had no idea we'd be seeing you again so soon, Amelia. If only I'd known, I'd have baked something special.'

'Well, Deirdre would,' teased Zoey.

Jilly turned to the group, her eyes appraising them one by one, her booted foot tapping on the ground. 'Really?' she asked, her words directed at Angus and Zoey. 'You didn't know anything about this?'

Angus and Zoey continued to deny any prior knowledge of Amelia's visit.

'Interesting.' Jilly swooped on the broom, banging its head against the palm of her hand three times, ostensibly to clear wisps of straw from the bristles, but using a rather alarming amount of force. 'Only, I'm sensing an ambush.'

For a few moments no one spoke, then Amelia decided she ought to come clean. 'Not an ambush, Jilly, no. Mac told me you're finding things difficult since your accident and —'

'Oh, he did, did he?' interrupted Jilly. Now it was Mac's turn to feel her furious glare.

'Yes, he did. Please hear me out.'

Ignoring Amelia, Jilly turned to Mac. 'What I decide to do, or not do, is Lochside's business.'

'Amelia is Lochside's business,' insisted Mac. 'Or have you

forgotten how she stepped in to help you out, putting her own life on hold while asking for nothing in return?'

'Yeah,' agreed Zoey. 'The least you can do is give Amelia time to hear what she's got to say.'

'OK.' Jilly propped the broom against the stable wall and stomped to the office.

The others followed, passing Euan who was packing up his tools. He grinned at them. 'Good luck you lot. Whatever this is about, I've been her farrier for a decade and she doesn't budge easily.'

'We know,' said Angus.

They gathered in the office, the sound of Euan's whistling fading away as he headed back to his van. Amelia had prepared her thoughts. She took a deep breath, then began. 'It started —'

'What did?' Angus butted in.

'You need to give Amelia a chance to tell us, Angus,' scolded Zoey.

'It started,' Amelia repeated, 'when I saw an advert while waiting for the tube. It gave me the idea of using the cottage for self-catering holidays, perhaps including a ride if there's interest. Then, I thought, what if we expand to offer more experienced riders a riding holiday? They could ride every day, help in the yard if they want to, even be assigned their own pony to look after. It would open Lochside up to a wider pool of customers. Some might not want to ride but would like to use the cottage as a base for walking holidays. We'd be making more use out of what we've already got.'

'It sounds doable,' said Mac. 'Many people rent properties out as holiday lets and I don't see why we can't too. We've got the bonus of a riding stables on the doorstep.'

'Offering holidays isn't something we ever thought of before,' admitted Jilly. 'Stan and I chose not to live in the cottage because we didn't want to be that close to the stables.

Stan was insistent he didn't want out lives turned into a busman's holiday. He knew I wouldn't be able to resist checking on the troops at all hours. We took the decision to allow the staff to live there if it suited them.'

'There are other opportunities too. We could have a route with a pub stop for lunch and even hire a horsebox for beach rides,' explained Amelia. 'After all, Lochside's surrounded by countryside perfect for riders and hikers. Even if you're not horse-mad, you could still rent the cottage for a holiday.'

'I like the sound of a pub route.' Angus rubbed his hands together with glee. 'A whisky's always welcome, especially on a cold day.'

'I was thinking more along the lines of soft drinks and sandwiches, but you've got the gist,' said Amelia. 'Then, of course, there's Lochside's Instagram page and a website.'

'Website?' Jilly spluttered. 'Instagram?'

'Technology?' Angus said, his expression aghast.

'Definitely. When people search for self-catering cottages or riding stables in the area, we need Lochside to come up as well as Three Stones Barn.'

'I like the sound of that,' said Zoey. 'Let's take some of their trade for a change.'

'That's the spirit,' cheered Amelia. 'We have to fight back.'

Angus pulled a face. 'I don't see what's wrong with sticking to leaflets rather than all that social media stuff.'

'Because Scotland has a high volume of visitors and we need to reach out to them. Social media is one of the best ways to do it,' Amelia insisted.

Angus and Jilly exchanged nervous glances at the thought of venturing outside their comfort zone.

'It's an ambitious plan,' said Jilly.

'It's ambitiously brilliant,' insisted Mac.

'OK, Amelia, I admit it all sounds plausible but why would you be interested in doing this? Your life in London offers you way more than I can up here,' said Jilly. 'I appreciate you coming up with all this but you must know it's way too much for me. I could no more turn Lochside into a modern business with internet and all that stuff than I could gallop to the moon.'

'Because I'm offering to take it all on as Lochside's Business Manager. I'd do it all for you.'

'Oh.' Jilly wasn't the only one who appeared stunned. 'There's an enormous difference between helping out for a few months and what you're suggesting, which is giving up a lot.'

'I know there is. I do believe this could work.'

'And if it doesn't? What then for you?' Jilly was determined to press her point.

'I guess I'd have to find something else. If I had to find another job I'd be willing to do anything. I'm done with office work anyway.' Amelia shrugged. 'The thought of Lochside being … well … no longer Lochside. I don't want that to happen. If I can keep it going and it gives you the chance to take a step back, then why not?'

'Go on, Jilly, give the lass a chance,' encouraged Angus. 'I don't see how you can lose. We're not stupid. We've noticed how much more of a burden you've been finding the physical work since your accident.'

'I admit it's tough at the moment but I'm still in recovery. While all this sounds wonderful in theory, I can't expect Amelia to do that,' insisted Jilly. 'I can't pay even a fraction of what I imagine a Business Manager would earn.'

Amelia was prepared for protestations about finances. 'I'm not suggesting a salary on a par with that. I'd only need a token wage and to stay in the cottage until I can find somewhere of my own. Then we can start renting the cottage out to holidaymakers.'

'Aren't there rules and regulations if you have a property

you want to rent out? We'd have to put all that in place before we could do it,' Zoey pointed out.

'I'm sure we're capable of sorting that out between us,' said Mac, confidently. 'Other people can do it. There's no reason we can't.'

Suddenly Jilly banged her fist on the desk, making them all jump and Gallus howl. 'Oh, very well then. We'll give it a try. I am not making any promises and I can't be responsible if it all goes wrong, Amelia, and you have regrets.'

'I won't,' Amelia said fiercely, her words lost in the cheers of Angus, Mac and Zoey.

When everyone had quietened down, Angus asked, 'Can we win back our customers from Three Stones Barn?'

'Yeah, I'd love to see their face when they realise we're taking the fight to them. Serves them right,' said Zoey.

'All you need to do is concentrate on proving to me I haven't just agreed to something crazy,' said Jilly, but Amelia could tell she was suppressing a smile.

'Yes!' Amelia couldn't resist a triumphant leap as she punched the air.

'I'm proud of you.' Mac grinned and kissed her forehead. 'I can't believe you got all that from a poster on the London Underground.'

'Seeing the poster it all made sense,' she replied, taking Mac's hand as they strode over to the cottage, which Jilly had agreed Amelia could stay in for the night. 'I was already working on a plan; I just didn't have the details sorted and then it all slotted into place.'

'As long as you're sure though. As Jilly said, you're giving up almost everything.'

'Yes, I know and yes, I'm sure.'

'Forgive me for being the voice of doom. I know you're aware what you're doing is a gamble.'

Amelia stopped walking and turned to face Mac. 'I never

take chances. I'm not getting any younger and I feel as if my life's been stalled for years. This is my chance and I'm taking it.'

Mac nodded. His expression was unreadable.

'What?' demanded Amelia.

'Just thinking how lucky Jilly is to have you and how lucky I am too.'

18

Deciding she didn't have the stamina for another long ride on the back of a motorbike, Amelia opted to return to London by train. Early on Sunday morning Zoey picked her up outside the cottage.

'Thanks for offering to take me to Inverness,' Amelia said appreciatively, 'and especially for getting up early on your day off. That's a real sacrifice.'

'Yeah, well,' muttered Zoey, releasing the Fiesta's handbrake and stamping on the accelerator. 'Once you said you wanted to go by train, Mac called in a favour I owed him so he could play that gig at Glasgow last night.'

'It must have been a big favour.'

'It was. He arranged for Chequered Pipes to play at my mate's twenty-first birthday bash free of charge. I don't remember much about it although I'm pretty sure they were good and I don't think that was just the beer goggles.'

Amelia chuckled. 'Mac messaged me earlier. He mentioned last night was a great success and they want to book the band again.'

'That's good feedback from such a popular venue. Really,

it's beyond me why he doesn't quit farting around at Lochside and fully commit to the band,' tutted Zoey, as she waited for a tractor to pass by on the road before leaving the lane with a screech of tyres and the roar of an overrevved engine. 'He'll never make it as a part-time musician.'

'I guess it's hard to give up the safety net and step into the unknown.' Amelia clung to the door handle as Zoey weaved around a pheasant trotting across the road.

'Can't be that difficult. You're doing it.'

'Yeah, I guess I am.'

'Thanks to you it won't be long before we're fighting off the customers with brooms.'

Amelia laughed and held up her right hand with the fingers crossed. 'I really hope you're proved right.'

The traffic increased as they neared the city. Aware of taking up too much of Zoey's precious day off, Amelia suggested, 'Why don't you just drop me here? It'll save you struggling to find parking.'

'Oh, if you're sure. That'd be good.' Zoey sounded relieved. 'Although I was going to keep you company because we're super early for your train.'

'Don't worry. I'll grab a drink and find somewhere to sit.'

Zoey indicated and pulled over to the kerbside while Amelia gathered up her belongings, then reached over to give her a hug. 'Thanks again.'

'No problem. See you in a month.' Zoey grinned.

Amelia waved until she could no longer see the Fiesta as it joined the queue of traffic ahead of a bus, then walked to the station concourse which was bustling with people, many pulling wheeled suitcases. Having had her ankles bashed by luggage twice while she was checking the departure board, she decided to get out the way and headed for a coffee shop. As she sat at a table, dipping an almond biscuit in the froth of her cappuccino, she wondered what it would feel like when she returned. It seemed unreal that next time she would be coming to stay. No more *Your Home, Your Castle*. She knew she wouldn't miss it, not at all. She wondered how the team would react to her leaving. She couldn't imagine they'd be that upset. In her experience, staff came and went and management never seemed bothered as long as someone was sitting in the seat. A chunk of biscuit snapped off. Plunging a teaspoon into the liquid to rescue it before it sank, she knocked the cup, spilling coffee all over the table. Swearing loudly, she mopped up the mess with napkins. The man at the next table looked up from his phone to watch her.

'Ooops,' she said.

The man grinned, shook his head and returned to his phone screen as the tannoy announced the next departure for Edinburgh, where Amelia would change trains for Kings Cross, was due to leave Platform Four imminently. Swallowing the last of her coffee, she grabbed her bags and dashed towards the platform.

Throughout the many hours of travelling, Amelia considered all the possibilities open to her. Some seemed daunting, others exciting. She scribbled notes with ideas for social media posts, designs for the Lochside website and planned the longer routes for the more experienced riders. Feeling inspired and passionate about the future, rather than simply following the routine, when she looked out the window, she was astonished to see the sandy coloured brick work and arched greenhouse style roof of King's Cross station come into view. Packing away her belongings, she waited for the hordes around the door to disperse before leaving her seat to join the crowd moving down into the underworld of the Piccadilly line. The heat was stifling and Amelia removed her cardigan with difficulty, trying not to accidentally elbow anyone. She grabbed a seat on the tube and eventually emerged onto the busy streets of Putney, glad to be free of the dust and hot air below. Carrying her bag, she walked to the place she would soon no longer be calling home.

As expected, the month of Amelia's notice period dragged by. She didn't know how the Editor felt about her resignation because Stephanie hadn't spoken to her since the day she'd returned to the office and informed Manju she was leaving. While the days carried on as usual, Amelia spent any spare time working on the marketing for Lochside's future, requesting Mac and Zoey take photos for her to add to the now up and running Instagram page. There was no point asking Jilly, who hadn't worked out how to use a smartphone beyond calls and texts, nor Angus who didn't possess a phone other than the landline at his home.

The Monday of Amelia's final week was a blustery day. Chewie took one look outside at the dark clouds racing across the sky threatening to shed their load in outbursts of thundery downpours and decided not to linger in the courtyard. It proved a good decision. The rain arrived, bouncing off pavements still hot from the recent heatwave. Steam rose up from the ground and puddles formed around drains blocked with leaves and litter. Passing cars sprayed unsuspecting pedestrians, foolish enough to stand too close to the kerb while waiting to cross.

Overnight the grimy window Declan once tried to open had sprung a leak. He must have managed to open it enough to break the seal and the driving rain was trickling in. Amelia chose to ignore it for a while until a patch began to form on the carpet. Having just dried her shoes after paddling most of the way to the office, she had no desire to get wet feet again. Shoving a wastepaper bin beneath the flow of water, she was about to return to her desk when the door cracked open a couple of inches, then swung shut. Ignoring it, she resumed working on the complicated spreadsheet she was wrestling with when the door opened again, fully this time, and Declan walked in. Amelia leaned sideways to see who was behind him and was surprised he was alone.

'Hey,' he greeted Amelia sheepishly.

'Hi. Oh … I've got your *Game of Thrones* person here.' Amelia held up the figurine she'd adopted, assuming Declan had come to collect it. 'I've started having conversations with it. I must admit, it's been the best colleague I've ever had! Never given me any trouble.'

'Er, thanks.' Declan chuckled, making no move to take it. 'Actually, I'd completely forgotten I ever bought it.'

Amelia lowered her hand, placing the figurine back on her desk. 'Well, it's here if you want it.'

'Cheers.' Declan shuffled his feet and slid his hands in the pockets of his beige chinos.

'I'd offer you a seat but as you can see there's only one and I'm in it … assuming you're staying?'

Declan coughed, clearing his throat. 'I … er … heard … well, Judith told me you were leaving at the end of this week. No one mentioned it to me until now, so I wasn't sure if it's true.'

'Yes, it's true. It's no secret and Judith's correct. My last day is Friday.' Trying to hide how happy saying the words made her feel, Amelia suspected she'd failed.

Declan thrust his hands deeper into his pockets. 'I wanted to …' The words appeared stuck in his throat. 'I wanted to apologise for the way I treated you.'

'You mean for the callous way you tried to get me in trouble for the damage to that yacht?'

'All right, all right. Yeah, OK, I overreacted and lashed out.'

'You did and I can't say it's been an enjoyable time but on the plus side it's pushed me to go for what I really want to do instead.'

'I didn't want to drive you away. I didn't mean everyone to take against you. You know what it's like.' Declan's whiny voice filled the confined space. 'I shouldn't have spoken to you like that in front of the others. Now they're all saying it's my fault you're leaving. That I drove you away. Even Judith had a dig at me earlier.'

'I see and you don't like being made to feel like that.'

'No … course not … I felt angry and threatened. You're good at this job, you always have been. It's unfair to show everyone else up the way you do.'

'You described me as tricky, yet I was only doing my job.'

Declan had the grace to blush. 'You can be tricky.'

'You could always have worked with me rather than against me.'

'That's not really my style.' A flash of the stubborn character Amelia knew well reappeared. 'I'd like to come to your leaving drinks though. Show there's no hard feelings and all that.'

'I've decided not to have any. I'm pushed for time before I leave.' Amelia smiled sweetly.

'You know,' Declan huffed, 'I came in here to apologise. You could be gracious about it.'

'Tell you what. I'll be gracious if you promise to treat my replacement kinder than you have me.'

'You're full of shit.' Declan turned away.

'Hey,' Amelia called out as he opened the door. 'I'd really like to know what happened on *Lucky Lulu*. Did you push me over on purpose to get me in trouble?'

'I …' Declan hesitated. 'Truth is, it was meant to be a joke. I was going to nudge you, scare you, that's all, but I slipped on that polished floor and crashed into you. Once all the glasses broke and the juice went everywhere I panicked. I knew the shit had hit the fan.'

'Well, I do appreciate your apology.'

Declan glanced back with a grin. 'I'm not all bad you know. If you were staying you could've got to know me better.'

Trying to conceal the shudder coursing through her, Amelia grinned. 'But I'm not. See you.'

Amelia stayed late, anxious to complete the fiddly spreadsheet. Eventually it was finished and, as she flicked off the lights and closed the door, the stillness of the editorial floor enveloped her. Chairs had been vacated, the standby lights on screen monitors were pinpricks of light in the semi-darkness and a phone rang unanswered on a nearby desk. A raincoat left on a stand resembled a figure loitering near the photocopier. The floor was devoid of people, yet to Amelia it didn't feel as if they were gone. Pausing at Declan's desk, she placed the figurine next to his chipped Arsenal Football Club mug, then hurried away.

Amelia lowered the window blind in the kitchen to block the bright sunlight, then finished preparing Chewie's breakfast, feeling under pressure from his hungry meows.

'I never thought any animal could be more demanding than Lochside's ponies,' she told the cat, as she placed his full bowl on the mat.

Friday had finally arrived. After today there would be no more reading equestrian magazines in her lunch hour while eating expensive sandwiches. Soon she could put all her plans into action.

She was singing in the shower when she heard the doorbell. Wrapping a towel around her wet hair and pulling on a dressing gown, she left damp footprints on the carpet as she rushed to answer the door. An enormous bunch of flowers had been left for her on the landing. Scooping them up, she read the card, smiling at Mac's message wishing her a good last day.

Later she tripped over a pile of rubbish bags left on the pavement as she sent Mac a thank you text. Usually that would have annoyed her, today she grinned and walked around them, ignoring the pungent smell. She bounced up the stairs at *Your Home, Your Castle* with the sprightliness of a newborn foal discovering its spindly legs for the first time. Her heel caught on the top step, sending her flying, sprawling across the landing like a snow angel.

'Careful,' said Judith, puffing up the stairs weighed down with shopping bags.

'No harm done.' Amelia picked herself up with a grin and straightened her grey trouser suit.

As she walked along the editorial floor, Declan caught her eye. He gave her a smile and waggled the figurine in the air. She discovered another colourful bouquet of flowers on her desk, this time from the editorial team. When she went into the kitchen to make her tea, plates of cakes had been laid out on the working surface alongside a note wishing her all the best. As she packed up her few personal belongings in a box she reflected that it was strange and rather sad how colleagues only made an effort when you were leaving.

Just before five o'clock there was brisk knock and Manju poked her head around the office door. 'Is it a good time or are you busy finishing up?'

'I'm pretty much done.' Amelia shut down the laptop.

Stepping into the office, Manju seemed to take it in properly for the first time. 'It is rather cramped and isolated in here and it looks like there's been a leak.' Frowning she pressed the sole of her leather boot into the dirty water stain on the carpet.

'Yeah.' Amelia shut the lid of the laptop. 'I didn't bother reporting it because no one seemed to care much.'

'I suppose it's too late for an apology?'

Amelia looked at Manju's expectant face and grimaced. 'I'm not going to change my mind and stay, if that's what you mean. If you want my feedback it's don't stick the new person in a cupboard and make them feel part of the team.'

'You know, it's funny, I was only saying to Stephanie the other day we need to do more team building —'

'I'm all set,' interrupted Amelia, who had no desire to hear Manju's plans for the company's future. 'I've emailed all my work in progress to the team and I'll leave my staff pass with security.'

Manju played with the tassels on her floral blouse. 'Sounds like you've got it all organised. I'm sorry to see you go. I know you'll give your new career everything and I'm certain it'll be a success but if it doesn't work out …'

'I know where you are,' finished Amelia.

'You do.'

Amelia gathered up her bags and the flowers and Manju held the door open for her.

Most of the staff had already left except Judith who had waited to say goodbye. She pulled Amelia into a hug, crushing the flowers between them. 'Take care, darling. We'll miss you.'

'Thanks,' said Amelia, stepping back to brush dislodged petals from her top. 'Although I'm not entirely sure that's true.'

'Nonsense, you'll be missed. There'll be fireworks once this lot realise they've got to do your work until a replacement's appointed.' From the glee in her voice, it sounded as though Judith was looking forward to watching it all unfold.

Before she walked away up the street, Amelia felt compelled to turn around and look up at the building. A silhouette was outlined in the window of Stephanie's office, a figure watching her go. Their eyes met briefly before the Editor backed away, having made no acknowledgement of Amelia. Seconds later the blind was lowered and Amelia turned her back. It felt symbolic, as though the curtain was coming down, with neither cheering nor applause, on her time at *Your Home, Your Castle*. Act Two of her career was about to begin.

19

Amelia was woken early by a pair of foxes engaged in an ear-splitting argument in the garden. Sleep had mostly evaded her anyway and the little she'd had was plagued by nightmares as her subconscious decided the night before her move to Scotland was the perfect time to run through all the scenarios of what could go wrong. She got out of bed to chase the foxes away, watched through the glass patio doors by an agitated Chewie, who was already disturbed by the appearance of packing boxes and the travel case, which usually preceded a trip to the vet. She'd only just finished chasing the foxes away when a persistent ringing of the doorbell diverted her attention from calming Chewie down. It stopped, then commenced again accompanied by a rattling of the letterbox. Through the living room window Amelia could see a van parked in the middle of the road and the driver was now on her doorstep.

'You Miss Hodge?' he asked gruffly. Amelia confirmed she was. 'This road's a nightmare for parking. I couldn't fit the van in your car park, it's too small, and I nearly clipped a wing mirror back there.' Pushing past her, he began collecting the boxes filled with Amelia's belongings. 'Need to be quick. I'm blocking the traffic.'

While he went back outside to begin loading, Amelia scooped up Chewie and secured him in the travel case. 'It's not for long. Once we get there, you can run around as much as you like.'

Between Chewie's hisses and the driver huffing and puffing backwards and forwards, Amelia felt relieved once all the boxes were gone and it was time to leave. As the final box was hurled into the van, Amelia hoping it wasn't one full of fragile items, the driver slammed the rear doors and hurried to get in the cab.

'See you then. I'll be in Scotland before you,' she sang.

'Ha, ha,' he shouted out the window.

Amelia grinned, watching the van depart with a crunch of the gears.

It was amazing how quickly Lochside felt like home to Amelia. She watched through the window as Chewie gambolled in the cottage garden. In the few days since their arrival, the cat had taken charge of his surroundings, putting Gallus in his place and taking control of the barns. He'd turned quite feral, thriving in the open space and freedom to roam. No longer fearing danger from the traffic, Amelia was more relaxed about him spending time outside. Today her focus was on showing the fruits of her labour to the team. As she made tea and coffee in preparation, she hoped they would approve of what she'd done.

An hour later everyone crammed into the cottage dining room for Amelia to run through the Lochside website and Instagram page on her tablet. Even technophobe Angus admitted it looked good. Jilly cooed over the 'meet the proprietor' page, which had a backdrop photo of her sitting astride a spotless Snowdrop.

'I have to say, Amelia, I'm impressed. If this doesn't drum up business, I simply don't know what will,' Jilly said, placing the tablet, its screen now smothered in numerous fingerprints, on the table.

'We have to be prepared for a slow trickle rather than an avalanche to begin with but we're on our way.' Amelia switched the device off and followed the others outside.

'A trickle's an improvement on the drip we've been reduced to recently,' said Angus.

'I could use a variety of photos, not just the ones I've already got. We could do with some different models.' Amelia's eyes swivelled towards Angus, who had steadfastly refused to be in any of them.

'Don't look at me,' he insisted. 'I'm not photogenic. I'll frighten people away faster than a ghost.'

Amelia closed the front door, protesting, 'That's not true, how about —'

'No.' Angus shook his head vehemently.

'Come on, Angus. We need to show we welcome all ages,' insisted Zoey. 'Amelia's done all the work on this. You only need to look happy and smile.'

'Grimace, more like,' muttered Angus.

'I really think —' Zoey began, then stopped talking as a vehicle playing loud music sped up the lane.

'I've told Euan many times to slow down,' tutted Jilly. 'He's a farrier not an ambulance driver.'

They gathered around Euan as he exited the van, looking puzzled. 'I feel as though I'm interrupting something. I'm sure I checked my diary earlier. Not got the wrong day, have I?'

'Not at all.' Jilly reassured him. 'We're excited because Amelia's just been showing us the fabulous new website and Instagram.'

'Cracking job. Well done team.' Euan winked at Amelia, knowing she'd done the bulk of the work. 'You'll soon be putting Three Stones Barn to shame.'

'That's the plan,' said Zoey. Watching Euan open the rear doors of the van to begin unloading equipment, she added, 'I don't suppose you can help us? We need some different models otherwise the same faces keep appearing in the photos. Would you be willing to do it?'

'Of course. You're welcome to take some action shots of me at work. I would've thought you'd rather use the model you've already got though.' Euan turned, pointing a steel rasp resembling a giant's nail file at Mac, who was creeping away. 'Weren't you once offered a modelling contract with an agency?'

'What?' Mac froze, feigning ignorance.

'Yeah, I remember there was a piece about it in the local paper. You turned it down to focus on the band. We all thought you were mad,' said Euan.

All five heads swivelled in Mac's direction.

'That was years ago —' Mac began.

'It's true?' squealed Zoey.

'Yes, I was in discussions with a modelling agency and yes, I turned it down. I was much younger then —'

'But you could've made a fortune,' interjected Zoey.

'Or I could have broken up the band for one of the toughest careers I can imagine. Who wants to be judged constantly on their looks? I'm an artist not a clothes horse.'

Sensing Mac's reticence to talk about it, Amelia spoke up. 'Well, it's a lovely day. Can we get some photos up by Loch Still?'

'All right, just to be clear on the rules, I'm not riding in a kilt. All that bouncing around in the saddle would chafe me in places I don't want to think about.'

Amelia sighed theatrically. 'I don't need a kilt. I just need you. This afternoon.'

'Then it's a date. Spending time alone with you sounds perfect.'

'Perfect,' Amelia repeated, smiling. 'I can't wait.'

'When we've all quite finished watching these two drooling over each other, I have horses that need to be shod,' huffed Jilly.

Euan saluted with the rasp. 'I've got my orders.'

As though they had overheard the plans for the photo shoot, any remaining clouds withdrew leaving a sunny afternoon with an endless blue sky. Amelia and Zoey brushed Hebrides and Pirate until they gleamed, then tacked them up with saddles and bridles scrubbed back to their original glory.

'They've never looked better,' praised Jilly, admiring the horses tied up outside their stables while Angus dabbed Pirate's hooves with oil. 'Doing a grand job there, Angus.'

Angus grinned and waved with the brush, spraying the dark liquid all over his jeans.

Mac, who'd changed into smart black jeans and a designer t-shirt, did a twirl. 'I figured I need to look my best if I'm going to be trending on social media at some point in the future.'

'I sincerely hope Hebrides doesn't slobber all over you and spoil it,' muttered Jilly.

Finally ready, Amelia and Mac rode the horses out of the yard, side by side.

'Do some good posing,' Zoey yelled after them.

Mac turned and gave a thumbs up.

The track was dusty. Hebrides sneezed and swished his tail at the midges lingering out of range of the repellent spray. Pirate tossed his head, aggravated by a persistent horsefly.

'Ah, the blighters,' Mac groaned, waving a hand to disperse a midge buzzing around his face.

'Yep.' Amelia flicked away a fly which had settled on Pirate's thick black mane.

'What's the plan for this photo shoot of yours?'

'I thought we'd use the ruin as background, then I can include some facts alongside the photos. Like how the locals refer to it as the Castle of the Shadows but its proper name is Brae Castle, which is the Scottish word for slope.'

'It's also the site of an ancient battle where a bloody clan fight took place on a date I've forgotten.'

'Not my area of expertise either. I intend to look it up.'

'I'm glad you're back.' Mac grinned, reaching over to take Amelia's hand, content to be in each other's company again.

As the track widened out, Hebrides shifted from walk to canter in one stride, turning sideways, ears pricked.

'Be careful,' warned Amelia, 'it looks like he's about to …'

Whether Mac heard or not, in an instant he was gone, leaving nothing but a trail of dust. Standing in her stirrups, Amelia watched anxiously as Hebrides bolted. He raced flat out. Mac appeared to have been taken by surprise and lost control. Amelia urged Pirate on, but Hebrides was at full pelt and had a head start. Pirate gamely took off in pursuit, Amelia hoping her mount's surefootedness wouldn't fail. The grass passed beneath them in a blur. Pirate's hooves skated over the ground. They were getting closer to Hebrides. Up ahead, Mac was pulling on the left rein, attempting a circle to force his mount to slow down.

'Sit back,' hollered Amelia.

Pirate's nose reached Hebrides' hindquarters, then drew level with Mac's knee and after a few strides Amelia stretched out for Hebrides' bridle. Her fingers grasped air as the horse veered. Ears back, Pirate ploughed on. Startled by the galloping horses, a flock of ducks took off from the waters of Loch Still, quacking their displeasure. A burst of effort took Pirate back upsides Hebrides and this time Amelia didn't miss, taking a firm hold near Hebrides' bit. Slowly bringing both horses back under control, she glanced at Mac, whose face was animated, eyes wide, wisps of hair escaping from beneath his hat.

'What a ride,' he whooped.

'You're OK?' Amelia's voice was pitched somewhere between a laugh and a sob. 'I thought you'd been run off with.'

'I know.' Mac laughed. 'And I wasn't about to stop you chasing after me.'

Before Amelia could decide whether she was angry Mac had tricked her, he leaned over and placed a smacker of a kiss directly on her lips. She hesitated momentarily, then in a flurry of dropped reins, tangled arms and bumping hat peaks, they kissed passionately. When they eventually broke apart, the horses had their heads lowered and were grazing.

'That was cheeky,' Amelia chastised Mac. 'I was worried you'd genuinely lost control.'

'Well, I do always lose control around you.' Mac gently pulled on the reins. 'Let's get these photos done.'

While Amelia snapped away, Mac posed in front of the ruins of the Castle of the Shadows, then beside the loch. Her favourite photo was of the four of them reflected in the dark still waters. She hardly recognised the carefree person gazing back at her as she took a selfie with the castle framed in the background, Mac kissing her cheek. As she lowered her phone with the camera still on, Amelia glimpsed a golden horse on the screen.

'Did you see that?'

'See what? I was only looking at you.'

'There's a horse up there.' Amelia flipped Pirate around and cantered up the mound, shouting, 'Hello.'

Roosting crows erupted into the sky but nothing else stirred. She encouraged Pirate over the rope boundary, delving deeper into the ruin where ivy creepers encroached and moss grew up the walls.

'Hello,' she called again, sure if another horse was present it couldn't move about unheard even if it was unshod. Pirate's ears were back and he refused to go any further. 'Walk on.'

He stood resolute, hooves planted, turning to glare at Amelia, then flicked his ears forward at the sound of a horse carefully picking its way behind them. Amelia whirled round in the saddle. Mac was approaching, leaning forwards to avoid a low frame. 'Amelia, I don't think there's anything else here. Can we go before we get stuck? I had to limbo back there. Much more of this and I'll be a headless horseman.'

Amelia sighed. 'I'm sure I saw that palomino again.' She looked at Mac, whose face was screwed up, lips tight. 'You don't believe me?'

'I'm not saying I don't believe you. I've seen it once myself —'

'You think I keep imagining it,' Amelia finished his sentence.

'No, except it's usually spotted around Lochside, presumably attracted by our ponies. Let's leave. We shouldn't be in here.' Mac turned Hebrides. Pirate followed automatically. 'And you must have more photos of me now than my parents.'

'I don't understand what's going on.'

'Neither do I. Whatever this horse is, whoever it belongs to, if it needs our help then eventually it will seek it from us.'

'I suppose.' Amelia relented.

'As you know I'm away with the band tonight. When I'm back I wanted to talk about the future.'

'The future?' Amelia repeated in alarm.

'Nothing to worry about. I've been thinking though that you can't live in the cottage forever. Soon it will be rented out for holidays. I thought maybe you'd consider moving in with me. Only if you want to, of course. No pressure at all and no sulking if you decline. I get that you're independent. I respect that.'

'Honestly, I haven't even thought about where I'll go.' Amelia pictured Mac's cosy cottage nestled in the hills outside Beauly and smiled. 'But I'd like that.'

The next morning Peewee managed to escape from the field. After the usual scrum of noses eagerly diving into their breakfast bowls, he'd suddenly ducked around Angus and galloped off.

'I can't find the wee chap anywhere,' Angus puffed in distress, having burst into the tack room breathless from running back to inform the others. 'It's my mistake. I left both gates open. I forgot to close the one at the end after I went to retrieve Gallus, then the field gate must have swung back in the wind. I checked halfway up to the Bothy before I came back.'

Amelia rose from her chair. 'OK, don't panic. I doubt he's gone far. I'll find him.'

Jilly placed her mug on the floor. 'Zoey can go too.'

'No need. We've got a group of novice riders arriving any minute now and you'll need Zoey to bring up the rear. Mac is already booked for the other ride. I can manage to find Peewee on my own.'

Leaving the tack room with headcollar in hand, Amelia felt confident she'd find Peewee just the other side of the fence, contrite at having given Angus the slip. She was sure he would follow the narrow track running along the rear of the fields rather than battle his way through dense undergrowth. Therefore, she was rather surprised to still be walking half an hour later as she took a right turn onto a path she hadn't seen before. Warm now from walking at a brisk pace, she removed her jumper and, as her eyes emerged from beneath the pink material, they widened in disbelief. Grazing contentedly, slightly ahead and just off the track, was a palomino, identical to the one she had spotted numerous times. She knew she wasn't imagining it because she could hear its teeth tearing up strands of grass. The horse swished its long, luscious tail, the silvery white hairs flicking its golden rump. Spotting her, it raised its head and snorted, sending flecks of spray across Amelia's bare arms.

'Hey,' soothed Amelia, stretching out a hand, 'you are real.'

Ears flicked forwards, the pretty mare took a few steps towards her, reaching out its elegant neck to nuzzle her palm. Suddenly, the horse squealed, half-reared and spun away. Simultaneously Amelia felt a nudge in the small of her back. She turned to find Peewee, head tilted to one side, looking at her.

'You rascal!' she scolded the pony, grabbing his headcollar although he seemed willing enough to be caught. 'Keen to return to your mates, are you? But what do I do with you?' she asked the palomino, who had retreated a few metres away.

Amelia clipped the lead rein of the headcollar she was carrying onto Peewee's, then, towing the grey, slowly approached the mare with the head piece in her hand. Gently she tried to slip it onto the palomino's head and the mare allowed her to fasten it without protest.

'Success. Now we need to make it back to Lochside and finally find out who you belong to and why you're lost,' she told the palomino.

Using a fallen log as a mounting block, Amelia clambered onto Peewee bareback and, leading the mare by the headcollar, turned back the way she'd come. The palomino accepted being with an unknown pony and walked placidly alongside, her nose level with Amelia's knee. Occasionally she would break into a jog, pulling on Amelia's arm, before slowing again when Peewee refused to increase his pace to match hers. They were halfway back and Amelia was starting to relax when a roaring sound approaching from the rear gave them all a fright. Unable to control Peewee in a headcollar alone Amelia was pulled to one side. The mare was turned sideways pushing her neck across Amelia's lap.

'Whoa,' Amelia sang, 'steady.'

Looking around she could see a quad bike was gaining on them. The mare whirled away from the bright red noisy machine, wrenching Amelia's fingers and buffeting into Peewee who laid back his ears and spun his head around, snapping his teeth. Seeing the furore, the rider stopped, cut the engine, then raised a hand in friendly acknowledgement.

'Thank you,' puffed Amelia, managing to turn both horses so they were facing forwards.

The rider removed his helmet and rested it on his thigh. He was a young man with messy red hair and a round freckled face above a yellow t-shirt, tucked into jeans. 'Not a problem. Sorry if I've upset your horses. I don't normally meet any on this track which is why I use it.'

'I don't usually ride along here but it's been one of those mornings. They'll settle down.' In fact, Peewee already had and was now picking at the cow parsley lining the sides of the track. The mare's eyes were rolling, her neck sweating as she lashed out a hind leg, aiming for the quad bike.

'Ahh, feisty, eh? That looks to be Hugh's Aurum you've got there.'

Amelia bolted upright. 'Hugh Douglas? This is his horse?'

'Aye. Well, actually, they bought the mare for his sister, Portia, but she never bothers with her much. Always in London and not interested in riding. I'm not one for telling tales …'

'I see.' Amelia smiled, keen to convey she wasn't bothered

about local gossip, although she was curious and the expression on the man's face gave the impression he did want to tell all.

'Oh, they look after their animals well enough, I can't fault them there,' he continued without encouragement, 'but this one's bored. A well-bred horse like that needs to be working, not left in a field all day with the Clydesdales. No wonder she's always escaping. We run the farm next door to Keilburn and I often find her roaming our land.'

'Right.' Amelia drew the word out, nodding in understanding. 'I've seen her too and I know it sounds silly but I thought she was a ghostly apparition or a trick of the light.'

The man laughed. 'No and I should know. She goes trampling through our veg patch regularly. I've complained to the Douglas family about it. Trust me, they're not being haunted by a ghostly horse and they're not taking responsibility.'

'Guess I'd better return Aurum to Keilburn then. I'm not sure of the quickest way to get there from here.'

'If you keep going straight, then take a right at the fork by the wishing well you can cut across the land which will bring you to a gate which takes you right next to Keilburn stables.'

'OK, thanks. The, er, wishing well?'

'Yeah, you can't miss it. It's a pool of water shaped just like one.'

20

Despite Amelia's doubts, she did find the wishing well and shortly after reached the gate to Keilburn. Jumping off Peewee, feeling every muscle complain about her riding without a saddle, she found it latched but not locked. The stable yard was directly opposite. She led Peewee and Aurum past a field where the Clydesdales were grazing in the shade of a huge oak tree.

The square-shaped spotlessly clean stable yard was empty of both people and animals. Unsure what to do, Amelia nosed around and discovered all the stables had metal nameplates screwed to the wall beside their doors. She found one labelled for Aurum and secured the mare inside. She was leaning on the door, watching Aurum pull at a bulging haynet secured to the back wall, when someone shouted at her.

'Oi. What're you doing in here? These stables is private.' A small elderly man, wearing brown breeches which billowed at the thigh giving him a bow-legged appearance, was marching towards Amelia. Beneath the tweed flat cap his expression was angry. 'You ain't stealing nothing today, missy. No more thefts, is what I've been told to prioritise.'

Holding her hands in a placatory gesture, Amelia turned to face him. 'I'm not here to steal. I found Aurum. She's in here.' She gestured into the stable.

'Oh. Sorry. We've had some trouble lately.'

'It might help if you locked that gate I just came through.'

'Aye.' The man stopped suddenly, appearing to notice Peewee for the first time. 'That's not one of ours.'

'No, Peewee's with me.' Protectively Amelia pulled her pony closer, interrupting him eyeing up a wheelbarrow full of hay.

The man's anger had been replaced with confusion. 'What's Peepee here for?'

'I was out looking for Peewee, not Peepee, after he escaped from his field and I came across Aurum alone, not I hasten to add, for the first time. I believe your mare is a serial escapee and I really ought to have a word with Hugh about it —'

'I've already spoken to Hugh and Leith about her escaping numerous times. The mare needs selling on. She's not doing nothing here. Birthday present or not, she needs to go somewhere they will exercise her and give her a more challenging existence than she's got. I've tried everything to solve the boredom problem but we've no one here to ride her regularly and Leith won't let her go.'

'Perhaps if I could speak to Hugh it would reinforce the message.'

'You can try but I doubt it. If you want to have a go, you'll find him in the big house on the second floor. Tell him Ron told you where to find him. That's me,' Ron added unnecessarily. 'Here, I'll look after your chap for you. I reckon he's after a bite to eat and some water.'

Leaving Peewee in Ron's hopefully capable hands, although the number of times he seemed to lose Aurum didn't fill her with confidence, Amelia hurried up to Keilburn House. Swallows swooped overhead, soaring across the fields, attracted by the midges which clustered around the barns and horses. As she neared the house, she came across crowds of people. Another Garden Party was in full swing. Marching into the house, she headed straight up the stairs, which curved gently to a landing off which doors stood open.

'Excuse me.' Amelia approached a staff member hovering in the first room. 'I'm looking for Hugh Douglas. I was advised by Ron I could find him on the second floor.'

The staff member's eyebrows raised suspiciously. 'Mr Douglas is in the family's private quarters which are on the third floor but I'm afraid they don't accept ad hoc visitors. If you wish to speak to him, you'll need to make an appointment with his secretary.'

'Never mind. It can wait. Sorry to bother you.' Amelia strolled away casually, moving further along the landing.

Although aware Aurum wasn't her responsibility, she wasn't giving up. If the mare kept escaping she could be injured or worse. Amelia felt compelled to insist Hugh address the situation. At the far end of the landing, in a quiet spot beyond the last bedroom and conveniently hidden around a corner, she came across a braided rope barrier strung between gold posts. Beyond was a small staircase leading upwards. Glancing over her shoulder to ensure she was alone, Amelia hopped over the rope, ignoring the dangling 'Private – No Public Access' sign as though she hadn't seen it.

The top of the steep flight of stairs was partially blocked by a coat stand bulging with jackets and caps. Fighting her way through the abundance of musty smelling material, Amelia emerged onto a small landing with walls covered in paintings surrounded by dusty gold frames. To her left, a white panelled door was propped open by an old copper kettle in use as a doorstop, through which was a corridor. One side had numerous closed doors, the other windows above shelves of dusty trinkets, giving the floor a less grand, more lived-in feel.

The faint murmur of voices drifted from the only open door at the end of the corridor. Amelia approached, her trainers making no sound on the garish mustard coloured carpet, careful not to trip on the rucked material which in places was worn through to the underlay. Reaching the door she paused, listening to the occupant's voices, one male, one female. Peering cautiously round the frame, she recognised the slender blonde in the checked shirt and skinny jeans tucked into cowboy boots, who was perched on the edge of an enormous desk. Behind the desk, Hugh sat hunched over a Macbook. The room was a study with floor to ceiling windows framed by heavy green velvet curtains tied back with gold brocade, providing views over the lawn to the loch. Another wall was decorated with a tapestry of Edinburgh Castle. Amelia was struggling to recall where she'd seen the blonde lady before when Hugh spoke.

'Give it a rest, Portia. I've offered her more and that's that.'

Now Amelia remembered the lady was Hugh's sister who she'd met at Stirling Castle months ago. There was movement as one of a pair of Red Irish Setters lolling on a rug between desk and door, raised its head. Before she could withdraw, the dog leapt to its paws with a howl, its bushy tail wagging.

'Be quiet, Bingley,' commanded Hugh, as Amelia ducked backwards, pressing fingers to her mouth to stifle a yelp.

'More? You'd think the woman would be biting your hands off for the money. All she's got at the moment is a tumbledown, worthless business and no future,' retorted Portia, followed by the sound of a can opening and liquid being poured.

Amelia remained still. As she hadn't been discovered she ought to either leave or make her presence known. Before she could do either, Hugh spoke again.

'Bloody Lochside. Still, let's see what Jilly makes of the

higher offer. She hasn't flatly refused it. I'm pretty confident she's going to go for it. The timing's good, what with her accident and the Colonel taking her interest away from those wretched ponies.'

Hearing Hugh's words, Amelia collapsed against the wall with a thud just as Bingley howled again. She felt like joining in. How could Jilly even consider selling to Hugh Douglas? It was Portia who voiced the question uppermost in Amelia's frazzled mind.

'Why do you want the place that badly anyway, Hugh? Without the riding school, it's only good for razing to the ground.'

'All in good time, Portia, all in good time.' Frustratingly Hugh said no more and the sound of fingers tapping on a keyboard filled the next few minutes. From further along the corridor a door clicked open and a man stepped out. Amelia recognised him as Hugh's father, Leith. He was looking down at his phone so hadn't seen her yet but he was blocking the only route back to the stairs.

Frantically Amelia scrabbled at the door behind her, relieved to find it unlocked. She slid through and found herself standing at the top of an uninvitingly dark, steep flight of stairs. The draught blowing up them ruffled her hair, bringing with it a smell of stale food. She could only see the top few steps. Lowering herself down onto the first step, it groaned like a ghoul under her weight. Pulling her phone from her back pocket, she switched on the torch and was relieved to see a thickly woven rope railing attached to the wall. Holding it with one hand, she lifted her phone with the other to shed light on the stairs below. At the bottom she walked into a basement kitchen with an open door leading to a garden. Breathing a sigh of relief that she was in the clear, Amelia was slipping her phone back in her pocket when a shadow appeared in the doorway, backlit by sunlight.

'Are you aware you're trespassing on private property?' asked an unfortunately familiar voice. Hugh stepped inside, smirking at Amelia's discomfort.

'Yes.' Amelia decided her only option was to be bold.

'If you're going to sneak up on people it's best to ensure there are no dogs around. They do have a frightful habit of giving one away.'

'I wasn't sneaking up —'

'I'm glad to hear it because you shouldn't be here. Only it does appear you intend to make a habit of this trespassing malarkey.'

'I don't. I only came because I wanted to speak to you about Aurum —'

'Aurum?' Hugh seemed to be struggling to place the name.

'Your sister's horse?' prompted Amelia. 'You know, the one that keeps escaping and trespassing on our land. I just returned her safely to your stables. It's you who needs to be thanking me for being here.'

'Oh, touché.' Hugh performed a brief, patronising bow. 'Good to know there's a reason for you being here beyond merely a desire to intrude.'

Amelia dithered. Part of her wanted to shout at Hugh, accuse him of trying to throw her aunt off her land and destroy a lifetime's work, but she wanted to hear Jilly's side before she confronted anyone. It might not even be true. If Hugh had known all along she was listening on the other side of the door, he might have said it just to upset her. She needed to keep cool. 'Just secure the mare, OK? Before she either has, or causes, an accident.'

'Ah, Amelia, such a good Samaritan.' Hugh chuckled in amusement, shaking his head. 'We've acres of land. Aurum won't come to any harm.'

Amelia folded her arms. 'Except she doesn't stay on Keilburn. I've seen her a few times up at Loch Still and in the castle ruins. She could get badly hurt. She also keeps coming to Lochside. It's like she's lonely and attracted by our ponies.'

Hugh's response was to laugh louder. 'Lonely? She's got two stonking great Clydesdales for company.'

'Fine. Have it your way.' Determined to end the conversation, Amelia marched past Hugh. 'Just don't say I didn't warn you.'

'Calm down. If it will appease you, I'll have a word with Ron about it and see if we can do better than his last idea which was to give Aurum a football to keep her occupied.'

'You will?' Amelia paused, turning to look Hugh in the eye.

'Yes, but only because I don't want your cantankerous aunt after me. If Aurum's causing trouble we will have to find a solution. Leave it with me.'

'It's for the best,' reiterated Amelia, unable to thank Hugh because she felt such anger at what she'd overheard. 'Why did you tell Portia … no, never mind.'

'It's best not to eavesdrop,' said Hugh with a sneer.

'Doesn't matter if you've got no secrets.' Amelia began walking away, hoping Ron hadn't lost Peewee in the time she'd been gone.

'Oh, um, Amelia,' Hugh called after her.

'Yes?'

'When it all goes wrong with that wannabe rock star you're dating do give me a call, won't you? Or you're welcome to drop by for a drink. You'll find me at the Gatehouse.'

Amelia led a weary Peewee back into a deserted Lochside. She was pleased to find no one around. She couldn't trust herself not to get overly emotional about the information she had stumbled across. Having fed Peewee and put him in the field with the others, she returned to the cottage and lay on the sofa. Pulling a blanket up to her chin, she fell asleep with Chewie curled up beside her.

. . .

Amelia was woken from a deep sleep by a loud roaring. Slow to gather her bearings, at first she thought she was back in London where lorries had used the road outside her flat in Putney as a short cut. She opened eyes dried out from the warmth of the still alight stove and, in the glow from the flames, saw Chewie up on his back legs, his paws resting on the windowsill, looking out. She sat up slowly, wincing at the pain in her neck from using the armrest as a pillow. The television had switched itself off and a bright light shone briefly through a slit in the curtains, fanning across the walls in an arc. Seconds later the roaring sound ceased. On the floor beside her Amelia's mobile phone screen glowed with notifications of unread messages and the clock read two o'clock in the morning. She'd been asleep for hours. Amelia was on edge especially when she realised in her upset state she couldn't be sure she'd locked the front door. Leaping from the sofa, tripping on the blanket tangled around her legs, she dashed for the door. Despite being hindered by Chewie scooting between her ankles, she'd almost made it when the handle began to lower. Extending her arm to its limit, she tried but couldn't push the door shut in time as it swung inwards. A figure dressed head to toe in black leather stepped into the cottage.

'What the hell happened to you?' asked a male voice.

Giddy with relief at recognising who it was, Amelia looked into the familiar, although tired, eyes of Mac.

'Never mind me. What the hell happened to you?' she asked in horror, taking in the enormous bruise spreading around Mac's puffed up, bloodshot right eye, below which three large scratches marked his cheek.

'The gig descended into a brawl.' Mac grinned, touching his face lightly with his fingers. 'We had the lot. Objects and drinks thrown at us on stage and then this bloke wrenched the antlers off a stag's head on the wall. He lobbed them at us.'

'What? No!'

'No one was bothering with our music anyway. There was too much shouting going on for anyone to hear us. In the break we'd agreed to pack up early and on the way out a drunk idiot knocked Digger over, nearly damaging the drums. Digger gave him a mouthful, the idiot swung a punch, I stepped in …' Mac tailed off with a shrug.

'I hope you're going to demand danger money from the venue.'

'I doubt we'll even get paid at all.'

'I wasn't expecting you back tonight. You scared me. I didn't know who it was turning up in the early hours of the morning.'

'I messaged you loads of times to let you know.'

'Oh, I didn't see them. I fell asleep on the sofa. Here, let me get some ice for your eye.' Amelia turned towards the kitchen, Mac protesting there was no need as he followed.

While Amelia bustled around transferring ice from the tray in the freezer to a clean tea towel, Mac sat watching her, grumbling, 'It would do me more good if you put that in a glass with neat whisky, you know.'

'Here,' she handed it over. 'Hold it against your cheek before it melts.'

'Ta.' Mac did as instructed. 'It's like a furnace in here.'

'I fell asleep with the stove on.'

'That's not clever. You shouldn't do that.'

'I didn't do it on purpose. I meant to go to bed early.'

'Sorry.' Mac sighed. 'It's been a terrible night. I don't know …'

'Well, they can't all be great gigs, can they?'

'I know, but we might just as well have not been there. It was a room full of boozed up revellers with no interest in our songs. When I think about the amount of work I put into it, I fear I'm getting too old and tired for this shit.' Mac took the now soggy tea towel away from his face, his expression downcast. 'Wasting my time, that's what I'm doing.'

'Nonsense,' insisted Amelia. 'You're overtired and overthinking. You'll be buzzing again once you've had some sleep.'

Mac put an arm around Amelia's shoulders. 'No, I don't think I will be. We're kidding ourselves. All these years Chequered Pipes have been playing pubs and clubs, parties, weddings … we'd even play a funeral if someone wanted us. Yet look where it's got us.' He stood up abruptly, waving his arms around aimlessly. 'Nowhere.'

Amelia stood and faced him, her hands on her hips. 'You need to stop this, right now.'

'Yeah, I do.' Mac nodded energetically. 'I need to pack up Chequered Pipes and all those stupid dreams and get a life.'

'That's not what I meant.' Amelia was shouting now. 'You need to stop this negativity and self-pity. It doesn't suit you and it's not who you are.'

Mac sank back down into the chair and placed his head in his hands. 'But what if we're just average? What have we achieved apart from years playing in dodgy pubs, ducking flying antlers, chasing visions of reward and recognition. Yet we're still in the same place, aren't we? Maybe it's never going to happen, Amelia. It can't for everyone can it? I'm watching it all slip through my fingers and I just can't … I just can't keep on plugging away.'

'I saw you play at Stirling Castle and you were brilliant. I guarantee you the rest of the crowd thought so too.'

'Yeah and nothing came of Digger's stories about a record executive being there, did it? I'm worn out.'

'Of course you're worn out. Look at the time.' Amelia

pointed to the clock on the wall. The hands stood at three o'clock in the morning. 'We both need some sleep.'

'Not so fast.' Mac reached out and held Amelia's arm. 'Your turn. What's the matter? Even with only one good eye I could tell you were upset the minute I saw you. Your face is all blotchy and you've obviously been crying.'

'I'll tell you about it later. Now's not a good time.'

'Yes, it is. You've listened to my tale of woe. Let's hear yours.'

Amelia sat opposite Mac and told him everything that had happened from Peewee's escape to her discovery that Hugh Douglas was the mystery prospective buyer Jilly wouldn't reveal. By the time she'd finished it was nearly four o'clock in the morning.

'I can't believe Jilly would do such a thing,' said Mac angrily. 'Sell to Hugh Douglas? It's got to be a mistake. She promised to give you a chance to turn Lochside around. It's hardly fair to continue conversations about selling behind your back. It shows a lack of faith. What will you do?'

Needing time, Amelia stood up, stretched, then filled the kettle. Once she'd made two mugs of tea, she returned to the table, placing them on mats. 'I have to ask my aunt straight. It's the only option. I hope what I overheard wasn't true but, if it is, Jilly's got some explaining to do, to all of us.'

'That she has,' agreed Mac, 'and I feel inclined to tell her exactly what I think.'

'Don't do that.' Amelia stood again holding out her hand for Mac to take.

'What's the plan?' he asked her. 'Stay up and head straight to work in a couple of hours?'

'No, come on, let's go to bed. I'm going to make you see just how unaverage you are.'

21

Suffering from lack of sleep a bleary-eyed Amelia and Mac stumbled into a tetchy atmosphere the next morning. Hebrides had thrown a shoe, meaning more unexpected farrier costs for Jilly and Angus was feeling unwell. Then Zoey returned from taking out two riders who had both fallen off. She'd spent most of the time at Loch Still rounding up a mischievous Pirate and Chess, who'd refused to be caught for nearly an hour. After the couple left, placated with colourful rosettes from Jilly, Zoey swore non-stop for at least five minutes that they didn't deserve them.

'They didn't even try and stay on,' she complained, 'one practically threw herself off Chess, then Pirate did the smallest buck I've ever seen and the other one hit the deck.'

'We can't all be perfect, Zoey,' said Angus magnanimously.

'True. What we can be is honest about our riding ability to ensure we get allocated a quiet pony rather than pretending we're an Olympic champion.'

Jilly clapped her hands for attention, waking Gallus who was snoozing on a pile of rugs. Amelia stopped midway through cleaning Snowdrop's bridle.

Mac dropped a spoon in the mug he was holding. 'We're not school kids, Jilly. Next you'll be requesting we raise a hand if we want to speak.'

'Not at all, Mac,' replied Jilly. 'It was the only way I could get anyone to hear me above the noise you're making stirring that tea.'

'Yeah, well, I'll try and do it in slow motion from now on.' Mac snatched a chocolate biscuit from an open packet and bit into it angrily.

'As we haven't got any bookings for the rest of the day, I thought we could all join in with poo picking in the fields. We haven't done it for ages and if we all do our fair share it won't take long. Amelia and Mac, can you join me with the geldings. Angus and Zoey, I thought you could take the mares' field.'

After their brief break, the team trudged round to the fields with shovels, wheelbarrows and a determination to get the chore over with as quickly as possible. They worked diligently, each engrossed in clearing their section of the field.

'You're not humming.' Jilly paused, glancing over at Mac. 'You usually provide us with a musical accompaniment.'

Mac straightened up to stretch his aching back. 'I don't feel much like singing today.'

'You shouldn't let that incident in the pub last night get you down. There's always going to be hooligans who don't know how to behave. Your eye will heal in no time.'

'It's not my eye or the pub brawl that's bothering me.' Mac resumed shovelling with his back to her.

'Sulking isn't productive.' Jilly didn't take the hint.

Mac stopped again and turned. From the look on his face, Amelia feared what might be about to happen but didn't have time to react.

'I'm not sulking, Jilly, I'm angry. We've heard the secret person you're considering selling to is Hugh Douglas and he's offered you more money. He thinks you're going to go for it this time. It's a poor way to treat us and how could you do that to Amelia? Your own niece! And why have you been encouraging her if you always knew you'd sell anyway if the price was high enough. No wonder you refused to tell us anything.'

'What?'

'Yeah, that's right, we know.' Mac shook the shovel in the air.

Amelia rushed over to stand between them. 'I accidentally overheard Hugh saying he's offered you more money for Lochside. I wasn't snooping,' she explained as Jilly stood still, showing no emotion. 'Why would he want Lochside? He's got more than enough acres of his own. Why take ours?'

'How exactly did you hear this?' Jilly's nostrils flared with fury.

As Amelia relayed what happened at Keilburn, Angus and Zoey arrived.

'What's all the yelling about and why does Mac look like he wants to hit someone with his shovel?' asked Zoey.

'Ask her.' Mac pointed at Jilly.

'All right. Everyone needs to settle down.' Jilly tried to take control of the situation as though they were misbehaving ponies.

'How can we? We've supported you and stuck by you and you're considering selling us out to Hugh Douglas,' protested Amelia.

'What?' Looking incredulous, Angus pulled his unlit pipe from his pocket and stuck it between his teeth. 'Jilly would never do anything as cowardly as —'

'Are you suggesting Amelia's lying?' Mac butted in aggressively, 'because I, for one, can guarantee you —'

'I don't care whether anyone believes me or not —' Amelia spoke over Mac.

'Has anyone actually picked up any poo yet because otherwise we're going to be out here for —' trilled Zoey.

'Will you lot be quiet,' Jilly roared at such volume the ponies took off around the field, galloping in circles, ears back, heads up, tails flaring. It was the tone she'd used for years to control naughty ponies and wayward children; it commanded you to obey. Everyone ceased talking. 'Stop with the accusations and let me speak.'

'Sorry, Jilly.' Angus shifted his feet, embarrassed.

'Right then. It's true I was approached by Hugh Douglas when I was in Orkney and feeling at a very low ebb. He'd got hold of my mobile number and was sounding me out about the future. I made it abundantly clear, once I'd recovered, I'd be continuing with the business and that interim plans were in place. He made me a significant offer for Lochside on the spot and said should I ever have a rethink —'

'Oh, the cheek of it,' growled Angus.

Ignoring him, Jilly continued. 'After Amelia's offer to work here full time as Business Manager, I put Hugh's proposal out of my mind. That's where it's stayed until he recently contacted me again with a higher offer. I've told him no, for now ...'

'So, there's still a possibility you might accept?' asked Amelia.

'I can't guarantee I won't. Think about it. The horses need to be fed and shod, someone has to pay the vet's fees and you all need to be paid regularly, then there's the bedding, the insurance, the upkeep. Do you think fairies break into Lochside every night and sprinkle dust over everything to make it all work? I know life doesn't work like that, no matter how much we want it to be easy. I've suffered. I lost my Stan, I could lose my business and who cares, eh? Who's going to hold my hand and make everything OK? I'll tell you who: me, that's who. If Hugh's money ends up the only option between me and nothing, then I'll take it.'

'I'm disappointed in you, Jilly,' said Angus sadly. 'The old you would never have given in.'

'It's not giving in, Angus. You're past retirement age. Surely sometimes you want to take it easy rather than being out all winter in all weathers. That occasionally you long to stay cosy in bed rather than trudge out in the dark.'

'No, never.' Angus shook his head. 'It's always a pleasure being here. Working with you and Stan all these years.'

'And you still will be because the gymkhana's going to change everything,' insisted Zoey. 'Amelia's working hard on the social media every night. She doesn't stop.'

'And the bookings are beginning to pick up,' added Amelia. 'We can do this, Jilly. We're all with you. We know how difficult it's been, especially since your accident.'

'I hope you're right,' said Jilly, 'because with winter costs coming down the track and no magic money tree, if business doesn't pick up soon … I do appreciate all of you and your support.'

'Tell you what, we'll finish up here. You take a break,' offered Mac.

Once Jilly was out of earshot, the remaining foursome looked at each other in disbelief.

'It's like the Jilly who went to Orkney stayed there and another Jilly returned in her place.' Angus was distraught. 'Stan would be livid. He'd have told that interfering Douglas chap where to go and then some.'

'But people do change,' said Amelia, gently stroking Pippin's face as the cob rested his head on her arm and closed his eyes. 'I guess I can see where Jilly's coming from. She's getting older and worrying more. We have to persuade her to give it more time.'

'I know the Colonel is a big factor in her life now,' said

Zoey. 'It's obvious she's not lonely anymore and she's got distractions she didn't have before she met him. They do things together. I'm glad she's got company even if it does mean the business is less important to her now.'

'I hate to sound negative but what if the gymkhana flops the second time around?' asked Angus. 'I don't see a way back for Lochside if it's a washout again.'

'It can't be.' Amelia frowned. 'It simply can't be.'

'It feels as though everyone's having a crisis at the moment.' Amelia sighed, then picked up her hot toddy.

Mac was lying beside her on a tartan woollen rug, hands clasped beneath his head, gazing upwards at the brilliant sunset lighting the horizon. Amelia couldn't recall ever seeing such a beautiful vivid orange as it reflected off the waters of Loch Still. The streetlighting in London meant stars, sunrises and sunsets were subdued. Here she got to see them in all their glory. It was another reason she had grown to love the Highlands.

'Yeah,' agreed Mac. 'Poor Angus had me genuinely worried earlier.'

After such a tense day, they had escaped the drama surrounding Lochside, albeit briefly, to unwind and clear their heads.

'He was terribly upset.' Amelia put her drink down beside the flask, then stretched out alongside Mac, who placed a hand on her thigh.

'I'm sorry I just blurted out that we'd found out about Hugh,' Mac apologised. 'I feel like a blithering idiot. I knew you wanted to discuss it with your aunt in a civilised manner. I should have kept my big mouth shut and let you deal with it instead of nearly giving Angus a heart attack.'

'It doesn't matter. It would only have festered if one of us hadn't said something and it's given me an appreciation of Jilly's point of view. We can't blame her. She's not had an easy time. I'd be devastated if she sold up and retired though. I just wish I could figure out why Hugh Douglas wants Lochside. It doesn't make sense.'

Mac exhaled, considering Amelia's words. 'I don't know either. I admit it seems odd. Possibly he's got some crazy plan for the site and he doesn't want to tell anyone about it yet.'

'But surely, Hugh doesn't have a burning desire to run a riding stables?'

Mac laughed with such gusto it disturbed the crows roosting in the castle ruins. 'I would say that's as likely as Paul McCartney calling and asking me to do a duet with him.'

'I suppose Hugh needs to learn not everyone can get what they want, as you said last night —'

'I did say that. What I forgot to add is that occasionally they get something better instead,' interrupted Mac. 'When I first met you, I always wondered why you were single. I'm glad you were because it gave me a chance.'

'I was in a serious relationship once,' Amelia confessed. 'He was ambitious for his career, whereas I was ambitious for us to have a life together. When we split up, I was devastated but now I look back and realise it would never have been this perfect dream. He'd have worked late every night and I'd have been sitting on my own, wanting to do things together which he didn't really want to do. He'd rather be at work or certainly working.'

'He sounds a rather sad individual to me,' said Mac. 'I never wanted to join the hordes of people who believe your career signifies how good you are as a person.'

'So, you've always been a maverick?' Amelia rolled on her side so she could see Mac's face.

'Always have, always will be and that's the good news. My crisis is over. I'll be playing "Bagpipes and Monsters" when

I'm old and I bet you I'll still be happier than all those career types, whether I've made it by then or not.'

'I'm glad to hear it.' Amelia sat up. 'What about relationships though? I've told you about mine.'

'Oh.' Mac sat up too and shrugged dismissively. 'I've been fighting off groupies for years.' The silence that followed was broken only by the splash of a duck landing on the loch. Mac began to laugh in huge snorts. 'I'm kidding, Amelia. Seriously though, I can be frustrating if what you're seeking is a home, a holiday and a steady income. Lochside is the longest I've settled anywhere. I'm single-minded about the band and Jilly's flexibility about time off for gigs suits me. There's none of that begging a manager to let you take leave at short notice.'

Dusk was falling fast, the light fading, casting shadows amongst the ruins of the castle. Amelia gazed over the water and shivered. 'It's getting cold.'

'Says the person who works outside for a living,' teased Mac. 'Here.' He tucked the rug around their legs and, putting an arm around Amelia, pulled her closer. 'Warmer now?'

They huddled together sharing the last of the snacks and the hot toddy. Once the flask was empty, Mac packed everything back into the hamper while Amelia folded up the rug.

'Let's walk back the long way,' she suggested.

'Is everything OK? You're not avoiding Lochside are you? I don't want you to feel like that about the place.'

'No.' Amelia reassured him. 'I committed to being Business Manager and I'm staying for as long as Lochside exists.'

'I'm glad to hear it. I'm sure it will work out OK in the end.'

'The worst scenario is me having to return to London if I can't find another job around here I'm qualified for.'

Mac leaned in and placed a finger gently over Amelia's

lips, then kissed her softly. 'We don't need to face any more obstacles tonight. Let's get the gymkhana over with and see how Jilly is after that.'

Holding hands, they walked around the shore of the loch, strolling at first but then picking up the pace when they realised they'd stayed out longer than intended and it was almost dark. As they passed the ruin, Amelia shivered again. Dark gaps in the jutting masonry and a squeaking from the metal posts as the rope fencing swayed in the breeze gave it a haunted feel. Unconsciously Amelia sped up, pulling ahead of Mac.

'Hey.' He tugged her back gently. 'Slow down, speedy. I'm carrying baggage, remember?' He waggled the hamper at her, clattering the contents against each other.

'Sorry.' Amelia glanced over her shoulder.

'It has a different vibe about it at night, doesn't it?' Mac's words showed he understood Amelia's desire to hurry.

'It's just earlier I thought … oh, never mind.'

Mac stopped, forcing Amelia to halt. 'Thought you saw someone?'

'Yes. I didn't mention it because you'll tease me and say I'm always seeing things, like with Aurum when we didn't know it was Aurum. It's probably someone setting up for night fishing.' It sounded an unconvincing explanation, even to Amelia.

'Unlikely unless there are two of them. They don't like to fish here alone at night because of the ghost of Gordon the Glorious.'

'Not Gordon the Glorious again.' Now they were on the track, out of sight of the open land and the ruin, Amelia felt braver. 'What would he be lurking around the castle for?'

'I looked it up after our photo shoot. The legend goes he hid there when a battle was going against him. His clan were annihilated but he survived and fled to safety, like I said when you found that book at Keilburn library. Hence, he always saw the castle as lucky and intended to return one day for the treasures he left behind. If you do see him, it's meant to bring you luck.'

'Oh, please. I did not see a ghost.'

'Don't be so sure, Amelia Hodge. There's much we don't understand.'

Once back at the cottage they found Chewie sprawled across the sofa cushions fast asleep. Looking at the comfortable cat forced Amelia to admit how tired she was, having had barely any sleep over the last few days. Mac flopped on the other end of the sofa, flicking through the messages on his phone. He looked up, frowning and shouted through to Amelia, who was in the kitchen, 'What did I tell you? Digger's had an argument with the landlord and he's refusing to pay us for that gig because of damage to his property caused by the fighting.'

'That's hardly your fault,' she called back, pausing in unpacking the hamper as Mac wound his arms around her waist. 'It seems unfair to blame you guys. And what about the damage to your face?'

'Don't worry about that now. Let's go upstairs. After all, it is your lucky night.'

'According to you. My theory is I probably saw a deer, after all they do exist, whereas ghosts granting good fortune do not.' Still, as she switched off the light, Amelia decided she might buy a lottery ticket in the morning, just in case.

22

The days leading up to the gymkhana were filled with frenetic activity. Intensely aware of the pressure to make the event a success this time, everyone moved up a gear. Tamsin and Mona were joined by two of their friends, Scott and Becky, who assisted as much as they could in any free time they had. Their enthusiasm knew no bounds. One afternoon Amelia found them in the field practising for the clear round competition by jumping the show jumps on foot.

'We're learning the course,' explained a breathless Tamsin, as she cantered by on her imaginary steed.

'Righto.' Amused, Amelia left them to it. They were working hard and deserved a break to let off steam.

Amelia's rising stress levels reached a climax when Chess stomped on her foot as she was trying to oil his hooves and refused to remove his weight until Angus came to the rescue. Once released, Amelia hopped on one leg while clutching her crushed toes and swearing. Sensing she needed a breather, Angus suggested it might do her good to go off on a quiet ride by herself. Having worked through much of the night posting gymkhana updates on social media and arranging PAT testing, fire assessments and gas safety checks for the cottage, she didn't need convincing.

'Yes, do take Pippin out for a stroll,' agreed Jilly. 'He won't be able to participate in the games as much as the younger ponies.'

Happy to be out on a jaunt, Pippin strolled along the lane, stopping to check both ways for traffic before crossing over to the woods.

'You know the routine better than me,' said Amelia, patting his sturdy neck.

They left the bright sunshine, entering the shaded woods. Surrounded by birdsong, Pippin trotted along, ears pricked, following the path without any direction from Amelia. She took the route she knew well, out to the boundary between Lochside and Keilburn, where a large bird of prey perched on the stone wall. Staying close to the tree line, she urged Pippin into a canter, revelling in the breeze against her face and having escaped from the cleaning, clearing and setting up. They went further than she'd been before, reaching a place where the wall snaked its way into a grove of trees. Pippin swung to the left intending to turn around. Keen to explore Amelia pressed him onwards through a narrow gap between two sturdy trees. Here there was no path. The grass grew high between entwined trees. Pippin slowed to weave through them. The air felt undisturbed and undiscovered. Gazing upwards, Amelia could barely see the sky through the dense green foliage. She was about to turn Pippin when they came upon a part of the wall which had crumbled, leaving only a foot high section. On the other side was a clearing, in the middle of which stood a small building tucked away far from anywhere. Pulling her phone out her pocket, Amelia checked the time and realised she should return.

Telling herself she wouldn't linger long, she guided Pippin over the low section of wall. He jumped willingly through the gap, as though eager for adventure too. Cautiously they moved towards the soft glow of lights, creeping up on a wooden cabin whose Scandinavian design appeared strangely out of place. A generator hummed somewhere beyond the building. From her perch high on Pippin's back, Amelia could see inside through the windows to a large room dominated by a stone fireplace. The décor of faux fur rugs and throws, white sofas, light-coloured wood and Art Deco wall lights seemed too extravagant for a hiker's Bothy. Pippin's ears flickered in reaction to the sudden boom of raised voices. He tossed his head, his nostrils smearing the glass of the window Amelia was spying through. She couldn't see anyone coming until suddenly a door slammed, followed by a male voice shouting: 'I'll do what I want.'

'No, you'll do what you mother wants otherwise you'll go to granny and grandpa's and stay there,' an older man's voice replied. 'I'm well aware just how much moaning you do about their fusty castle, as you call it.'

'That's because it is. Grandpa's only interested if it's covered in cobwebs or it's whisky.'

'That's no way to talk about your family's history. Do you believe this came easy?'

'Portia has it easy. You bail her out all the time. She can't afford that place in London and she's never done a day's work to deserve it. I work on the estate all the time … for scant reward, I hasten to add.'

Amelia recognised the voices as belonging to Hugh and Leith.

'You've got the Gatehouse. I gave you the Gatehouse. That's more than a scant reward.'

'Yeah, the damp old Gatehouse while Portia got this lodge.' Hugh strode through an archway into the room and spun around with his arms outstretched to reinforce his point. 'And the London flat.'

Moving quickly before she was spotted, Amelia ducked, lying along Pippin's neck, urgently tugging his left rein. The cob obediently reversed a few steps.

'Portia has friends who are high profile names. She needed somewhere to invite them to stay where they could relax in privacy. You know this already and that's why we've always ensured the lodge isn't widely known about. I intend to keep it that way.'

'Yeah, this is the best hiding place I know of. That's why I came here to get some peace. Perhaps I'll stay here and not do any of that work you've set aside for me.'

'Stop changing the subject. Hugh, your mother is concerned about your obsession with buying Lochside. She feels it's a waste of money and she doesn't want the family perceived as chasing a widowed woman off her land. That would not be a good look for us.'

'I don't care. I want it. I want to have it.'

'Enough of this,' Leith bellowed, following Hugh into the room.

'It's my inheritance money to spend though,' Hugh retorted. 'And it's better spent on property than wasted on handbags and shoes. Portia has plenty of those, doesn't she?'

'Why don't you think about the family's reputation and not just yours? We don't want the locals complaining you closed down Lochside.'

'Surely no one's really bothered about that woman and her bratty ponies. From what I hear most of her customers abandoned ship as soon as Three Stones Barn opened its doors.'

'That may well be the case but Lochside's been established in the area for years and the locals have a certain sympathy and admiration for how Jilly's kept going since Stan died. Use your common sense. We don't want Jilly telling everyone you forced her out.'

'I'm not forcing her out. I'm offering her good money for the place.' Hugh's words were followed by the sound of a door being flung wide, its handle smashing into the timber wall. Pippin shied, scraping his hindquarters on a tree trunk, dislodging a shower of leaves. Amelia fought to bring him back under control as Hugh charged down the steps from the cabin, fortunately so distracted by his conversation he didn't look to his left for he would have seen them. Amelia cleared the leaves from Pippin's mane and waited a few minutes in case Leith left too.

'Looks like the coast is clear, Pippin.' Amelia gathered up the reins. Before Pippin could move there was a loud knocking on the window. Starting guiltily, Amelia turned to see Leith glaring out at them. Raising her hand in what she hoped would be seen as a friendly gesture, she apologised as Leith opened the window. 'Sorry. We lost our way.'

'What?' he demanded.

'I said I'm sorry. We lost our way.'

'You're local. I recognise you from somewhere. How can you be lost?'

'Well … I haven't ridden this way before. We're leaving right now.'

'Wait a minute, what are you …'

Leith's words faded as stiffly Pippin jerked into action and Amelia trotted him briskly back to the gap in the wall. They retraced their steps and, as she urged the cob into a canter through the woods, she reached a decision. She was done tiptoeing around everyone. It was time to confront Hugh and find out what he wanted Lochside for and if there was any way of persuading him to back off.

On Friday the last-minute preparations for the gymkhana kept everyone busy. While Angus and Jilly checked out the jumps in the arena, Mac and Digger set up a pair of pop-up gazebos in a corner of the field. Angus had eagerly volunteered to use one for refreshments. The other would be for Chequered Pipes, who were providing entertainment before and after the games. Amelia watched Digger fussing over where the drums would go and wondered whether Angus had considered bringing headache tablets. Hopefully he wouldn't need any because Mac had promised they would keep the volume down to avoid upsetting any of the animals and she watched as he firmly told Digger to return the amplifier to the van.

'I said this will be the halfway point where the ponies and riders will turn,' Zoey repeated, 'if you would just listen to me, Amelia.'

'Sorry. I was miles away.' Amelia shook her head and turned her attention back to Zoey, who was holding a pole in place aligned with the others to ensure they were all at regularly spaced intervals. She gave the top of the pole a tap with a mallet, securing it a few inches in the ground, then looked down the line. 'Couldn't be any straighter if we'd used a ruler.'

'Perfect.' Zoey gave a thumbs up. 'It's all going well. I called Euan and he's confirmed he'll be here for the farrier demo. We agreed to base it in the yard, then we're not overcrowding the fields.'

'Great.' Amelia rubbed her hands on her thighs and gazed at the sky. 'I hope the weather is kind to us this time. I know the forecast is for a warm, sunny day but it's only a forecast, isn't it? They don't really know, do they?'

'Worrying about the weather never changed anything. Come to think of it, worrying about anything never changed anything either.'

'True. I was thinking if we're low on customers we'll have to use the helpers to bump up the numbers for each game, otherwise there won't be enough participants.'

'I'm sure they won't mind. I overhead Mona saying she's so excited she won't sleep tonight.'

'Neither will I.' Amelia sighed. 'If the helpers win all the rosettes it's going to look like a stitch up.'

'Stop fretting, Amelia.'

Amelia couldn't help it. She felt the weight of expectation following her around and she couldn't shake it off. This was their chance to prove what Lochside had to offer but only if anyone was interested enough to come along and find out. She strolled back to the stables where Tamsin was shampooing Pirate's tail. Streaks of grubby water flowed from the tips of his black hairs.

'Jilly said not to put them back out in the field today once they've been washed. I don't know where they find all the dirt,' Amelia called over.

'OK.' Tamsin looked up with a huge grin. 'The others are tack cleaning.'

With everything under control, Amelia picked up a small stepladder and a pile of the homemade signs directing visitors to the parking area. She set off down the lane, Gallus trotting in her wake. As she was securing the last sign to a tree branch a flatbed lorry loaded up with portable toilets arrived. Stopping alongside her, the driver lowered the window and called out, 'Expecting a delivery for Lochside?'

'Oh, yes, thanks, that's for us. Do go on up the lane.'

Jumping down, she folded the stepladder and followed the lorry, arriving at the gates to find a heated discussion underway between Jilly and the driver.

'Look, it isn't gonna fit down there.' The driver pointed to the narrow gap between the buildings. Amelia could see his point. There was no way the lorry would squeeze through. 'We'll have to strap the toilets to a trolley and wheel them out to the field.'

'Be careful, oh, do be careful,' called Jilly, as she watched the trolley go by with the toilet cubicles wobbling on it. Gallus ran alongside, ears flapping, occasionally leaping into the air to try and catch a piece of dangling webbing strap in his teeth. 'My nerves are frayed. Why did I agree to all this?' she asked anyone who would listen.

'Because it's better than having everyone nipping behind the bushes,' Amelia told her sternly. 'Besides we've found a solution. None of the buildings are going to be knocked down by a lorry … not today anyway.'

'How many hours until this is all over?' Jilly rubbed above her left eyebrow. 'I can feel a migraine brewing.'

Just then Becky, a slim girl with blonde bunches and rosy cheeks, poked her head out the office door. 'Can they bring dogs with them tomorrow?' she yelled.

'What?' Jilly snapped.

'Can they bring dogs with them tomorrow? Someone is on the phone asking if they can. It's a chihuahua called Doughnut.'

Amelia and Jilly exchanged a look. Amelia called back, 'I don't see why not as long as they keep them on the lead.'

'Good because that's what I've already told them.'

Tamsin walked over, pulling a piece of paper from her pocket. 'We've put these new posters up everywhere.' She held up a colourful advert.

'Fantastic.' Amelia admired the artwork. 'I'm sure they will have grabbed people's attention.'

'I put them everywhere I could get permission. Becky lives up the road from Three Stones Barn so we made a huge one to go on her garden fence.'

Amelia and Jilly burst out laughing at the thought of what the proprietors of Three Stones Barn would make of Lochside's big event.

'They probably won't feel threatened and assume we'll fail,' sniffed Jilly.

'We don't have to worry about what they think of us. Most importantly everything's under control,' Amelia reassured her aunt.

The words were hardly out her mouth when Angus arrived from the fields, walking so fast he was almost jogging, arms pumping, legs scurrying. 'You'd better come quick. Gallus is stuck in one of the toilets.'

'Seriously?' Amelia assumed she must have misheard.

'Yes. We can't get him out. The lock's jammed.'

'Surely it can't be completely broken?' she asked, hurrying after Angus. 'They've only been here five minutes.'

'I don't know. I left them trying to sort it out to get reinforcements.'

The ponies were gathered at their fences, noses thrust over the rails, ears up, watching the drama unfold as the lorry driver tried to wrestle open the door of the toilet cubicle on the end of the row.

'We didn't notice until it was too late,' he explained, pausing to draw breath. 'The dog was sniffing inside, then the wind slammed the door shut. We can't get it open. It looks as though the lock's got bent and is jammed.'

Despite heaving with all their might on the lever, none of them could shift the door lock an inch. Seeing the commotion, Mac and Digger came over to try, accompanied by Gallus howling mournfully from within. Despite numerous attempts, no one was able to set the hound free.

Mac turned to the driver. 'What do we do then? He can't stay in there.'

'Don't know, mate.' The driver appeared nonplussed. 'This has never happened to me before.' He pulled his mobile phone from his jacket pocket. 'Guess the only option is to call the Fire Brigade. Get them to break him out.'

'What! Do we have to?' Amelia cringed. 'Can't you speak to your Head Office or something?'

'My Head Office is in Sunderland. What're they going to do?'

'But surely the Fire Brigade will assume it's a crank call, requesting emergency services for a basset hound stuck in a toilet.'

'No choice, mate. I'm not prepared to break the door down. I could be accused of destroying company property.'

'How about if we break it down instead? Then you can blame us,' asked Digger hopefully.

'I can't permit you to do that, I'm afraid.' The driver raised his phone ready to dial.

'What about a locksmith?' asked Amelia hopefully, just as Jilly arrived having been summoned by Angus.

'Hold on,' she commanded, 'and do shush, Gallus. No one can concentrate with you wailing like a banshee.'

The howling ceased and everyone watched as Jilly examined the narrow crack between the door and the frame. Producing a hoof-pick from her back pocket, she inserted the slimmest part of the pick in the gap, pulled sharply upwards and seconds later the lock pinged. The door flew open, Gallus tumbled out and Amelia grabbed him before he could cause any more trouble.

With one crisis averted, half an hour later Angus bashed his thumb with a mallet while knocking pegs into the ground to mark the show jumping arena. After holding it under the cold tap for a few minutes, he declared it was only bruised not broken. Amidst everything else, the feed merchant arrived and accidentally dropped a sack, which split open, spilling pony nuts all over the cobbles. Chess managed to grab a few mouthfuls before being stopped by Zoey.

'It's for your own good, you don't want to be ill,' Zoey told the piebald, as she secured him in his stable still chewing a mouthful.

'I hope that was the third disaster of the three they're

supposed to come in,' Amelia said, stopping to lean on the door beside Zoey.

'My drama tutor used to tell us there's an old saying in theatre: a bad dress rehearsal means a great first night.'

'I hope we don't turn out to be the exception to that and become the show that closes early.'

That evening, an exhausted Amelia and Mac crashed on the sofa in the cottage.

'I'll cook,' offered Amelia. 'You've done more than enough today.'

'Not true, you did more than the rest of us. I'll give you a hand.'

Flitting from one thing to the next, Amelia felt unable to relax. 'What if I've forgotten something?' she asked, stirring pasta absentmindedly.

'Hey. Deep breaths. The sun's forecast to be shining on us tomorrow. We're good to go.'

Amelia failed to muster a smile. 'I'll try but I can't stop feeling déjà vu. What if it's a repeat of last time? It's like being the kid who invited the entire class to their party and is now wondering why they did that and whether anyone's actually going to turn up.'

'They will turn up. They'd be crazy not to with no entry fee. There's nothing to lose. Even if they just come, have a look around, hear the best band in the universe play a few songs and then leave, they'll still have a great time.'

'But they didn't last time. Not one single soul came to Lochside.'

'You don't know that for sure. We cancelled early in the day because the weather was shocking and we assumed no one would want to do outdoor stuff.'

'I need everything to go smoothly. I suggested it. There's no way it won't all be my fault if it's a disaster.'

Mac towed Amelia to the sofa, placing his hands on her shoulders, forcing her to sit down. 'Amelia, you … we, all of us, have done so much but in the end you can't control everything, you simply can't. Whether one hundred people turn up or one, you've tried and that's huge. No matter what, no one's going to blame anyone for anything. Everyone willingly agreed to it.'

'Only because I sold it to them as the answer to our prayers.'

'Uh-uh.' Mac wagged his forefinger, then mimed zipping up Amelia's lips. 'No more of this negative talk.'

They sat together, hands entwined, watching Chewie playing with one of the many ping pong balls Amelia had purchased to use in the egg and spoon race.

'He's reminding us, you know,' said Amelia.

'What?' Mac jolted upright, having almost dozed off.

'Chewie.' Amelia pointed at the cat, who was now on his back with the ping pong ball trapped between his front paws. 'That the point of tomorrow is to have fun. That's why I suggested it and that's what it's all about.'

'Then I suggest you stop worrying about it and enjoy yourself.' Mac leaned over to kiss Amelia's cheek. 'This time nothing can possibly go wrong.'

23

Amelia and Mac arrived in the stable yard at six o'clock on Saturday morning. The sky was the predicted cloudless blue and it looked set to be a dry, warm day, possibly one of the last before autumn arrived. Standing in the centre of the lawn, Jilly attempted to take charge but soon gave up, allowing Tamsin and her friends to get on with plaiting manes and tails and tacking up the ponies while making an extraordinary amount of noise.

'They've got excitement overload,' observed Amelia.

'I can't keep up. They only arrived a short time ago and have everything underway already. We'd be struggling to get it all done without them,' said Jilly.

The ponies sparkled and even Pirate conceded to wearing a glittery purple browband on his bridle, although he didn't seem impressed. Angus and Mac went out to check on the show jumps. Zoey collected the spare hats and boots from the tack room and followed them, cautiously pushing a wheelbarrow piled high with all the gear.

Picking up the spare poles for the bending race, Amelia turned, then almost went flying over Gallus who was under her feet. As the hound slunk away, Jilly made a grab for him.

'I'm going to keep him in the office today. It's for the best.' After Jilly closed the door, shutting him in, Gallus's face appeared at the window. 'I can't have him running amok with unfamiliar dogs around.'

Amelia checked everything was ready in the fields. By the time she returned, Euan had arrived and was preparing his equipment. Beside him, Pippin dozed, oblivious to the buzzing atmosphere and his role as guinea pig for the farrier demonstration. Angus was supervising the unloading of a crate of cakes from a van with the name of a local bakery printed on its side, while the lads from Chequered Pipes carried their instruments out to the gazebo.

'I don't think I've ever been awake this early in the morning,' Digger informed Amelia as he walked by carrying a guitar case, his eyes hidden behind aviator sunglasses, his t-shirt on back to front.

'We're grateful to you for coming,' Amelia told him. 'We hope you'll join us later for drinks at the cottage, if you're able to stay.'

'Got my emergency supplies until then,' Digger said, pulling a small silver hip flask from the pocket of his jeans.

'All right everyone, gather in the tack room,' Jilly yelled. 'It's time for the pre-gymkhana briefing.'

Being engrossed in their tasks everyone ignored her, instead carrying on with what they were doing.

'Bacon rolls, tea and coffee are available in the tack room.' This time Jilly's voice came through a loudhailer and there was no ignoring it, not that anyone wanted to. The announcement that food was available caused a stampede as they all crammed indoors.

Jilly struggled to make herself heard over the chattering and laughter and resorted to banging a spoon on the side of a mug until everyone stopped talking. 'OK. We've about an hour until gates open. I'll be locking the office and tack room for security so please make sure you take anything you need and all valuables are locked in the desk drawer. Angus will have a cool box with refreshments and snacks for you to help yourselves. Now, before you all disappear, I've a surprise for you.' With that, Jilly produced a large cardboard box which had been hidden beneath some rugs. Peeling the Sellotape off, she pulled up the flaps to reveal a pile of clothes. She lifted one of the items, holding up a mint green polo shirt with Lochside Riding Stables written in black circular italics around a horse's head logo. 'There's one for each of you —'

'Including us?' interrupted Digger, through a mouthful of bacon.

'There's plenty to go around. Feel free to take one. I had assumed they wouldn't be cool enough for you guys though.' Jilly grinned cheekily.

'Nonsense, we're here to support our mates. Besides I've always looked fantastic in green.' Digger swooped on the box and began handing out the shirts.

'Any questions?' Jilly called in vain above the melee.

'Can I ride Jellybean in the clear round?' asked Scott.

'Yes. As a thank you for your help, you can participate in one game. I've drawn up the rota —' Jilly got no further as the children charged off to check the list pinned to the wall, discussing swapping if they hadn't been allocated the pony they wanted.

At ten o'clock Amelia stood in front of the main gate, fiddling with her nails. She had hoped a few cars would turn up before opening time. There was no sign of any. At quarter past the hour, Mac joined her.

'Where are they all?' she asked anxiously.

'It's early yet,' he reassured her.

'But the posters and social media posts all clearly stated a ten o'clock start. If anyone's coming I'd expect them to be here by now.'

'I've got to go get ready with the band.' Mac squeezed her hand. 'Keep the faith.'

He walked off, leaving Amelia feeling alone and exposed as she stared down the empty lane willing a car, even just one, to appear.

Minutes passed. The strains of music as Chequered Pipes warmed up for the welcome session drifted in the air. Euan discretely checked his watch while smoking over by the cottage. Angus, chewing his unlit pipe, watched the farrier enviously. Amelia turned to the group gathered in the yard behind her. Tamsin and her friends stood patiently with their ponies. Her eyes scanned them. They looked amazing, never better, as did the team, smart in their matching polo shirts. Tamsin caught Amelia's eye and gave a shrug, the happy smiles of earlier beginning to waver. Unable to take the tension, Amelia walked down the lane towards the road.

She marched, head down, unsure what she was doing, uncertain if she would stop or just keep going. Could she walk far enough away to obliterate her failure? It was obvious to her now that her old-fashioned idea wouldn't appeal to a generation more interested in electronic devices than reality, more comfortable inactive indoors than out in the fresh air. Her aunt would sell Lochside now, she was certain of it. All her cards had been played and the joke was on her. She'd left a secure life in London without a backward glance, convinced quaint gymkhana games would be the answer. A robin hopped across the path ahead, then flew up to watch her from a low branch. She paused. The robin ruffled his feathers. Now that her feet had stopped crunching on loose stones, Amelia thought she could hear something. It sounded like mooing. Not just one moo but loads of them. Setting off again, she jogged to the end of the lane where a herd of Highland cattle with shaggy brown coats and large horns were passing by in succession, taking up the entire width of the road. Bringing up the rear was a farmer carrying a stick, chivvying them along. Behind him a line of cars waited patiently.

'Sorry to have held up your customers, me dear,' the farmer apologised, as he drew level, tipping his cap. 'My silly lad left the gate open this morning and the whole herd broke free. One went and they all followed.'

'It's OK, can't be helped. Did you, er, did I hear you say something about my customers?'

'I did indeed. They're all in a hurry to get to the gymkhana. I'm grateful they've been most understanding about the delay. Rural living, you see. You can't rush a cow or fifty.'

To the farmer's surprise, Amelia burst into a mixture of laughter and tears as the lead car turned into the lane, the lady in the passenger seat giving her a cheery wave.

'Straight on … parking straight on,' directed Amelia, standing back as car after car filled with excited children drove by. 'Well, I never,' she said to the robin now pecking around her boots, feeling the weight of disappointment lift from her shoulders.

By the time she'd walked back to the stable yard, Jilly was busy greeting people and directing cars, now parking on both sides of the lane. 'Good morning. Yes … do go on through, follow the signs.'

Amelia waved to Euan who was preparing Pippin for the demonstration. He raised a hoof scraper in acknowledgement, then turned away to chat with a child who had stopped to talk to him.

Standing beside her aunt, Amelia gazed around in amazement at the constant stream of cars rapidly filling the space. Having previously been convinced no one was coming, she asked, 'What do we do if we run out of parking places?

We can't let them leave cars out on the main road. That would be dangerous.'

They both groaned as an estate car reversed into the gap alongside Amelia's Mini with millimetres to spare, leaving the people carrier behind it nowhere to go.

'I haven't given it any thought,' admitted Jilly. 'I never dreamed anywhere near this number would turn up.'

'Me neither.'

'We'll have to open up the meadow to use as an overflow car park.'

'The meadow. Where's that?'

'On the other side of the road.'

Amelia visualised the land opposite the end of the lane. All she could picture was an overgrown field encompassed by a straggly hedge and guarded by a tumbledown gate. 'Can we do that?'

'I don't see why not. I own it.'

'Really? I didn't know that.'

'Well, the ground's no good for pasture so Stan and I always left it to its own devices. We didn't have any use for it. You'll see what I mean when you get there.'

'OK.' Amelia made to head straight down the lane.

Jilly stopped her. 'Best get someone to give you a hand. That gate hasn't been opened in decades.'

Running off to find Mac, Amelia located him eating a cupcake and chatting to Zoey.

'Need your help,' she panted.

He shoved the last of the sponge cake into his mouth. 'Dare I ask what disaster has befallen us this early in the day?'

'Parking. We've filled all the spaces set aside and now the lane is clogging up fast.'

'Really.' Mac was staggered. 'That's fantastic. I thought it seemed to be getting busier —'

'We need to open up the meadow,' insisted Amelia urgently. 'Can you give me a hand.'

They ran the entire way, stopping only briefly for Amelia to collect the gate key from the office. The lane to Lochside was crammed with cars and the queue was now reaching the road.

'Bear with us, we're getting it sorted,' Amelia reassured the harassed drivers of cars filled with children impatient to be let out.

To their dismay the meadow's gate was rusted and rotten. Having been neglected for years it had dropped on its hinges and sunk into the ground. The padlock and chain were badly corroded and it took Amelia several attempts to insert the key in the misshapen lock and then turn it. After a few failed tries, there was a click, followed by a shower of rusty flakes. Pulling the chain free, they both heaved but the gate refused to shift. Sitting on her heels, Amelia inspected the bottom rail which was submerged into the earth as though it had taken root.

'What do we do?' she asked, trying not to let the constant sound of car horns tooting add to her stress. 'It's not budging.'

'Try jiggling it.'

As best they could they hooked their feet under the lowest bar and bounced the gate up and down. Nothing happened.

'We can't turn people away because of lack of parking.' Amelia felt angry with herself for overlooking the possibility this might happen. She redoubled her efforts, hauling hard on the rails, the metal biting into the palms of her hands.

'I'll try from the other side,' Mac suggested, climbing the gate cautiously in case it didn't support his weight. He landed in unkempt coarse grass, his ankles peppered with spikes from the thistles, straddling a particularly vicious looking plant as he heaved.

Suddenly and with a terrific squeal, the gate wrenched free, clods of earth dangling from the bottom as Mac raised it a few inches, pulling it inwards. 'Go, Amelia,' he said through gritted teeth.

Not needing to be told twice, Amelia dashed out to the road, waving her arms to direct the cars through the now open gate. 'Park anywhere you like … anywhere you like.'

As the traffic began to snake its way into the meadow, Amelia walked over to stand with Mac, who had pulled the gate as wide open as he could. She stumbled a few times on the ruts hidden under the thick carpet of grass.

'I can't understand why Jilly let this get in such a state. I expect there'll be a few scraped exhausts,' said Mac.

'Yeah, it appears I'm a victim of my own success.' Amelia smiled, waving to a family in a Range Rover.

'You're never a victim.' Mac picked up the padlock and chain, placing them out the way. 'I reckon we can leave them to it. It's obvious this is the overflow parking. They'll follow each other.'

Back at the stable yard, Amelia helped Angus to carry a box full of bean bags. Picking up the ones he dropped on the way, she plonked the loudhailer on top. 'That's everything.'

Having no hands free, Angus nudged the loudhailer with his chin. 'I don't know why Jilly wants that.'

'She said when she reads out the rules of each game everyone will need to hear her. Her voice isn't loud enough. She's also keen to provide a commentary for the clear round jumping.'

'I don't think it's necessary. You've heard her when the ponies are misbehaving. She can reach a volume where climbers on the summit of Ben Nevis can hear her.'

'Now, Angus, that's cheeky …' Amelia's attention drifted for they had reached the gymkhana area and the field was busy with families unpacking picnic hampers, unfolding portable chairs and placing blankets on the grass. Children played with friends and a small crowd had gathered to dance to the jaunty jig Chequered Pipes were playing. As the song finished to applause, Mac took a bow, then winced at feedback whining through the air.

Jilly had picked up the loudhailer and, after some brief crackling, managed to get it to work. 'Attention everyone. You won't be permitted to participate without a hat and appropriate footwear. Don't worry if you haven't brought your own. Zoey can sort you out with some to borrow for the day.'

To draw attention to where she was located Zoey waved both arms above her head and some children scurried over. While she was busy swapping trainers for boots and fitting hats, Tamsin and Mona led the ponies out from the stable yard. The games were about to begin.

'It's just how I imagined it would be,' Amelia said happily, turning to Angus who was no longer standing next to her as a queue had formed to buy refreshments.

24

Once the participants for the first game were ready, Amelia stood on the sidelines with Mac.

'The first one needs to go well,' she muttered nervously. 'It sets the tone.'

'Angus told me Jilly's a pro at this. They used to hold gymkhanas regularly when Stan was alive. They loved it,' Mac replied, between mouthfuls of cake.

'I wonder why they stopped.'

'Jilly didn't feel like doing it on her own without Stan.'

Back on the loudhailer, Jilly was explaining the rules of the bean bag race to the riders seated on excited ponies who had assembled at the start in a rather unruly line.

'What do they have to do?' Mac asked.

'Once Jilly blows the whistle, they have to grab a bean bag from the top of the barrel beside them, then ride as fast as they can up the course, drop the bean bag in the bucket, circle around the marker and return. The first four to cross the finish win a rosette if their bean bag landed in the bucket. It's good fun.'

As soon as the whistle sounded a frantic scramble began,

accompanied by cheering from the onlookers. Riders clutching bean bags urged their ponies up the course, some moving faster than Amelia had ever seen before unless it involved food. While it looked chaotic all the riders and ponies made it safely back over the finish line, where Zoey presented the first four with their rosettes.

Soon Jilly was back on the loudhailer again. 'OK folks, the next game is the walk, trot and canter. You walk up, circle clockwise around the marker, trot back, turn again, then canter back. If your pony breaks into a trot when they should be walking or into a canter when they should be trotting, my eagle-eyed assistant Angus won't miss it and you must turn a circle as a forfeit before you can continue.'

Amelia and Mac couldn't resist laughing as they watched the riders and ponies trying to beat each other. Pirate didn't manage to maintain a walk, bolting off the course until he was brought back by Tamsin. Meanwhile Chess, who usually needed a lot of urging to trot, cantered when he should be trotting. It didn't matter. The air was filled with giggles, the children's faces shone with excitement as the crowd urged them on.

While the second round of rosettes were being handed out, Euan appeared. 'The demo went well. The adults seemed to find it interesting too. One lady asked me to trim the claws on her miniature poodle. I politely declined. My tools aren't designed for that.'

Amelia gave him a high five. 'You're the best.'

'I keep telling people that! Seriously, I've got to go but I'll try and join you this evening for drinks.'

'Cool.' Mac nodded, then took Amelia by the arm. 'We're up next. It's the egg and spoon race.'

'You're mistaken. We're not taking part in that,' protested Amelia.

'Oh yes we are.'

'Oh no, we are not.'

'We are. I put our names down earlier.'

'You did what?'

Tamsin and Zoey sided with Mac, insisting Amelia join in and she found herself hoisted onto Whisky, as Mac mounted Pumpkin.

Balancing her ping pong ball carefully on the spoon, Amelia waited at the start line for the whistle. Despite her protests, she could feel her competitive spirit rising. Next to her Mac was biting his lip in anticipation, while restraining an eager Pumpkin. At the starting signal, Pumpkin shot forwards, Mac adopting a standing canter, while Amelia kept Whisky at a steady walk. Halfway up the course, her patience paid off when Mac's ping pong ball went flying.

'You see,' teased Amelia, drawing level as Mac dismounted to retrieve it. 'The tortoise always beats the hare. See you later.'

Pumpkin swung his hindquarters towards Whisky causing him to stumble which dislodged Amelia's ping pong ball, forcing her to stop and dismount.

'Oi, that's my one,' argued Mac, grabbing the ball rolling past her boot.

'No, it's not, yours is that one over there.' Amelia turned, pointing to a ball which had rolled into the path of Jellybean, who knocked it with his hoof, sending it flying further away. Laughing at Mac's dismay, Amelia was unprepared as he snatched her ball off the ground, then vaulted back onboard, cantering off with his feet dangling out the stirrups.

Amelia straightened up. Beside her, Whisky had lowered his head to pick some grass.

'He's not taking this race seriously,' she complained to Becky, who had run over with a replacement ball for her.

Mac was turning round the marker. 'You're going to finish last. Loser!'

'At least I didn't cheat.'

Mac was right. Amelia and Whisky did come last, walking slowly over the finish. Angus handed Amelia a bottle of water. 'We're taking a breather before the sack race, flag race, clear round jumping and apple bobbing. Still lots to come and the good news is we've reached the maximum number of participants for them all.'

Shortly afterwards, Amelia gave out rosettes to the those placed in the sack race who had successfully managed to dismount and lead their pony back while hopping down the course holding a sack up to their waist without falling over. The crowd moved over to gather around the arena eager for the clear round jumping competition to begin.

Mac assisted Angus checking the jumps were all intact before returning to the waiting area. 'Hey, Amelia, you should have a go at this.'

'Nope. No way,' Amelia replied firmly. 'I'm not volunteering to make a fool of myself in front of everyone.'

'Oh, go on,' Zoey joined in. 'Be daring.'

'No,' repeated Amelia. 'Besides Angus told me it's fully booked.'

'Not where you're concerned, it isn't,' said Jilly, striding over with a box of rosettes under her arm. 'If you want to have a go, you'll get one of these if you don't knock anything down.'

Admiring the lilac and yellow rosette Jilly was holding, Amelia almost relented, the child in her desperate to win the pretty ribbons. 'But I don't like jumping. I'd rather just watch.'

'What good is watching?' asked Mac. 'You need to be a participant in life not an observer.'

'You do it then,' snapped Amelia.

'I'm not the one who needs to prove to myself I can,' he said softly.

'I know what you're doing. You're trying to make me face

my fears and I'm telling you I don't want to.' Amelia looked down at the ground, thinking. 'No, I don't want to.'

'Yeah, you do,' said Tamsin. 'Some of the ponies are having a rest but Pirate's ready. Here.' She propelled his reins into Amelia's hand.

'I can't do this,' Amelia said nervously to Mac, as he walked at Pirate's shoulder, accompanying them to the arena entrance.

'You're the most capable person I've ever met. I don't know why you don't see it. For some reason you don't.' Mac placed a reassuring hand on Amelia's left knee. 'Leave your fears here. Jump free, Amelia. Do it.'

At Mac's encouraging words, Amelia trotted Pirate into the arena, her heart thumping. Ears pricked, Pirate gave a snort, launching straight into a canter which caught Amelia off guard. His eyes swept the colourful jumps, sizing them up. Jumping was his favourite activity and, as they cantered the circumference of the arena to warm up, she felt him tug on the reins keen to be off. She aimed Pirate at the first jump, a plain red and white striped pole. Taking a fierce hold, he charged at it, soaring over, then flicking his heels to show his disdain at how easy it had been. They cleared the cross rail, Pirate flying over the centre of the crossed poles. Then they were at the wall, a solid looking fake fence painted to resemble stone bricks. Despite her efforts to steady him, Pirate charged at the jump and had to put in an extra stride, which brought him in too close. He rose steeply, Amelia tangled her fingers in his mane as his hooves brushed the hollow wooden brick. Hearing a loud rattle, she glanced back to find the wall still intact. She switched her focus ahead, for the combination loomed: two jumps set only two strides apart. Pirate bounced over them like a tennis ball. With only a couple of fences remaining, one a plain jump of a single plank which Pirate cleared as though he had springs, they then faced the final, most difficult, jump: the oxer. Amelia stared ahead at the two poles, placed close enough together to form a single jump but with the first pole set slightly lower than the other. The gap between had been filled with plants. Pirate's ears flickered, summing up the size and width of the obstacle which, as they got closer, appeared dauntingly wide. Amelia considered aborting and forfeiting her clear round. She didn't need a rosette. Pulling up, she slowed Pirate to a trot.

'Go on, Amelia. Let him go.' It was her aunt's voice roaring over the loudhailer. 'You can do it.'

A chant went up around the arena, cheering her on. Amelia felt the outpouring of support, willing her not to retire. She nudged Pirate with her heels, wondering if it was too late to gain enough momentum to clear the jump. Her pony was not to be defeated. He quickened his pace, the fence loomed closer, Amelia's pulse soared higher than Pirate as he rocketed, legs tucked neatly beneath him. They landed to a round of applause. Pirate bucked playfully. Amelia patted his sweaty neck with relief.

'Well done,' congratulated Tamsin, clipping the lilac and yellow rosette to Pirate's bridle. 'You made it look easy.'

Pirate bounced around his lap of honour with Amelia feeling ridiculously proud of the fluttering ribbon held together by a circle of card attached to his bridle. She didn't refuse the challenge. She stroked Pirate fondly, grateful for his skill.

'How about that,' she trilled to Mac, who was waiting for her by the exit. 'What an amazing feeling jumping clear, after all these years.'

'You weren't just jumping clear, Amelia, you were jumping free.'

'I was, wasn't I?' Amelia untied the rosette and gazed at it, reflecting on Mac's words as Mona led Pirate away.

Mac swooped, lifting Amelia up, swinging her round,

hands clasped around her waist, as she playfully tried to stick the rosette in his hair.

'Oi, stop that,' he joked, dropping her gently back on the ground. 'You'll wreck my carefully crafted rocker image. Remember once the jumping's over, I'm back on with the band.'

With the final clear round completed as Tamsin and Snowdrop leaped the oxer in a display of perfect jumping, Chequered Pipes struck up the first notes of 'Lazy Loch Days'. The crowd cheered before making their way over to dance as the band brought the day to a close.

'Looks like some of the non-drivers have been on the wine,' observed Angus, watching a lady in a pink dress remove her wedge espadrilles to attempt the twist.

'I hope they all join in soon,' replied Amelia. 'It's a perfect way to end the day. I'm due to take Gallus for a walk. It's over an hour since Zoey last checked on him.'

As she strolled back to the office, Scott came running up to her. 'There's a posh car stuck in the lane,' he gabbled breathlessly. 'This way.' Grabbing her hand, he dragged her over to the gates where the driver of a blue BMW X5 was trying to turn the car around in a narrow gap between the gates, the cottage and some of the parked vehicles.

Walking up to the driver's window, Amelia was surprised to find a man dressed in a smart charcoal grey suit, white shirt and pink tie sitting behind the wheel. He pressed the release button and the window lowered smoothly and silently. Assuming he was lost, she asked if she could help.

'This is Lochside?' he asked. 'Lochside Riding Stables?'

'Yes, that's correct.'

'Then I don't need directions, thanks. I'm already in the right place.'

'Oh.' Amelia placed her hand on the top of the door. 'I'm

afraid you're rather late in the day though. We've just finished the clear round.'

'That's OK. I'm here now which is what matters to my family.'

Scott reappeared, beckoning to Amelia. 'The dog in the office keeps howling. Jilly said you need to take him out.'

Feeling she couldn't ask the man to park in the meadow, Amelia directed him to pull in behind her Mini. 'I won't need to get my car out,' she told him. 'Then do go on through. There's still plenty going on and refreshments are available. We've got one more surprise bonus game and a band.'

'Who's the band?'

'They're called Chequered Pipes. Enjoy.'

Thinking no more of it, she rushed off to collect Gallus who was making a lot of noise from behind the door. She clipped a lead on his collar, watching the smartly dressed man tiptoe across the yard in his shiny tasselled brogues, looking out of place, like a workaholic forced to indulge in some leisure time. Avoiding the crowds and other dogs, she headed down the lane, Gallus stopping regularly to sniff scents. Crossing the road, they walked through the meadow, keeping to the edges where the grass grew less wild, to climb the hill beyond. Amelia could hear 'Lonely Loch Days' playing and hummed along with the catchy chorus. Shading her eyes, she gazed at the vehicles parked below her, each one a potential new customer for Lochside. The day had been a resounding success, more than any of them had dared to hope. She saw Zoey emerge from the lane, jog across the road and up through the meadow, calling her name.

'A good crowd turned up in the end,' she noted, when she was close enough for Amelia to hear.

'I'm relieved. I don't know the exact numbers yet. Once we have them, I'm sure we'll find we've exceeded all expectations.'

'Overshot the mark completely. Well done, Amelia.'

'Cheers, although it's been a team effort. We should all take the credit.'

'Chequered Pipes are wrapping up and it's time for the bonus game. Apple bobbing.'

'Yikes! I was hoping to give that a swerve.' Amelia frowned at the thought of plunging her face into a bowl of cold water while trying to catch an apple with her teeth.

They arrived back at the gymkhana together, Zoey keeping Gallus on the lead. Amelia paused for a moment, gazing around, taking in the crowds gathered at the games area where Jellybean was trying to get his teeth into an apple floating in a bowl of water before his rider. Others were walking dogs while chatting to children. Becky and Mona waved from the centre of a large circle of grazing ponies. The smell of fresh coffee and doughnuts drifted over from the refreshments table and Amelia sniffed appreciatively, acknowledging how tired and hungry she was. She was about to go and get herself something to eat and drink when Jilly stepped up to the microphone, surrounded by the band.

Panicking, Amelia grabbed Zoey's arm. 'Please don't tell me she's going to burst into song.'

'Of course not. She knows it would spoil everyone's day.'

'May I have your attention please.' Jilly's voice sounded oddly distorted by feedback from the speakers. Everyone stopped to look in her direction. 'All of us at Lochside hope you have enjoyed your day.' Jilly paused as loud cheers erupted. 'Thank you for coming. Any child who didn't win a rosette, please see Zoey. We would like everyone to go home with a memento of the day and we do hope to see you back at Lochside soon. As a reminder, we offer riding in beautiful countryside, pub rides and soon we'll be booking beach rides, which are sure to be very popular. Keep an eye on our website and Instagram.'

There was another round of cheering and applause as Mac stepped up to swap places with Jilly. 'We do have one special thank you to make to the person whose idea today was and who made it all possible. Step forward and take a bow, Amelia Hodge.'

Blushing, Amelia shook her head and mouthed the word 'no'. She didn't need praise. For her it was enough the day had been a success. Zoey, however, wasn't going to allow Amelia to dodge the moment. Placing both hands on Amelia's back, she propelled her forwards, almost tripping over Gallus's lead in the process. Digger produced an enormous bouquet of pink roses from behind the drum set and kissed Amelia's cheeks. His breath smelt strongly of whisky; Amelia suspected the hip flask was empty.

'Three cheers for Amelia,' shouted Mac.

Everyone joined in, including, Amelia noticed, the man in the charcoal grey suit.

25

With the gymkhana drawing to a close, Amelia finally managed to find a moment to grab a cup of coffee and a biscuit.

'Sounds like we're definitely branching out into pub lunches and beach rides,' she said to Angus and Mac. 'Jilly's grown ambitious.'

Mac nudged her in the ribs. 'I wonder who she's caught that from.'

'It doesn't mean I'm ever doing this again though. It's been exhausting. No, we will not be doing this again,' Amelia insisted.

Jilly swept by with a huge smile on her face. 'Same again next year. Oh, what the heck! Let's make it an annual event.'

Mac grabbed Amelia as her fatigued legs wobbled.

'We're putting the ponies to bed,' called Zoey, leading Jellybean and Whisky away.

As they packed up, Amelia received positive feedback from the crowd as they returned to their cars, carrying empty picnic baskets and accompanied by children wearing rosettes and smiles. She was delighted to hear one boy say to another: 'I can't wait to come back here. That was fun. Not like that other place where they tell you off all the time. It's boring there.'

'I know,' his friend replied. 'I want to come here too. I heard they let you gallop flat out and take you swimming at the beach.'

'Cool,' the first boy agreed. 'I'm gonna ask my mum to book me in before we leave. I don't want her to forget.'

A surge of happiness pulsed through Amelia, making her emotional as she collected Chess and led him over to the field where Tamsin was laying out buckets of feed. She yawned noisily as she removed the pony's bridle and undid the plaits from his mane, feeling the silky hairs between her fingers.

'I'm going to shut the gate to the meadow,' Mac shouted over. 'There are only a few stragglers left and they're leaving now. Angus doesn't want it left unlocked. He's concerned we'll get an influx of wild campers. I told him it's unlikely.'

Jilly rushed over, her cheeks rosy, her smile wide. She looked invigorated, even the fine worry lines between her brows less pronounced, resembling more the carefree aunt of Amelia's youth. 'There you are,' she puffed, clutching her side as if troubled by a stitch. 'You'll never believe it. We're getting lots of requests to book in and there's already interest in the pub ride. I only mentioned it once in my speech.'

'That's fabulous.' Amelia grinned. 'We'll give the ponies a few days off and then we'll be raring to go.'

'Jolly good, jolly good,' chanted Jilly absentmindedly, her attention elsewhere. 'If you'll excuse me, here's Arthur.'

'Arthur?' Amelia repeated, taking in the short man in a tweed suit giving her a friendly smile as he walked towards them. He had bushy white hair, an equally bushy moustache and a walking cane with a dog's head carved into the handle.

'Hello, I'm Arthur. Jilly's told me all about you. Good to

meet you at last and on such a glorious occasion.' He extended a hand and shook Amelia's firmly.

'Wait … you're the Colonel?' asked Amelia.

'Oh, well, technically yes. I don't refer to myself as that though … I'm Arthur.' He took Jilly's arm gently. 'I look forward to seeing you all again at the drinks later.'

As Jilly and Arthur walked away, Amelia and Angus exchanged a glance. 'Well, well. We got to meet him at last.'

'Aye. I saw them with their heads together earlier … plotting, if you ask me.'

With a bounce in her step, Amelia packed away the last remnants of a most pleasurable day, Gallus chasing in and out of her legs as she loaded bean bags onto a wheelbarrow.

'You're the only one with any energy left,' she told him, as he loped beside her to the barn.

Inside Angus was sitting on a bale of hay, with a sack of overflowing rubbish between his feet.

Amelia stopped beside him. 'What a day it's been. Drinks, then bath and bed for me.'

'Aye, it's been a good day,' Angus agreed, sucking on his unlit pipe. 'Brought back fond memories of when we held gymkhanas regularly. I don't really know why we stopped. Suppose they simply became less popular as technology advanced.'

'Could be. There's an awful lot of competition for kid's time and attention now. We did it though. It's been a success.'

'It needed to be. Keep that Douglas clan from snapping at our heels.'

'I intend to speak to Hugh about it.'

'Do you, now?' Angus reached down and stroked Gallus, who rolled on his back, squirming with delight.

'Yep. Maybe we can reach an agreement for him to leave Jilly alone.'

'Just be careful, Amelia. That family has a certain status

and won't take kindly to the likes of us telling them what we think.'

'I will be. Don't worry.'

Their conversation ended as a departing family stopped by to offer their thanks and give the children a chance to show off their prized rosettes. When they had gone, Angus rose to his feet, joints cracking and gathered up the rubbish bag. 'I'll chuck this here in the bin and see you at the cottage. I'm ready for a wee dram.'

With everything finally cleared away, locked up and the ponies fed and settled in for the night, they gathered in the cottage garden. An assortment of chairs had been brought from inside, boosted by a couple of rickety deckchairs from the shed. They sat in a circle around a portable fire pit Mac had set up in the centre of the chairs. With dusk approaching, they watched the flames dancing, the adults sipping whisky and the children soft drinks. Chewie purred contentedly from Zoey's lap and Euan arrived carrying a huge pile of pizza boxes.

'I guessed you'd all be hungry,' he said, taking an empty seat, then handing the boxes out.

By the time they'd finished eating and sharing tales from the day, it was almost dark, the garden lit only by flames and the light from the kitchen spilling out through the window. Jilly stood suddenly, disturbing Gallus who was asleep beneath her chair, and raised her glass high. 'Please join me in a toast. To pulling off a gymkhana which I know we'll all agree was a roaring success … to Lochside.'

'To Lochside,' everyone chanted, clinking their glasses.

'I want to add a huge and well deserved thank you to Tamsin, Mona, Scott and Becky for helping us out today,' Amelia added warmly. 'We could never have done it without you. Therefore, I believe a free hour's ride on the pony of your choice is the least we can do to repay you.'

'Yippee,' the children cheered.

'Can I add that we're already fully booked up next weekend,' announced Angus, trying to convey enthusiasm at the thought of being rushed off his feet.

'And that's just from people booking on their way out,' said Zoey proudly. 'There's already five messages on the answerphone we'll need to call back tomorrow.'

Gradually the children's parents arrived to collect them and, with an early start the next day, Euan left soon after, along with Zoey who said she'd drop Angus home. Having bid goodbye to Arthur, Jilly put the empty pizza boxes in a bin bag while Amelia and Mac carried the chairs inside, until only two remained around the fire pit.

'How's it going with Arthur?' Amelia couldn't resist asking her aunt as she folded up a deckchair, while Jilly washed up the glasses.

'Good.' Jilly winked at her niece. 'It's nice to have a companion again. He's got a plan for turning the meadow into an outdoor school. He feels it would be a real bonus if we could provide lessons.'

'Really? Sounds interesting.'

'It is and I agree with him. That space has been wasted for far too long and ought to be earning its keep, same as the rest of the place.'

'OK.' Amelia propped the deckchair against the wall. 'If we go ahead, and I know it's some way off actually happening, we'll need to think about hiring an instructor. I imagine it won't be easy finding someone qualified and available nearby. It isn't likely to happen overnight.'

'Actually, it is. Beatrice is a British Horse Society Accredited Coach.'

'Beatrice? Who's that, Jilly?' asked Mac, joining the conversation.

'Arthur's niece. She's currently working abroad but wants

to return home. Since his divorce, Arthur's been rattling around in the manor alone so suggested she stay with him while she finds work.'

'Which we're going to provide her with?' asked Amelia.

'Eventually, yes.' Jilly nodded. 'But right now, it's midnight and time for me to head to bed.'

'Before you go, can I ask, does this mean you're definitely not going to accept the increased offer from Hugh Douglas? If you're investing in Lochside, I assume not.' Amelia looked her aunt in the eye.

Jilly tapped the side of her nose. 'Trust me. I've got it sorted.' Refusing to elaborate, she gave Amelia and Mac a hug and said goodbye.

They sat outside beneath a starlit sky listening to Jilly's car engine fading away.

'I know she's your family but she can be bloody infuriating. Why not just give a straight answer to your question?' Mac grumbled.

'She's not selling. I know she's not. She's committed to giving this Beatrice a job.' Amelia stretched out her legs and waggled her feet. 'I don't know about you but I'm knackered. Time for bed. Can you put the fire out?'

'I can but were you aware there's a superstition in these parts that whoever puts the fire pit out will have good fortune for a year.'

'Really?' Amelia jumped out of her chair, keen now to do it herself.

'No, I just made that up on the spot.' Mac laughed.

'Then why bother saying it?' Unimpressed at Mac teasing her, Amelia glared at him.

'Because that's the thing about luck. People always believe it comes to them, when in fact it comes from them, from what they do.' Mac walked over to Amelia, pulling her into his arms. 'As you proved today. You've changed Lochside's fate.'

. . .

In the days following the gymkhana, bookings steadily increased, some from former customers keen to return, others were new names. On Tuesday morning, Angus declared he was coming down with a cold, insisting it was brought on by all the extra work. Eventually he agreed to go home and rest up rather than continue working outside in a persistent drizzle which, as Jilly pointed out, wasn't going to do his chesty cough any favours at all.

Aware the next few days were the only quiet time scheduled before a busy weekend, Amelia made her excuses to pop out. The team, each preoccupied by their own commitments, were unconcerned by her sudden departure. Zoey was due to visit Glasgow for a few days in preparation for her return to University and Jilly was booked on a flight to Orkney the next day to stay with Donna. Mac had come up with a new lyric for a song and kept disappearing to make notes. Amelia didn't feel guilty leaving them to it and sneaking off. She flicked on the wipers and turned up the demister to clear the Mini's windscreen as she drove down the lane. Beeping the horn, she waved at Zoey who was up a stepladder removing the temporary parking signs, the soggy paper disintegrating in her hands.

A short while later Amelia pulled up to the imposing gates at Keilburn. Seeing they were secured by a formidable padlock, she lowered the window and stuck her head outside looking for a means to request entry. She couldn't see one. Feeling conspicuous as she left the warmth of the car, she stood waiting beside the bonnet in case there was a concealed CCTV camera on which she would be spotted. No one came to ask her what she wanted and after five minutes it was clear uninvited visitors weren't welcome. She could wait a long time before anyone noticed her.

She drove on up the road following the boundary of the estate, searching for another entrance or even the Gatehouse she was seeking. A mile further on, she was rewarded by the sight of a gate concealed within the green railings. As she drew up, stopping the Mini inches away from the metal bars, she could make out the hinges. What seemed to be missing was a way to open it. There was no handle or latch. She jumped out the car, shivering in the damp air and walked up to the gate. Her first impression was right, it was embedded into the railings with no apparent means of release. Banging the top rail in frustration, she pushed against the barrier. It didn't budge. A vehicle approached, swinging in to stop sideways behind the Mini, blocking it in. An older man leaned out the window of a Land Rover, calling over, 'Can I help you?'

Thinking quickly, Amelia decided a version of the truth was probably the best option. 'I'm here to see Hugh Douglas. I found the main entrance was locked …' She tailed off with a little shrug, hoping to appear puzzled and innocent.

'It would be.' The man appraised her with grey eyes beneath black hair. 'If you've an appointment, I'm surprised you weren't already aware of that.'

'Yes, me too. You'd think Hugh would've mentioned where to meet up, wouldn't you?' Amelia giggled falsely. 'I guess that must have slipped his mind. It's been a while since we arranged it.'

The man got out the Land Rover, clutching a mobile phone. 'I'm the Estate Manager for Keilburn. I'll give Hugh a call for you. Let him know you're here, save you waiting.'

'Oh … no … really, it's no bother. I'll just …' Amelia waved a hand over her shoulder, indicating she'd get back in her car and leave. It was too late, the Estate Manager was already talking on the phone. Listening to his side of the conversation, it was obvious Hugh was saying he didn't know anything about her reason for being there.

'What's your name?' the Estate Manager asked, holding the phone away from his ear.

'I …' Amelia hesitated. She'd got herself into this, now she'd have to go through with it. 'Amelia. Amelia Hodge.'

The Estate Manager repeated her name into the phone, while looking at Amelia with suspicion. He ended the call and turned to her. She waited, fully expecting to be asked to leave and was taken aback when, with a loud squeak, the gate began to open slowly inwards.

'Hugh tells me he wasn't expecting you. That said, he's happy for you to meet him at the Gatehouse. When you reach the junction take a left.'

Amelia watched him get back into the Land Rover. 'Wait. How will I find the Gatehouse? Isn't it by an actual gate?'

'It was when we had the old boundaries but that was way back.' The Estate Manager had to shout over the engine noise. 'It's been situated within the grounds for years, ever since Leith's father expanded the estate.'

He drove off before Amelia could ask anymore. As soon as the rear of the Mini passed through, the gate began to swing shut behind it, as though invisible eyes were watching. She daren't take her eyes from the road which was carved out of the banks of the river that fed into Keilburn Loch. The right-side tyres were perilously close to the edge with its steep incline down to the water and occasionally dirt and stones slid away, tumbling downwards as the overhanging tree branches scraped the car. There was no option to turn back. Amelia remained hunched over the steering wheel, feeling fear not dissimilar to being on a runaway horse. She felt a burst of relief when a downhill section led to a quaint stone bridge, then levelled out. Now she was driving over a rutted track through fields, which were soon replaced by woodland.

Following the winding route she eventually reached the place where the track split. To the left a puddle strewn pathway headed into the trees, wide enough for a vehicle. Amelia turned onto it, as instructed.

The suspension bouncing beneath her, Amelia drove timidly, pressing the button to fold in the wing mirrors which were perilously close to being damaged by the trees lining either side. She suspected she'd gone wrong until she pulled up in a clearing facing a grey stone, gothic style building with narrow windows. It was tucked away amongst the trees and looked out of place with its steep roof and gargoyles crouched on the points above the guttering. She'd travelled some distance from the main road but a sign confirmed she had found the Gatehouse.

As she switched off the engine, Amelia began to have doubts. She hadn't been invited, not really, and it occurred to her the family must have all sorts of security in place. She looked around nervously for a gang of Dobermans, but all seemed peaceful. Deciding it was safe, she left the car, marched up the path and banged on the door knocker. Nothing happened. She knocked again, harder, with no response. Raising her arm to knock for the third time, the door suddenly opened revealing Hugh, a white bath towel slung around his waist.

'Hey, you caught me.' He twinkled. 'In fact, you got me out the shower.'

Determined to remain focused on Hugh's face rather than his toned body, which was resting casually against the door frame, arms folded over his bare chest, Amelia suspected he had done this on purpose to disconcert her. She could imagine him chucking off his clothes and leaping in the shower seconds after the Estate Manager's phone call. Well, his ploy was not going to work. She was absolutely not going to dwell on his appearance, nor his lack of clothes.

26

'Aunt Jilly …' Amelia announced determinedly.

'No, Amelia, I'm Hugh, not your aunt. Are you OK? I hope you don't mind me saying you look a little flustered and glassy-eyed. Are you feeling ill? Would it be a good idea for you come in and sit down?'

Recoiling, Amelia shook her head in alarm. To her horror, the words she had practiced on the drive over had evaporated from her mind. She couldn't place them in the order they were supposed to come out, probably because in her imagination Hugh had been fully dressed, not parading his rather spectacularly muscled torso in her face. 'I don't want to come in. I want to ask you what you want.'

'How on earth should I know what I want?' Hugh raised his hands in baffled amusement. 'You're the one who's sprung a visit on me. Shouldn't it be me asking you what you want?'

'I need … to know.' Blushing, Amelia tried to pull herself together as the speech she had rehearsed in her head for the last few days fell apart like a shredded script. She found she couldn't remember any of it.

'Please can you either come in so I can put on a robe or get to the point. I'll catch a chill standing here like this.'

'Well, perhaps you should have postponed your shower until later.'

'I'm not arguing on my doorstep especially while wearing a towel. Either come in or leave … your choice.'

'Lead the way.' Surrendering, Amelia followed Hugh into a dark and narrow hallway with wood panelled walls. Opening a door, Hugh ushered Amelia into a lounge with pine green walls and windows overlooking the front lawn. She took a seat on a sofa beneath an art nouveau wall light.

'I'll be back in a tick.' Closing the door behind him, Hugh left Amelia alone in the small room.

Fidgeting, she considered leaving immediately and was halfway up out her seat when Hugh reappeared wearing a black towelling robe and carrying a tray with a full cafetiere and two mugs sliding on its surface. Catching the delicious whiff of freshly brewed coffee, Amelia sat back down deciding she was there to talk. A brief chat wouldn't do any harm and she was thirsty.

'What is it you need to know?' asked Hugh, pouring coffee into the mugs and handing one to Amelia.

'Why you want to buy Lochside.' The words were out before Amelia could phrase them less bluntly.

Hugh didn't falter, nor did he spill hot liquid. Instead he sighed dramatically, raising his eyebrows. 'And why should I tell you that?'

'I didn't mean to overhear you and Portia talking. I was trapped outside the door and couldn't leave.'

'That's not strictly true though, is it? After all, no one was holding you hostage. You were free to walk away at any time.'

'And I didn't. Why do you want Lochside?' Amelia pressed on.

Hugh rolled his eyes upwards in exasperation, stood up and walked over to the window. 'Have a look at this, Amelia.'

Putting her mug of half-drunk coffee on a table, Amelia joined him. For a few moments neither said anything as they watched a blackbird pecking on the lawn.

When Hugh spoke, his voice was soft. 'All of this, everything, is owned by my father. My father and the estate committee. You can't change anything, do anything, without their permission. I've tried hard over the years. I've come up with good suggestions, all of which have been ignored. I want my own piece of land, my own property, where I run the show. Is that difficult for you to understand?'

'But Lochside has been my aunt's business for years. It's been her life. She needs Lochside and Lochside needs her.'

Hugh turned to Amelia, scowling. 'That's not the impression she gave me when I first approached her. We had a good chat and she struck me as fed up and keen to consider selling.'

'She'd just had an accident,' Amelia protested. 'She was struggling, vulnerable, in pain and scared about the future. She was probably muddled. None of us make good choices when we're feeling low.'

'Tell yourself that if it makes you feel better.'

'I don't need to. We had our gymkhana —'

'So I heard,' interrupted Hugh. 'As if a bunch of kiddies playing games is going to save a business from going under.'

'It was a huge success. We don't need you or your money.' Amelia was yelling now; she couldn't stop it. 'Leave us alone. Back off. We won't be going anywhere.'

'Arrogance doesn't suit you.' Hugh turned on Amelia. 'You don't get to barge in here and tell me what I can and can't do.'

'And you don't get to drive my aunt off her land because you want to be the boss.' Realising no one knew where she was and she'd left her phone in the car, Amelia walked out the room, up the hall, wrenched open the door and stepped outside into the sunshine, startling the blackbird who flew away squawking in protest.

Hugh followed her until he reached the doorway. 'Running away doesn't answer the question I know you're now consumed by.'

'Which is what?' Amelia snapped, looking over her shoulder.

'Do you really know your aunt?' Hugh smirked. He knew his words had hit their mark. 'Has she lied to you, misled you or can you trust her?'

'I know my aunt better than you ever will and she would never sell Lochside.' Opening the car door, Amelia glared over at Hugh. 'Despite your selfish mind games.'

'Before you go, I've got one other thing to tell you. Don't ever turn up here uninvited again or I'll have you escorted off the premises. You can pay the entrance fee if you want to visit again.'

Reversing at speed, Amelia spun the Mini and whizzed back along the narrow gap in the trees, inches away from denting the car. She didn't care if it got scratched. What she did care about was how Hugh had tried to make her doubt her aunt when she was sure Jilly's mind was made up. Was Hugh's vicious mood due to disappointment?

Switching off the alarm on Wednesday morning, Amelia was surprised she could still hear a persistent noise. Her phone screen was flashing on the bedside table signalling the arrival of a text from Angus's wife saying his cold was worse, he was ill in bed and wouldn't be at work for a few days. She lay listening to the rain bouncing off the window, trying to get herself in the mood for a busy day. With Jilly and Zoey away and now Angus out of action, Amelia and Mac would have to do it all between them. As they would already be short-staffed, Jilly had only booked in one ride. Amelia couldn't resist hoping they would cancel, as she forced herself to leave the comforting warmth of the shower. She was running behind when she heard Mac's motorbike pulling up outside, followed by the clanging of the gates being unlocked. Taking her unfinished piece of toast with her, she got to the barn as Mac was piling feed into bowls.

'Good morning,' she greeted him cheerfully.

'Not sure what's good about it.' Mac chucked the feed bowls onto the wheelbarrow, ready to take them to the fields.

'It's just light rain.' Amelia grabbed some tools. 'I'll start mucking out.'

'Knock yourself out. There's plenty of that to be done.' Mac grabbed the handles and lifted the wheelbarrow, steering it to the barn door.

'Is everything OK?'

'Yeah. Perfect.'

'Only it doesn't seem to be.'

'I'm annoyed.' Mac dropped the handles, turning to face Amelia.

'OK. I'd kind of figured that out by myself.'

'With Jilly, not you.' Mac rubbed his hands on his jeans. 'I mean, she knew Zoey was off for a few days sorting out Uni stuff, then she goes and books herself a holiday to Orkney at exactly the same time. Now Angus has gone down with the lurgy and we're left to do everything between us.'

'It is unfortunate timing,' Amelia agreed.

'It's bad planning, is what it is —'

A shrill whinny coming from the direction of the fields pierced the air and soon turned into a chorus as the herd joined in.

'It sounds like the ponies are getting impatient for their breakfast,' Amelia pointed out gently.

'Honestly, she's become obsessed with that Colonel Arthur,' Mac continued, as though he hadn't heard. 'He's really wormed his way in, hasn't he? Arthur tells her to take a break and she rushes straight off. Must do what Arthur says with no thought to the business picking up, which is what she wanted. Well, what she said she wanted.'

'You're being a little unfair, Mac. Arthur's company. She's been without that for a long time.' Amelia felt it necessary to defend her aunt even though she couldn't disagree with all of Mac's points.

'Get out the way,' Mac snapped at Chewie, who was sprawled in the barn doorway keeping dry. 'By the way, your cat shredded another rug earlier. That's two he's destroyed this month.'

'He's not supposed to be in the tack room.'

'Well, tell him that. He's everywhere.'

They worked on their chores without speaking until the two friends booked in for a ride at ten o'clock arrived as Amelia was brushing the tangles out of Snowdrop's tail. She heard them telling Mac they were both competent riders.

Once they were mounted on Pirate and Chess, Amelia led them out the yard, Snowdrop jogging beneath her.

'We'll take the circular route around Loch Still,' she told them.

As they rode, Amelia made a conscious effort to release the tension in her shoulders and not let Mac's bad temper affect her. Despite the light drizzle it was a calm day. Two tiny brown birds flitted in the hedgerow, twittering and hopping slightly further ahead each time Snowdrop drew near. Chess followed on, with Pirate bringing up the rear. Confident the riders knew what they were doing, Amelia felt able to relax and listen to their friendly chatter.

'We're touring,' the girl on Chess, called Kirsty, informed Amelia. 'Tomorrow we're going up to the Castle of Mey.

Right up near John O'Groats. You can stay there. We're already booked in.'

'It sounds amazing.' Amelia smiled. 'I've seen photos. It looks beautiful up there.'

They had reached the place where the track widened out onto open ground and the ponies broke into a trot, keen to be off.

'All OK for a canter?' Amelia checked, although if they weren't there wasn't a lot she could do because the ponies were already on tiptoes in anticipation.

'Bring it on,' Tara whooped, giving Pirate some rein.

Three abreast, the ponies surged into a fast canter. Their ears pricked, they raced each other across the grass, enjoying the opportunity to stretch out properly, unhindered by novices on their backs. With no one else around it was safe to let them choose their own pace. They laughed at their mount's eagerness, matched equally by their own. Amelia heard a yell and glanced back to check it was from joy, not terror; it was. As the ruin loomed in the background, Amelia slowed Snowdrop.

'How about we go up to the castle and I can take your photo as a memento?' she suggested.

'Fab idea,' agreed Kirsty. 'It'll look great on our Instagram page. We've set up a Scottish Adventures one.'

They rode on up the mound and, after some nifty manoeuvring, positioned the two ponies beside each other with the circular turret of the castle as a backdrop. Amelia snapped away on her phone, getting some nice pictures of Pirate and Chess posing with their necks arched and their ears up.

'This place is creepy,' commented Tara, glancing behind.

'But interesting,' added Kirsty.

'I'm hoping it'll be a draw for walkers to hire the cottage once it's available for rent,' said Amelia. 'Don't forget to lean slightly back as you ride down.' As the words left Amelia's lips, Snowdrop's forelegs slipped from under him. He bounded down in two gigantic leaps, throwing her briefly airborne. She regained her seat with a grimace.

They rode on around Loch Still, admiring the trees which were starting to turn their autumnal colours and a red squirrel who scampered across their path. A swan glided along the smooth water, keeping them company for a while.

As they trotted up to the gates at Lochside, Kirsty and Tara declared they'd had a wonderful time.

'My pleasure, it's been nice to —' Seeing Mac sprinting towards her waving his arms above his head, his face contorted, Amelia stopped abruptly.

'Guess what? Guess what? Guess what?' He sounded excited rather than panicked. Picking up on his urgency, Snowdrop shied, bumping into Chess who kicked out with a hindleg, narrowly missing Pirate.

'Steady,' soothed Amelia.

'It's happening. It's finally happening.' Mac was dancing.

'Have you won the Lottery or something?' asked Tara, 'because you're behaving as if you have.'

Having been oblivious to their presence moments earlier, Mac noticed the customers and calmed down. 'Sorry,' he whispered to Amelia, 'tell you in a minute.'

With Kirsty and Tara gone, Amelia was putting Snowdrop's saddle on its peg when Mac burst in, unable to contain his news any longer.

'You remember the guy in the grey suit … the one who seemed out of place at the gymkhana?'

'Yep.' Amelia nodded that she did.

'Turns out he works in the music industry and his daughter was taking part in the gymkhana. He arrived late because he was delayed at work. It's brilliant that he made it though because he was very impressed with Chequered Pipes and he wants to meet us to discuss doing a demo and possibly signing us up with his company.'

'Bloody hell. That's amazing.' Delighted for him, Amelia threw her arms around Mac.

'Yeah, the only thing is, he wants to meet us this afternoon.'

'But you must go,' insisted Amelia.

'At five o'clock … in Edinburgh.'

'Doesn't matter. I'll be fine. I've got all day.' Amelia unzipped her jacket pocket and handed Mac a key. 'Here, take my Mini. I won't be going anywhere and it'll be an easier journey than on the bike.'

'Cheers.' Mac kissed Amelia. 'Are you sure you'll be OK?'

'Absolutely.'

While Mac got ready to leave, Amelia led Chess and Pirate out to the field. The other ponies were waiting for them by the gate. After letting them go, she sat on the top rail, swatting away the irritating midges. Pirate bucked playfully, narrowly missing Whisky with a flying hindleg, then galloped in circles with Fergus and Pippin. In the adjacent field Brutus leaped and snorted.

'All right boys. Calm down. I'm keeping an eye on you.'

Mac's news had given Amelia mixed feelings. She was thrilled for him; this could be the realisation of all his hard work and dreams. The flip side was that it could take him away from Lochside. The sound of the latch on the gate at the end of the path clicking open caught Amelia off guard. She looked over as a couple dressed in bright yellow hiking gear and carrying walking poles stepped through. Their friendly smiles suggested they were harmless and had probably lost their way. Amelia made a mental note to buy a padlock for that gate. She called to the ponies again to settle down.

'Ahoy there.' The man gave a cheery wave, stopping in

front of Amelia to lean on his poles. 'We're glad to see you. We've got in a muddle and have no idea where we are.'

'No problem. I thought you might be.' Amelia jumped down from the fence, gently pushing a curious Whisky aside.

'Your ponies are lovely,' said the woman admiringly, just as Fergus galloped by with his tail in the air emitting a huge fart, while Pirate and Peewee started an argument by the water trough.

'They have their moments. Where do you need to get to?'

'Beauly,' replied the man.

'Gosh. You're a long way off.'

'Are we?' The woman sounded distraught. 'I'm exhausted.' She flopped down on the damp grass. 'Would it be possible to order a taxi to collect us from here?'

Amelia thought for a second. She knew Mac was heading that way and could probably take them. 'I know someone who might be able to drop you off. If you want to follow me.'

'That's wonderful. Thank you so much. My legs are eternally grateful.' The woman got to her feet with a smile.

Although he was taken aback when Amelia walked into the yard with the hikers, Mac agreed to take them to Beauly.

'Are you sure?' she whispered to him in the office. 'I'd never give strangers a lift myself, only the words were out my mouth before I'd thought it through, and they seem OK. If you prefer, we can call a taxi for them. I imagine they'll have a long wait.'

'Nah. I'll do it. It'll take ages to get a taxi out here.' Mac's phone beeped. He glanced briefly at the screen. 'It's Digger. He's pestering me to get a move on. I've got to pick him up because Verity's got their car today.'

'Of course. Good luck this afternoon. You'll smash it.' Sensing he was keen to get going, Amelia gave Mac a brief kiss.

As soon as he was in range of the Mini, Mac pressed the

key fob to unlock the doors, then ushered the man into a rear seat. Before getting into the car behind him, the lady turned to Amelia. 'Sincerely, thank you. You've been kind and helpful, unlike that awful man we spoke to at that Bothy on the hill. He was incredibly rude. I almost told him to fu —'

'All aboard,' Mac shouted, pressing the horn impatiently.

'What man?' Amelia asked urgently. The lady appeared not to hear as she joined her partner in the car. 'Excuse me, what man?' Amelia repeated her question to no avail. Mac was already reversing away and seconds later the Mini was out of sight, leaving Amelia alone and wondering what to do.

She knew she should check on the Bothy and the welfare of the rude man. Whoever he was, he was on their private land and she felt it was her duty to make sure he was OK. If he was looking for somewhere to stay he wouldn't be able to access the Bothy. If she took one of the horses she would be quick and Spirit needed exercising. The mare hadn't been ridden for a few days and tended to be skittish if she wasn't doing enough. It would be a jaunt to check all was well and then back to get on with the chores. After all, as she'd just told Mac, she had all day.

27

Locking the cottage and main gates, Amelia set to tacking up Spirit. The mare swished her tail and stamped a hoof as she tightened the girth. Deciding to take the key to the Bothy just in case she needed it, she sprinted to the office and pulled open the drawer. It was empty; the key wasn't there. She tried to recall whether she'd ever put it back before she returned to London. She couldn't be sure. No one had mentioned it was missing. Rather than turn the place upside down searching for it, she decided to get going.

She trotted Spirit out the yard, ignoring the mare's goggle eyes and swivelling ears while remaining alert for any objects she was likely to spook at. With everyone away and Mac having left suddenly she'd felt rather directionless. Her mood had perked up now she had something to focus on. Once through the gate, Spirit took off, cantering effortlessly up hill to the Bothy. A pheasant dashed out from the undergrowth, then disappeared again, frightened by the pounding hooves. By the time they reached the Bothy both horse and rider were breathless and, as Amelia reined Spirit to a walk, the mare snorted. Overhead a buzzard circled and ferns rustled as a deer slipped away to hide in the trees. Amelia didn't notice for her eyes were fixed on the Bothy door and the familiar Loch Ness keyring dangling from the lock.

Amelia steadied Spirit who was dancing on the spot beneath her. A faint scraping sound was coming from inside the Bothy. Dismounting, Amelia looped the mare's reins over a branch then ran the stirrup irons up the leathers. Nothing seemed to quite fit. They key shouldn't be there and the Bothy should be locked. With a deep breath, she crept over to the door, pushing gently to make a gap wide enough to peer inside. She could see the outline of a crouching figure, torch in one hand, while the other was poking between the wooden floorboards with a metal trowel. Withdrawing from the doorway, Amelia considered her options. She could call Mac and ask him to return but she couldn't be the cause of him being late or perhaps missing the most important meeting of his life. Glancing over at the grazing Spirit, she thought about leaving, but what about the key? She wasn't sure if there was a spare and she wanted to know what was going on and why someone was damaging her aunt's property. Deciding to use the element of surprise, she pushed the door again with such force it smashed against the wall and startled the figure, who jumped up and spun around to face her.

'What is going on here?' Amelia demanded, using as much authority as she could muster considering she was scared. 'And how did you get the key from ...' As the figure stepped into the daylight near the door, her words tailed off for she recognised him. The face above the green jacket was undoubtedly that of Hugh Douglas.

'Hello,' Hugh answered, with a grin. 'I might have known you'd be the only one at Lochside with enough persistence to figure it out.'

'I don't ... I don't understand. Figure what out? What are you doing here? How did you get the key?'

'The key. Ah, well, that was quite simple. I swiped it from the kitchen counter. You don't believe you genuinely won the champagne in the raffle, do you?' Hugh laughed, his peals echoing like church bells in the empty space. 'I thought I'd have quite the job stealing it even though I knew which one I needed. I overheard Mac telling you in the Hiker's Hope before the Garden Party. I figured after a few glasses of champagne and a stressful day you'd fall asleep, leaving me unhindered to search the office. Can you imagine how delighted I was to discover what I needed was right there in your kitchen?'

Engrossed in his words, Amelia failed to notice Hugh manoeuvre himself around her until it was too late. Grabbing the key from the lock, he slammed the door with a wellington booted foot. As soon as it was closed, he locked it from the inside.

'And now you're trapped.' Hugh shrugged, dropping the key into one of the jacket's deep pockets.

Carefully Amelia moved further inside the Bothy, trying to maintain space between them. 'I don't understand why you wanted the key. Surely all your efforts to buy Lochside haven't been because you wanted this old wreck.'

With the trowel, Hugh indicated Amelia sit in the rickety wooden chair in the corner furthest from the door. She obeyed, keen not to antagonise him, although her mind refused to accept that she was in any real danger. Hugh was Lochside's neighbour, she didn't believe he would harm her. This was all some sort of weird misunderstanding soon to be cleared up.

'You see, you really are quite clever sometimes,' mused Hugh, crouching down to scrape at the floorboards again. 'That's precisely what I wanted, only —'

'You know that's vandalism,' Amelia interrupted, wincing as a floorboard cracked beneath the pressure of Hugh's prising. 'Being Scottish, I'd expect you to know the Bothy code: respect for other users, respect the Bothy, that kind of thing —'

'Yeah,' sneered Hugh, 'because Jilly really subscribes to that, doesn't she? Locking this place up so no one can use it.'

'She thought it was for the best.'

Hugh ignored Amelia, as he slowly, carefully, dug in the earth beneath the broken floorboard. Amelia watched Hugh as, lips pressed together in concentration, he plunged his hand into the space and withdrew a small package wrapped in cloth. He held it with a reverence which seemed unworthy of such a tiny, grubby object. 'I've found it … finally.'

'Found what?' Amelia asked, surreptitiously glancing in her pocket at her phone. The screen showed emergency calls only. She may need it soon, but Hugh was speaking again. She didn't want to draw his attention to the fact she had a phone, so looked him in the eye.

'The dagger of Gordon McTavish. Once considered lost forever. Not anymore. I've found it. I knew it was here.' Hugh lifted the package onto his lap, his eyes sparkling in the torch light.

'Wait a minute. Surely you don't believe that folk tale about Gordon the Glorious, do you? Isn't it supposed to be nonsense?'

There was, however, nothing nonsensical about the glittering gold dagger emerging from the cloth as Hugh unwrapped it. Even in the dim light filtering through the grimy little window beside her, Amelia couldn't restrain a gasp at the size of the emeralds and opals which adorned the delicate handle. The sound appeared to remind Hugh she was there, for he stood and turned on her. 'I knew you'd be a nuisance from the moment you first arrived,' he snapped angrily. 'I was sure I could convince Jilly. You were different, with your single-minded determination. I almost had Jilly set on selling until you interfered. I know she would have sold eventually. She's changed since Stan died. If you hadn't kept encouraging her to keep the business going after the accident, she'd have done the sensible thing. She'd have taken the money and run.'

'But what's any of it got to do with you?' Amelia's voice surged with rising fury. 'Is this why you suddenly wanted to push my aunt out? To prevent you having to steal from our land? Although you've hardly behaved with integrity.'

'Because then I'd have owned the Bothy and could claim the dagger as mine. I had it all worked out until late yesterday when I got a call from Jilly informing me she'd decided to never sell.'

'Really? She said that?'

'Don't act like you didn't already know that.'

'I …'

'She hasn't told you?' Hugh scoffed. 'Her precious niece. She said she'd got other plans. Good job I did too after all those nights I spent traipsing around up here by torchlight, sinking in the stinking bog —'

'The lights,' gasped Amelia. 'Those mysterious lights I saw from my bedroom. I didn't imagine them. It was you.'

'I've been trying to work out where the dagger was hidden since that television crew filmed a documentary at Keilburn and mentioned it. This historian with wild hair told me most of the clues were said to be in a book he spotted in our library but it was all a hoax anyway and not worth bothering about. I've got time. I thought I'd check it out. I figured it out: how many paces from the well, the coordinates hidden in the text placing it on Lochside's land. I've lost track of the time I spent pacing around up here with a compass and then … bang! I discover it's buried right under where they built Lochside's Bothy. That was a complication I hadn't foreseen.'

'What did you decide to do then?'

'Well … I heard about Jilly's accident and believed I could persuade her to sell. Annoyingly she kept dithering, so I upped my offer. Yet still she wouldn't bite. I resorted to a back-up plan to dig up the dagger, bury it on Keilburn's land and make a miraculous discovery. No one would be any the wiser unless archaeologists were to ask exactly where I found it, then I'd have to blag. I hit another snag. I couldn't break down the Bothy door, it's impossible to destroy —'

'It's reinforced,' Amelia interrupted boldly. 'It's wood with a hidden steel core. Jilly didn't want any other animals getting trapped inside so she bought a door that would never weaken.'

'Ha! I should have guessed Jilly would put animal welfare before anything else. That's when I realised, to get inside, I'd have to get my hands on the key. Then Jilly seemed to be faltering again about selling so I held off … until now.'

'Why did you visit Gordon's grave?' Amelia blurted out, before realising she wasn't supposed to know Hugh had been there.

'What? You've been following me? You little sneak.' Hugh paused to catch his breath; his cheeks flushed.

'No, we just happened to be out that way when you went there.' Amelia knew it was a feeble explanation, but she was intent on keeping Hugh talking while she slipped one hand in her pocket and tried to unlock her phone. If she pressed the screen randomly enough times she might just hit the emergency call button.

'I thought it might be buried with Gordon himself. When I visited the grave, I realised it was too obvious. If it was there, it would have been found long ago. No … it's here. I'm the only one who believed it existed and I've found it. Me, the son of Leith Douglas, will have discovered one of the most significant archaeological finds for decades. The recognition will be mine.'

With that, Hugh raised the dagger high above his head.

Shrieking, Amelia cowered in the chair, petrified. Hugh was crazy, all of this was crazy. What wouldn't he do to keep secret the dagger was found at Lochside, not Keilburn. If anyone knew, they could challenge him and the only person who knew was her. Feeling vulnerable and scared, Amelia raised her hands defensively.

'Don't panic. I'm not going to hurt you. I'm not that foolish.'

'But … but … you tried to rip my aunt off. Tried to take Lochside from her for less than it was worth. That's coercion.'

'No, it's not, it's persuasion.' Hugh sighed dramatically, shaking his head. 'I tried to do this the honourable way and, if Jilly had sold up, I could have legitimately claimed the dagger. Of course, it would have been unfortunate timing for Jilly and a lucky find by me, when I was restoring the area after years of neglect. You forced me to take this option.'

'But surely you can't expect me to let this go? That discovery belongs to Lochside.'

'And yet it's your word against mine, isn't it?' Hugh nodded slowly. 'I found the dagger on Keilburn land, didn't I? How are you going to prove I didn't, eh?' The word of a respected son of a local landowner versus a nobody from a dilapidated riding stables. I know who I'd believe and … newsflash … it isn't you.'

Amelia's brain was fizzing, trying to put all the pieces of the past few months together, trying to grasp what had gone wrong on a day that had begun like any other. 'But the book, it places the dagger here. If you can work it out, so could someone else. I'll tell the police to search Keilburn's library for it.'

The smirk on Hugh's face confirmed to Amelia he was ahead of her. 'Too late. I've burnt it. I'd tell them it's missing and you're a liar trying to claim a priceless treasure to save your failing business.'

Reaching in her pocket, Amelia pulled out her phone, unlocking the screen with shaking fingers. Realising what she was about to do, Hugh moved fast, snatching the phone from her hand, then running to the door. In a second, he had it unlocked and was outside locking it again.

'Hey.' Amelia ran over, pummelling the door with both fists. 'Unlock this immediately.'

She heard Hugh's footsteps moving away and dashed over to the chair, dragging it to the window. Standing on it, hoping the seat wouldn't give way under her weight, she watched through a tiny patch of glass as Hugh untethered Spirit, then slapped her on the rump, yelling, 'Yaaahh.'

The startled mare took fright, galloping away into the trees, as Hugh walked off, leaving Amelia alone. She tried to open the window she could reach but it was jammed solid, the frame glued shut by the swollen wood. The panes of glass were too narrow for her to fit through if she broke one. She banged her fists against the door with all her strength despite knowing she was trapped. All she could do was wait until Mac returned to Lochside and hopefully found Spirit, which would prompt him to search for her. From somewhere outside she could occasionally hear her phone ringing or the tone for messages as the patchy signal came and went. Hugh must have tossed it in the undergrowth nearby.

Time passed and darkness came. With the loss of light, the creaking sounds of the old Bothy took on a different feel, especially to a cold and tired Amelia. She jiggled her legs agitatedly, trying not to think about ghosts or much at all, but nothing could stop her mind whirring through the questions that remained unanswered. Had Hugh slipped a sedative in her champagne that night so he could search for the key in peace? There would never be any proof, the glasses long since washed up and put away, but she had her suspicions. She knew he wouldn't bury the dagger straightaway, not in the middle of the night. Where would he take it for safekeeping? Somewhere the likelihood of anyone finding it was minimal. Somewhere hidden, where visitors wouldn't drop in. He'd need to be careful in case she reported him to the police and they insisted on searching the Manor and the Gatehouse.

Exhausted, she finally dozed off in the chair, her head lolling uncomfortably, before waking disorientated to the sound of hooves outside. Climbing back on the seat, she looked out the window. All was pitch black. Hoping it wasn't Spirit returning alone, she sat down. The hooves sounded closer. She peered outside again to see a bright light approaching in mid-air. She followed the light as it drew closer. She was banging on the window when Mac's face loomed the other side of the pane. He was sitting on Hebrides and leading the riderless Spirit. He looked utterly bemused. She watched him dismount and lead the horses out of sight around to the door. Shortly after the lock clicked and the door swung open, revealing Mac holding the horses.

'How the heck did you manage to lock yourself inside with the key outside? Surely only a magician is capable of doing that.' Mac seemed baffled. 'Or did the Spunkies do it?'

In no mood for jokes, Amelia rushed outside as Mac handed her a hat with a light strapped to it. 'It wasn't the Spunkies, it was Hugh Douglas,' she said, searching for her phone.

'What? What's gone on here? The floor's all broken up by the fireplace. Are you hurt?'

'No, I'm OK,' she answered distractedly, spotting her phone screen lighting up within a cluster of ferns. Standing upright, she took Spirit's reins from Mac's hand. 'Hugh's been searching for something, a valuable something, a dagger. He found it in the Bothy. I interrupted him. He's stolen it and is going to claim it as his discovery.'

'But that's crazy. What for?' Mac was struggling to keep up.

Amelia shrugged. 'From what he said he's desperate for recognition and attention and he knows finding a rare artefact like the dagger will be a huge story and make him rich.'

'This is unbelievable.' Mac shook his head in disbelief. 'And he already is rich.'

'No, Leith is and that's part of the problem. I'm not making it up. How did you find me?'

'I returned to find the stables in a mess, the ponies unfed and Spirit waiting at the gate. I thought you must have fallen off and hurt yourself. It gave me quite a fright.'

'Oh … Mac. Your meeting. How did it go?'

'It went brilliantly. We agreed a deal today, or rather yesterday now. We've got to go to London to meet the main team and check out the contract. If that goes well, we sign.'

'Oh, Mac, congratulations. That's amazing.'

'There'll be time for celebrating later. Right now, we need to get you safely back.'

'But what do we do then? Hugh burnt the only evidence the dagger was on Lochside's property. Without that, what proof do I have?'

'Hugh can't imprison you without being held accountable. We need to call the police,' said Mac, springing onto Hebrides.

'If he admits anything it'll be that he found the dagger at Keilburn and he never locked me in.' Amelia turned the key in the Bothy door and zipped it in her pocket.

'I'm a witness too though. It's our word against his.' Mac whirled the chestnut in the direction of the stables. 'And that thieving git deserves everything he's got coming.'

Amelia settled into Spirit's saddle. 'Wait, Mac, I've been thinking it over for hours and our only option is to steal it back.'

'We can't do that. How do we even know where the dagger is?'

'Hugh will have taken it to the place he doesn't know I know exists. The best hiding place he knows.' Without waiting for a response, Amelia steered Spirit towards Keilburn, nudging the mare into a gallop.

They raced through the bracken, splashing through a brook then on into the trees, their way lit only by moonlight and the narrow beam of the head torch on Amelia's hat. The mare's stride never faltered. She was bred for endurance; this was her purpose and she covered the ground easily. From behind came the sound of Hebrides racing to catch up. Ahead a clump of trees clustered close together and suddenly a huge fallen tree trunk was blocking the path. With no option to go around, Amelia felt her old fear rise again as her hands instinctively adjusted to rein Spirit back. She may have conquered jumping small poles designed to come loose if a pony knocked them but the trunk was unforgivingly solid and twice the height of the clear round jumps. Spirit ignored the pressure on the reins and took off, soaring high into the air, so high Amelia felt she could touch the moon. When she'd gained her breath, she let out a fierce whoop.

'This is wild,' she yelled, adrenaline buzzing in her veins.

'Way to go,' Mac cheered, as he drew alongside.

Soon after they eased their mounts to a walk and Amelia put a forefinger against her lips signalling to Mac to keep quiet. They approached the cabin. Midges were buzzing around a lit lantern fixed to the porch. Securing Hebrides and Spirit, they crept up to the cabin. Mac tried the door handle but found it locked. Meanwhile, Amelia tiptoed along the side to the rear of the building. There was a back door which she found was also secure. She spotted a window had been left ajar.

'What do you reckon?' she asked Mac, pointing to it as he approached.

Mac surveyed the window. 'Hmm. It's a risk. If there are cameras or an alarm it's going to undermine our case that we're the ones being honest if we're caught breaking in. Listen, Jilly never knew about the dagger. I'm not wishing to play devil's advocate, but should we let this go? Hugh's clearly sad and a bit mad. Is it worth riling him and his family?'

'Remember when Angus told us about Stan's metal detecting? I believe my uncle had an inkling something was there. It's not for Hugh to profit from the dagger. He's being dishonest. It belongs to Jilly and ultimately to a museum.'

Mac sighed, glancing around as though for inspiration. 'Well, we can't stand here all night. I'll go in. You stay here, then at least you're not involved if it goes wrong.'

Reaching up to his full height, Mac pushed the window wide. It opened effortlessly. 'Pretty complacent about security. Here goes.'

With a groan, Mac heaved his body upwards. He was too large to fit through the gap. He began to wriggle frantically. Terrified he was stuck, Amelia grabbed his ankles.

28

Yanking backwards on his legs, Amelia pulled Mac out the window. They landed in a heap on the grass.

'Ouch.' Mac sat dazed, rubbing his elbow. 'Can I request you take a gentler approach next time?'

'You're not doing it again. I'll do it. I can fit through.' Amelia stretched upwards and placed her hands on the frame. 'Boost me up.'

'I'm not sure it's a good idea for you to go alone.'

'I'm doing it anyway but if I have to climb up there myself it'll take longer and make more noise.'

'Crikey.' Mac lifted Amelia and, seconds later, she landed with a soft plop inside a marble bathtub. Glimpsing a shadow in front of her, she almost screamed, managing to suppress the sound when she realised it was her reflection in a full-length mirror opposite.

'What's happening?' hissed Mac.

'I'm in a bathroom,' Amelia whispered back.

'Be careful. I don't like this.'

Stepping out of the bathtub, Amelia activated the torch on

her mobile and opened the door as quietly as she could. Outside was a narrow corridor. She gazed up the dark passageway. The only sign of movement was a flickering light coming from the room she recalled contained the fireplace. She moved carefully in that direction, peering around the archway, then rapidly ducked back, switching off the torch. Hugh was slumped, head resting on his folded arms, at a table in front of the fireplace. The glow of the flames was flickering off the glass of a bottle of Vodka. There was no drinking glass, he had been swigging directly from the bottle. To Amelia's relief, the firelight also twinkled off the gems on the hilt of the dagger, lying on the table near Hugh's left arm. A loud snort indicated he was asleep, possibly a Vodka-induced one. Amelia couldn't be certain as she crept into the room. She reached the table and was inching towards the dagger when Hugh suddenly turned his head away from facing the fireplace. She was close enough to see the drool on his chin.

'Told you,' he muttered, 'told you I'd make it one day. Told you …'

Amelia remained still. Seconds ticked by. Hugh snored. Seizing the moment, she reached for the dagger, sweeping it off the table and, with restraint, managed to tiptoe away again. She ran back along the passageway to the open window. Hauling herself up on the side of the bathtub, she clawed her way back through the window and was prevented from landing headfirst on the ground by Mac's quick reflexes as he caught her.

'I've got it,' she whispered.

'Was the cabin empty then?' Mac asked.

'No. Hugh's in there. He's been celebrating with Vodka. We need to get out of here.'

Grabbing each other's hand, they ran as fast as they could back to the horses.

. . .

It took a few days for everything to settle down. Amelia found herself exhausted by constantly having to explain what had happened. Jilly arrived back early from Orkney and sat in the office in stunned silence while Amelia and Mac updated her.

'Stan knew,' she insisted. 'I'm sure he did. At the very least he suspected there might be something buried here. I teased him ruthlessly over his metal detecting and, glory be, he was right all along. Always was, my Stan. What happens now?'

'Mac and I have done some research and we understand you need to contact the Treasure Trove Unit and report it.'

'Do we get paid a fortune for it?' asked Zoey eagerly, spilling tea over her jodhpurs. 'How much are we likely to get?'

'Is Jilly likely to get,' Mac corrected her. 'If it's confirmed as genuine and significant, it'll probably be allocated to a museum —'

'But it's Jilly's,' interrupted Angus. 'It's on her land.'

'Look, Angus, Amelia and I are no experts, however Jilly may well receive a reward payment for the dagger,' Mac reassured him. 'And as for Hugh, we feel it's best to let that go. We've heard nothing from him. I'm staying at Lochside with Amelia in case he pays her an unscheduled visit. We can't take the chance that he could seek some type of revenge.'

'Well, hopefully Hugh has more sense than to cause a fuss over something he should never have taken in the first place. It would get very messy because I won't go down without a fight.' Jilly rose to her feet with a groan. 'All this excitement is making me feel tired to the bone. Amelia, will you join me for a walk please?'

They strode along the path between the fields, where the geldings and mares were grazing beneath a sun which still held some warmth despite autumn's rapid approach.

'You know, it's true I'm not finding it as easy as I used to,' Jilly began, 'and therefore I've made a decision —'

'You've not changed your mind again?' Amelia was incredulous. 'You're not selling Lochside to someone else? Not after everything.'

'Of course I'm not. Far from it. No, what I'd like is for you to take over from me. I intend to handover the business to you … if you want it and I'll semi-retire. You won't be rid of me completely but I promise not to interfere.'

'Are you serious?' Amelia fell against the railings, studying her aunt's expression for clues.

'I'm absolutely serious. I wouldn't joke about something like this. You know, Amelia, your mother told me —'

'Told you what?'

'That you needed a little push to realise the potential you've always had.'

'Oh, she did, did she? But did she mention opportunities never came my way. She knows that. They always went to someone else. Eventually I stopped trying. I knew that's what I'd done but it was easier that way.'

Jilly clambered up on the top rail and tapped the space beside her. Obediently, Amelia jumped up to sit next to her. 'When I moved here all those years ago and started this business, I did it because I couldn't get anywhere. I was never the one chosen and gradually I realised there's no logic to it, no skill, no one person better than another, it's simply the way it is. I decided to stop letting other people control my life. It's been tough and it's been lonely, especially since I lost my Stan. My advice is stop waiting and do it yourself. Plough your own furrow, don't try to sow the seeds of your future in someone else's.'

'That's good advice, if not always easy to follow.'

Jilly grinned. 'The truth is all three of them could have run this place for a few months while I recovered from my accident. After all, Zoey's halfway through a degree in Business Administration, Angus has been my assistant forever and even Mac offered to have a go. Although he'd probably have turned the admin into song lyrics, he's more than capable.'

'Then why am I here?'

'Because if you weren't you'd still be sitting at the same desk, doing the same job for the same salary. Unappreciated and underutilised.'

'Are you telling me this was all a ploy to get me out of a rut?' Amelia felt her hackles rising at their presumed interference in her life.

'No. The accident was exactly that but it provided the opportunity. You still had to take it though and aren't you glad you did?'

Amelia scratched her head and thought about it. 'Yeah, I am glad, although I wish you'd all been honest with me.'

'But then you wouldn't have found out anything for yourself and you'd have probably hot-footed it back to London. Mac told me at the time you were tempted to do that.'

'I was.' Peewee approached, pushing his nose into Amelia's lap. She stroked him. 'Are you sure that you want to do this? You're not doing it for me.'

'I live with ghosts, Amelia. Of Stan and my ponies who I've been so fond of over the years and lost. Memories of the good old days. It's about the future now and that's you. You're good at it. There's no other pair of hands I'd rather place Lochside in.'

'I'd be delighted to take Lochside on. I feel excited for the future here.' Amelia leaned over to kiss her aunt's cheek. 'Thank you.'

'No, thank you. It'll allow me to have the best of both worlds. I'm keeping my troops yet easing off. Now's the time for me to take life easier, see more of Donna and the grandchildren and spend time with Arthur. We have a lot in common and at our age you've got to make the most of it. Don't worry, I'll have a discreet word with Angus to make sure he doesn't panic.'

'I'm glad you've found someone to share the next stage of your life with.'

'Yes, Arthur and I have plans. He's chatted to Beatrice and she'd be delighted to join the team here if you want her. We'll be losing Mac soon, as you know. It's kind of ironic that you moved from Scotland to London and now he's going the other way.'

They walked back to the tack room where Zoey was waiting for them, along with Angus and Mac.

'Have you heard?' she demanded, 'about Three Stones Barn?' They shook their heads in bewilderment. 'It's being turned into a wellness retreat. Apparently Jake's wife always wanted to do it and now she's had enough of the riding stables and it'll be offering Yoga, Pilates and what's the other one … Gong baths. That's it.'

'Gong baths?' Angus repeated.

'You know, you bathe in the sounds of the gong. It's meditation.'

'Sounds like an expensive alarm clock to me,' Mac tutted.

'Most of their horses were livery anyway. It means riders coming our way,' cheered Zoey.

'Well, I'll be,' muttered Jilly, slumping down in a chair. 'A wellness retreat. Whatever next.'

'I'm definitely going back to Uni,' added Zoey. 'It would be nice to stay. I've decided you lot are all right but I still want to go around the world.'

Angus shook his head in dismay. 'Whatever for? There's nothing out there that's not here.'

'Technically that's not true. Sunshine for one thing.'

Later, Mac found Amelia in the barn having a clear out. 'I hear congratulations are in order. Jilly told us you're taking over.'

'Thanks.' Amelia paused, gazing out the open doors to the fields beyond where the sun was setting. There was no comparison between Lochside and spending your day sitting in a hot stuffy office above the crowded streets of London.

'It was wrong of us not to have told you that you didn't have to step in at the time of Jilly's accident. That one of us could have done it rather than making you feel obliged to run the place.'

'You're all right.' Amelia smiled. 'I didn't have to. I had a choice and I chose to.'

Mac took Amelia's hand. 'I've just found out that "Lazy Loch Days" has entered the streaming charts.'

'Amazing, Mac.' Amelia threw her arms around him in celebration. 'Oh, that's wonderful. Everything's working out for you. So, what's next, then? A world tour, sold out stadiums.'

'Steady on.' Mac laughed. 'Actually next is a mundane meeting in London. I'm taking a few days off. Hope that's OK with my new boss!' Mac jumped on a hay bale, leaping off high into the air. 'The future's looking bright. Perhaps a tour.' At the sound of someone calling his name in the distance, Mac stopped jigging. 'That's Digger. He's collecting me on his way to the airport. Wish me luck. Will miss you loads.'

With a brief kiss, Mac was gone, like a whirlwind. Amelia leant back against the hay bale. Everything was happening too fast. In a strange way she felt she had gained and lost. Gained Lochside and lost Mac. She was pleased for him. He deserved it, had worked hard for it. This opportunity would take him on a completely different trajectory to hers and for some reason she felt the urge to cry. She wiped her eyes then laughed at herself. Everything was working out. She shouldn't be crying.

'Don't get upset.' She looked up to find Zoey standing in the doorway. 'He'll be back. He won't leave you behind.'

Amelia smiled weakly. 'He might not have a choice once he's signed a contract.'

Zoey plonked herself next to Amelia. 'The one thing I know for sure about Mac is he's no fool. He's not going to lose who he is. Of course he's overexcited right now, who wouldn't be in his shoes. It'll settle down. Give it time.'

The next morning, Amelia rode out alone on Pirate. She wanted to take some time out. It was Zoey's last day and Beatrice was due to start work at the end of the week. As she trotted around Loch Still, a brisk wind lifting Pirate's mane, she heard hooves approaching fast from behind. Assuming it was the late morning ride from Lochside catching her up, Amelia turned. Her face fell. It wasn't the string of familiar ponies. A golden blur was cantering straight towards her. Hugh's face was grim as he pulled on Aurum's reins, bringing the palomino to a halt inches away from Pirate, who stood his ground. They glared at each other, neither speaking. Amelia wanted to turn away and leave with dignity. Anger made her stay.

'You,' Hugh spat, 'ruined everything. I know you broke into the cabin and stole the dagger from me —'

'I took back what was rightfully ours,' snapped Amelia. Pirate whirled in a circle in agitation. 'For your information, I own Lochside now and you'll not push me around. You'd better stay away from my family, my team and my business. You brought it all on yourself and you've got what you deserve.'

Hugh's sneer was vicious. 'You wish. Your business will fail.'

'Not while I have any say in it. Go away, Hugh, and stay away.'

'I'll never go away,' threatened Hugh, 'and you will pay for what you've done, Amelia Hodge. I suggest you never stop looking over your shoulder. I'll see to it your life is ruined in every way. You don't play games with me and win.' Whacking his heels into Aurum's sides, the startled palomino launched into a gallop, leaving Amelia and Pirate coughing in a cloud of dust.

Jilly led a group of youngsters over at a steady trot. 'That dreadful man. Is everything all right?' she asked, concerned.

'Yeah. I warned him to keep away from us.' Amelia dropped Pirate in alongside Chess.

'I'm sure he will. He might be mouthing off but he's not going to want any trouble for himself.'

'Let's hope not. He threatened to ruin me and Lochside.'

'He's got to act tough because he's been caught out. The Douglas family are of no consequence to us. We have more important things to think about, like how much of the reward money we're going to spend on our outdoor school.'

'Really?' Amelia shrieked.

'Yes, I heard this morning …' Jilly paused, glowing. 'Arthur and I are going to spend some on a Mediterranean cruise. The rest I'll put into providing the best outdoor school for Beatrice to teach lessons in. We've got a waiting list going already.'

'Well, that's fantastic.' Amelia grinned, delighted.

'I've got my eye on a Norwegian Fjords cruise too.' Jilly lowered her voice so the children couldn't hear her. 'Arthur and I want to spend time together. I doubt I'll be around much. Good old Gordon the Glorious and his dagger, eh?' Chuckling, Jilly rode over to rescue a girl who couldn't lift

Pumpkin's head from the grass. 'Give him a good firm instruction, Joanne,' she barked.

Smiling, Amelia looked around at the loch, the castle ruins and the bunch of ponies cantering in a straggly line with Jilly and Chess leading the way. This was her life now and she wouldn't change it for the world.

EPILOGUE

With business thriving, rides booked in every day and enquiries about renting the cottage coming in at a rate Amelia could barely keep up with, she knew she ought to feel delighted at how Lochside's fortunes had turned around.

Zoey had returned to University in Glasgow and with Mac away too, Amelia had advertised for staff. A steady flurry of applications was coming in. Soon she'd need to sit down with Angus and Beatrice to go through them all and decide who to invite for a chat. *I'll need to make sure none of them is on the run*, she thought with a smile, recalling Mac's joke at their first meeting. He had been in London a month now and, although she received many messages and the occasional video call, she missed him and longed for more. She understood, or at least thought she did, the demands of long sessions in recording studios and evenings spent writing and rewriting lyrics, so she kept her feelings to herself.

As she turned into the lane leading to Lochside, the Mini gliding smoothly over the recently repaired potholes, she reflected that generally life was good and she had no cause for complaint. The feed merchant's truck was waiting by the gates, the driver chatting to Angus, whose bike was propped against his hip. They both greeted her cheerfully.

Frost spattered the cottage lawn as Amelia unlocked the door and placed fresh-cut flowers in a vase as a welcome gift for their first ever self-catering holidaymakers, due to arrive that day. The heating was faintly humming, the rooms felt toasty warm and Amelia was pleased with the work that had been done to transform the cottage. The day was due to be bright and cold, meaning their guests would arrive to see Lochside at its best. Even the most scenic of surroundings looked better without a downpour.

She was in the kitchen setting out fresh scones on a plate when the front door began to tremble beneath incessant knocking.

'One moment,' she yelled.

Dashing through the living room, she opened the door to a man dressed in motorbike leathers, a helmet tucked under his arm.

'Hello, Jilly's niece. I need you,' he said.

With a cry of delight Amelia ran outside and leapt into his arms. 'You're back.'

Mac picked her up, spinning around and laughing as her feet flew through the air. 'Course I am.' He grinned. 'I'll always come home to you.'

ALSO BY JAY ANN FOLEY

The Misfit

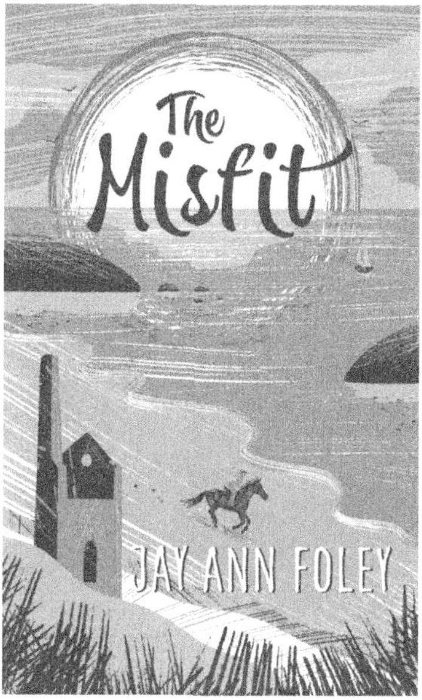

Georgie Wright is feeling frustrated. Her career as a jockey is more stuck at the start than flying at the finish. Meanwhile her partner, the talented Sam Christie, moves ever closer to his goal of being crowned champion jockey.

When Georgie finds herself blamed for an accident on the gallops and ostracised by her colleagues, she flees to a farm on Bodmin Moor and a temporary position working with father and son team, Fred and Tom Pengelly. There she is introduced to The Misfit, a highly talented thoroughbred whose temperament makes him an untested contender for the Epsom Derby. Can Georgie bond with the horse and earn herself the ride in such a prestigious race?

With a spate of rural crime in the area and under pressure from jealous rivals, Georgie struggles to keep The Misfit safe and sound. Will they ever get to participate in the horse-race of the year and prove their critics wrong?

From the romance of the Cornish moor to the bustling home of British horse-racing in Suffolk, The Misfit will take you on a journey right up to the final furlong!

Printed in Great Britain
by Amazon

58224923R00179